TARK'S TICKS DARK VALLEY

A WWII NOVEL

CHRIS GLATTE

SEVERN RIVER
PUBLISHING

Severn River Publishing
www.SevernRiverBooks.com

ISBN: 978-1-64875-567-5 (Paperback)

ALSO BY CHRIS GLATTE

Tark's Ticks Series

Tark's Ticks

Valor's Ghost

Gauntlet

Valor Bound

Dark Valley

War Point

A Time to Serve Series

A Time to Serve

The Gathering Storm

The Scars of Battle

164th Regiment Series

The Long Patrol

Bloody Bougainville

Bleeding the Sun

Operation Cakewalk (Novella)

Standalone Novel

Across the Channel

To find out more about Chris Glatte and his books, visit

severnriverbooks.com/authors/chris-glatte

1

First Lieutenant Tarkington crossed the finish line etched into the sand. He'd sprinted the final one hundred yards and now simply wanted to fall down and breathe. He resisted the urge and turned to watch the others instead. Henry finished a close second, with Vick, Raker, Stollman, and Winkleman crossing just behind him.

Tarkington got control of his breathing and lifted his chin toward Henry. "You let me win?"

Henry shook his head. "You know I'd never do that, Tark...I mean, sir." He gave him a half-hearted salute.

Tarkington scowled. "Save that bullshit when we're around other troops, *Sergeant*."

Henry gave him his sideways grin and spit onto the sandy beach. The brass had given the entire team promotions. Tarkington didn't want the rank, but Colonel Bradshaw and General Krueger insisted. Krueger elevated him past second lieutenant and straight to first lieutenant, saying it would instill more respect from other officers. A month had passed and he still couldn't get used to being saluted.

They found shade beneath a nearby grove of coconut palms and drank from their canteens. Staff Sergeant Winkleman asked, "Any word?"

Tarkington shook his head. "Not yet. Something's in the offing, though.

They finally have Buna and Gona under control, and the Aussies have their sights on Lae and Salamaua. Both have airfields and deepwater ports."

Winkleman nodded. "Your rank's good for something, I guess. We're usually out of the loop on that kind of information."

Tarkington wiped the sweat from his brow. "Yeah, guess so. I'm still not used to it, though."

Corporal Stollman touched the new stripe on his shoulder. "The extra pay's nice."

Corporal Raker agreed. He touched his own new stripe. "Draws in the ladies like moths to a candle."

Winkleman shook his head. "That sounds right. They all end up burnt and dying."

Raker leveled his blue eyes at him. "Still not getting laid, Staff Sergeant?"

Winkleman flipped him the bird.

"Shame to see a grown man struggle like that." Raker grinned. "Just say the word, Wink. I can get you laid tonight, easy."

"I'm not interested in your cast-off trash, Raker."

Raker looked affronted and mockingly grasped his chest. "Trash? That's why you fail, Wink. You're too damned picky."

Winkleman retorted, "Yeah, I guess I like my women to have teeth."

The squad guffawed, and Raker held up his hands. "That only happened once. She was sweet, just"—he shrugged—"flawed."

Stollman punched Corporal Vick's arm. "You got in late last night. You holding out on me?"

"I don't kiss and tell, Stolly. You know that."

Raker pointed at him. "You sly dog. Who is it?"

Vick scowled at Stollman. "See what you've done?" Stollman smiled but didn't look apologetic. Vick focused his glare at Raker. "None of your business. She's out of your league by a mile." That brought a flurry of catcalls and whistles.

The sounds of multiple engines overhead made them all squint up at the sky. A descending flight of B-25 Mitchells appeared over the towering Owen Stanley Mountains. They flashed out over the sea, continuing to lose altitude. Above them, a flight of P-38s circled, watching their charges like sheepdogs.

A jeep skidded to a stop, and a soldier that looked as though he'd just been assembled in a factory hopped out the passenger side and approached them. His immaculate new uniform, short haircut, and shining white skin, mottled with fresh red mosquito bites, screamed of a new arrival. His lapel shone with the single gold bar of a second lieutenant.

Tarkington faced him, and the soldier snapped off a perfect salute. Tarkington returned it haphazardly. The rest of the squad barely reacted to the new arrival, and the officer scowled at their lack of outward respect. When it was apparent Tarkington would not correct his men, the officer addressed him. "Sir, I'm Lieutenant Spaulding with G2. Captain Gronlin requests your presence."

"Jesus. Makes it sound like he's being summoned by the king," Stollman murmured. Spaulding's eyes narrowed, but he did his best to ignore Stollman.

Tarkington plucked the handkerchief from Spaulding's front pocket and wiped his sweaty face. He finished by wiping his hands, then stuffed it back into Spaulding's pocket. "Thanks." Spaulding's jaw rippled as he tried to contain his anger. Tarkington stepped aside and held out his arms. "After you, Lieutenant."

Spaulding nodded and led him to the Jeep. Tarkington grinned at his squad. "Get cleaned up. I'll see you back at the barracks."

They watched him enter the front seat of the Jeep and drive toward town. Sergeant Henry drawled, "That kid compared to Tark..." He shook his head. "Looked like a before and after."

"I don't think Tark ever looked like that butterbar," Vick said.

"Sure he did. Hell, we all did. Remember back on Luzon when this whole thing started? We were green as grass."

They all nodded as they reflected. The Japanese assault on the Philippines in December of 1941 happened over a year ago, but it seemed like ten lifetimes had passed.

∾

Tarkington entered the sweltering Quonset hut, surprised to see Colonel Bradshaw. He and General Krueger had left Port Moresby on a C-47 soon after awarding the squad their battlefield promotions. Nearly a month had passed, and the only orders he'd received were to stand by.

After a crisp exchange of salutes, Bradshaw greeted him with a hearty handshake and a backslap. "It's good to see you again, Lieutenant Tarkington. Keeping your men out of trouble?"

"Yes, sir. Just finished a run around town, in fact. They're getting antsy for more action though, sir."

Bradshaw released his grip and escorted him to a large table holding a map of the northern coast of Papua New Guinea. Captain Gronlin and various lieutenants, including Spaulding, stood in a semicircle. None looked too happy to see Tarkington.

He wasn't used to saluting yet, but he'd adjusted to the disrespectful glances and snide, barely concealed remarks from his fellow officers. Since he hadn't gotten his commission from a military academy and hadn't been through Officer Candidate School, those that had could hardly stomach him.

Despite his obviously extensive combat experience, they called him a mustang and an opportunistic lowlife. He didn't mind being called a mustang. Indeed, he kind of liked it. He held his tongue mostly, knowing the prepubescent little shits were just blowing smoke. It riled his men more than him, and he had to rein them in a few times before they assaulted a disrespecting officer and got thrown in the brig.

Bradshaw put his thickly calloused finger on a point northeast of Port Moresby. "This is Huon Gulf. The port town of Lae sits astride the Markham River. The Japs own this entire region, but the Aussies have a toehold in the Bulol Valley." He moved his finger southwest. "Since the Japs lost Buna-Gona, they're reinforcing Lae and probably Salamaua on the coast here." He moved his finger directly east from the Bulol Valley. "In order to understand this region better, I'll fill you in on some recent history. Back in May, our air force flew two companies of Australian commandos into Wau to put pressure on Lae and Salamaua." He put his finger on a tiny dot far up the Bulol Valley and due west of Salamaua about fifty miles. "The airstrip could barely take a C-47. The commandos, along with a few hundred New Guinea Volunteer Rifles cadre, got to work improving the airstrip and boosting the defenses. They mounted a successful raid on Salamaua airfield, destroying buildings and killing about sixty Nips. They even captured valuable intelligence documents. Right after that, the Japs landed at Buna and attacked over the Kokoda Track. The Allied focus shifted, leaving the Australian commandos with little support. They were told to monitor Lae and Salamaua and hunker down."

He clasped his hands behind his back and continued. "Earlier this month, the Japs reinforced Lae with about three thousand troops from Rabaul. The NGVRs and commandos observed them moving along the coast to Salamaua. Now they're pushing inland toward Wau. The commandos and NGVRs won't last against such a sizable force, so the Australian Seventeenth Brigade will be airlifted into Wau." He pointed at the Owen Stanley Range separating Port Moresby from Wau. "The only way to get men and supplies there quickly is flying over the Owen Stanleys through a gap. They used it before the war. It's usually clear in the mornings, but fog shuts it down by late morning most days. It's a tight window and can change quickly, especially this time of year."

Tarkington nodded his understanding. Bradshaw continued. "Besides using our air assets, the battle shaping up around Wau is strictly an Australian operation. Our troops are still mopping things up in the Buna region, but US command has shifted focus to the deepwater bay at Lae and the surrounding airfields. Air assets will soon hit the area hard, softening things up for a possible amphibious landing, but reconnaissance flights have had trouble pinpointing concentrations of enemy aircraft. Before we send in bombers to hit troop concentrations, command wants to clear out the land-based fighter squadrons they suspect are hidden throughout the Markham River Valley. That's your mission. Fly into Wau, move into the Markham Valley on foot, find the enemy aircraft, and call in air raids."

Tarkington nodded and studied the map, noting how much they had improved since he'd first been in the region. Even the best map couldn't show how truly tough the terrain was, however. Maps made everything look tidy and close, but even moving a mile could sometimes take days.

New Guinea's thick jungles and high volcanoes could make the strongest man whimper for mercy. Besides the unforgiving terrain and climate, there were also countless beasts and vipers that could kill a man instantly or painfully slow. Hell, even the damned bugs could kill a man. "Any idea how far the Japs are from Wau?"

Bradshaw scowled and pressed a finger to the map. "Last we heard, they were in a tiny village here, called Mubo. It looks close to Wau, but don't let that fool you. The terrain is steep and treacherous. It's only fifty miles from Wau to Salamaua as the crow flies, but it could take more than a week to traverse those mountains, and the commandos and NGVRs will dog them all the way. You should have plenty of time to be out of the region before the fireworks begin."

Tarkington wondered about that but didn't comment. Instead he asked, "When do we leave?"

Bradshaw grinned and slapped his back. "Tomorrow morning. The Seventeenth Brigade is still in Milne Bay, so it'll be a few days before we shuttle them into Wau."

Captain Gronlin stepped in and pointed at the map. "A C-47 will fly you and your men in." He traced the valley north. "You'll patrol downstream towards the Markham Valley. The commandos and NGVRs have a good handle on enemy troops in the region, but if you come across any, we'd like to know about it. Your primary mission, however, is to find those hidden airfields and enemy planes." He circled an area on the map. "We think they're in this region, near the village of Nadzab."

Tarkington nodded but asked, "Begging your pardon. But why don't the Aussie commandos do the job? They're already there."

Gronlin looked mildly annoyed as he replied. "They've been there for months. Captain Grumskey, the Aussie commander, says half of them are suffering from malaria and fever. With the enemy pushing in from Sala-maua, they're the only troops holding Wau. They need to stay put and assist the Seventeenth Brigade when they arrive. Your squad was sitting on their hands here, so..." He shrugged.

Colonel Bradshaw gave Gronlin a scathing look, then told Tarkington, "You'll fly out tomorrow morning at 0600 hours. Take enough provisions for a week."

"Yes, sir."

Bradshaw looked down his prodigious nose at Gronlin. "You have anything else for Lieutenant Tarkington, Phil?"

Gronlin scowled. "No, sir."

"That'll be all. I need a private word with Lieutenant Tarkington."

Gronlin expected Tarkington to be dismissed, and he hesitated for an instant, then gave Tarkington one last glance before following his entourage of underlings out the door of his own CP.

Bradshaw smiled. "Sorry about that."

"I'm used to it, sir. Word about my promotion spread through the officer ranks quickly. They're resentful, but I don't give a shit...sir."

Bradshaw chuckled. "I wanted you to know that we're still figuring out the Alamo Scout training. We've started building a training facility on Fergusson Island."

Tarkington smiled. "Fergusson? Right next to Goodenough Island, right?" Bradshaw nodded and Tarkington added, "Good choice. Get 'em acclimated to where they'll be fighting."

"Their mission will be reconnaissance, mostly. This mission would be perfect for them, but," he folded his beefy arms across his broad chest, "your men are ready now."

"The men'll be happy to get back into the war, sir."

"Eventually, we'll find a mission tailored for your squad's unique skill set. Your demo work in Buna was outstanding. General Krueger would like to see more of that."

"My men would like nothing more, sir."

Bradshaw shifted the conversation. "The handheld radios have been problematic. I'm sending a new radio set on this mission, an SCR-300. One of your men will have to learn it and carry it. It's capable of long-distance transmissions, which you'll need."

Tarkington frowned, wondering which team member he'd turn into a radioman. Vick was used to carrying extra gear, but he was also his best knife man. He'd be severely hampered carrying a bulky radio on his back.

Bradshaw shrugged. "Commandeer one of the Aussies if you need to. I'll send a message to Captain Grumskey. He's a good man and will be happy to help in any way he can."

Tarkington nodded, then asked, "I don't mean to have the wrong attitude, but what happens to us if the Nips take Wau? Far as I can tell, that airfield's the only way in or out of there."

"The Seventeenth Brigade will come in right behind you. They'll be able to stop them." He rubbed his chin. "But to answer your question, you'd be on your own. Getting to the coast for pickup on a barge could work. The radio will help with that." Bradshaw extended his hand, and they shook. "Keep your men healthy, Tark. We'll see you in a week or two."

Tarkington nodded and mumbled a reply. But his mind was already going over the thousand things he needed to get done before boarding the C-47 the next morning.

2

They took off just as the sun burst over the edge of the world. The C-47 pilots weren't Americans, but Australians. Like most Aussies they'd met, they were jovial and easy to get along with.

When Lt. Tarkington saluted the pilot, a captain, he extended his hand, and they shook instead. "Welcome aboard, Yank. I'm Captain Wainwright, and this here's Lieutenant Spanaour." He indicated the grinning copilot. He was flicking knobs and switches, preparing for takeoff. "We normally have a few Sheilas serving drinks, but they've all come down with the crud."

Tarkington snapped his fingers. "Just our luck I guess, Captain."

"Make sure everything's strapped down back there. We have to get over the Owen Stanleys, and it can get bumpy, even this early."

The copilot pulled his headphones off. "Not to mention the occasional Zero."

Captain Wainwright nodded. "Yes, them too."

Tarkington remembered the Zeros that jumped them on their flight from Brisbane to Milne Bay. They'd been saved when a pair of Australian-flown P-40 Kittyhawks appeared and chased them off, but not before taking fire and thinking they were all going to die in a ball of flames. It wasn't one of his fondest memories.

"You know any of the Kittyhawk pilots out of Milne Bay?" he asked.

Captain Wainwright rubbed his chin. "They pop in occasionally, but fighter jocks don't mix with us lowly transport pilots much."

Tarkington grinned. "Thought all you Aussies stuck together."

The lieutenant sneered and said, "They *think* they're winning the war, we *know* we are."

Tarkington didn't know what to make of that. Lieutenant Spanaour explained, "Shooting up a few Japs is one thing, but delivering hundreds of men and their supplies so they can shoot up Japs by the bushel is quite another."

"We gonna have any of those useless sonsofbitches watching our tails on this trip?"

Captain Wainwright laughed heartily but shook his head. "They're too busy winning the war to waste time escorting us, Lieutenant." He flipped a few switches, and a humming filled the cockpit. He turned serious. "We haven't been jumped in a week or more on this run. Once we're through the gap, it's a quick trip to Wau. We'll be all right."

Tarkington asked, "The gap?"

"It's a slot through the mountains that keeps us at seven thousand five hundred feet or so. Fog can be a problem, but usually not this early in the morning. It usually shuts down in the afternoon."

Tarkington nodded and turned away, not happy to hear they wouldn't have an escort. The rest of the squad sat in the back. They'd stacked their gear in the center and strapped it down with the various tie-off points. In the back of the plane, six Australian soldiers sat stoically, looking across the aisle at one another. They were replacements for commandos who'd succumbed to various jungle maladies.

Tarkington sat down on the steel plank sticking from the side and buckled in. He pulled the strap tight across his lap, remembering being thrown around when the Zeros had attacked on their trip across the Coral Sea. He'd nearly broken his neck.

An Australian sergeant poked his head into the open hatchway. "'Ave a pleasant flight, Yanks." He pulled the door shut and latched it. The small, dirty windows allowed some light inside, but not enough to make much of a difference.

First one, then the other engine roared to life. The smell of engine exhaust overwhelmed the cabin. The engine's roar made conversation impossible. Lieutenant Spanaour leaned from his copilot seat, waving to get Tarkington's attention. He pointed at his headset, then indicated one hanging nearby. Tarkington pulled it from the hook and put on the headphones.

He heard Spanaour's tinny voice. "We've got clearance. We'll be taking off. Make sure your mates are strapped in tight."

Tarkington gave him a thumbs-up signal. "We're all set."

Spanaour nodded and turned back to his duties on the flight deck. They taxied, then braked abruptly while the engines revved to takeoff power. It was a bumpy ride down the metal Marston matting. It smoothed as the plane lifted off gracefully and darted out over the bay, climbing steadily.

Tarkington watched the world go by through a window. The vibrant colors of the sea mesmerized him. He closed his eyes and leaned his head back against the plane's metal siding.

There was a space left on the bench between the Aussie commandos and the GIs. Corporal Raker leaned across the divide and yelled to be heard. "You wanna cigarette?"

The nearest Australian soldier nodded and extended his hand. Raker handed him a Lucky Strike from a brand-new pack and fumbled in his shirt for a lighter. An Aussie sergeant across the way shook his head and yelled, "Oi. No smoking in flight. Against regulations."

Raker stopped feeling for the lighter. The soldier tried to give the cigarette back, but Raker held up his hand. "Save it for later." He grinned at the Aussie sergeant. "Thought you Aussies liked to bend the rules."

The sergeant's face looked to be chiseled straight from granite. He leaned forward and Raker did too, until they were both straining against their belts. The sergeant scowled. "Not this time, Yank."

Raker smiled at him and leaned back. He put his mouth near Stollman's ear. "Got a stick up his ass or something."

Stollman leveled his gaze at the sergeant, who glared at both of them. "He sure the hell does. Looks ready to tear both our heads off. What the hell did you say to him?"

Winkleman sat across from Raker and one seat away from the surly sergeant. His eyes were slits, but he saw and heard the exchange and saw his men getting agitated. He glanced at the Aussie sergeant, who continued glaring. Winkleman pulled his head from the side of the plane and leaned toward the sergeant. "What's the problem, Sergeant? He was just being friendly—making conversation."

The sergeant tore his simmering eyes from Raker and centered them on Winkleman. Staff Sergeant Winkleman had more stripes than the Aussie, but that didn't seem to matter to him. "Tell your men to mind their own business, Yank."

Winkleman wanted to let it go but couldn't. He leaned closer and seethed, "You'll address me by my rank, and you'll mind your tone, Sergeant." The Aussie lifted his chin and seemed ready to let it go, but Winkleman wasn't finished. "What the hell's the matter with you, Sergeant? Somebody shit in your soup this morning?"

The Aussie lurched forward and glared at Winkleman, who stared back unflinchingly. The Aussie squinted and raised his voice for everyone to hear. "Don't care to be friendly with a bunch of American cowboys."

Winkleman exchanged a glance with Tarkington, who had opened one eye, then shut it, not wanting to get involved. Sergeant Henry chewed on a piece of grass but kept staring straight ahead. Winkleman said, "Cowboys? None of us are cowboys. But what you got against cowboys, anyway?"

"You're Alamo Scouts, or some bullshit like that. Sound like cowboys to me. Hear you're loose cannons—unprofessional and dangerous."

Winkleman grinned. "Well, you got that last part right. We are dangerous."

"My men can run circles around you and your dandy-boy uniforms."

Winkleman looked at his mottled green and brown camouflage as though offended. It wasn't standard issue and set them apart from every other unit in the field. Even clean, they looked unkempt and sloppy. They were that way by design. They blended into the jungle environment perfectly.

He shook his head. "Don't let the uniforms throw you, Sergeant." He leveled his icy blue eyes at him. "If you can run circles around us"—he gave him a sideways grin—"then why're they sending us to do *your* job?"

The sergeant's eyes blazed and his jaw rippled as he gritted his teeth.

Winkleman remained calm and held up his hands. "Take it easy, Sergeant. We can settle this once we land, if you like." He looked at his men, who were watching the exchange like hungry wolves.

The sergeant's commandos didn't look as eager to tangle with the veterans. Besides the sergeant, there wasn't a single combat veteran among them. But he couldn't back down now. "You're damned right we will," he seethed.

Winkleman nodded and leaned his head back against the airplane skin. He sighed. "It's settled, then. See you on the ground."

The C-47 flew low through the gap. The thin, cold air kept everyone awake, and the buffeting from thermals kept them on edge. Thunderheads already formed around the lofty peaks, even though it was still early morning. The tallest peak in the Owen Stanley Range, Mt. Victoria, rose to over thirteen thousand feet. The gap kept them low enough to avoid having to use oxygen. The plane banked and dipped, weaving through clouds and mountain peaks. Tarkington looked outside. Seeing how close they flew to impossibly green and impassible hillsides made his stomach lurch. The plane jinked and banked, flying as though being pursued by the devil himself. He focused his attention back to the inside of the plane and held onto the seat.

Finally, they passed beyond the gap. The banking and jolting lessened, and the air temperature rose. They flew comfortably for five minutes. The air smoothed out, and Captain Wainwright leaned over and his voice came through the headset. "We're through the worst of it. Smooth flying from here. Not long now."

Tarkington leaned forward. "Coulda really used one of those Sheilas back here."

Wainwright grinned. "I'll file an official complaint for you, Lieutenant."

The plane suddenly banked and dropped, pulling Wainwright's attention back to the cockpit. Tarkington's stomach lurched, and the seat belt cut into his waist. Men gasped and called out, their voices laced with fear.

The copilot screamed, "Zeros twelve o'clock high!"

Wainwright took the controls back, and they continued diving. Tarkington could hear the engines screaming as they pushed to full power. He leaned forward and glimpsed the green ground through the cockpit window growing larger. It looked as though they'd fly straight into the looming jungle. At the last moment, Wainwright pulled up, and Tarkington suddenly became aware of his own body weight. He felt as though someone stood on his shoulders as the g-forces grew.

The plane leveled, and his weight returned to normal. The plane banked suddenly, and over the din of the engines he heard the zipping sound of machine-gun fire. He stayed leaned forward, remembering the last time he got caught on the wrong end of a Zero's machine guns.

The roar of an aircraft flying past in a whir made him look out the window near his shoulder. He glimpsed a flash of green. The enemy plane's speed made it feel as though the C-47 stood still. He imagined they must look like an irresistible target to the high-performance fighters.

They banked hard the other way. Tarkington's head slammed into the airplane's curved wall, and he saw stars. He struggled to lean forward and stay forward, but it was difficult. More zipping machine guns, and this time he felt and heard the impacts. The right engine's noise changed from a steady roar to a whining scream.

He heard the copilot's calm voice. "Lost number two."

Wainwright's strained voice answered, "Shut it down and feather the prop."

"Done," came the curt reply a few seconds later.

Wainwright yelled, "Where are they?"

Spanaour finally answered, "I—I don't see 'em. I think they're gone."

"Keep your eyes peeled, but help me with the stick. She's heavy and losing altitude. Must've damaged the elevator."

Tarkington keyed the mic. "Can we do anything to help you?"

Wainwright's strained voice answered, "Stay strapped in. We will not make the airfield. Have to ditch, and it won't be pretty."

Tarkington's stomach felt as though he'd swallowed a beehive. All the soldiers stared at him, hoping for information. They looked as scared as he felt. He whipped the headphones off. He yelled over the whine of the single engine trying to keep them aloft. "Stay strapped in! We're crash-landing!"

The news didn't make anyone happy. His men braced themselves, and the Australians mimicked them. Tarkington didn't have the slightest idea how to brace for a crash landing. He pulled his knees to his chest and wrapped his arms around his knees, figuring the smaller and more protected he could make himself the better. But he knew—in the end—survival was a roll of the dice.

The plane shook and shimmied and seemed to slide sideways through the air. Tarkington couldn't believe they hadn't hit the ground yet. He regretted taking the headphones off but didn't want them to yank his head off upon impact. Perhaps they'd make the airfield after all.

He was about to uncurl himself and chance a peek out the cockpit window when Captain Wainwright yelled in a raspy voice, "Brace for impact!"

Tarkington felt the nose of the plane lift and then felt the bottom drop out. Seconds later, a horrendous wrenching noise and he was thrown sideways toward the cockpit, then up, then down, then back. He felt like a rag doll. The seat belt would either give way and he'd fly and splatter against the metal sides or he'd be cut in half by its tenacious grip.

Intense light suddenly shone in as the plane ripped open in the middle with an ungodly tearing sound. Before the front section spun away, he glimpsed the back section tumble along the ground, sending up huge divots of dirt and vegetation.

The plane seemed to plunge along forever. Finally, it stopped with a shuddering groan and settled onto its side. Tarkington faced up, staring at Sergeant Henry. Henry hung by his belt and looked to be either dead or unconscious. Tarkington's head swam in and out of darkness, and dizziness swept over him in waves.

Something dripped onto his forehead, and for a moment he thought it was gasoline. He forced himself to focus and recognized blood dripping from Henry's head. He reached blindly for the safety belt release and finally found it. He felt weak, and he couldn't make the simple mechanism work. He desperately pulled and pushed, but it wouldn't budge. He reached for the knife along the outside of his shin. He clutched the handle and pulled the razor-sharp blade out. It took a single stroke to cut the belt loose.

The tension across his waist immediately released, and he rolled from the steel plank and pulled himself to his knees.

His ears roared as though a river ran through his head. Gradually, he heard groans and men calling out in the gloom. A hand touched his shoulder, and he heard his name. "Tark! Tark! You okay?"

He recognized Winkleman's voice. He nodded and answered groggily, "Yeah, I'm okay...I think." He pointed to Henry, still unconscious and hanging from the belt. "Let's get him down."

Winkleman got as close to Henry as he could. "He's alive. Strong pulse and he's breathing."

Tarkington felt relief flood his system, and he nearly collapsed.

"Stay put, Tark. You might have a concussion. Stolly, help me get him down."

Tarkington watched them work to release Henry from the belt. They finally had to cut him loose and catch him. His weight collapsed them both, and they ended up in a pile.

Tarkington took in the scene. The back section of the airplane was gone. The front lay on its side; broken wires sparked and sizzled. He felt as though he had sharp nails wedged in his throat. "Where's Raker and Vick?" he rasped.

Winkleman unwound himself from beneath Henry and pointed. "They must be in the back section." He propped Henry into a sitting position. His head lolled, and he moaned.

Stollman poked his head into the cockpit but didn't linger too long. "Jesus, Joseph, and Mary." He stepped back, shaking his head. He looked at Tarkington. "They didn't make it."

Tarkington noticed the small stream of thick blood running from the cockpit and pooling against a metal strut. He turned away and pushed himself to his feet. Stollman came to his aid, but Tarkington pushed him away. "Gotta find the others." Stollman nodded and gingerly stepped over twisted metal and their strewn combat gear.

Tarkington followed him, finally stepping from the inside of the twisted airplane and onto churned-up black soil. He stood to his full height, glad to be out of there. He could see the tail section. The plane had dug a trench in the ground, and it looked as though half a tunnel had been dug, connecting the two airplane sections.

Stollman trotted toward the smoking carnage, and Tarkington followed, but much slower. He noticed gear and bits of unidentifiable airplane parts strewn everywhere. He leaned down and picked up a carbine rifle. It looked to be undamaged, and he slung it over his shoulder. He noticed a body sprawled on the lip of the ditch. The uniform told him it wasn't one of his men, but that of an Australian commando. The body glistened with blood, and his limbs bent unnaturally. The sightless eyes stared up at the clear morning sky. The soldier's mouth hung open as though about to take a spoonful of soup.

Stollman made it to the tail section and called out, "We've got survivors."

Tarkington tore his eyes from the dead Aussie and stumbled the rest of the way. Once at the edge, he saw bodies sprawled everywhere. Some moved, some didn't. Stollman stumbled from the back, helping a dazed and bloody soldier in a torn mottle-camouflaged uniform. It was Raker, and he helped another soldier along, an Aussie. Along the edges of the plane, more Australian commandos pulled themselves upright and stumbled their way toward the jagged opening.

Tarkington continued scanning the carnage but didn't see Vick. Stollman helped Raker and the wounded Australian sit down. Raker's uniform dripped blood, and Stollman nervously searched for the wound. Raker shook his head. "It's not my blood, Stolly. I'm fine."

Tarkington kneeled, feeling the micro-cuts which seemed to be all over his body, pulling and stinging. He placed his hand on Raker's shoulder. "Have you seen Vick?"

Raker met his worried gaze and shook his head. "He's not back there." Then he asked, "He's not in front?"

The Aussie sergeant stumbled from the wreckage, helping a limping soldier along. Stollman went to him and helped him step down. The sergeant grunted, "Thanks." He helped his man to the ground beside the others, then stood. His cheek had a deep cut, which bled freely. He pressed his hand over the wound and looked at the surrounding carnage. "My God." His eyes stopped on the body propped on the lip of the trench. He shook his head. "Dunworth." He looked back at the tail section. The stunned survivors coughed and moaned. He saw another mangled body beyond them. "Bing didn't make it."

Tarkington added, "The pilots didn't either. We're still missing a man, Corporal Vick."

The sergeant's head snapped up as though remembering. "I saw a man get flung out when the plane ripped in half. Might be your man."

Stollman shot to his feet, and Tarkington joined him in the search. His mind cleared slightly, but he still felt groggy. He moved carefully but with renewed purpose.

Walking past the tail section, he saw the long, furrowed trench marking the doomed C-47's path. On either side, large trees loomed, and he marveled at the dead pilot's skills. If they'd hit one of those, they'd all be dead. One wing marked where it had clipped a tree and torn loose from the fuselage. The engine smoldered and sparked. The propellers bent back nearly ninety degrees. He surmised the plane had broken in half at that point.

Winkleman caught up to him. "Henry's fine. He took a hard hit, but he's coming around."

Tarkington nodded. His voice was heavy with emotion. "Vick's missing. Probably got thrown."

Winkleman's color drained as he took in the scene. Stollman yelled Vick's name and frantically searched the area. Winkleman patted Tarkington's shoulder. "We'll find him, Tark."

3

Vick opened his eyes a slit and saw blurry green. Pain lanced into his head as though someone had thrust a spike through it. He evaluated his body. He lay on his back. He felt pain, but nothing specific. His head hurt worse than anything else, but that might change once he tried to move. The greenish world slowly came into focus. The light shooting into his eyes made him wince, as though he stared directly into the sun.

For a moment he thought he might be dead but then shunned the idea, hoping death wouldn't be this pain-filled. He suddenly remembered the plane crash. He looked around in a panic. Was he mistaken? Where was the wreckage? Perhaps he really was dead. Then he remembered seeing the gap open in the side of the plane right beside his seat. He remembered feeling his seat belt snap and flying through the air. From there, a blank... until right now. He wished he could descend back into the painless blackness he'd emerged from. Where were the others?

He forced himself to sit up and look around. He saw the gash in the ground marking the path of the plane. He'd been thrown nearly fifty yards. Bits and pieces of unidentifiable parts of the airplane littered the area, but he heard no sound beyond the normal jungle noise and his own heartbeat in his ears. He didn't see anyone.

He focused on a distant stream of smoke lazily drifting through the sky.

That would be where he'd find the others, he thought. Would he find bodies? It didn't seem possible that anyone could survive.

He rolled to his hands and knees and crawled through a stand of brush. Thorns and branches held him, but he pushed and finally broke through. The tail section poked from the ground and looked wholly out of place in the lush jungle. He heard voices. He strained to see who they belonged to. He tried to get to his feet, but the pain and dizziness overwhelmed him, and he only managed to get to his haunches before he fell sideways, suddenly breathless.

More voices called out, and he thought he heard his name. Blackness impinged on the periphery of his consciousness. He struggled to stay awake. If the others couldn't find him, he'd be alone and left for dead.

He focused on staying conscious. He opened his mouth and tried to yell, but nothing came out. His throat felt like it had filled with glue. A shape emerged from around the front of the wreckage. He recognized his best friend, Stolly. Was he imagining things? No, Stolly was real.

Relief coursed through him. He felt a weight lift from his shoulders, knowing his friend had survived. But the worry returned as he thought of the others. Who'd made it, and who hadn't? Perhaps it would be better to simply descend into the darkness.

A hand on his shoulder shook him awake, and he winced. He opened his eyes and saw Stollman's fire-red hair gleaming in the tropical sunlight. His eyes shone through his blackened, soot-streaked face. Stollman's smile stretched, and he said, "There you are, you son of a bitch."

Vick smiled. He tried his voice again, and it came out like dry gravel. "You found me."

Stollman hollered, "He's over here."

Vick cringed. "You hafta yell?" Shapes emerged, and soon familiar faces surrounded him. "Tark's Ticks," he murmured and passed out again.

Once they found Vick, they got to work tending to the wounded as best they could. Two pilots and two Australian commandos were dead. One of the Aussie survivors had a badly broken leg. His face blanched white as a bedsheet and beads of cold sweat streamed from it. He rocked slightly and clutched his right leg. It canted at an odd angle.

The Aussie sergeant, who introduced himself as Sergeant Omar, cut the commando's pant leg away and pulled back in revulsion. The pallid white skin near the wounded man's lower thigh stretched tight over a mass of broken bone threatening to push through. "God almighty," Omar seethed.

Tarkington left Vick's side and joined Omar. He saw the grisly break, then looked the commando in the eye. "What's your name, soldier?"

The commando tore his eyes from Omar and refocused on Tarkington. "I'm Stuart." He shook his head. "I mean, Private Gordon."

Tarkington nodded and kept his focus on Gordon's eyes. "Don't look at it, son. You've got a bad break. Gonna hurt like hell, but we need to get a splint on it."

Private Gordon's eyes flashed with fear. "It—it's not bad right now. Feels numb."

"Good. That's good."

Gordon looked hopeful. "Just leave it for now. It's fine. I'll wait for rescue."

Tarkington glanced at Sergeant Omar, who gave him a hard look. Omar leaned forward and looked into Gordon's eyes. "We've gotta get a splint on it, or you'll lose your leg, mate."

Tarkington scowled at Omar. "He's blunt, but he's right, Private." He held up a small syrette. "This is morphine. I'm gonna give it to you before we set your leg. It'll help with the pain."

Winkleman came from the tail section, along with Stollman and Raker. Winkleman checked on Sergeant Henry as he passed. He had a bloody bandage on his head. He'd gotten his bell rung and probably had a mild concussion. He wanted to help, but Tarkington insisted he rest.

Winkleman made his way past the line of Aussie commandos. Besides gashes and cuts, they'd escaped serious injury. Winkleman kneeled beside Tarkington and took in the nasty leg break. He forced himself not to react, seeing the private's fearful eyes upon him. He addressed Tarkington. "Found most of the weapons and gear. We cobbled enough together for everyone. Also found a charred but usable flight map. From the few landmarks and our flight time, I think we're about ten miles from Wau."

Tarkington nodded. "Good. I didn't hear the pilots calling in an emergency, so Wau probably has no idea where we are. We're definitely overdue by now."

"Think they'll send out a search party?"

Tarkington exchanged a look with Sergeant Omar. "If they weren't healthy enough for a reconnaissance mission, doubt they are for a rescue mission. I think we're on our own."

Winkleman grinned. "Wouldn't be the first time."

Tarkington nodded his agreement, then indicated Private Gordon. "Gordon's leg needs to be set. Have the men scour the wreckage for anything that can be used for a splint. Twine or wiring too. If we need to, we can get into our own ropes."

Winkleman stated, "Henry and Vick got their bells rung, but they're already coming around."

Tarkington said, "We were damned lucky." Omar glanced at the four dead men lined up near the front section. Tarkington added, "Obviously not everyone was." He raised his voice and said, "Sergeant Omar, get your men collecting and divvying up the ammunition. Water and food too. Most of the packs came through okay, but find the best ones and get us ready to leave. We'll also need to fashion a stretcher for your man here."

Omar hesitated for a fraction of a second, then nodded. "Yes, sir." He stood and started ordering his men to the task.

Soon, Tarkington sat alone with Private Gordon. The young commando's eyes darted like that of a wild animal searching for a place to hole up and die. The pain was obviously becoming more of an issue. Tarkington gave him his most fatherly smile and touched his shoulder. "It's gonna be all right, Private. When we get the splint ready, I'll give you the morphine. Don't wanna give it too early. We want you nice and loopy for as long as possible." Gordon's eyes took on a feral look, and Tarkington squeezed his shoulder, bringing Gordon's full attention back. "Understand? I need you to be strong." Gordon closed his eyes and nodded quickly. Tarkington smiled. "Attaboy."

Gordon smiled through the pain. "*Attaboy*? American slang." He lay back and gazed at the incredibly blue sky.

A few minutes later, Winkleman and the others returned holding lengths of charred metal torn from various points of the aircraft and wiring cut from the rudder and aileron controls.

They stacked it next to Gordon. The noise made him sit up, and his face blanched from the pain. He clutched at his leg, and his eyes gaped at seeing the grisly wound for the first time. Panic rose and he tried to back away, but Winkleman got behind him and held him fast. "Easy—easy does it."

Tarkington held up the syrette. "I'm gonna give this to you now."

Gordon struggled to get control of himself, and Tarkington plunged the tiny needle into his leg. The effect was immediate. Gordon's eyes went from sheer panic and pain to glassy warmth. He settled back down, and Winkleman rested his hands on either shoulder, ready to hold him down.

Tarkington looked at the others. "Anyone know how to set a break?" All eyes went to Vick, who acted as their de facto medic.

Vick still felt considerable pain, but the dizziness had passed. He shook his head. "Just 'cause I carry more medical supplies doesn't mean I'm a trained medic." He added, "You guys got the same training I did, and none of it involved setting a compound fracture." He rubbed the back of his neck. "Besides, I'm not ready to do a hell of a lot."

Henry got to his feet and carefully wove his way to Tarkington's side and crouched. "Get outta the way, Tark."

Tarkington looked sideways at him. "You sure you're all right?"

Henry shrugged as he looked the leg over. "Good enough."

"You done this sort of thing before?"

Henry nodded as he ran his hand over the wound. The skin felt hot to the touch. He sighed and drawled, "This is gonna be a group effort." He pointed. "See how the leg's getting pulled to the side? We gotta pull it down, straighten it, then splint the hell outta it."

Tarkington nodded. "Okay, he's on morphine."

"He'll still feel it, but he'll most likely pass out. We need to brace his body, otherwise we'll just pull him down. Those muscles and tendons are stronger'n you think."

"The others can hold him in place," Tarkington suggested.

Henry shook his head. "That won't work. He needs to be braced against something solid." He looked around at the wreckage. He pointed at one of the plane's wheel struts. It had been torn loose from the wing's undercarriage and stuck vertically in the ground, as though shot from a bow. The shredded wheel hung and slowly rotated in a light breeze. "Take him over there and put the wheel between his legs."

They moved him as gingerly as possible. Gordon's eyes shot open, and he grinned at Winkleman, who held his right shoulder. He mumbled something incomprehensible. They set him down, straddling the firmly planted wheel apparatus, and Gordon closed his eyes and floated into the ether with a soft moan.

Henry directed them. "Okay, Wink and Stolly, hold his upper body firm. He'll wanna rotate. Don't let him. Tark and I will pull his leg down and try to get it lined up." He looked at Raker, Vick, and the four remaining commandos. "You assist where needed, but get ready with the splints. Once we let go, they've gotta be in place or his leg'll twist again."

Sergeant Omar looked Henry straight in the eye. "You sure about this, mate?"

"He'll lose his leg if we do nothing." Henry shrugged. "This might kill him. His femoral artery's intact or he'd already be dead, but there's a risk this'll shear it."

All eyes went to Sergeant Omar. It was his man, so his call. He reached forward and adjusted Gordon's crotch around the wheel structure. "At least we won't crush his knackers."

Henry nodded. "All right...on the count of three. One, two, three."

Henry, Tarkington, and Omar pulled. The sound of crunching, grinding bone nauseated them. Gordon fought to sit up, his eyes suddenly blazing, but the men kept him down. Winkleman lay across his chest and felt as though he rode atop a bucking bronco. Soon Gordon relaxed, and his body went limp.

They pulled on the leg and the strain of straightening it was clear on their sweating brows. They grunted and gasped and were finally able to pull the leg into place.

Henry ordered, "Now. Put the splint on now."

They quickly put the six lengths of metal rods around the leg and used all the metal wires they had salvaged to keep them in place.

Henry nodded. "Now we see if it holds. Let the pressure off slow." They released their grips in increments until they no longer touched the leg at all. Henry smiled. "That's looking good." He looked at Vick, who felt the side of Gordon's neck. Vick gave him a nod. "Okay, let's move him and raise his legs over the level of his heart."

They moved him off the wheel strut a few yards and propped his legs on a spare pack. Gordon was still blessedly unconscious. His face had a pasty, yellowish tinge but was improving by the second.

Henry touched the leg. It looked discolored and swollen. "The artery's still intact. If he doesn't go into shock, he'll be all right."

Sergeant Omar asked, "He won't lose the leg?"

"Don't think so, but he'll need to go under the knife soon, or he'll always have a limp. Hell, he probably will anyway. That's a bad break."

Tarkington asked, "How many of those have you done?"

Henry gave him a sideways grin. "Including that one? One."

Tarkington raised his eyebrows. "Dammit, Henry. How d'you know what to do?"

"Uncle Theo told me about doing it on a boy that got attacked by a gator. Nearly ripped his leg off. His bone was sticking out of the skin, so not exactly the same."

Tarkington shook his head. "The boy live?"

"Nah, they tore his artery clean in half. Sprayed 'em like a firehose. Died in under a minute." He rubbed his forehead. "Gonna sit down for a spell. My head's acting up."

~

They fashioned a stretcher out of metal stanchions and parachutes that they'd found in the plane wreckage. They hefted Private Gordon's limp body into it and took turns hauling him.

The farther they travelled, the more their respect for the skill of the deceased pilots grew. As far as they could tell, they'd put the plane down in the only open ground long and wide enough for such a task. Perhaps it had been luck, but the soldiers realized the pilots had saved their lives.

They moved generally northeast. The walking was relatively easy, but they kept the pace slow. They didn't know for sure how far from Wau they were, so they didn't push and expend their supplies and energy too quickly.

Although it felt like they were in the middle of nowhere, Tarkington sent Raker forward as a point man. There'd been no reports of Japanese south of Wau, but he didn't want to bet his life or those of his men on it.

Raker stopped and waited for the others when he came to a sloping hill. Tarkington joined him and pulled out the flight map he'd found in the cockpit. Since arriving on Papua New Guinea, their maps had improved markedly. However, the Australian's flight map had much more detail than the maps they'd been given.

Tarkington looked around and noted the surrounding hills. He glanced back and forth between the map and the real world and finally placed a finger on the map. "I think we're right about here."

Raker nodded. "I agree. Looks like we just get over this mountain, and the valley beyond will lead us right where we wanna go."

Tarkington kept staring at the map. "We might run into locals in that valley. They can get word to Wau or give us a hand getting there."

They slugged water and ate a few bites of their meager food supplies. Everyone felt sore from the crash, but no one complained. Refreshed, they slowly climbed the hill. The foliage thickened, and the stretcher made it tough going, but soon they crested the hill and looked out over a good-sized valley.

The day waned past noon. The temperature hung near eighty degrees, and the humidity made it feel oppressive. Sweat ran off their bodies as though they'd been sprayed with a garden hose. All of them had been in the region for months but would never truly be comfortable. At least it wasn't as hot as being at sea level.

They sat and drank, hoping they'd find water in the valley. Streams usually dotted the region and they could refill canteens, but they hadn't come across any on the way up. Henry pointed into the valley. "Smoke down there."

Tarkington squinted and finally saw what his eagle-eyed scout saw. A stream of white smoke wound its way from the valley floor on a thin tendril. "Good eyes. Looks like a cooking fire. Must be a village down there."

Sergeant Omar wiped his brow. "Gordon's waking up some. I think the morphine's wearing off."

Tarkington nodded. "Hopefully we'll be able to borrow a cart or something for him in that village."

Omar noticed the tendril of smoke and frowned. "Might be Japs."

Tarkington shook his head. "I don't think so, but we'll be careful just in case."

They moved down the hill. The terrain eased and they made excellent time, but the area where they'd seen the smoke didn't seem to get closer. Raker heard water babbling over a small waterfall. His thirst spiked. He grinned and hurried toward it. He called out, "Hey, over here. I found water."

The others quickly joined him. Raker had his head dunked, and he slurped the clear water deeply. Soon, the others drank and filled canteens. A feeling of unease came over Tarkington, and he looked around for his lead scout, Henry, but he couldn't find him.

He turned in time to see a scantily clad native emerge from the forest like a wraith. He'd painted his face in cracking red and white, and his bloodshot eyes stared intently from within deep-set eyebrows. He held a spear at head level, ready to hurl its deadly point into Tarkington. More emerged until they were surrounded. The others noticed and stopped in mid-slurp. Most of their weapons were out of reach.

Tarkington smiled and raised his hands. "Don't do anything stupid," he said from the corner of his mouth. "The natives are normally friendly toward us. Don't give them a reason to skewer us." The rest of the soldiers raised their hands and smiled.

The native closest to Tarkington had his eyes locked on him. He spoke, and it mystified Tarkington. They'd studied rudimentary native speech, mostly Pidgin English, but the more they learned about New Guinea, the more they realized how many varied languages and dialects there were. Even villagers living only a few miles from each other couldn't understand one another.

Tarkington continued smiling. "Americans. Australians. Friends."

The head man didn't lower his spear but raised his voice. It didn't sound like anything Tarkington had ever heard. He continued smiling until his face hurt. The head man cocked the spear, and Tarkington thought about what he'd do if the man threw it. The Americans and Aussies were outnumbered. They might get a few, but by the time they got to their weapons, they'd most likely be skewered.

From behind the head man, Henry emerged and placed the barrel of his carbine against the back of the man's head and muttered something very Cajun and just as baffling, but the intent was obvious; throw the spear, you die.

The other natives turned in surprise, and Henry pressed the barrel harder. The head man uttered something, and his men lowered their spears. Henry backed away and allowed the native to turn and look at him. The native spoke again, and Henry replied in Cajun. There was no chance either man understood the precise content, but they didn't need to. Mutual respect flowed between them like the babbling creek they stood beside.

4

The natives guided them to their village in the valley. They couldn't communicate with spoken language, but Tarkington felt confident the natives hadn't mistaken them for Japanese. Some tribes had never seen a white man, let alone a Japanese soldier. But this village wasn't far from Wau or Salamaua on the coast, both of which had been occupied by the Japanese. Through hand signals and gestures, Tark's group had made it clear they wanted to go to Wau. The leader they'd met in the woods seemed to be the chief of the entire village. He nodded, gestured, and made airplane noises. He mimicked flight with arms spread and indicated they'd take them to Wau tomorrow.

Sergeant Omar wanted to leave right away, protesting that his wounded man needed proper medical care. Tarkington pulled him aside. "You're going to have to trust me. We've got a lot of experience with natives. It's best to let 'em treat us as guests. They want us to stay and feast, so that's what we'll do. To do anything else might very well lead to our throats being cut."

"But what about Gordon? He could die out here."

Tarkington pointed. A topless native woman had Private Gordon's head resting in her lap as she stroked his hair and cooed a soft song. He looked as content as any man with a freshly broken leg could look.

Despite the hospitality, the Australians kept their guard up, careful to keep the natives in sight and in front. But for Tarkington and his men, it was all too familiar. They relaxed and allowed the native women to fawn over them. The villagers provided food and fruit-infused water.

Tarkington sat between Henry and Winkleman. He propped his carbine against a log. "Well, Henry, you've done it again. If those had been Japs, we'd all be dead by now."

Henry shook his head. "Japs can't move like that. And by the way, you'd be dead—I'd be fine."

"I don't know how you do it."

Winkleman shook his head and lifted his chin toward Raker. "And I don't know how Raker does it. I mean, he doesn't even speak the language. He's said nothing, and they're flocking over him."

Raker lay on his back, his head in the lap of another topless native woman. She smiled and stroked his thick hair while another woman dropped bits of food into his mouth and muttered. Tarkington said, "He really has a way with women."

"I'll never hear the end of it," Winkleman lamented.

Tarkington laughed and clapped Winkleman on the back. "I'd take him up on his offer."

Winkleman looked offended. "You mean, setting me up?" Tarkington raised an eyebrow in the affirmative. "Never happen!" erupted Winkleman.

"You only live once, Staff Sergeant, and out here, time gets short quick."

As the day faded to evening and finally darkness, even Sergeant Omar let his guard down. The natives regaled them with delicious meat, cooked over a bed of coals and sprinkled with fruit and herbs. Omar tore off a size-able chunk of meat, and the savory juices dripped off his chin. "This is bonzer meat. What is it?" he asked Tarkington.

"Best not to ask too many questions," he responded with a wry grin.

"What d'ya mean by that?" he asked, wiping the meat juice from his chin.

Winkleman chimed in, "They're probably head hunters. Could be long pork."

Omar glanced at the remaining meat in his hand. "Long pork? That different from regular pork?"

Winkleman looked him straight in the eye and without an ounce of mirth said, "Might be Jap or maybe an enemy tribesman."

Sergeant Omar stopped chewing and stared at the bone he was sucking the meat from. He blanched for a moment. "You mean human meat?" He guffawed. "You're pulling my leg." He put the meat aside, eyeing the bone suspiciously, and dug into a potato-like root.

~

The soldiers sat around the fire pit and stared into the dying embers. The feast had been a welcome change from bully beef and C-rations. Soon, wood-carved cups were passed to each man. Tarkington sniffed the warm liquid. Sergeant Omar sat up and put the cup to his lips.

Tarkington leaned close and muttered, "Careful. It might have..."—he paused—"medicinal effects."

Omar looked from Tarkington to the cup, then to Private Gordon, who'd been sipping from a similar cup for the past thirty minutes. Omar thought his increasingly odd behavior was delirium from the pain of his broken leg. Gordon had his hands up, and he moved them slowly in bizarre arcs, as though dancing. He seemed to be utterly mesmerized by their movement, and the grin on his face reminded Omar of men he'd seen in opium dens before the war.

Omar sniffed at the steam coming off the top. Tarkington shrugged and took a mouthful, swallowing loudly. He watched Omar watching him. "If they wanted us dead, they'd a-done it a long time ago." Omar watched the others sipping. His commandos upended their cups. Omar took a sip. It had a slightly bitter taste but wasn't unpleasant. He drained the rest and set the cup down.

Tarkington grinned. "See you in the morning."

Omar looked at him with surprise. "You're not staying up?"

"I am, but you might not remember much from this point."

Omar looked alarmed, but Tarkington assured him, "Don't worry, we'll look out for you and your men."

Ten minutes passed before Sergeant Omar suddenly laughed. He stared at the coals, leaning forward intently as though trying to read from afar. His eyes widened and sparkled, and he laughed again. His men across the circle stared at him in wonder, then joined him. Soon the circle filled with grinning, laughing soldiers and natives.

Tarkington felt the buzz in the back of his head, but he'd dumped most of his drink into the dirt. It wasn't for prudish reasons; he'd experienced similar concoctions in the Philippines and enjoyed the experience, but he figured someone needed to be in control, at least a little.

His men had no such qualms, and soon the entire group was hooting, laughing, and carrying on. A steady drum beat began and the lead native stood and danced in a stomping circle, and his painted warriors joined him. They stoked the fire and their darting, dancing shapes stood in silhouette against the orange and yellow flames. GIs and Australians soon became part of the mix. Tarkington grinned and clapped along with the drumbeat. Women joined the circle of gyrating, dancing men, and soon the dancing turned sensual.

He watched Winkleman rubbing against a topless young woman. The sultry look on his and her faces reminded Tarkington of Nurse Gallop. He hadn't seen or even thought of her in months. He wondered what she was doing at that exact moment. He wished he could describe what he was seeing unfold in front of him at that very moment. He was sure she'd delight in the seductively sensuous scene. He decided he'd look her up if he ever got back to Australia.

A young woman appeared in front of him. She reached her hand out to him as her hips flexed and thrust. He looked around the village, but the glare of the fire didn't allow him to see more than a few yards. He didn't fear a Japanese attack. If the enemy did ambush them, they'd be dead whether or not they were inebriated. The fire might attract the attention of a passing Japanese aircraft, but he thought the likelihood of that happening was slight.

He got to his feet and felt a wave of well-being flood through him. The woman smiled seductively, her hand reached for his. "Aw, why the hell not?" he uttered to himself and took her hand.

Tarkington awoke with a start. He felt refreshed, as though he'd slept soundly for many hours. The warm body beside him brought the night's events into focus as though he were watching a movie. He pressed into the young woman's back and felt her smooth skin emanating heat. She cooed but stayed asleep.

He heard the noise that had brought him from his dream-laced sleep— a low-flying aircraft. He reluctantly left the naked young woman's warmth, slung his carbine, and stepped from the little thatch hut. The sun blazed, but it lay low in the east; still early morning. The village sat deeply in the trees, but Tarkington noticed a small clearing nearby. He trotted toward it, maneuvering around the fire pit. Two Australian soldiers slept on thin reed mats, entangled with naked native women. They had taken Gordon into a nearby hut, and the older women attended his leg and kept him comfortable.

He didn't see Sergeant Omar. The last time he'd seen him, he'd been dancing and gyrating like a crazy man between two topless women. He wondered if the drug-induced experience would dull the sergeant's hot temper. Since the crash, the altercation on the plane hadn't come up, but he doubted his men had forgotten.

He broke into the small clearing and shielded his eyes as he gazed into the blue sky. The droning engine noise seemed to come from everywhere and nowhere. It bounced off the valley walls, making it impossible to pinpoint which direction it came from.

Henry touched his shoulder, and Tarkington jumped in surprise. "Dammit, Henry. Why you always sneaking up on me?"

Henry ignored the question. As usual, he had a long piece of green grass between his teeth. He squinted into the clear sky. "See it yet?"

Tarkington shook his head. "Not yet. Sounds low."

Henry nodded his agreement. "Think it's one of ours?"

"Yeah. Bet they're searching for us, or at least for the wreckage. We're way overdue."

"Think a few flares survived."

Tarkington scowled. "I'm not *that* sure. But that's a good idea. Got any nearby?"

Henry turned. "Be right back." He adjusted his slung carbine and trotted back toward the village.

The droning engine noise got louder and seemed to come from the north. Henry returned carrying a pack and a flare gun pistol. He handed the flare gun to Tarkington. They both watched the sky to the north. The sound grew louder and louder until it seemed right on top of them. A flash of dull green painted metal got their attention. A C-47 flew a couple hundred feet above the treetops. The roar of the dual engines became the only sound. The plane turned, and Tarkington could clearly see the right-seat copilot. Tarkington stepped forward, his face catching the sun, and he waved frantically.

The plane sped past. Henry stepped beside him and asked, "Think he saw you?"

The engine noise changed as the pilots added power and the plane rose a few more hundred feet and made an arcing turn back their way. Tarkington loaded the flare gun, and when the C-47 faced their way, he fired. The red flare streaked into the morning light in a graceful arc.

The plane continued winging its way toward them. The engine pitch changed again as the pilot pulled power and slowed. The rest of the soldiers emerged from the forest. Excited natives bounced on the balls of their feet, babbled, and pointed.

The pilots took a slow pass over them, giving them a good look. They took another pass and tipped their wings in greeting. "Wish we had that damned radio," cursed Tarkington. The bulky radio they'd been issued hadn't survived the plane crash. The spare batteries had but were useless to them, so they'd buried them near the pilots and commandos.

On the third pass, the pilot opened the cockpit's side window and chucked something out. It fluttered into the center of the grassy field. Raker ran to it and brought back a notebook held closed with twine.

He held it up and grinned. "Some post for you, Tark."

Tarkington snatched it from him, untied the twine, and read the note. He grunted, then relayed the message. "They found the wreckage. They've drawn a map of sorts to Wau. Says we're about ten miles away. They wanna know if we need help." He looked for his second-in-command. Winkleman stared at him with glazed eyes. He had the look of a man who hadn't slept the night before. Tarkington scowled. "He wants two flares for yes, one for no." He looked at Henry. "We got enough?" Henry nodded and pulled two more flare shots from his pack. Tarkington fired two off, and the plane made another pass, waggled his wings, and disappeared back north.

The villagers jabbered and laughed. It reminded Tarkington just how far from modern Western civilization they were. Seeing airplanes certainly wasn't new for the natives, but seeing them fly that close and dropping gifts onto their village caused quite a stir.

Henry rubbed the back of his neck. They all still felt sore from the violent, wrenching crash the day before. The effects of the medicine had worn off, and they became reacquainted with their aches and pains. Tarkington had a general full-body ache, but Henry's head throbbed with a persistent headache. The medicine had allowed him to sleep, but now the pain assaulted him with a vengeance. He uttered, "Glad we're getting help. I'm not feeling too spry at the moment."

Tarkington looked concerned. If Henry complained, he must really be in bad shape. "Headache?"

Henry spit out the grass and nodded. "More like a sledgehammer hitting me over and over. *Ache* doesn't do it justice." He lifted his chin. "I'll be fine. Just need a few hours."

Tarkington nodded. "You'll get it. No reason for us to move out until help arrives. It'll give us time to cobble together a cart for Gordon. I'm sure the chief here'll let us borrow a few of his men too."

Sergeant Omar heard the exchange. "The men coming from Wau aren't in the best of shape from everything I've heard. It's why they asked for us in the first place."

"I know," Tarkington replied, "but with the villagers' help and your troopers' knowledge of the terrain around Wau, we'll make good time. They won't have to do much work. The natives are young and strong and willing to help. Besides, they won't send anyone who can't hack it."

Sergeant Omar nodded and pulled Tarkington aside for a private word. "Sir, Captain Grumskey's in command of the garrison in Wau. He's a bit of a stickler, especially when it comes to drinking and imbibing of any sort." Tarkington looked surprised. Omar shrugged. "I know us Aussies have a reputation for drinking. It's earned, but Grumskey's not that type of officer.

He loathes the reputation and damn well doesn't allow it in his command. It's earned him the nickname Granny, although no one would dare say it to his face. He'd literally tear a man limb from limb if he heard it." He licked his lips and continued. "I don't think he'd be too keen on last night's..." He searched for the proper word.

Tarkington grinned and filled in the blank. "Shenanigans?" he offered.

Omar's chiseled features softened as he considered the foreign-sounding word. "That sounds right."

Tarkington slapped his back. "Last I saw you, you were having a good time, and out here that's worth celebrating, but I understand completely. Your secret's safe with me, Sergeant."

Omar smiled, and it looked unnatural for him. "It was quite a night. Feel like a fool now, though."

"Nonsense. You were no more foolish than anyone else."

"What was in that drink, anyway?"

Tarkington shrugged. "I don't know for sure. Probably tree bark or maybe frog excretion."

"A frog? Fair dinkum?"

Tarkington gave him a quizzical look.

Omar said, "I mean, is it true?"

Tarkington grinned at the slang and answered, "It's true. As long as the natives are drinking the same stuff, I don't worry about it. It seems to be part ceremony, part just having a good time. Kinda like how we drink more during the holidays back home."

Omar tipped his jungle hat back off his forehead. "I've gotta admit," he held up two hands as though weighing, "if offered a pint in one hand or frog sweat in the other..."

Tarkington tilted his head. "One's a lot easier to come by than the other. Probably a good thing." Omar nodded his agreement, and Tarkington got back to business. "Let's get the men fed and working on a solution for getting Gordon outta here without damaging him more. I'd like to be ready to move first thing in the morning, assuming your pals make it here today."

Omar braced smartly. "Yes, sir."

5

Native villagers intercepted the Australian contingent from Wau and led them the last mile. Six Australian commandos, led by Captain Grumskey himself, strolled into the village in the early afternoon.

Tarkington had his shirt off and sweated profusely as he helped work on a cart to make Private Gordon's trip more pleasurable. Grumskey stepped into the village boundary, took a long look, then barked, "Who's in charge here?"

Tarkington turned at the unfamiliar voice. He wiped his brow with the back of his hand, wiped his hand on his filthy camouflage pants, and stepped forward. "Me. I'm Lieutenant Tarkington, US Army Alamo Scouts." He didn't salute in case an enemy sniper lurked nearby.

Grumskey nodded back. "I'm Captain Grumskey. I think you're expecting us."

"Yes, sir. Thanks for coming. We made it this far, but one of your men has a badly busted leg. The more men we have to help, the better."

Sergeant Omar emerged from a hut, followed by the two other uninjured commandos, Corporal Dobbs and Private Dawbry. Omar strode up to Grumskey and braced. "Sergeant Omar reporting, sir."

Grumskey nodded and looked around furtively. "Good to see you in one piece, Sergeant."

Omar pursed his lips. "Yes, sir."

"What's the situation, Sergeant?"

He pointed at the two strapping young commandos behind him. "Corporal Dobbs, Private Dawbry, and myself survived the crash with cuts and bruises. Private Gordon suffered a severely broken leg. He's in the hut resting, sir." He lifted his chin. "We lost Private Dunworth and Bing. Both pilots too. They died instantly, sir."

The corners of Grumskey's mouth turned down, and Omar added, "It's a wonder anyone survived."

Tarkington nodded his agreement. "The pilots saved our asses. They threaded the needle and avoided most of the trees. They deserve a lot of credit."

Grumskey stated, "When you didn't arrive, we checked in with Moresby, and they sent out another transport. They found the crash site easily enough." He shook his head. "We can't afford to lose planes. What happened?"

Sergeant Omar stiffened. "Jap Zeros jumped us soon after we got over the Owen Stanleys. The pilots avoided them for a while, but that's not a fair fight, sir."

"I've been telling them we need fighter escort even for these short flights." He shook his head in frustration. "What a waste." He looked around at the gawking natives. "Good thing the natives are friendly. If they sided with the Nips, your heads would be on spikes by now."

"Can't understand a word they say," Tarkington said, "but they're certainly friendly." He grinned slyly.

Sergeant Omar gave him a worried sideways glance, but Captain Grumskey didn't pick up on the innuendo. "Can we move Private Gordon? I'd like to get back to Wau as soon as possible."

Tarkington stated, "Judging by your timing getting here, we won't make it to Wau before dark."

Captain Grumskey squared his shoulders. "That's correct. But the Nips are coming over the Black Cat Track from Mubo. The Seventeenth Brigade is due to fly in tomorrow morning to reinforce us. I'd like to be there when they land. Is there a problem?"

Tarkington shook his head. "No, sir. Just assumed you'd rather get a full night's sleep and move out in the morning."

Grumskey pushed his bush hat off his forehead. "You assumed wrong, Lieutenant." He glared at Omar. "Now, what's Gordon's status?"

Omar pointed at the cart. "We can use this. We think the natives will help us push him, but without an interpreter, we can't be sure, sir."

Grumskey waved it away. "If they want to help, I won't stop 'em." He lifted his chin toward the six soldiers he'd brought along. "These are my best men. They're up to the task." They looked tired, and hearing they'd have to retrace their steps without a break didn't sit well. They exchanged glances with one another but didn't speak up. Grumskey directed, "Fill up your canteens and get some food. We leave in thirty minutes."

They made good time while the daylight lasted. The further down the valley they traveled, the wider and easier the track became. A few young men from the village helped them along but halted when the valley turned from northeast to northwest. Tarkington tried to figure out why. He coaxed them to continue, but they simply smiled and shook their heads.

He finally gave up, and Grumskey explained, "There's another village up ahead. They probably don't get along. I see it all the time. Their worlds encompass a relatively small area, and they don't encroach on others unless they're on a raiding party."

"A raiding party?" asked Tarkington.

Grumskey nodded. "Yes, they'll go to war with their neighbors sometimes and raid them. They'll take food and women, that sort of thing."

"You passed through that village this morning?"

"We skirted around it, but I'm sure they noticed us."

"Anything we need to worry about?"

"They're not overly friendly, but they're not outwardly hostile either. We'll skirt around them to the west. There's a well-used footpath."

Tarkington looked at the darkening sky. "Be dark in another quarter hour."

Grumskey nodded. "My men know the way. They'll find the footpath and get us past safely."

Grumskey moved ahead, and Tarkington watched him go. Winkleman strode up beside him, and Tarkington grumbled, "He's going to push his men to the brink."

Winkleman agreed and indicated the cart. Now that the natives were gone, Private Dawbry and Corporal Dobbs pushed and pulled the cart along the bumpy track. "This pace isn't doing Gordon any favors."

Tarkington noticed Gordon's strained features. Every bump and jolt made him wince. He didn't call out, but his lip was bleeding from biting down constantly.

Tarkington went to the side of the cart and put his hand on Gordon's shoulder. "How you doing?"

Gordon forced a quick smile. "Fine, Lieutenant. Fine."

Tarkington adjusted his sling and pushed Corporal Dobbs aside. "I'll take a turn. We'll switch out every fifteen minutes." Winkleman took over for Dawbry.

Sergeant Omar walked behind them, covering their tail. He saw the exchange and moved closer. He looked embarrassed. "Thanks for helping out, sir."

Tarkington shrugged. "Your boss says we're going to skirt a village that may or may not be friendly. So keep your eyes peeled for trouble."

Omar nodded and took his rifle off his shoulder. "We've gotta worry about the natives, too?"

"Probably not, but you never know. Frankly, I'd rather deal with Japanese than angry natives." He thought back to Luzon and the trouble he and his men had had with a group of rogue villagers. He realized that had been over a year ago. It staggered him to think of how much had happened since. He shook his head. They'd been through a lot together. Would it ever end?

He grimaced, reminding himself of the vow he'd made to himself. He'd do whatever he could to end this war as quickly as possible. His resolve hadn't changed. If anything, it had increased.

The last letter he'd received from his brother, Robert, stated he looked forward to getting into the fight. Against his older brother's wishes, Robert had dropped out of college and joined the Marines, of all things. The censors had a field day with the letter, but Tarkington knew he would be in the thick of things. He'd hoped to keep Robert out of harm's way, but he'd failed.

The cart jolted as they strained to push the wheels over a thick tree root. Gordon couldn't keep from yelping. He bit down on his lip, reopening the cut. Darkness encroached on them. Soon they moved along a narrow path, just barely wide enough to accommodate the cart. A quiet descended on the group, as though they instinctively knew danger lurked nearby.

Tarkington saw Henry a few yards ahead. He had his carbine off his shoulder and held it at the ready. Tarkington looked around, trying to get a sense of the surrounding jungle. He heard creek water babbling nearby and the incessant buzzing of insects. Night animals would be coming from wherever they'd spent the sweltering day to hunt for food. He hoped the natives weren't hunting tonight.

Tarkington and Winkleman gave up their spots on the cart but stayed close by. The Aussie commandos on point slowed as the darkness made staying on the trail more and more difficult. No orders had been given, but each man had his weapon in hand and ready. When they needed to talk, they did so in hushed voices. The night air felt oppressive and close.

Henry slowed until he and Tarkington walked side by side. He hissed, "I don't like it." Tarkington shut his eyes, knowing his lead scout's hunches and feelings never steered him wrong. His sixth sense had saved them countless times. "We're being followed."

"Japs?"

Henry shook his head slow. "Nah. I'd know that for sure. Think we're being tailed by the natives from the village we passed by."

Tarkington nodded. "I'll tell Omar. He's tail-end charlie."

"Have him tighten up. He gets too far from the main group, they'll take him."

Tarkington wanted to ask Henry what he was talking about but thought better of it. He faded back, allowing the cart to pass along with Winkleman and the two Aussies who were now on cart duty.

Winkleman came closer. Tarkington could barely see the features of his face. Winkleman asked, "What's up?"

"Henry's buzzer's going off. I'm checking on Omar. You seen him?"

Winkleman nodded. "Saw him a few minutes ago. He's not far back there." They both stopped and waited. The darkness suddenly felt heavier and more foreboding. After a full minute, Tarkington raised his eyebrows. Winkleman couldn't see the motion but understood Tarkington's concern. "He shoulda been here by now," Winkleman whispered.

They both crouched and aimed their carbines into the blackness. Tarkington ordered quietly, "Tell the others to stop."

Winkleman hesitated for an instant, then moved off, whispering, "Be right back."

Tarkington concentrated on every sensory input. Something had happened to Omar. He didn't know the Australian sergeant well but knew he wouldn't stop without first telling someone. The darkness pushed in around him. The insect and night animal noises should be louder. He gripped his carbine and clicked the safety to the off position. He had the distinct and wholly frightening feeling that eyes watched his every move.

The fading creaks and moans of the cart stopped. Winkleman had caught up and warned the group. Tarkington crouched and stayed perfectly still. He listened, watched, and smelled the jungle.

He felt, rather than heard, Henry crouch beside him. Raker arrived a few seconds later. Each aimed their muzzles in different directions. The feeling of being watched disappeared, and the darkness suddenly didn't seem as oppressive.

Henry said in a conversational tone, "They're gone."

"And they took Omar," Tarkington said.

Henry drawled, "Yep."

They moved back to the cart and found the rest of the squad and the Australians waiting nervously. Captain Grumskey strained to see past them. He growled, "Where's the sergeant?"

Tarkington answered, "We think warriors from the nearby village took him."

"Taken?" The captain looked as though someone had slapped him. "You mean killed?"

Tarkington shrugged. "I don't think so." He looked abashed. "I don't know for sure, but I've heard of it in some of the more remote villages we've come across before. Are you familiar with the Native American Indians' practice of counting coup?"

Grumskey shook his head, and Tarkington explained. "It's a bloodless way of disgracing your enemy. Before us white men came around, the Indians would have turf wars, just like the tribes around here do sometimes, but instead of outright slaughter, they'd count coup. Getting close enough to touch an enemy without them seeing you was a major victory and a major disgrace to the warrior they touched. No one died, but the victory and defeat were no less real. I'm thinking this is the same sort of thing, but instead of just touching the enemy or stealing their horse, they've taken him."

"That's—that's ludicrous. It's—"

Tarkington interrupted, "I'm not worried about his safety. Not yet, anyway. I think maybe the villagers don't appreciate us walking back and forth along their path, and this is their way of telling us to knock it off. Or maybe they expect a toll or something."

Grumskey shook his head and pinched the bridge of his nose. He finally looked up and said, "Well, let's get him back."

Tarkington rubbed his chin. "Gordon's hurting, sir. He needs to get on that plane back to Port Moresby. My men and I have a lot of experience dealing with indigenous people. Let us get your man back. We're over halfway to Wau. We can find the way from here."

Grumskey pursed his lips, mulling it over. "You sure you can handle it? I could send a few of my men with you. More men might make negotiating easier, particularly if it comes to blows."

Tarkington shrugged. "You've been marching almost twenty-four hours, sir. We had an entire day of rest. Besides, I doubt they'd be intimidated by more men."

Grumskey squinted and looked around the darkness. His men kneeled, taking advantage of the break. Tarkington added, "If we're not back by tomorrow evening, send help."

Grumskey finally nodded. "Okay. I'll allow it, Lieutenant."

Tarkington smiled in relief. "I'll take the two spare rifles in case we need to do some horse trading." Grumskey looked at him curiously, and Tarkington explained, "You know, trading. In case they want something in return for Omar."

~

Tarkington waited until he could no longer hear the squeak and rattle of the cart. He motioned his squad to gather round and filled them in. "We're gonna find this village and get as close as possible without being seen. It'll be our way of counting coup against them. At the very least it'll earn their respect."

Stollman shook his head. "How the hell you know all that Indian crap, Tark?"

Vick smacked Stollman's shoulder. "Jiminy Christmas, Stolly. Read a book once in a while, would ya?" Stollman looked around the group for help, but they all acted as though the concept of counting coup was common knowledge, so he didn't persist.

Tarkington lowered his voice. "Okay. I want Henry and Raker leading. From here on out, no noise."

Winkleman touched Tarkington's arm. "What if we find them cutting on him—or he's already dead? What if you're wrong about their intentions?"

"Then we'll fade away and tell Grumskey he's got a hostile village on his flank."

They moved east from the path. Small game trails weaved between thickets and vine-laced trees. The stars overhead put off just enough light to discern the paths, and they kept one another within sight. They moved slowly and silently, making sure of each footfall.

An hour passed before Henry stopped and held up a fist. Tarkington figured they'd only made it a couple hundred yards from the path. Sweat dripped off his nose, but he ignored everything except staying quiet.

After a full two minutes passed, Tarkington slithered up to Henry and settled in beside him. He didn't need Henry's help to see the village. The flickering glow from a small fire drew his attention. Thatch huts on stilts surrounded the area, but he saw few villagers. Two painted warriors stood near the fire, and between them, Sergeant Omar sat stripped and bound. The warriors held long spears and smug expressions. Relief flooded Tarkington. If they'd meant to harm Omar, they would have done so by now.

The juxtaposition of last night and tonight almost made him laugh out loud. He wondered what Sergeant Omar thought of his captors. He certainly wasn't having as much fun as he'd had the night before.

Henry moved glacially and pointed to his left. Tarkington leaned forward and peered into the gloom. A thick stand of brush and trees sprouted from the lush ground. Tarkington couldn't see anything out of place, but Henry's eyes and sixth sense were better tuned than his own. If Henry believed the bushes and trees held warriors, they did.

Henry held his hand up, telling Tarkington and the others to stay put. Tarkington nodded and slowly lay onto his belly and pushed back into a thicket. Someone would have to step on him to find him. Henry moved off like a dark wraith. One second he was there, the next he wasn't.

Raker slithered close and whispered into Tarkington's ear. "More of 'em to the right."

Tarkington nodded and signaled that Henry had gone left. He whispered, "Can we get by them?" Raker nodded. Henry would try to get close to the warriors on the left. He didn't know what end-game plan he had, probably just get as close as possible. Perhaps if they could get past the others on the right, they could get behind the warriors guarding Omar and sneak up on them. Tarkington got Winkleman's attention. He was a few yards behind, on his belly and nearly invisible. Tarkington signaled for him to stay put, then signaled Raker to lead them right.

Raker crawled into a slight defilade, and Tarkington followed. They moved painstakingly slow but finally got past the thicket where Raker had seen the warriors. A commotion from Henry's area made them both freeze. Movement only yards away revealed an unseen warrior's position. The warrior trotted toward the commotion silently. Once he'd gone past, Tarkington shared a relieved glance with Raker.

They increased their pace and soon found themselves behind the raised huts and the two warriors guarding the hapless Sergeant Omar. The

GIs lingered in the darkness beyond the glow from the fire. From across the clearing, they saw more warriors emerge. They held Henry between them and brought him to the fire, forcing him to sit beside Omar. Tarkington heard him cursing in full-blown Cajun. He grinned, sure he was making a fuss to cover them.

He motioned for Raker to follow. The warriors faced the fire and struggled to contain Henry between them. With their carbines up, Tarkington and Raker ran silently across the clearing and were upon the group before they could react. The warriors froze, seeing the carbine muzzles pointed at their heads and the grinning soldiers behind them.

More warriors emerged from the darkness. They ran forward with spears and bows and arrows cocked and ready to throw and fire. Behind them stepped the rest of the squad. They held their weapons ready but kept the muzzles aimed toward the sky.

Stollman grinned like the Cheshire Cat. He nodded toward his friend, Corporal Vick. "This counting coop enough for you, asshole?"

Vick shook his head. "*Coup*, not *coop*, you dumb-ass."

6

Tarkington awoke again to the sounds of nearby aircraft engines. He rubbed his eyes and sat up painfully. Soreness wracked his body, and he decided this must be how old men felt in the morning. He stepped from the thatch hut, surprised to see that the sun had already peeked over the eastern horizon.

Other squad members moved about, and Tarkington saw Sergeant Omar among them. They'd traded both spare Lee-Enfield rifles for his release, and the villagers insisted they stay with them for the rest of the night. Despite taking Omar by force, there was no more hostility.

He joined the men watching two C-47s winging toward Wau. Tarkington shaded his eyes. "Must be shuttling in the Seventeenth Brigade. We better get on our way. I'd like to get word out that we're alive and we need a new radio."

After a breakfast of dried meat and roots, the villagers walked them to the path skirting the village, and the chief regaled them with a speech no one understood. When he finished, he chambered a round into his newly acquired Lee-Enfield rifle and fired into the sky. He whooped, and the other villagers joined in and waved their spears and bows.

The GIs took that as their cue to leave. They nodded and waved, then turned away and walked along the path without looking back. The natives continued hooting and whooping until they disappeared around the corner. Winkleman shook his head. "Thought they'd never stop hollering."

Tarkington nodded. "Let's pick up the pace."

None of them felt recovered from the crash. Their bodies still ached, but Raker increased the pace and the others pushed through their pain and kept up. The path wound haphazardly but continued generally north. More C-47s flew over them, both coming and going. The squad could judge how far from the airfield they were based on how low they flew.

"How many troopers can they squeeze into one of those?" Tarkington wondered aloud.

Winkleman shrugged. "Ours wasn't near full. I'd say at least twenty fully loaded men."

"We've seen at least six today, so figure they got one hundred and twenty men down? Maybe a light company."

"That's a good guess. More on the way, probably."

Tarkington shook his head. "Captain Wainwright told me the gap through the Owen Stanleys only lasts till midmorning, then gets shut down by fog. Probably won't see more today. Don't forget, they've gotta fly back too."

"Hope they got Gordon out," stated Sergeant Omar.

Tarkington added, "Me too. We won't get our radio until tomorrow at the earliest. If we don't get there before the last flight out, we'll need to send word by radio."

Raker continued leading them along the track. The path diminished in width somewhat, but the deep tracks left by Gordon's cart left little doubt that they were on the correct path.

The roar of a nearby aircraft made them all look up through the thin layer of leaves. A C-47 flew low overhead. The wheels disappeared into the underside of the wings, telling them it had just taken off. It roared mightily, then faded as it moved past the ridge and out of sight.

Raker stopped at the edge of a clearing. Tarkington stepped forward and got his first glimpse of Wau village. Dust marked the airfield along the southern edge. No planes remained. Men holding packs and weapons sprinted off the airstrip. A hissing screech made Tarkington duck. The men at the airfield, merely stick figures from this distance, dove for cover. A second later the screech ended with a dull thump, and a dirt-filled explosion erupted near the edge of the airfield.

"Mortars," Tarkington said.

Three more shells arced through the sky and exploded near the airfield. Raker pointed to a low hill overlooking the village. "I saw smoke from over there. Think that's where they're shooting from."

Tarkington nodded. "How'd they get so close? Thought the Aussies had 'em bottled up and accounted for."

"Apparently not," drawled Henry. He pointed back to Wau. "Looks like they're sending out a welcoming party."

From the eastern edge of the village, a line of soldiers spread out and moved along a dirt road. The mortar barrage ended. The GIs strained to see the Japanese mortar crew but couldn't.

Tarkington waved them forward. "Let's get into town and find out what's going on."

~

They entered Wau using the same road the troopers had used to pursue the mortar crew. A few foxholes and trenches dotted the area, but mostly, the town was wide open. No one challenged or even acknowledged them until they walked into the center of town.

The soldiers who'd been there a long time were easy to distinguish from the new arrivals. Some looked more like civilians. The only thing distinguishing them were the rifles slung over their shoulders.

One of them took notice and approached. He wore a filthy, floppy jungle hat that covered thick dark hair. His most striking feature was an untended thick beard. He was tall and thin but carried himself like a combat veteran. He stopped in front of them and looked them over. He smiled, and his teeth barely showed through his beard. In a thick Australian accent, he said, "'Allo there. Who the bloody hell are you?"

Tarkington stepped forward. "I'm Lieutenant Tarkington, and these are my men. We're US Alamo Scouts." He pointed at Sergeant Omar. "And that's one of yours."

The Australian's eyes lit up and his smile grew, pulling his beard up and rounding his head like a plate. "You're the blokes from the plane crash," he stated. "Grumskey's lot went to find you. Americans, right?"

Tarkington nodded. "That's right. Now, who the hell are you?"

He slapped his chest with a closed fist as though mimicking a legionnaire from Roman times. "Corporal Nance of the NGVRs at your service, Lieutenant."

"NGVR? Thought you were being airlifted out of here."

Nance's smile disappeared, and he looked affronted. "I've been here from the start. Wau's my home. They suggested we leave, but most of us chose to stay on."

"Suggested? I thought they ordered," growled Sergeant Omar.

Nance's smile returned, and he looked squarely at Omar. "New Guinea *Volunteer* Rifles. That's our name. They can't bloody well order volunteers around too much. We'd just quit and do what we bloody well wanted anyway."

Omar's jaw rippled as he clenched his teeth. Tarkington grinned and looked behind the big man. Troopers in uniform scurried about carrying gear recently offloaded from the C-47s. In contrast to Corporal Nance, they looked like brand-new shiny coins. Tarkington pointed their way. "Is Captain Grumskey that way?"

Nance turned and pointed. "He's near the airfield last I saw, briefing the general, I think."

Omar asked, "Did they get Private Gordon out today? He had a broken leg."

Nance smiled and nodded. "Yes, yes. He got out just fine. Rode out with other injured commandos and one or two NGVRs who chose to leave." The sound of distant gunfire made them all turn back toward the hills. Nance said, "Nips got past our pickets on the Black Cat Track somehow."

Tarkington nodded. "We saw the mortar attack."

Still staring toward the gunfire, Nance continued. "Yes. That's the first time they've done that. I don't think it's the main force, though. We got word that they moved through Mubo only yesterday. There's no way they could travel that quickly. Most likely an advance element."

A group of Australians, some wearing standard new AIF uniforms and some wearing torn and faded commando uniforms, rounded the corner and entered the block. They surrounded an older man, and Tarkington saw he wore the rank of a brigadier general.

Tarkington cursed under his breath. "Dammit. I wanted to avoid this."

The entourage of officers noticed them and approached. The general's smile looked crooked on his face, and it made his well-manicured mustache twitch. The GIs and Omar snapped to attention but didn't salute. The general didn't seem to notice or care. "What do we have here? Americans?" His deep voice made Tarkington think of his father.

"Yes, sir. I'm Lieutenant Tarkington, and excluding Sergeant Omar, these are my Alamo Scouts."

The general pursed his lips and then focused his blue eyes upon him. "I'm General Murray Moten, good to meet you. Alamo Scouts. Hmm, I'm not familiar with that unit." He leaned forward and inspected the small Indian head sewed onto the shoulder of Tarkington's camouflage uniform. He shook his head. "I wasn't informed of an American element here in Wau."

Tarkington nodded. "It's an honor to meet you, sir. We were...delayed. We were supposed to pass through here two days ago and be out of your way by now."

General Moten glanced at the commando commander, Captain Grumskey. "These are the men that got shot down?"

Grumskey nodded. "Yes, sir." He pointed at Omar. "Sergeant Omar... well, they had to deal with the villagers down the road. That's why they didn't come in with us."

Moten looked from one to the other. He clasped his hands behind his back. The distant sound of a firefight wafted on the breeze. "Well, I'd love to hear the entire story someday, but it seems the bleeding Japs are knocking at the front door." A smattering of agreement from the officers, and Moten continued. "We got almost a full company in today, but the fog shut the pass down earlier than expected. Tomorrow, we'll get two more companies in, hopefully. Until we're reinforced, I'll need to fold you and your Alamo Scouts into the defense of Wau."

Tarkington ground his teeth and finally said, "We have orders from Colonel Bradshaw, sir. All we need's a replacement radio and we'll be gone."

Moten's eyes hardened. "It's not up for debate, Lieutenant. The situation's dire. Unless I hear from MacArthur or Blamey personally, I need every available man to repulse the Japanese regardless of your original mission. Understood?"

Tarkington stiffened and nodded. "Yes, sir. Understood."

"Good. Get your men fed and settled, then join me in the CP."

"Yes, sir." He watched the group of officers move past. He noticed Captain Grumskey's sympathetic gaze. When they were out of earshot, Tarkington addressed the GIs. "You heard the man. Find us a place to hole up, Wink. Henry, see if you can find a proper medic and get your head looked at. You too, Raker."

Raker shook his head. "I'm—"

Tarkington interrupted, "Do it." Raker noticed the instant change in Tarkington's mood and nodded. He joined Henry, who asked Corporal Nance for directions. Tarkington rubbed the back of his neck as he walked away from the others. He headed toward the building the officers had disappeared into and muttered, "Dammit. Can't things ever go as planned?"

By midafternoon, Tark's Ticks followed a bedraggled group of Australian commandos up a dirt path they called the Black Cat Track. Despite their sore, battered bodies, General Moten wanted their unique skills as reconnaissance soldiers to match up with his own special units and find the main Japanese force.

Tarkington listened in while Captain Grumskey briefed the general and brought him up to speed on the area surrounding Wau and the Bulol Valley. He used a well-worn map. Tarkington kept his distance but took in the information.

He learned that the Black Cat Track connected Wau with Salamaua. The name derived from the Black Cat Mine, which sat along its winding path. Any force coming from Salamaua would have to use the BCT, so the NGVRs, who'd proven their reliability countless times, watched it. They'd reported seeing the force at Mobu but hadn't seen them since.

The mortar attack and ensuing firefight in the hills beyond had come as a complete surprise. It made Grumskey and Moten think the enemy soldiers might have found an alternate route. The commandos' and Alamo Scouts' job was to find them.

The commandos led the way up the winding track. They quickly climbed higher than Wau's three thousand five hundred feet and soon looked down upon it. The surrounding hill vegetation was relatively light. The further the BCT dove into the hills, the thicker the jungle became. But so far, walking was easy.

Tarkington kept his men separated from the commandos. Grumskey's men, led by a veteran officer, Lieutenant Willoth, moved well and obviously felt at home. Grumskey stayed at the CP but, before they'd pushed off, told Tarkington that Lt. Willoth had played an integral role in the raid upon the airfield at Salamaua several months before. Tarkington saw the hardness in Willoth's eyes, formed by months of deprivation and combat against a tenacious enemy. It only took a few minutes of patrolling for Tarkington to trust him completely.

After an hour, Willoth called a halt. His men spread out, unslung their packs, and drank from their canteens. The weather looked to be taking a turn for the worse. Tarkington made sure his men had what they needed, then strode up to Lt. Willoth. "Looks like it's going to piss on us any second."

Willoth glanced at the darkening sky and towering clouds. "It's the beginning of the rainy season. We're in for it."

"This trail must suffer."

Willoth finished gulping water, then wiped his mouth with the back of his hand. "It holds up better than you'd think, but parts of it wash out further along around Mobu."

"Maybe the Japs are trying to get in place before the rains begin."

Willoth nodded. "That and before too many reinforcements from Moresby arrive."

"One under-strength company of commandos, a couple hundred NGVRs, and a company of AIF troopers. Will it be enough?"

Willoth shook his head and pointed to the hills to the east of Wau. "As you can see, once the Nips get in those hills with any kind of numbers, they can sweep through us easily. Conservative estimates counted two thousand soldiers heading our way. We'll need the entire brigade if we're going to stop them."

"Two thousand?"

"I hear the original force numbered five thousand, but our flyboys whittled down their convoy."

Tarkington pointed at the trail. "And this track is the only way through?"

Willoth looked concerned. "I thought so, but maybe they found another way. That forward element should've been spotted."

Tarkington nodded. "I've been wondering about that, too. If they're the forward element, why give themselves away with a mortar strike? They didn't do any damage, just gave away their position."

Willoth asked, "You think they're trying to draw us out? Like a feint from the main thrust?"

Tarkington shrugged. "We gotta find the main force."

Willoth screwed the cap back onto his canteen and clipped it to his belt. "Black Cat Mine's another two miles. From there, we'll meet up with more NGVRs and see if they have any news."

The remaining miles took a full hour to complete. The track wound into valleys, through ravines, and alongside cliffs. A soaking rain added to their difficulties. By the time they crested yet another hill and saw the telltale signs of a large mining operation, everyone felt exhausted and ready to enter the shelter provided by the mine's old run-down buildings.

Willoth stopped them with a raised fist. The commandos went to their knees, and the GIs instantly followed suit. They watched the camp from a slightly raised position. It looked quiet and dark, reminding Tarkington of a ghost town from the Old West.

Willoth signaled his men to move out with caution. Tarkington scooted forward until he could see the camp better. Nothing looked out of place, but something had spooked Willoth. The commando glanced back at Tarkington and signaled for him and his men to stay put. He swallowed his pride and nodded back.

The GIs spread out and watched the commandos move stealthily toward the outbuildings. Tarkington kept the muzzle of his carbine aimed at a dark, glassless window on the second floor of the largest building. Winkleman asked, "What's the trouble?"

Tarkington shrugged. "Willoth didn't like something, and it's his show."

Stollman chimed in, "This rain's making my ass chafe."

Vick swiped a fat mosquito off his nose. "Least it's cutting down on the damned mosquitos."

Stollman whispered, "Never happen. Your blood's too sweet."

The sudden sound of gunfire erupted from the camp. Henry put his carbine to his shoulder and aimed. "Muzzle flashes from inside."

Tarkington hissed, "Don't fire. Could just be startled NGVR troopers. Let Willoth take care of it. Watch our flanks."

The Australian commandos hadn't fired a shot but continued closing in. Yelling and sporadic firing continued from inside the camp. Three commandos closed in from the back of the largest building and burst through the door. No shots rang out, and the rest of the commandos poured in from side doors until no one remained outside.

For half a minute, nothing happened. Tarkington felt odd, as though the buildings had somehow swallowed the men whole. A shiver ran up his spine, and he felt goosebumps on his arms. He shook his head and silently cursed his imagination. Finally, Lt. Willoth emerged from a dark doorway and waved the all clear.

The GIs moved cautiously, keeping their eyes on the surrounding jungle. More commandos exited the buildings. Their faces looked grim, weary, and disgusted. The steady rain dripped off the brims of their hats. Tarkington approached and raised an eyebrow to Willoth.

Willoth took off his hat and ran a dirty hand through his hair. "The shots came from a wounded Volunteer—thought we were more Japs. It's a slaughterhouse inside. They left him for dead but cut on the others." He lowered his eyes and shook his head. "He had to listen to their screams. He was too far gone to save. He's gone along with the others." He pinched the bridge of his nose, remembering the grisly scene. He blew out a long breath. "Before he passed, he said he heard a lot of men, but he didn't know how many exactly."

Tarkington nodded grimly. "Didn't pass by us, but we'll be able to track them easy enough, if the rain doesn't interfere too much."

7

While the GIs watched the trail for more Japanese, the commandos buried the four NGVR soldiers. No one wanted to stay in the blood-soaked mining facility, so despite the rain, they huddled deep in the jungle brush and watched.

Winkleman leaned close to Tarkington's ear and whispered, "If more come, we gonna take 'em?"

Tarkington heard the venom in his voice and turned to search his camouflaged face. Winkleman's eyes smoldered with hatred. Tarkington wondered what had happened to the strong streak of morality that used to course through his second-in-command. The rain dripped through the branches and wetted their backs with fat drops. He shook his head. "The mission is to find them, not kill them."

"After what they did to those Aussies?"

Tarkington flashed on the scene, which he was sure would be added to his stream of nightmares. The soldier who'd been shot and played possum was the only man who hadn't been tortured. The others had been bound and cut to shreds with bayonets. Tarkington leveled his eyes at Winkleman. He seethed. "We'll get payback, but not yet."

Henry and Raker came out of the rain like apparitions and kneeled beside them. Henry drawled, "Found their tracks. Easier than finding a herd of cattle. They split off. They're following a different trail. It heads due south toward the lowlands overlooking Wau."

Tarkington got to his knees. Dirt and mud slid off his mottled tunic. He pointed at Winkleman. "Stay here. We'll tell Willoth we found their trail." Winkleman nodded and focused on the trail. Tarkington turned to leave but stopped and said, "Anything comes down that trail—you let it pass, unless it's unavoidable. That's an order." He didn't wait for Winkleman to reply.

Halfway back to the mining camp, Henry asked, "What was that all about?"

Tarkington shrugged. "Wink wants payback."

Raker nodded and seethed, "Dirty sons of bitches—we all do, Tark."

Tarkington shook his head. "You think I don't? We can't just do whatever the hell we want. The mission comes first." Their boots sunk into the soft ground and squelched with each sodden step. "They're moving on Wau fast. We'll get our chance soon enough."

The commandos had finished putting their countrymen into the ground and were busy stowing their entrenching tools. Lieutenant Willoth's face was a mask of disgust and hatred. Tarkington indicated Raker and Henry. "They found their tracks. They're on a different trail heading south."

Willoth wiped his muddy hands on his pants. "South? None of the maps show a path, and the NGVR troopers never mentioned another track." He asked, "Any idea how many?"

Henry exchanged a glance with Raker. Raker rubbed his chin and answered, "Hard to say on a single track like that, but the rain has softened the ground enough to make deep imprints. I'd say it's a sizable force."

Willoth splayed his hands, wanting more. Henry added, "Only way to know for sure is to get a look-see on 'em."

Willoth stated, "Narrow path, following a superior force...could walk right into an ambush."

"We'll be careful," Henry said with an edge to his voice.

The corners of Willoth's mouth turned downward, and he shook his head. "I don't like it." He waved them into the nearest mining building. "Take a look at this." They stepped into the largest of the buildings. It was dark and smelled of rot and blood. Puddles of oily water covered the floor where it sagged. He moved to a window and spread a map on a rickety table. The map had seen better days. The corners were frayed, and the paper looked thin. Willoth placed a finger on a zigzagging trail. "This is the mine we're sitting inside now. Show me where the Japs split off." He added under his breath, "The Jap Track."

Henry grinned. "Jap Track—I like that." He looked sideways at the map, then placed a finger. "Here." He traced the map's contour lines. "Are these accurate?"

Willoth shrugged. "For the most part. This is a gold mine—a profitable one too. A lot of money went into its development, and the surrounding ten miles have been mapped fairly extensively for that purpose."

Henry nodded. "Then it would make sense that the Jap Track follows this ridge line. The contour lines suggest that it isn't too steep and leads south to the bluffs overlooking Wau."

Willoth moved his finger back down the BCT an inch, then moved due south. The contour showed a hill that rose above the rest. "The top of this hill might have a commanding view of the area south. We could spot them as they come off the ridge."

Tarkington squinted at him. "Might?" he asked.

Willoth tipped his hat back. "Better'n walking into a bloody ambush, mate." He shrugged. "I'll leave a squad here in case more Japs show. The old landline still works from here to Wau. We'll check in, tell 'em what we've found and what we plan to do. They need to know the Nips are coming from an unexpected direction. If we can give them a force size, that'll be bonzer."

Tarkington nodded. "Makes sense to me. We better get going or we'll miss 'em."

After relaying the information to Wau, they split the force. Willoth left one commando squad to watch the track, and Tarkington and the rest moved back down the BCT until they surmised they were abreast of the hill, then moved into the jungle.

It didn't take long before they were climbing. Raker led the way. The slope steepened, forcing him to move across the hill. The GIs followed a few yards behind, and the commandos kept good spacing. They didn't expect trouble, so Raker moved quickly. The rain continued but turned into a mist rather than a downpour. In spots, the jungle floor was shrouded in thick, wafting fog.

Raker saw the peak a half hour later and crouched. The jungle thinned, and Tarkington wondered if they had logged the area. He noticed old stumps, wet with multicolored moss and vines. He looked back and saw Lt. Willoth making his way. When he crouched beside him, Tarkington kept his voice low. "We're close to the top."

Willoth nodded. "We'll move left. You blokes head straight in."

Tarkington watched the Australians move to the left flank. He signaled the squad to spread right and move forward slowly. Raker nodded and moved, using the natural cover. Tarkington followed, keeping ten yards between them.

As they approached the top, Tarkington noticed a wooden structure. Raker glanced back, making sure the others were seeing the same thing. Tarkington gave a quick nod, and Raker continued his advance. Tarkington could see a few commandos off to the left, and they stalked the structure like lions hunting gazelle.

The structure looked abandoned. The walls were faded to dirty gray, but the roof's thatch looked intact. He flicked the safety off his carbine and scanned the surrounding area. He heard a distant whistle and wondered if he'd imagined it. The sound seemed to emanate from inside the building. He thought it might be the wind, but the leaves and trees were as still as stone.

Raker heard it too and crouched, bringing his carbine to his shoulder. Tarkington moved to his side. The whistling stopped. From the corner of his eye, he caught the commandos moving toward the back. The front door suddenly burst open and a scruffy, bearded man holding an old metal pot stepped into the open and flung dirty water.

He turned but stopped suddenly, as though he'd sensed something. He lifted his nose and sniffed, then turned in their direction. His deep-set eyes widened, and his mouth formed an O in the center of his gray beard. Raker kept his carbine aimed and stood. "Stay where you are, old timer," he said with a dangerous edge.

The man dropped the pot and raised his hands high over his head. The pot clanged and rolled a few feet. The man's eyes shifted right and left, taking in the camouflaged forms that suddenly emerged in his front yard.

Tarkington stepped past Raker, who kept the man covered. The rest of the squad moved to the perimeter, searching the area for more unexpected people. As he approached, Tarkington got a strong whiff of the man. He lowered his carbine and gave the man a good look. He didn't wear a shirt, and his skin hung off his thin frame like pale sheets. He wore pants that had either been cut off above his knees or had simply rotted away. His feet were bare and splayed, reminding Tarkington of the countless natives he'd encountered. The commandos moved from the back of the hut, and the man's eyes went even wider. He shifted from foot to foot as though ready to bolt.

Tarkington slung his carbine and held out his hands. "Easy does it. We're not the enemy."

Willoth approached. "Oi, what do we have here?" He stepped beside Tarkington. "Search the shack." Two commandos entered the house carefully, their rifles leading the way.

The old man watched them enter, his face changing from surprise to worry. Tarkington soothed, "They're just checking it out. No need to worry."

"Unless you're hiding something, eh?" added Willoth.

The man's arms still extended straight over his head, but his initial fear faded like melting snow, and his eyes took on a steely glare that bore into Willoth. "Australian." His voice sounded like wet gravel grinding beneath tires. His eyes shifted to Tarkington, and the condescending tone disappeared. "And American?"

Tarkington lifted his chin and nodded. "That's right. What about you? Where you from?"

Before he could answer, Willoth sneered, "He's a bloody Kiwi. Aren't you?"

The man's wiry arms came down, and he smiled, showing off a cavernous hole devoid of teeth. "You bloody well got that right."

The two commandos came out of the shack and shook their heads. "Nothing inside except filth."

The man's smile disappeared, and he squinted at PFC Dawbry. "Keep your filthy hands off my things!" he rasped.

Dawbry adjusted his jungle hat. "I wouldn't touch your trash, yobbo."

Before the old man could respond, Tarkington asked, "Anyone live out here with you, sir?"

The old man's eyes simmered, and he shook his head. "The missus died five years ago." His eyes glistened, and he pointed to a cross on the far side of the clearing. "Addy," he whispered.

Tarkington extended a hand. "I'm Lieutenant Clay Tarkington of the US Army." He indicated his men. "And these are my men." He shifted, indicating Willoth, who continued to scowl with distaste. "And this is Lieutenant Willoth of the AIF."

The old man's cavernous smile returned, and he shook Tarkington's hand. The diminutive man's calloused hands dwarfed his own. The old man hesitated as though trying to remember, then he said, "Name's Clemson Callico."

Tarkington smiled. "Did you work at the Black Cat mine?"

Clemson's face darkened, and he shook his head emphatically. "Hell no. I'm not a bleeding crook, am I?" His eyes lit up. "I've got my own mining operation, and those greedy cocksuckers can't bloody well have it." His eyes went to slits, and he released Tarkington's hand as though it were on fire. "You're not with them, are you? You'll have to skin me to—"

Tarkington held up his hands and interrupted, "No. We're soldiers. The mine's been out of commission for years now. Ever since the Japs invaded. That's why we're here, to kill Japs."

Clemson smiled and asked, "Those Black Cat whores are out of business?"

Willoth answered, "They'll be back after the war, no doubt."

Clemson shot daggers at Willoth, but his interest was piqued. "War? I don't want any part of your war." He took a step toward his open door. "That why you're here? Conscription? I won't go! I'll—"

Again Tarkington interrupted, "We're not here to conscript you, Clemson."

Willoth murmured, "Your bloody stench might shorten the war, though. Nips would take their own lives rather than face you."

Before Clemson could respond, Tarkington said, "We're here to find the Japs. Have you seen any Japanese troops?"

Clemson held up a bent and battered finger. "There has been more commotion than normal lately."

Willoth shook his head. "You backwards bleeding Kiwi. You haven't noticed the war till now?"

Tarkington spun on Willoth. "Give it a rest, Lieutenant. Let the man speak."

Willoth ground his teeth, but he kept his mouth shut.

Clemson nodded. "I can show you."

"Show us what?" Tarkington asked.

"The commotion," he sputtered with exasperation. He turned from his shack and waved them to follow. He moved like a jungle cat as he weaved through the sparse forest. Hand-dug canals snaked through the area, connecting creeks with one another. Sluice boxes were placed in strategic areas to collect rocks and hopefully gold from the little creek's confluence. The whole operation looked like an engineering feat of epic proportions— held together by a thread.

Finally, Clemson led them along a thin ridge line and onto a large mossy rock promontory. The view took their breath away. The moss on top was matted. Clemson obviously spent time here, probably watching the world pass by.

The men spread out. There was plenty of room for all of them. Tarkington shook his head and made an appreciative low whistle. "What a view."

Clemson had a wistful smile on his deeply lined face. "Addy loved it here."

Tarkington nodded. "I can see why. It's beautiful." The hills and valleys rolled out below like a smooth green tapestry. Clouds covered the higher peaks all around, but shafts of sunlight lanced through in spots and turned the dark green to vibrant, almost neon green.

Willoth had his compass and map out. He pointed. "Wau's over there somewhere beyond those hills. You must see aircraft occasionally?" he asked.

Clemson nodded but spoke to Tarkington. "More lately, yes." He pointed to the distant cloud-enshrouded mountains. "They come from the mountains in the morning and drop out of sight. Then they fly back to the mountains. I wonder what it would be like to fly into the mountains."

Willoth sneered, "You woulda found out if you'd been evacuated along with everyone else."

"Evacuate?" Clemson shook his head as though the notion of leaving was impossible to even consider. "Leave my home?" The thought muddled his brain and he spluttered, "I—I could never leave Addy."

Willoth shook his head. "Crazy old loon."

Clemson pointed. "Are those your Japs?" He said the word as though testing it on his tongue.

Tarkington looked where he pointed but couldn't see anything except endless waving grasses and splotches of vibrant colors where wild flowers sprouted. Henry stepped forward and squinted. "I'll be damned. I see 'em." He looked at Clemson with awe. "He's got better eyes than a damned eagle." Clemson gazed at Henry, and his slight smile showed solidarity. They had both lived off the land for years, surviving through backbreaking work, smart decisions, and sheer tenacity.

Willoth pulled a set of binoculars from his pack and focused on the area. He finally nodded. "Now I see 'em." He scanned back and forth for a long time before handing the binoculars off to Tarkington. "Looks like an entire regiment, if I'm not mistaken."

Tarkington finally found the distant enemy troops. They moved in one long continuous line, snaking through the grasses. Their greenish uniforms blended well, and they seemed to appear and disappear as they passed through the tall grass. "Regimental size at least." He kept scanning. "We've found their main force."

Willoth pulled out his map and spread it on the lush greenery atop the rock. He found their position and estimated where the enemy troop column was. The town of Wau was circled on the map. "They're about ten miles from Wau. They could attack any day now."

"Wonder if any more troops came in from Moresby." Tarkington asked Clemson, "You see any more airplanes the past couple of days?"

Clemson nodded. "A few the other morning, but nothing today."

Tarkington exchanged glances with Willoth. Willoth said, "They might've gotten another company landed."

Tarkington frowned. "We're going to need more men to stop them. Once they take the airfield, it's all over."

"A bloody air strike would go a long way right about now."

Tarkington nodded his agreement. "The flyboys are thin out here, and the weather's not on their side today." He looked skyward. "That goes both ways, though."

Willoth took the binoculars back and stuffed them into his pack. "We should get back to the mine and call this in. Maybe our boys got artillery delivered." Tarkington nodded but thought it was wishful thinking with little merit.

They hustled off the promontory, led by Clemson. Despite looking old, he moved like a lithe sixteen-year-old. When they got to his shack, he stopped beside his front door. Willoth smiled. "You staying here? You can come down the mountain with us if you want. We could get you on a flight out of here tomorrow, probably."

Fear crossed Clemson's face, and he shook his head stonily, thinking about the terrifying prospect. He couldn't make himself answer. Henry put his hand on his shoulder. "He's staying right here. You'll be fine. The Japs haven't bothered you by now..." He shrugged. "Stay here with Addy, Mr. Callico."

Clemson beamed, his gums shining through his gray beard. "You've seen her?"

Henry looked him straight in the eye. "She's all around you. You know that," he stated, as though it were obvious.

Clemson looked around his humble surroundings, then darted into the shack, disappearing into the blackness within. He emerged a minute later, holding a large gold nugget between his fingers. He extended it to Henry with a toothy grin. The marble-sized nugget shined brightly between his dark fingers. He plopped it into Henry's hand, and Henry felt the weight. Dark creases and folds crisscrossed through the precious stone. The gold gleamed where it had clearly been buffed and rubbed smooth. Henry beamed. "Thank you. It's beautiful." He tried to hand it back. "It's a hell of a gift, but you should keep it. Might need it later when this whole thing's over."

Clemson shook his head and held out his hands. "Keep it. That's a small one."

They left Clemson Callico at his doorstep, waving.

8

Lieutenant Willoth used the landline at the mining site to report their findings to headquarters. At first he spoke to a sergeant, then Captain Grumskey. Grumskey was excited and told him to stay on the line.

"What's going on?" asked Tarkington. He didn't like being inside the mining building. It reeked of decay and death. He was eager to get back to Wau and hopefully onto his original mission of finding airfields.

Willoth answered, "We've created quite a stir, I think. Grumskey wants me to hold the line."

Soon Willoth stiffened to attention and spoke quickly into the headset. "Sir, this is Lieutenant Willoth reporting." He covered the mouthpiece and whispered to Tarkington, "It's bloody General Moten." His voice returned to normal. "Yes, sir. I'm here. I hear you loud and clear."

Tarkington listened to Willoth explain how they found the Japanese. He failed to mention Clemson Callico's role, and Tarkington wondered if it was out of malice or respect for the man's privacy. Either way, Tarkington thought it best to keep the old codger out of it. Willoth laid out his map and tried to explain the enemy position by referring to landmarks and distances from Wau and the Black Cat Mine. Coordinates would have been easier, but the maps weren't sophisticated and rarely matched and so could be wildly inaccurate.

Willoth finally signed off. He deflated visibly as he hung the handset on the hook on the wall. "General Moten wants us to stay here for the time being. He wants us to wait for reinforcements." Tarkington looked surprised. Willoth continued, "Apparently your Army Air Corps has been busy. They managed to get two hundred men from the Sixth Battalion into Wau over the past two days. Moten's sending two platoons up the track to join us. Once they arrive, we're to lead them to the Jap Track and keep command updated on enemy movements."

Tarkington wasn't happy about the news, but it wasn't wholly unexpected. He wondered if Colonel Bradshaw knew they'd been shanghaied by the Australians.

He joined his men outside. The rain had stopped, but the sky still looked dark and ominous. It was the commandos' turn to watch the Black Cat Track for more enemy troops. The GIs sat beneath dripping trees and ate C-rations. Mosquitos buzzed around their heads like dirty halos, but they'd long since given up on waving them away. Bug spray was useless, and they joked it seemed to attract insects rather than repel them. The longer the men stayed in the jungle, the less they seemed to be bothered by the bugs. It was as though they built up a natural immunity. Everyone except Stollman, whose fair complexion seemed to draw mosquitos in like moths to the flame.

Winkleman made room on a rock, and Tarkington sat down. "What's the dope, Tark?"

"Settle in. We're waiting for a couple platoons to join us, then we'll go down the Jap Track and keep tabs on those sons of bitches."

"Shoulda done that in the first place."

Tarkington shrugged. "Willoth's playing it careful. That's not a bad thing."

"Why're we beholden to the Aussies, anyway? We should cut out of here."

Raker sat a few feet away on the grass, cleaning his pistol. He looked up at Winkleman. "Why you so uptight, Wink? You didn't get laid at the village, did you?" Winkleman's cheek twitched, and he sent daggers with his eyes. Raker continued tormenting him, "If you can't get laid there..." He shook his head sadly. "Then there's no hope for you, Wink."

"Fuck off, Raker." He got up and strode until he stood in front of Raker. His fists were balled tightly, and his veins popped through his bulging forearms. "Get up. I'm done taking shit from you."

Raker set his pistol aside and got to his feet slowly. He stepped forward until they were nose to nose. Raker seethed. "You start it off, Staff Sergeant. Let's see what you've got."

Tarkington considered interfering and stopping the fight, but Raker's relentless attacks had earned him an ass whooping. Both men were vicious, deadly fighters, and both needed to blow off some steam. There'd be black eyes and maybe even a broken nose. But they wouldn't kill one another...he hoped. He turned his back to them. The others watched, wholly entertained.

Winkleman struck first. He pushed Raker back and jabbed with a quick right. Raker ducked and blocked the blow with his forearm, then delivered an uppercut to Winkleman's gut. Winkleman curled over, and Raker brought his fist up toward Winkleman's chin. Winkleman saw it coming and shifted left. Raker's blow missed and unbalanced him. Winkleman jabbed with his left fist and connected with Raker's left cheek. Raker's eyes glassed with tears, and he stepped back, stunned. Winkleman didn't give him a chance to recover. He feinted with another left jab, but the roundhouse right connected and sent Raker sprawling. He went to his knees and spit blood.

Winkleman shuffled his feet like a boxer in a ring. "Come on, you fucking pussy. That all you got?" The GIs whooped and egged them on. Money came out, and they made hasty bets.

Raker lunged and wrapped Winkleman in a low tackle. His powerful legs lifted Winkleman off the ground, and he slammed him onto his back. Winkleman lost his breath for a moment, but adrenaline took over, and soon he was landing blows into Raker's back and kidney area.

Raker released him and rolled off, getting to his feet like a feral cat. Blood dripped from a cut on his cheek, and his teeth were covered in a thin film of red, which turned his sneer sinister. They sized each other up as they circled.

Raker spit. "Come on, Wink. Why don't you—"

Winkleman didn't let him finish. He lunged forward and extended his chin like a prize pig. Raker took the bait, aiming an off-balance roundhouse at him. Winkleman easily avoided it, then he stepped forward and landed two quick jabs. Raker's head snapped back each time, and he stumbled backward. He finally tripped and fell onto his back.

He scrambled to get up, but Tarkington turned back to the action and barked, "All right—that's enough. Put your dicks back in your pants."

Raker got to his feet, but he swayed unsteadily. "That—that's not fair. He—I—we were just getting started."

Stollman cursed as he handed greenbacks over to Henry. "Dammit, Raker. All that training and you fall for that shit? Never betting on you again."

Raker spit blood onto the wet ground. "Fuck off, Stolly. He just got lucky. It'll be different next time."

Tarkington shook his head. "All right, you've had your fun—now let's get our heads back in the game." He leveled his gaze at Raker. "That's an order, Raker."

Raker took a long slug of water from his canteen. He drained the rest over his head to wash away the blood and sweat. He swished and spit a pink stream, then smiled. "Yes, sir, Tark."

The two platoons from the Sixth Battalion showed up a few hours later. An athletic-looking officer, Captain Dane, led the force. Despite his impressive stature, his pockmarked face and darting eyes made him look uneasy and unsure of himself.

The day waned toward evening. The GIs and commandos gave the newcomers disdainful glares. Stollman leaned close to Vick. "They look like toy soldiers in their brand-new duds."

Vick shook his head, "Don't be mad at 'em for showering now and then. You should give it a try, Stolly."

A few NGVR troopers had led them up to the Black Cat Mine. Tarkington recognized Corporal Nance from Wau. Nearby, he also saw Sergeant Omar and a few of his men from the doomed C-47. The crash was still fresh in his mind.

Next to the spit-shined AIF troopers, Omar's men, and particularly the NGVR troopers, looked downright gritty. After introductions and handshakes were made among the Aussies, Nance and Omar broke away and approached the GIs, who'd stayed in the background. Nance's grin was sincere and infectious. "Oi, Americans!"

Handshakes and back slaps ensued. The animosity from the flight had disappeared like the sun behind the clouds. Omar asked, "How's it been out here?"

Tarkington shrugged and indicated the four gravesites beyond one of the buildings. "Not good for the Volunteers."

Nance looked at the shining white crosses marking the Volunteers' final resting place. He took off his jungle hat. His smile disappeared, and his voice lowered. "Heard they didn't die well by all accounts." Tarkington shook his head, remembering the severed parts, hacked-up bodies, and the pain frozen onto their dead faces. Nance continued staring at the graves. "They were good men. Hard workers and dedicated soldiers. They'll be missed." He turned back, placing his hat upon his greasy, long hair. His smile returned, but it had an edge of malice to it. "We'll see about making that right."

Omar gave a quick shake of his head. "Now, now, Corporal—you assured Captain Dane that you'd be professional. No vendettas to cloud your judgment."

Nance's smile didn't waver. "Course not. Doesn't mean I'm not looking forward to seeing the sadistic bastards get what's coming to them. Doesn't matter who does it—as long as it gets done." Omar tilted his head, unsure how he should take that. Nance didn't give him long. He clapped his hands together. "Now, let's get on with it, shall we?" He moved off and joined the three other shabbily dressed NGVR troopers.

Tarkington asked Omar, "How's Captain Dane? He looks scared out of his wits."

The corners of Omar's mouth turned down. "He's a famous rugby player. I remember reading about him before the war." Tarkington raised an eyebrow, and Omar continued. "I'd prefer if Captain Grumskey came along, but General Moten wanted him nearby." He lowered his voice. "Dane fought in Africa. Hear he had a bad time of it and lost half his company. Made a bad decision." He shrugged. "Least that's how I heard it, but you know how rumors spread."

"Looks nervous as a mouse in a room full of cats."

Sergeant Omar agreed. "That's why Grumskey sent my squad along. Wanted me to let Lieutenant Willoth know to keep an eye on him. Dane's in charge, but Grumskey told him to rely heavily on Willoth."

"Think he listened?"

Omar shrugged.

Winkleman shook his head. "Sounds complicated. Here he comes now." Winkleman made himself scarce as the brawny captain approached.

Tarkington stiffened and greeted him with a nod. Dane looked Tarkington up and down, taking in the mottle-camouflaged uniform. "You must be Lieutenant Tarkington?" He extended a hand. "I'm Captain Dane."

Tarkington took it and they shook. "Yes, sir. Good to meet you."

Dane's eyes passed over each GI. His gaze lingered on Raker's cut and swollen face for a moment, then moved on. "Only six men? For some reason I thought you had a full squad of twelve."

Tarkington nodded. "We're not a normal line unit, sir. We're a team of Alamo Scouts...just six of us."

Dane grinned. "Not much of a command, Lieutenant. Seems like a waste of leadership." Tarkington ignored the jibe, but his icy gaze made Dane look away. Sergeant Omar looked away too, suddenly interested in his boots. Dane continued, "Well, we'll take the lead on this one. Your *team* will take up the rear guard. Understood?"

"Understood, sir."

~

They had little trouble finding and following the route the Japanese had taken. Taking the rear guard didn't faze Tarkington or his men. They had confidence in the commandos' abilities to keep them out of an ambush.

The narrow track followed the ridge line but rarely broke out onto the top. Parts of it were no wider than a boot print. Falling would be a spectacular ride before splatting into the winding valley five hundred feet below. Winkleman crept along at a snail's pace in those spots, drawing jeers from the others. The rain started again in earnest, and their progress slowed to a crawl.

Just before nightfall, the trail dropped off the ridge, widened, and broke out onto green, grassy plains. The rain filled in the Japanese boot prints with muddy water. The long, snaking line of soldiers stopped, and word passed for Tarkington to move up.

He left the squad sitting beneath trees and vines, sipping water and eating C-rats. He found the group of Aussie officers huddled beside a sizable boulder. Lieutenant Willoth saw him and waved him over. They made room for him, and he adjusted his short sword and crouched beside them. Captain Dane said, "Welcome to the party, Lieutenant." Tarkington grunted but otherwise ignored him. Dane and Willoth had their maps out. Dane pointed at his much newer map. "We're here, and we think the Japs are somewhere in this region." His finger traced a large area. "I doubt they'll move at night, so we'll set up along the edge of that tree line and find them in the morning."

Tarkington exchanged a glance with Lt. Willoth. Willoth pinched his chin and studied the map as though considering Dane's words carefully. He finally said, "The Japs might continue moving through the night and attack in the morning, sir." Dane looked surprised, and Willoth continued, "We've found the Nips would rather move and even fight at night, sir." Dane's jaw rippled, but he didn't rebuke his subordinate. Willoth gazed at Tarkington and suggested, "When it's fully dark, why don't we send out a patrol to find them? They can move faster, pinpoint their position, and report back here before morning."

Tarkington spoke up. "My men have had it easy. Let us find the Nips. This sort of thing is right up our alley, sir."

Willoth was about to protest, but Dane spoke first. "Keeping our forces separate would cut down on confusion."

"Yes, sir. We'll just need a radio with fresh batteries. We can shove off as soon as you give the word."

Dane nodded but didn't agree right away, as though considering other options. He finally said, "Okay, Lieutenant. Find them and get back here." He held up a finger as though about to scold a child. "But whatever you do, don't let them see you."

Tarkington just grinned and nodded.

~

It felt good to be on their own again—more natural. Henry took point and led them alongside the route the Japanese had taken. Even in the blackness, the trail was easy to follow. The steady, light rain soaked them to their skin, but their movements kept them warm. The trail led them through supple, waist-high grasses and occasional patches of cutting kunai grass.

They approached a line of trees. The trees' outlines against the dark sky looked menacing as they swayed in the light wind. Henry stopped and crouched, and the squad spread out around him. Tarkington eased in beside him and focused on his senses. The air smelled thick with wetness and the hint of jungle rot. The chirping insects and distant calls of wild animals sounded subdued in the steady rain.

Henry glanced at him and nodded. Tarkington nodded back, and Henry moved into the tree line. Just before the darkness swallowed him up, Tarkington waved the others forward. Under the trees some of the rain was blocked, but fat drops plopped on them from pools on the leaves. The impacts on the back of their necks sounded loud.

Henry slowed with the increased darkness. The obvious trail they'd been following changed. The Japanese soldiers had spread out, making many different tracks through the trees. Henry stopped often, making sure he still followed the main track.

Tarkington gazed at the dark treetops, wondering if they were being watched by monkeys or something more dangerous. If there were snipers in the trees, he doubted they'd be able to see his squad slithering silently through the blackness below. He could hardly see Henry only yards away, and the men to either side were merely dark, silent shadows. Tarkington concentrated on each step—careful to avoid fallen branches and sticky mud. The trees seemed to stretch on forever.

Finally, they came to the edge of another grassy expanse. They'd set out two hours before and needed a break. Tarkington waved them closer, and the squad silently fell in beside him. He signaled them to take a break, and soon he heard canteen lids being carefully unscrewed. Stollman pissed against a tree while staying crouched, and Henry pulled a fresh stalk of grass to chew on.

The drips falling from the branches overhead lessened, and the grassy expanse brightened noticeably as the clouds parted, allowing starlight to penetrate. From the blackness of the trees, the field seemed to glow. Without the incessant drips, night sounds amplified. Tarkington slid his canteen back onto his belt and took in the scene. New Guinea was a terrifying place to fight a war, but it was also undeniably beautiful.

Everyone froze at the same instant. An unnatural sound caught their attention. At first it was difficult to tell where it came from. Then the sound of slipping feet and shaking branches and leaves pinpointed it. It came from above and behind them and sounded close.

The squad turned in place and faced back toward the dark trees. The noise again, and this time Tarkington caught movement in the trees. A shadow shimmied down the trunk of a massive tree. The dark shape could've been any large animal, but the outline of a long rifle across its back left little doubt. Tarkington felt an icy shiver course through him. They'd moved directly beneath a sniper but hadn't been seen.

No one moved as they watched the sniper descend, branch by branch. Tarkington wondered if the soldier was moving to a better position or simply had to take a shit. Whatever—he'd sealed his fate.

Keeping him in his peripheral vision, he scanned the treetops for more signs of snipers. He decided there could be an entire company of them and he wouldn't be able to see them unless they moved.

He turned away from the descending sniper and looked at the dark faces of his squad. Despite the darkness, he could identify each man without question. Vick was staring back at him. His eyes seemed to glow. Tarkington gave him an exaggerated nod, and Vick returned the signal.

He already had his knife drawn. He waited until the sniper took another step down the tree, then moved closer to the base of the tree. The sniper's movements masked his own. The squad readied their carbines and covered their teammate. Each time the sniper took a step, Vick moved until his dark shape blended with the wide base of the tree. Their paths would soon cross.

The sniper continued his downward journey. He moved faster the closer he got to the ground. Tarkington had his muzzle steadied on his black mass. He kept both eyes open—his peripheral vision working over-time. The sniper's shape stopped six feet from where Vick waited. A whistle mimicking a common jungle bird came from the sniper. Tarking-ton's breath caught in his throat. The sniper waited a few seconds, then whistled again. This time, two similar whistles answered from the treetops.

The sniper continued working his way down the trunk. Tarkington wondered if the others would see Vick waiting and warn the sniper or simply shoot Vick. Tarkington didn't dare move his muzzle to the new threats. Any movement might draw enemy attention now that they could be focusing on this area.

Vick was his best knife man, but if he didn't make a clean, silent kill, they'd be in trouble. He couldn't see Vick but knew he waited for his prey at the base of the tree. Would he choose to let the sniper live? He'd kill him if he thought he could do it quietly. Tarkington kept his muzzle immobile but moved his eyes toward the other unseen snipers. If Vick drew their fire, he hoped to see a muzzle flash.

The sniper dropped the last few feet from the tree with a soft plop. Tarkington held his breath, listening for the sound of metal slicing through flesh, but nothing happened. He figured Vick must be within feet of the soldier.

From the corner of his eye, he saw the dark silhouette of the sniper against the lighter backdrop of the trees beyond. The pith helmet and long rifle he assumed to be an Arisaka Type-38 betrayed his identity.

A sudden, lightning-fast movement erupted from the shadows and clashed with the outline. The brief struggle sounded like church bells to Tarkington, but it soon ended with barely a hitch in the surrounding jungle sounds. He waited to hear the crash of a rifle, but it never came. Relief flooded through him, and he slowly let out the breath he'd been holding.

No one moved for fifteen minutes as Tarkington wondered what the hell to do next. At least two snipers were above them somewhere, and soon they'd wonder why they hadn't heard from their buddy. Perhaps Tark-ington and his men should stay put and wait for the snipers to investigate, but would they? If the GIs stayed until daylight, the enemy might spot them. But what if there were more? Firing their weapons would certainly give away their position and bring nearby troops.

He moved his hand slowly and signaled. He pivoted his body until he faced directly away from where Vick had dispatched the sniper and inched his way forward. The sole of Winkleman's boot appeared, and he kept pace with his second-in-command. They slithered under and over thick roots and fallen branches. The wet ground kept their movements mercifully quiet. Bugs and various unseen creatures crisscrossed over his arms and back. He did his best to ignore them.

He expected to be shot in the back at any moment, but after forty minutes of painstakingly slow crawling, he finally followed Winkleman into a thick stand of brush. Despite the relatively cool night, sweat ran off his nose as though from a spigot. Raker and Winkleman smiled at him as they continued deeper into the thicket. Behind him, Henry moved silently, and beyond him Tarkington saw Stollman's dim outline.

It took another ten minutes before Stollman entered the thicket, and Tarkington whispered into his ear, "Where's Vick?"

Stollman slowly turned until he faced back the way he'd come, searching for his friend. Tarkington saw concern in his eyes as he scanned. He whispered, "He was farther back. He'll be along."

"He okay?" Tarkington realized he didn't have confirmation whether or not Vick had actually killed the sniper. Perhaps he'd met his match. The thought made him queasy, but he realized if that were the case, the sniper would've called out by now.

A whistle from the treetops froze them all in place.

9

Vick watched the sniper descend toward his position. He'd made it to the base of the tree without being spotted. He concentrated on keeping his breathing and heart rate under control. The knife in his hand felt good, but the sweat pooling in his palm worried him. He didn't dare wipe it on his pant leg. Any movement now might be seen.

The sniper stopped just above him, and Vick wondered if he'd been spotted. When he heard the bird whistle, he nearly lost control of his heart rate. His mind whirled—the only reason the sniper would whistle would be to communicate with other soldiers. His suspicions were soon confirmed. The two answering whistles were much farther away, but he figured they must be looking toward their comrade. He barely breathed, wondering if he was about to be shot. He closed his eyes, hoping it would be quick and painless. He thought how mad Stollman would be to lose another friend.

The sniper continued moving toward his position. The good news was he was still alive, but what the hell would he do now? The sniper was getting closer and would be close enough to kiss in seconds. Vick's mind whirred like a top. Would the sniper see him? *Hell*, he thought, *he'll probably smell me.*

Sweat dripped from his chin. He had his carbine tight against his back.

The sniper would be right on top of him. With the addition of the other snipers, he wanted to slink away and leave this one alive. Perhaps the sniper would do whatever he came down to do, then scurry back up the tree, or perhaps a different one.

The sniper dropped from the tree and landed lightly. Vick felt a slight breeze and smelled the man's body odor. Vick froze and thought he might crush the leather-laced knife handle. The sniper's dark form filled all his senses, and he stopped breathing. Time slowed to a crawl. He'd be seen— or his presence would be felt—any second. He had to strike now.

He sprang from his crouch, and his left hand wrapped around the sniper's face at the same instant he rammed the tip of his razor-sharp knife into the base of his neck, angling into the brain. The body spasmed wildly for a few seconds and hot blood washed over Vick's hand, but he held tight, bringing his full weight onto the dying soldier, keeping him from thrashing.

He waited for the crash of a rifle or the questioning twirling whistle from the dead man's comrades, but nothing happened. The night sounds continued unabated, as though nothing had happened. He thought he'd made far too much racket, but his overcharged senses could have manufactured more sound than he'd actually made.

His heart felt as though it would erupt from his rib cage. The stench of death washed over him, but he dared not release the body. He watched the shadows, knowing Stollman was close but out of sight. What would Tarkington do, he wondered. There were at least two more snipers nearby.

Finally, he saw the slightest movement in the darkness. Stollman was moving away from him. Tarkington must've signaled a move. Vick slowly unwound himself from the dead sniper. He released the body, and the coagulated blood made a sickening sound as his arms broke loose. He guided the body until it stabilized against the base of the tree. He wondered if he should try to hide it. It might buy them some time if he could just tuck it beneath the leaves and branches. He had hours before daylight, and the others would wait for him. Stick by stick, he slowly covered the body.

He'd nearly finished when he heard another twirling whistle. His breath caught as he realized it came from ground level this time. Perhaps it was a spotter or one of the other snipers—and he'd expect an answering call.

Vick thought back to his time on Luzon. While fighting the Japanese using guerrilla-style tactics, they'd sometimes communicated using bird whistles, but he did not know how to mimic the call the Japanese were using. Could he fake it? If he flubbed it, he'd only give away his position. He wondered what the rest of the squad would do. They might maneuver to intercept the enemy soldier. He strained to see them, but it was no use. The call came again, this time a few yards closer.

He licked his lips, trying to wet them with a suddenly dry mouth. He wondered if he'd be able to whistle at all, let alone sound like anything remotely close to a jungle bird. He pursed his lips and, against all his instincts, tried to whistle. The high-pitched sound made the entire jungle stop. Vick cursed himself and waited for the shot that would end his life.

A twirling, beautiful whistle came from the darkness from the area he figured the rest of the squad to be. He instantly recognized Henry's bird call. He'd regaled them with his bird-calling abilities while trying to teach them on Luzon. The jungle noises didn't return, as if the animals watched a tense show play out before them.

The enemy didn't respond. Vick wondered what they'd be thinking. The whistle had come at least thirty yards away from where they'd last heard from their comrade and sounded nothing like the original. Despite the beautiful call, Henry had elevated it above the natural sounds, leaving no doubt it came from a human.

Vick took the opportunity to move to the other side of the tree. He hugged the tree, blending with the large base, until the tree's girth separated him from the enemy snipers. He kept his eyes on the blackness. There'd been no response from the Japanese. No whistles and no movement that he could see. They must be confused and trying to piece it all together.

Vick inched himself to a standing position and leaned against the tree. The sniper he'd killed had probably picked this particular tree because the base had an easy entry point and the thick, evenly spaced branches would make an easy climb. He sheathed his bloody knife, then pulled himself carefully onto the tree, keeping the trunk between himself and the danger.

He moved slowly until he figured he was ten feet off the ground. The ground looked black and bottomless, and he realized why the snipers hadn't seen them when they passed beneath. It felt like looking into a black hole. He could be ten feet or one hundred and ten feet off the ground. He pulled his knife from his sheath again and settled in.

A quick movement caught his eye. He used his peripheral vision and saw the dim outline of a man's shoulders and helmeted head. He knew he watched the soldier who'd whistled from the ground. But now he was much closer and moving between Vick and the rest of the squad. If he'd tried to move with the squad, he would've been discovered.

Vick tried to put himself into the mind of the soldier. He'd whistled and gotten an odd response from the base of the tree, then another odd response from the blackness on the left. He couldn't fire for fear of hitting his own man, yet he knew something wasn't right. How many others were out there, and what were they thinking? Most likely sighting through their sniper scopes, searching for something to kill.

Vick kept watching the shadowy figure. Now that he'd identified him, he was easier to pick out against the blackness. The soldier moved slowly and with the precision of a man accustomed to stealth. A veteran jungle fighter.

The Japanese soldier stopped, now directly between Vick and the rest of the squad. He didn't move for a few minutes, and Vick tried to control his breathing. Time passed eternally slow. Sweat dripped off his nose and chin, and he hoped it blended with the plops from the recent rain. A low voice, no doubt calling to his comrade. The soldier's first mistake. Now the others would know his position, if they didn't already.

Vick tasted bile rising in his throat as the soldier turned and moved toward the base of his tree. He expected it, but it still turned his sweat cold. He'd hidden the body but knew the soldier would find him if he felt around in the darkness. Or perhaps he'd simply climb the tree and Vick could greet him with his cold blade. Either scenario would be loud and dangerous. *How the hell did I get myself into this?*

The soldier kept on coming, and Vick still didn't know what he should do about it. If the soldier stumbled onto the body, all hell would break loose. Vick hadn't pulled the dead man from where he'd killed him for fear of making too much noise. If the soldier continued on his present course, he couldn't help but find him.

Vick calmed his breathing and concentrated on staying quiet. The enemy soldier was nearly directly beneath him. He knew what he had to do. There was no other choice.

The soldier moved two more feet and stopped. Vick stared down at his dark back. He could see the pith helmet and the metal from a gun glinting dully. He doubted the soldier would see him, even if he looked directly up at him. The soldier called someone's name, the voice barely above a whisper.

Vick dropped from the tree. The ten-foot drop took an instant but felt like an eternity. The soldier either sensed the danger or heard the rustle of Vick's body sliding from the tree and turned at the last instant. Vick crashed into the soldier and drove his knife into the man's upper back. He'd been aiming for his neck, but the last-second move caused him to miss. The soldier screamed from surprise and the agony ripping through his back.

Vick tried desperately to wrap his hand across his mouth, but the soldier instinctively spun and shed Vick from his back.

Vick lost the grip on his knife as he rolled away. He whipped his carbine off his back in a practiced, smooth motion. The Japanese soldier's scream cut through the night, and Vick saw him clutching desperately at his upper back. Without thinking, Vick aimed, flicked off the safety, and fired once into the man's head. The muzzle flash lit up the scene momentarily, and the screaming instantly stopped. His shot was immediately answered with a flash from the treetops. Vick felt the heat of the bullet, and his carbine was torn from his stinging hands. He threw himself sideways and rolled away from the spot, hearing multiple gunshots from the darkness.

He rolled until he hit something solid. He lay on his back, breathing hard. He pulled his sidearm and tried to get control while he searched for more enemy soldiers and muzzle flashes. Movement nearby made him spin to his feet, his .45 pistol shaking slightly. He saw the muzzle of a carbine aimed at his head and Stollman's grinning face beyond the sights. "Jesus Christ, Vick. You trying to wake the whole neighborhood?"

Reunited with the squad, Vick quickly explained what happened. Tarkington stated, "We've gotta get the hell outta here before the entire Jap regiment comes a-callin'. We got the other sniper—at least we heard him fall through the branches. He's either dead or too far gone to matter." He touched Henry's shoulder. "Take us north along the edge of the clearing. We'll see what our commotion attracts—if anything." Henry hesitated for a second, and Tarkington explained, "We still haven't pinpointed the Nips. If they come, we can assume they're close."

Vick stiffened, as if remembering something. "I left my knife in that Jap's back. My carbine's over there too."

Tarkington pushed him. "Take Stolly with you. Hurry." Vick and Stollman ran into the darkness and soon returned. Vick wiped his bloody hands on his pants and held up his carbine. The barrel was bent at an odd angle and the forestock splintered badly. "Son of a bitch ruined my carbine. Nearly punched my ticket too."

Tarkington ordered, "Get the ammo and disperse your mags. Chuck that thing where the Nips won't find it when you get a chance."

Vick nodded and asked, "Should we cover the bodies?"

Tarkington shook his head. "Nah. If they heard us, there's no time." He waved them forward, and Henry moved quickly along the edge of the tree line. The grasses to their right swayed in a light breeze.

When they'd moved a hundred and fifty yards away from the dead snipers, Tarkington halted them, and they pushed themselves closer to the edge of the grasses and watched and waited. Minutes passed before Raker got Tarkington's attention and pointed toward the other side of the field.

Tarkington watched the darkness beyond the grasses. Shapes suddenly appeared like apparitions and slipped into the field. They were far from his position and, unless they changed direction, wouldn't come close. He checked his watch. The glowing dials showed it had been less than fifteen minutes since they'd fired their carbines. The Japanese must have been close, perhaps in the stand of trees.

The shapes finally stopped emerging from the tree line, and Tarkington counted at least twenty men—maybe two squads. Was this part of a bigger group? He wondered if more soldiers were maneuvering around the edges of the clearing, avoiding exposure or keeping them looking one way while they closed in from the other. Once this group found their dead comrades, would they comb the area?

Tarkington signaled, and they went to their bellies and slithered forward into the tall grasses. Being out of the trees made him feel exposed, but they'd be invisible to anyone from the trees if they remained prone and motionless.

They turned back toward the trees they'd come from. Tarkington could just make out the tree line and a few yards into the darkness. His paranoia was warranted. He saw shapes moving in the darkness of the trees. Unlike the soldiers who'd crossed the field, these men moved slowly and carefully. He only saw six soldiers but assumed there were more in the shadows beyond.

They stayed completely still as the enemy soldiers passed. There was no reason for these soldiers to suspect Tarkington and his men had moved into the field, and he doubted they'd be able to pick up their trails in the darkness. To find them, they'd have to step on them.

They waited nearly an hour, and Tarkington realized time was becoming a factor. He didn't relish being this close to the enemy force in daylight. He assumed they'd found their dead comrades by now, but he'd heard and seen nothing since they'd passed. Were they searching the trees, or had they backtracked their own trail toward the commandos and AIF troopers? He decided to move.

He signaled the others, and they crawled through the grass foot by foot until they reached the furthest northern corner. They got to their feet and crouched, watching the surrounding darkness for any movement. They'd be crossing the path that the Japanese had taken in their flanking maneuver. If they were unlucky, they might meet them as they returned to their regiment. The odds were against it, though, so Tarkington tapped Henry and covered him as he stepped from the grass and into the trees. Raker went next, then Winkleman, Vick, and Stollman. Tarkington took one last look across the swaying grasses and followed them into the murk. The rain started again. It pelted his neck as he left the field, and the temperature dropped a few degrees.

His senses worked overtime as his vision adjusted to the heavy darkness. The rain increased, and the sound of it muffled their passing. Soon great drops found their way through the leaves and branches and soaked them once again.

The morning light diffused across the village of Wau and through the open windows, lighting up the map spread out on General Moten's table. The welcome droning sound of aircraft drew him outside. Gray clouds filled most of the sky, but shafts of sunlight penetrated in spots. Rain squalls slowly moved across the mountains in gray sheets. He searched for the American transport plane, a bit surprised that they'd made it through the pass so early. They must have done it while it was still mostly dark.

Over the past few days, they'd landed a quarter of the Seventeenth Brigade and he'd dispersed them to defend the airfield. But he knew a concerted Japanese push would make quick work of his thin line.

The news from the Black Cat Mine about the Japanese finding an alternate route changed his defensive plans. He still needed men watching the trail in case more Japanese came over land, but instead of sending the bulk of his forces, he redeployed them closer to the airfield. He wanted to extend his defensive perimeter into the outlying areas but needed more of his brigade. The C-47 would bring another load of thirty men. Perhaps even a few of the twenty-five-pounder artillery pieces he'd been clamoring for.

His assistant, Sergeant Crimpton, pointed. "There they are, sir."

General Moten squinted and saw the dark outlines against the gray clouds. His hope changed to alarm. "Those are Jap bombers!"

Sergeant Crimpton's mouth dropped open as he noticed the three approaching planes marked with the glowing red meatballs. He pushed General Moten. "Get to the cover, sir." He stopped, cupped his hands to his mouth, and bellowed, "Air raid! Take cover!" Then he took off after Moten.

Moten slid into the slit trench along with other men from his command. The only anti-aircraft weapons, two .50-caliber machine guns, opened fire from the airfield. Moten thought they were premature and made a mental note to address the issue later.

The twin-engine bombers came fast and low, and Moten watched as they unleashed one bomb each. Moten dropped his head below the level of the trench and cringed as the ground shook with the impacts. The roaring of engines and bombs filled the air, and he covered his ears as debris rained down on his cover.

He lifted his head and saw the planes flash down the valley, then arc high into the sky for another pass. "They're gonna strafe us!" he yelled. The .50-caliber machine guns opened fire again as the planes closed the distance. Yellow tracers reached out but fell behind the bombers. The front of the planes winked and red tracers chewed up the ground, walking across buildings and equipment. Moten pressed himself into the dirt walls, and he felt the bullets impacting the ground through the walls. A private cursed and raised his rifle, trying to track the aircraft. He fired and screamed, "Bugger off!"

Moten glanced at him, and the private noticed him for the first time. His face went from raging red to white in an instant. He stammered, "Sorry—sorry, sir—I..."

Moten held up his hands. "Did you hit him, son?"

"I—I don't think so, sir."

"Hit the bugger next time and I'll put you in for the bloody Victoria Cross."

The hammering from the .50 calibers stopped, and the engine noise diminished to nothing as the enemy planes disappeared over the mountains to the east.

Moten hopped from the trench and surveyed the damage. The three bomb craters smoldered. Fire licked up the sides of a nearby building. Men emerged from trenches and foxholes, shocked by the sudden, violent destruction. Sergeant Crimpton brushed dirt from his pants and joined his commander. "Hope that doesn't become a habit, sir."

Moten gazed toward the socked-in mountains separating them from Port Moresby. "Get Moresby on the horn and let 'em know about this. Ask about the C-47s too. We need those men here now." The sergeant gave a quick salute and hustled off to the radio room, dodging bits of burning debris. Moten clenched his fists and seethed, "Where the hell are our bloody fighters when we need 'em?" He turned from the carnage and looked at the highlands surrounding the valley to the east. He placed his hands on his hips. Captain Grimerson from the NGVRs strode up and asked, "Well, that hasn't happened for a few months. Can't say I miss it much."

Moten kept peering into the distance. "Somewhere up there's an entire Jap regiment. We've gotta keep them off our backs for a few more days."

Grimerson nodded. "Lieutenant Willoth's platoon and that squad of Yanks are up there, sir."

"Captain Dane's two platoons, too."

Grimerson's mouth turned down, and he hedged, "They're raw and untested. They might just get in the way."

Moten looked at the scraggly Volunteer. He'd been out here for years, and the craggy lines in his face proved it. Some of the regular troopers looked down on the NGVRs, but Moten had nothing but respect for them. He'd heard their stories of sacrifice and bravery and seen some of it himself. Despite their unorthodox outward appearances, they were excellent soldiers who hated the Japanese even more than his regular troops did. They'd experienced their brutality firsthand.

Captain Grumskey stepped forward. Moten hadn't noticed him before. Grumskey said, "That's not a bad idea, sir."

"What idea?"

"Willoth and the Yanks hitting the Japs and slowing them down."

Moten pursed his lips. "It's an entire regiment. They'd get slaughtered."

Grumskey crossed his arms. He was used to having to explain the role of commandos and special units to line officers. General Moten and most other senior officers weren't familiar with the skills these specially trained men brought to the table. "They trained my men for hit-and-run tactics, sir. I'm not as familiar with the Yank Alamo Scouts, but I think they're cut from the same cloth, sir. They can slow 'em down. I'm sure of it."

The exhausted GIs moved faster on their way back. Raker led them on a circuitous route, avoiding retracing their steps. Finding their camp turned out to be more difficult than they expected, but an outpost sentry finally challenged them three hours after daybreak. Tarkington directed the men to get some rest while he went to find Captain Dane.

An uneasy corporal scurried off to find Dane, muttering about how his commander ordered him not to be disturbed. Tarkington took off his floppy jungle hat and ran his hands through his soaked hair. Exhaustion hung off his limbs like sagging moss, and he hoped to get this over with quickly and get an hour or two of shut-eye. Even half an hour would do wonders, but he didn't get his hopes up.

Captain Dane emerged from the tree line, yawning and rubbing his eyes. The corporal pointed at Tarkington, muttered something, and veered away. Dane checked his watch and squinted in the light. "Criminy sakes, Lieutenant. You boys were out all night."

"Yes, sir. We have a good idea where the Nips are."

"An idea? Did you or did you not find them, Lieutenant?"

Tarkington explained what had happened, and by the end, Dane looked more angry than concerned. "So they know we're here? I thought I told you not to be discovered. You assured me," he stroked his chin, trying to remember the exact phrase, "this was right up your alley."

Tarkington felt his anger growing in the pit of his stomach. He was too tired for this kind of horseshit. "Doesn't always go as planned. We were lucky to get out of there in one piece."

Dane shook his head. "Now the Nips know they're being followed. Hell, they might be getting ready to wipe us out as we speak."

Tarkington wanted to throttle him but kept his voice from showing his simmering anger. "We would've seen them on our way back. We didn't. Their target's the airfield, not us."

Lieutenant Willoth showed up. Unlike Captain Dane, he looked as though he'd barely slept. He had his rifle slung over his shoulder, and his hat sat at a jaunty angle on his head. "Welcome back, Tarkington. Your sergeant told me about your night. Glad you all made it back safely."

Tarkington nodded, thankful for Willoth's cool head. "Thanks. Me too."

Willoth addressed Captain Dane. "A runner from the mine just delivered orders. Command wants us to slow the Nips down while they wait for more reinforcements."

Dane looked shocked. "Attack? But we're not even a full company. We'll be—"

Willoth interrupted, "Your platoons are to stay in reserve. My commandos, the Yanks, and a few of the NGVR troops will do the attacking."

Dane's face darkened. "Reserve? Let me see this order." Willoth handed him the sheet, and Dane read it. His face turned red, but there was nothing he could do. "This—this is highly unusual. What are we supposed to do, sit on our hands?"

Willoth said, "You'll watch our backs, sir. We'll need your support, particularly if things go badly."

"You mean bail you out when you put your foot in it," he stated glibly.

Willoth didn't rise to the bait. "Possibly, sir." The tension in the late morning air hung between them like unwashed laundry.

Tarkington lifted his chin and interjected, "If there's nothing else, I'd like to join my men and let 'em know about this."

"Ah, yes, fine. You're dismissed."

Tarkington walked toward where he'd last seen his men, and Willoth came up beside him. "Your men need anything? Sounds like you had quite a night."

Tarkington answered tiredly, "Vick needs a new rifle if you can spare any...and we all need a few hours of sleep, but I assume we'll be leaving soon."

"We're waiting for the NGVRs to join us from the mine. It'll take 'em a few hours. I'll take care of the rifle, and I'll see that you and your men aren't disturbed for a few hours." Tarkington mumbled his thanks, and Willoth added, "Dane's a bit of an ass, but he'll come around."

Tarkington waved but didn't respond.

10

Corporal Nance and three other Volunteers arrived a few hours later. The cloud cover had thickened, and a steady rain kept everything wet and miserable. Nance waved and called out as though arriving for a festival. "Hallo, hallo. Thanks for waiting, wouldn't bloody well want to miss out on this one, mates."

Lieutenant Willoth heard Nance's unmistakable booming voice and turned in time to see him nearly skipping into their camp. He couldn't keep the smile off his face. He'd known the man since first arriving in theater many months before.

He'd been suspicious of Nance's constant happy-go-lucky outlook, assuming it was all a farce. But the more time he spent with him, the more he realized he was just a genuinely cheerful person, despite their grim circumstances. He was also a crack shot. He enjoyed nothing more than killing Japanese, almost to a fault. He'd been a mine worker living in Wau when the Japanese first invaded and shut everything down. He could've left at any time but chose to stay and make the Japanese pay for their sins by his ruthless hand.

Willoth extended his hand and they shook. "Welcome, Corporal." He nodded to the other three—men he'd fought alongside countless times.

"Lang, Culler, and Winger, huh? Really scraping the barrel these days, Nance."

All of them were bearded and looked filthy. "Fuck off...sir," Private Culler hissed good-naturedly.

Nance's smile broadened, and he released Willoth's hand and reared back, laughing. "You're bloody right about that, Willi." Nance was the only man able to get away with calling him that.

Captain Dane heard the commotion and trotted from beneath the stand of trees. "What's all this bloody yelling about?"

He stomped up to the newcomers, and Willoth spoke low to the Volunteers. "Easy now, this one's new."

Nance ignored him and stepped forward with his filthy hand extended. Dane looked at it as though he'd contract leprosy if he touched it. "Who the hell're you, exactly?"

Nance glanced back at Willoth, straightened up, and snapped, "Corporal Nance of the New Guinea Volunteer Rifles at your service sir." He indicated the now braced men standing behind him. "And this is Privates Lang, Culler, and Winger, respectively, sir. We've just arrived from the mine." He grinned. "Here to help exterminate some bloody Japs, sir."

Dane shook his head. "Where's your bloody uniform, Corporal? I don't see any insignia on any one of ya."

Nance's shirtsleeves had been cut off, showing off stringy muscles and fat veins. "Our uniforms along with the insignias rotted off a long time ago, sir." He smiled again. "Just have to trust us, I guess, sir." He gave him a smile, his teeth barely visible behind the thick beard.

Dane looked him up and down and Willoth stepped forward. "I can vouch for them, sir. I've known these men a long time." He nodded and slapped Nance's shoulder hard, making a cloud of dust. "They don't look like much, but they're fine soldiers." Nance was about to insult his friend right back but Willoth spoke first. "I'll get 'em settled in, sir. Need to go over our equipment with the Yanks before stepping off."

Dane nodded and stepped aside. "Yes, see that you do. After you get them settled in, I want you men on your way. No more delays."

Willoth waved. "Yes, sir. We'll be ready to go in an hour."

When they were out of the captain's earshot, Willoth shook his head. "You just can't keep your mouth shut, can you?"

Nance feigned offense. "What'd I do? Hell, I nearly saluted the poor sod." They wove their way through regular AIF soldiers who didn't try to hide their disdain for the commandos and especially the NGVRs. Nance smiled and said hello to anyone close enough to hear. He leaned closer to Willoth and said, "Hear we're taking the Yanks along on this one."

Willoth nodded. "Yeah. They're a good sort. They ran into some trouble last night. Snipers." Nance raised an eyebrow and Willoth continued, "Killed all three of them and got out clean as a whistle."

"Sound like my kind of Yanks."

Willoth remembered and asked, "That reminds me, have you ever heard of a bloke named Clemson Callico?"

Nance stopped in his tracks, and for the first time, Willoth saw alarm and even fear in his eyes. "Jesus, Joseph, and Mary. Where'd you hear that name?"

Willoth stopped and looked at the other Volunteers, who looked just as surprised as Nance. "Met him the other day on a hill overlooking this entire area."

Nance looked stunned. "Met him? I thought that bloody Kiwi was long gone. What hill? Take me there."

Willoth's face screwed up in astonishment. "I'm not taking you there now. We've got more important things to do."

"The son of a whore killed my sister," he seethed. "I thought he fled long ago or I'd have killed him myself."

Willoth gripped Nance's shoulders. His sinewy muscles felt like steel cables. "Take it easy. I'll take you to him when this is all over, okay?" Nance's jaw rippled, but he gradually relaxed. Willoth added, "He—he seems like a nice fella, actually. Eccentric maybe, but solid. He's got quite an operation going, too."

"He killed my Adelaide."

The corner of Willoth's mouth turned down. "Ah, that must be Addy? He showed us her grave."

Nance spun from his grip. "More'n he ever showed me." They moved down the hill to find Lt. Tarkington and his men.

Tarkington and the squad were cleaning weapons and sorting their ammunition when Nance and Willoth approached. Tarkington rose, recognizing Nance from Wau. Nance's smile returned, and he extended his beefy hand. "Tarkington. Have I got that right, mate?"

Tarkington grinned and took his hand. "Corporal Nance of the Volunteers."

Nance looked at the other GIs and gave a low whistle. "Don't you men look dangerous?" Winkleman exchanged looks with the others, wondering if the gangly son of a bitch was poking fun. Nance rubbed his hands together in a quick motion. "You blokes ready to kill some Japs?"

The GIs stepped forward and they made introductions all around. Tarkington raised an eyebrow to Lt. Willoth. "What's this about killing Japs?"

"We got orders to harass and slow down the Japs as much as possible."

"With Dane?" Tarkington asked with some trepidation.

Willoth shook his head. "Nah. His men will stay back in support. It's my commandos, Nance's men, and your Alamo Scouts."

There was muttering from the GIs, and Tarkington forced a grin. "A match made in heaven, no doubt."

They moved out an hour later and moved fast, hoping to get around the Japanese force before they'd gotten too far toward Wau. The map showed multiple plateaus separated by small valleys and interspersed with forests, but no one put too much stock in their accuracy.

Nance had brought more line-of-sight radios and dispensed them to Tarkington and Willoth. They wouldn't do much good for contacting Wau unless they got much closer but would come in handy if they had to separate and coordinate their movements.

Vick had been given a spare Lee-Enfield rifle. It wasn't all that much different from the Springfield he'd used most of his military career, but he would've rather had his shorter, lighter carbine back on his shoulder. He felt as though he carried a howitzer on his back.

Since the GIs had been in the area the night before, they led the way. Raker and Henry were both on point. They kept forty yards between them, but in the waist-high grass, they could keep tabs on one another. Everything looked different in daylight, but when they got to the forest where they'd encountered the snipers, they detoured far to the right and slowed.

They soon dropped into a canyon, which cut deeply through the fields and led straight toward the Wau Valley, miles distant. The thick trees, heavy underbrush, and slippery rocks near the creek burbling at the bottom made travel more difficult, but they could move faster not worrying about noise or being spotted.

They jumped from boulder to boulder and hustled along the banks of the creek. No one spoke as they trotted along, concentrating on every step. Falling and twisting an ankle, or worse, was a genuine possibility. Nance and the Volunteers moved like gazelles, easily matching Henry and Raker. The line of soldiers spread out as the fittest and most agile outdistanced the slower men.

They ran for two hours before the canyon widened. The tiny creek had become more like a river as more and more water trickled in from countless feeders. The sound of water crashing through rocks and cascading over sheer walls into deep pools drowned out all other noise.

Henry halted, and soon everyone caught up and rested near the base of a waterfall. Their eyes shone from the exhilarating run. Nance's heavy beard dripped with sweat and drops of water that mirrored the beautiful surroundings like tiny diamonds.

Willoth pulled out the map while the others drank straight from the creek and refilled canteens. They risked tainted water, but the creek was gin clear and Nance assured them he'd been drinking from such creeks most of his life without an issue. One nasty bug could wipe a man out, but they chanced it anyway. The water tasted sweet, and the cold refreshed them as it coated their insides.

Willoth spread out the map and pointed. "I think we're here."

Tarkington leaned close and studied the map. "I'd agree with that."

"You estimated the Japs were somewhere in this area here last night," Willoth stated. Tarkington nodded. Willoth continued, "We can assume they're moving, but based on their tracks, they're a large group. They'll move slowly." Nance came over and peered between them. Willoth continued, "I think we're ahead of them, but there's only one way to know for sure."

Tarkington glanced up the steep canyon walls. "We can climb out of here and take a look-see." Willoth nodded and tucked his map back into his pack.

Nance led the way, his men close behind. The slippery slope made it tough, but they finally crested the canyon walls and waited for the rest of them. Soon they were spread out on top, facing southeast. The view took Tarkington's breath away. Green grasses swayed in a light breeze. Holes in the clouds allowed shafts of golden sunlight to shine through, turning the grasses they shone upon vibrant green. The air smelled clean, with just a hint of saltwater from the distant sea. The grasses angled down to the west. The high Owen Stanleys in the distance were shrouded in clouds. Between where they stood and the mountains, but out of sight, was Wau village. From here it looked as though no man had ever walked these hills.

Tarkington and Willoth searched the area through their binoculars. They carefully scanned. Tarkington pointed. "See that farthest patch of forest up there, as far as you can see?"

Willoth nodded.

"I think that's where the snipers were, which means the Japs might be close." He turned his binoculars toward where he figured Wau to be. "There are a few more plateaus that way. See the little valley between the first and second one? See how the trees kind of pinch the grasses down?" he asked. Willoth grunted the affirmative, and Tarkington finished. "If we hustle, we can set up some of our surprises in there, then fade back to this river and see what happens."

Willoth glassed the entire area, then nodded. "I agree." He handed Nance his binoculars and asked, "You up for a little reconnaissance, Corporal?"

Nance scanned quickly, then handed the binocs back and smiled. "Yes, sir."

Willoth pointed straight across the field. "While we move down into that little cut over there, I want you and your men over there watching for the Nips." He held up a finger for emphasis. "Don't engage them." He patted Nance's ruck. "Once you've got 'em spotted, fade away and report in with the walkie. That way we'll know how much time we've got."

Nance's smile faded slightly, but he nodded. "We can do that, Lieutenant. But are you sure you don't want us to nibble off a few of 'em? Maybe take out a straggler?"

Willoth's face darkened. "No. Absolutely not, Corporal. If you do that, they'll be on the alert and might find our surprises before they go off. Don't alert them to your presence unless it's life and death." Nance nodded and Willoth continued, "When the fireworks go off, we'll meet along this creek about a thousand yards further downstream. Once we're all back together, we'll decide how to hit them again." He looked at Tarkington. "That sound all right to you, mate?"

Tarkington exchanged glances with his men, then nodded. "We should get going."

~

Willoth and his commandos spread out up the slope and watched for movement while the GIs went to work in the defilade. Stollman and Vick carried most of the explosives. Back in Port Moresby, Tarkington had questioned Stollman about bringing the extra weight along on a reconnaissance mission, but Stollman insisted, and now Tarkington was glad he had.

Stollman doctored the grenades, tying an extra stick of TNT to them. Then they tied a thin wire to the grenade's pin and scooted it out as far as possible without activating the fuse. They placed these carefully near the base of a tree and strung the wire to another tree, keeping the wire inches off the ground. Then they camouflaged the wires and grenades and stepped away carefully.

Stollman wanted to fashion bombs he could string to a small portable plunger he carried with him for just such occasions, but there wasn't time. They'd only gotten three trip wires set before the radio crackled and Nance warned them of advancing enemy soldiers.

The GIs hustled toward the bank of the river only four hundred yards away while the commandos covered their move, then joined them. The four NGVRs showed up twenty minutes later, and they all hunkered in the grass and waited.

The calm silence of the day carried the sounds of a large group of men and equipment on the move. Tarkington lay at the base of a tree. He used the trunk for cover and got to his feet slowly. He peeked around the trunk and saw the Japanese. They moved through the grasses, their green uniforms blending well. They spread out the leading elements moved cautiously. Behind the first group, the main force emerged from the forest and were much less cautious.

He brought his binoculars slowly to his eyes and scanned them carefully. He ducked and moved toward Lt. Willoth. "I'd say regimental strength. They're hauling mortars and heavy machine guns too. They've got a line of carts, probably full of ammunition. They're serious about taking the airfield."

Willoth shook his head. "Too bad we don't have any artillery support. We could ruin their bloody day."

Tarkington continued. "They're heading straight for the booby traps. I think their forward element will run into them in a few minutes. When we hear the first one, let's get back into the canyon and move downstream and get in front of them again. We can do it all over."

Willoth stroked his stubbled chin. "They'll be alerted."

"A couple booby traps will just slow 'em down a little. We need to do more."

Nance pushed through the grass and entered the conversation. "Let us sneak out there and harass them from the rear. We're crack shots. We'll kill their officers."

Willoth and Tarkington exchanged glances. Tarkington shrugged. "It would give us more time to set more traps."

Willoth looked Nance straight in the eye. "A couple of shots each. If you get pinned down, we can't come for you."

Nance's eyes lit up, and his grin widened. "Of course. Couple of well-aimed shots might make 'em think twice."

Tarkington grabbed Nance's shoulder before he went to tell his mates the good news. "Don't worry about getting back to us afterwards. Do it if you can, but getting away's the key thing. Okay?"

Nance nodded and leaned in until he was just inches away. "I don't have a death wish, Yank. We'll do what we have to do. We'll be okay. This is our backyard."

The sudden crack of an explosion echoed across the grasses. From the treetops, smoke and dirt shot up and dissipated. "That was fast," Willoth remarked.

Tarkington found Henry and Raker nearby. "Take us back into the canyon and downstream." He noticed Stollman and Vick congratulating one another as though they'd scored the winning touchdown in the championship game. "Keep your explosives handy—we're gonna do it again." They hustled back into the canyon as the sound of another explosion rumbled across the hills.

11

Corporal Nance led the other NGVRs across the grassy field until they found the Japanese regiment's tracks. Two explosions had gone off, and he knew the Americans had set three. He wondered if the enemy had found it or were simply moving more cautiously now. Either way, the Japanese would be spooked and moving slower, allowing him and his men to get close enough to harass their flank.

Nance waved them close, and they crouched in the swaying grasses. He whispered, "We'll spread out. I'll stay on the trail. Winger and Lang go left, and Culler, you go right. Remember, find their officers if you can. Don't fire more than twice from the same spot." He pointed away from the canyon. "We'll meet over there somewhere, don't want to lead the buggers to the others." He looked each man in the eye. He knew them better than he knew his four brothers back in Broken Hill. They'd worked in the mines together for years before fighting side by side against the Japanese. Each man had saved the other's life countless times. "Good luck, and good hunting." He watched them disperse and quickly disappear into the grass.

He turned down the hill and hustled in a low crouch. He held his trusty Lee-Enfield rifle in his right hand as he trotted and took in his surroundings. The grass was trampled from the many Japanese boots and carts that had recently passed. He sniffed the air, catching the faint whiff of burnt gunpowder. The explosions had sounded bigger than mere grenades, and he wondered how many of his sworn enemies had perished. He licked his lips, eager to add to the tally.

He came to the lip where the field angled down into the small valley and woods below. He got onto his belly and crawled until he could see over the top of the grass and into the forest. The remnants of smoke still drifted through the canopy, and he heard faint voices.

Movement caught his eye, and he saw dark shapes moving just inside the tree line. He pulled his pack off and set it in front. He carefully braced the rifle onto it and tucked the buttstock into his shoulder. He'd asked for a scope, but his request never amounted to anything. He'd grown accustomed to the open sights but knew he'd be more effective with a proper scope. Without one, it just meant he had to get closer.

He scanned the Japanese soldiers. The rear echelon spread out in a long line, their rifles ready for trouble. Nance was glad to see the booby traps had done their jobs and slowed their advance. He passed over ordinary soldiers one by one. He would've liked to put bullets through each of their heads, but he was hunting officers, or at the very least, NCOs.

Another explosion erupted. It was much louder, and from the corner of his eye, he saw smoke and debris arcing through the trees. As the rumble swept over his body, he took his eye from the sights. He saw a soldier standing, and even from here he could hear him issuing orders. He adjusted and found the officer. The officer had his back to him. Nance centered his sights on the man's upper back. He calmed his breathing and pulled the trigger. The rifle kicked solidly into his shoulder. It felt good, and he knew before the slight smoke cleared that his target was down.

The noncom beside the officer saw him pitch forward, a dark bloodstain spreading across his back. The Japanese NCO turned toward the sound, but before he could shout a warning, Nance fired. His bullet pierced the NCO's chest, and he dropped beside his twitching officer. Nance quickly chambered another round and pushed himself straight backward until he could no longer see his quarry. He heard a shot from the right and smiled grimly, knowing Private Culler rarely missed with his Lee-Enfield.

He got to his feet and ran to his left. Answering enemy fire grew in intensity. He was beyond the slope and completely out of sight, but he could still hear and feel the zings and snaps of passing bullets. A rifle shot from his front made him veer uphill. He didn't want to accidentally stumble into Winger or Lang and catch a bullet from them. A second shot from Culler behind him brought a new flurry of shots from the Japanese. He hoped Culler had the sense to get the hell out of there.

Nance slowed to a walk and veered back down the hill. When he thought he was close, he went to his belly and crawled forward until he could see the forest again. He scanned for more targets. Muzzle flashes winked from the darker background of the forest. He probably wouldn't be able to distinguish an officer from an enlisted man now, but he searched anyway. There were far fewer targets. He heard another shot from his left, either Winger or Lang. It sounded relatively close but further forward.

He heard the distinctive sound of a Japanese Nambu machine gun. It sounded like a woodpecker hammering away against a particularly stout tree. He lifted his eyes from the sights and saw the smoke coming from the tree line. He aimed at the smoke and flickering muzzle blast. He concentrated and finally glimpsed the gunner's dim outline.

The gunner had taken the time to weave jungle grasses through his helmet, breaking up his outline, but the gun smoke gave him away. Nance checked for windage—nothing. He aimed carefully, squeezed the trigger, and the rifle bucked satisfyingly. The gunner had just depressed the machine gun's trigger, but Nance's shot brought it to an abrupt stop.

Nance chambered another round and rested his sights on the loader, who looked around as though being stalked by a tiger. Nance relished the soldier's fear, remembering his youngest brother for an instant. He pulled the trigger, and the loader flopped backward.

Bullets ripped into the grass, and dirt exploded in front of him. He ducked and pushed himself backward as fast as possible, hoping the NGVRs were already gone.

He pushed past the lip, turned, and fast-crawled straight away. Bullets snapped overhead, but they were shooting at shadows now. He got to his feet and heard a high whistling sound. He dove forward and covered his head. The crump of an exploding mortar shell shook the ground. Dirt and grass sprinkled his back. He heard more whistling shells and tried to make himself as small as possible. This one was closer, and he felt the heat of it.

He shot to his feet and sprinted right until he heard the low whistle again, then dove and buried his nose in the dirt.

Four more shells dropped nearby, and after each shell exploded, he ran as fast and as far as possible. By the time the last shell impacted, he was well away and breathing hard. He wiped the dirt and grime from his beard. He continued through the grass field, listening for pursuing Japanese. He hadn't heard any more shots from his mates and figured they'd cleared the area.

He pushed through a particularly thick section of grass and faced two rifle barrels. He blanched for an instant, then smiled broadly, recognizing Winger's and Lang's bearded faces. "Seen Culler?" he asked.

They shook their heads, and Winger said, "Not yet. Thought maybe they blew your arse up, mate."

Nance brushed the dirt still covering his shoulders. "They got close. Buggers set up faster'n I thought they could've."

"The Nambu had us pinned for a bit."

Nance grinned. "That crew won't be bothering anyone again. Hopefully gave the Yanks enough time." He pointed east. "Let's find cover and wait for Culler."

~

By the time the third explosive went off, the GIs and commandos had moved half a mile down the canyon. They moved fast along the banks of the river, which had calmed as the gradient lessened. The underbrush grew thicker, but the ground above the floodplain was hard-pack and easy to move along.

The distant sounds of rifle fire drew their attention, but they kept moving. Tarkington gave a quick whistle, getting Henry's attention, and he pointed east. Henry nodded and moved toward the grassy fields. The gunfire sounded like insignificant pops.

Another plateau spread before them. Instead of lush grasses, this area contained harsh, cutting kunai grass. The intensity of the Japanese fire increased up the hill. Tarkington and Willoth searched downhill for a suitable place to set up more explosives, but there was nothing obvious.

Multiple lanes of travel could be used, and if they chose incorrectly, the Japanese could simply bypass them.

Willoth shook his head in frustration. "Bloody tough spot, Tarkington."

Tarkington finished scanning and pointed downhill. "Let's move further down. Hopefully, there's something beyond the next valley." He pointed his thumb toward the increasing firefight. "Let's get it done while the Nips are occupied." He slapped Henry's shoulder. "Double time." The sound of a Nambu machine gun made him look back up the hill. "Sounds like Corporal Nance is doing more than nibbling at the corners, dammit."

Willoth nodded but assured him, "I've seen them get out of worse scrapes. They'll be all right."

A few minutes later, they heard the distinctive thumping of mortars. Tarkington raised an eyebrow. "Still think they're okay?"

Willoth tilted his head. "Hope so."

They went back into the canyon to avoid the kunai grass. They marched another quarter. Instead of kunai grass, the area was mostly short grasses and runty scrubs. "Now we've got no cover to speak of," muttered Tarkington. He scanned west. "I can see the far edge of the valley. We're running out of real estate. Vick, see if you can raise Wau from here." Vick nodded and unslung his pack. Tarkington continued, "The Jap commander might think about setting up his CP somewhere nearby." He pointed at a distant cluster of boulders. "Wonder what you can see from the tops of those? Probably the whole damned valley."

Vick tried raising Wau but only got static in return. "Nothing, Tark."

Tarkington cursed, "Damned radio."

Vick carefully stowed the radio back in his pack. Stollman stepped close. "Can I see those binoculars?" Tarkington handed them over, and Stollman scanned the area, paying close attention to the distant rock formation. "If we can get there before the Japs get there, I think we can hurt 'em bad." Tarkington furrowed his brow, and Stollman explained, "We could string that whole area up with explosives and set 'em off from cover."

Vick shook his head. "We don't have enough wire. We've only got a few yards' worth. We'd be too close."

Stollman stroked his chin, considering other options. "True," he murmured. He finally added, "I'll bet the Japs take those carts along the easiest route through all the scrub and boulders. If we could put explosives in their way, we could destroy a good bit of their supplies."

A breeze blew down the hill, and the absence of gunfire and mortars added to the tension. Tarkington looked at Willoth, then back to Stollman. "Let's get moving. We'll head to the rocks and see what we can see. The kunai grass will slow the Nips, but I expect we need to hustle across that open ground before they clear it or they'll see us for sure."

Running across the open ground felt all wrong to them. The commandos kept slowing and would search uphill for any signs they'd been spotted. They zigzagged their way through the surprisingly tenacious scrub brush. Needle-sharp thorns extended from every limb, catching their clothes and cutting exposed skin. The short green grass looked inviting from a distance, but it was sparse and clumped, increasing their chances of rolled ankles.

They finally made it to the large rock feature. The rocks had a reddish hue and looked as old as the earth itself. As they rested, Tarkington wondered how the hell the rocks had gotten there. Were they left over from some long-forgotten ice age, or had they tumbled down a long-extinct river?

Stollman found his way to the top of the tallest boulder and called down to them. "View's amazing from up here."

Tarkington was astounded by how quickly he'd scaled the rock. He'd expect it from Henry or Raker, but not Stollman. He stepped back and called up to him, "See any Japs?"

Stollman looked up the hill and shook his head. "No. I can see the kunai grass, but you could hide an entire division in there and I wouldn't see 'em."

"How about Wau?"

Stollman turned and shielded his eyes. "Not the town but certainly the valley."

Tarkington motioned to Vick. "Get up there with the radio."

Vick interrupted the drink he was taking from his canteen and wiped his mouth with the back of his hand. "Dammit. Can't a guy get a break around here?" he muttered under his breath. He twisted the lid back on and stormed away.

Tarkington handed Henry his binoculars. "Get up there and keep an eye out." Henry and Raker trotted to the other side of the boulder.

Willoth stood beside Tarkington. "You planning on staying here? I don't like it—feels like too much of a landmark. The Nips are sure to come here, if only out of curiosity."

Tarkington raised an eyebrow, an idea forming, then called up to Stollman. "Stolly, you still got those long fuses in your pack?"

Stollman nodded and smacked his pack lovingly. "You bet I do. I never know when I'll need 'em."

"Help Vick get up there, then come down. I've got a job for you."

Minutes later, Vick appeared beside Stollman on the boulder. He took out the radio and tried to connect. After a few attempts and adjustments, he looked down and shook his head. "I think we're still too far away." Henry and Raker appeared beside Vick and took in the view. Henry scanned the area slowly with Tarkington's binoculars.

Tarkington hollered up to them, "Stay put and watch for the Nips. But don't get too comfortable. We won't be staying long."

Stollman scampered off the boulder and soon trotted around the edge of the rock, dusting himself off. "We're leaving?" he asked.

Tarkington nodded. "This place will be crawling with Japs soon. Hell, they might even set up their HQ here. Might become a jump-off point for 'em." Stollman adjusted his carbine's sling and nodded. Tarkington gave him a sly grin. "You think you can rig a timed explosive in case they do?"

Lieutenant Willoth grinned. "You devious bastard."

Stollman studied their surroundings, becoming excited. He pointed to where one rock met the dirt. "I could tuck it in there. Pack loose rock in front and on top to give it more punch." He stroked his chin, seeing the carnage in his mind's eye. He held up a finger as though coming up with a new idea. "I've got a few of those acid fuse charges left. Longest I can set it is about four hours. Think that'll be enough time?"

Tarkington checked his watch. "If they come, they should be here by then. Just be getting dark too—maybe you'll catch 'em during dinner."

Stollman stepped back and hollered up to Vick, who'd just sat down and gotten comfortable. "Vick, get your lazy ass down here and bring your pack."

Vick leaned over the edge of the rock and cursed, "You know we're the same rank, right, asshole?"

Stollman shook his head. "What's that got to do with anything? We're gonna rig this place to blow."

Vick got to his feet, muttering the whole way down.

Henry leaned over and called down in his slow Louisiana drawl, "I see 'em, Tark. They're in the grass."

12

General Moten stood in front of his HQ and watched the last C-47 lift off from Wau airfield. The rains cut down the dust but turned the airstrip to mud. The natural tilt of the airfield kept large puddles from forming, but the ground was spongy, and chunks of mud dripped off the plane's wheels as it lifted and gained altitude.

Major Connaway stood beside him. "That's the last plane we'll see today. Hope this weather improves or we won't see another tomorrow."

Moten asked, "How many did we get in today?"

Connaway answered, "We got all of C Company and a third of Able Company. They also brought in more food, ammo, medical supplies, and those new submachine guns." Moten raised an eyebrow, and Connaway walked a few steps to an open box. He lifted out a stocky green weapon. "The Owen submachine gun. The thirty-three-round magazine should help our lads out there."

Moten hefted the weight, then handed it back. He smoothed his mustache and said, "Not much to look at. We'll see how it stands up in the muck."

Connaway returned the weapon, and Moten continued, "Let the officers know I want to brief them at noon. That should give them enough time to get their men settled. We need them on the line as soon as possible." Connaway nodded his understanding. Moten asked, "Any word from Captain Dane?"

Connaway shook his head. "Not yet, sir. They only have the handheld radios, so they'd have to be close and have a line of sight."

They both turned away from the airfield and looked east toward the foothills beyond the valley. "I suppose there up there somewhere," Moten said. "I'm planning on sending C Company up past Wardumi. They'll be the closest to Dane's men."

"We could send a patrol out to link up with them, sir."

Moten's lips pursed, and he shook his head. "They're too green; they need time to adjust. I don't want them getting in over their heads just yet."

Connaway said, "Captain Grumskey's been itching to take his commandos up there, sir. They're better trained for it, too."

Moten motioned Connaway to follow and stepped into the thatch hut he'd claimed as his HQ. He went to the table and looked at the map. He found the tiny town of Wardumi, which had been penciled in by an aide. It was about a mile due east of Wau. It could hardly be called a town. Only four dilapidated structures sat there, but the dirt track road leading through it was well traveled by villagers. He tapped it with a meaty finger. "Have Grumskey lead Lieutenant Pringle and C Company to Wardumi."

Major Connaway nodded and put his finger on a spot a half mile further east from Wardumi. "There's a farm up here with an excellent field of fire. C Company might be more effective here, sir."

Moten left the more minute details to Major Connaway, who'd been there longer and knew the area better. He nodded. "Agreed. Whatever you think, Dan. Once they're dug in, I want Grumskey's men to head further east and either link up with Dane or find the Japs. Either way, I need to know where that Jap regiment is. We need more men, and this weather's going to shut down our reinforcements for a while."

Connaway nodded. He knew all too well what they faced. There wasn't an accurate count, but the lowest estimate was two thousand enemy soldiers. The recent influx of reinforcements only brought the Allied total to three hundred fifty. He didn't like those odds. "Sure would be nice to get some twenty-five pounders in here, sir."

Moten sighed. "No doubt. But the priority is men. Artillery takes up too much room on the planes. Our 60mm mortars will have to do for now." He glanced outside. Curtains of rain swept the airfield. "Hope those last pilots got over the hump in time. Nasty flying weather, and it doesn't show signs of getting any better."

Captain Grumskey and his commandos led the newly arrived C Company from Wau to Wardumi and beyond. He'd been to the farm before, and once they arrived, he helped Lieutenant Pringle set up a formidable defensive line. The company had one Vickers machine gun, which they dug in behind a rock wall. It faced northeast, across an open field, which the Japanese would have a hard time crossing.

Once Grumskey and Pringle were satisfied with their efforts, Grumskey said his goodbyes and led his men further east. The AIF regulars looked at them as though watching dead men walking.

Soon, the commandos were climbing the sloping hills overlooking the Wau Valley. The airfield and farm were soon out of sight as they dipped into and out of verdant valleys.

The rain swept over them in waves. Sometimes it was a downpour, other times a light mist, but it never stopped altogether. They used the natural cover and moved quickly. From Wau, the foothills looked close and, besides grass and scrubs, featureless. But between each undulating hillside, they had to descend into unseen valleys and climb up the other side, where they'd find another plateau and another valley beyond. By the evening, Grumskey thought they'd only moved two miles from Wardumi, despite having walked twice that far.

He kept them moving well past nightfall. They moved carefully, not wanting to blunder into the enemy. At around 2100 hours, a tremendous flash in the distance, followed by a rumbling cascade of sound, made them stop and crouch. The chirping insects stopped suddenly but resumed their cacophony after a few seconds.

Grumskey conferred with Lt. Blakely. "What the bloody hell was that?"

Blakely answered, "Can't be artillery, and I didn't hear any aircraft. Big explosion, though, so it wasn't a grenade. Has to be Willoth and those Yanks. From what I hear, the Yanks brought explosives."

"I'm guessing that wasn't much more than a mile from here."

"I agree, sir."

Grumskey watched the distant glow slowly disappear into nothingness. The night's blackness settled over them once again. He whispered, "Corporal Gaines." Corporal Gaines edged closer, and Grumskey ordered, "Get on the radio and see if you can raise Lieutenant Willoth or the Yanks." He raised his voice. "Rest of you, take a ten-minute break."

Gaines switched on the radio and tried four different frequencies before the static broke and he heard a faraway, tinny voice. "I've got something, sir. It's faint, but..." He listened intently, but the words were garbled. He stood, hoping for a better position, and called again, "This is Cutthroat. Do you copy? Over."

He listened, and this time he could make out the reply. "Cutthroat, this is..." The signal cut out, then returned. "Have a weak signal. Over."

"Sounds like a Yank, sir." Gaines's voice cracked with excitement.

Grumskey nodded and held out his hand. "They've got one too." Gaines handed it over, and Grumskey depressed the transmit button. "Read you faintly. Were those your fireworks? Over." He didn't want them to give away their position over an open channel. The handhelds, though underpowered, could be picked up by the enemy if they were close enough.

The crackling response: "Roger..." Garbled words followed and the static increased, finally cutting out.

Grumskey cursed, "Losing the signal, dammit." He pressed the button and said, "Moving your way. Repeat. Moving your way. Over." He listened and heard more garbled words before they faded and the static filled the airwaves. He turned the volume low and handed the radio back to Gaines. "Keep it low, but on. We'll move toward the explosion and check in every five minutes." He tapped Blakely's shoulder. "Let's move out, Lieutenant."

∼

Captain Dane paced the grass into a muddy trough. The commandos and Alamo Scouts had left hours before, and his AIF soldiers reported from the forward outpost that they'd heard distant gunfire and explosions. He tried raising the commandos on the short-range radios but couldn't make contact. He didn't enjoy being a forgotten afterthought. Men under his command were in contact with the enemy, and sitting here on his hands didn't do them any good.

He barked, "Sergeant Millcutty."

Staff Sergeant Millcutty's blocky shape stepped from the shade of a nearby tree. "Sir."

"Inform the men. We're moving out. We need to reacquire contact."

Yelled orders got the men moving. Fifteen minutes later, they formed into a skirmish line and advanced into the verdant grasses. Dane addressed Millcutty, "We'll move forward until we can raise them on the radio. Have Huggins keep trying every few minutes." Millcutty nodded and passed it along to Corporal Huggins, who took out the handheld radio and turned it on low. He pressed it to his ear as he walked.

Dane glanced at his watch. It would be dark in another hour. He cursed himself for waiting this long to move forward. He hadn't planned on doing so but felt compelled after hearing about the distant gunfire. If his men were in trouble, he needed to be able to respond quickly. He hoped he wasn't already too late. "Sergeant, let's double time. I want to be in contact before the sun sets."

Millcutty came closer and lowered his voice. "Sir, there might be Japs close by. We heard their gunfire."

"Precisely why we need to hurry. Once it's dark, we'll have to slow down. Those men might be pinned down and need our help. Hell, we might already be too late."

Millcutty nodded and trotted forward to tell his men to double time. The men gave him fearful, exasperated looks, but they obeyed and were soon trotting into the unknown. Millcutty didn't like it. He'd seen combat on the burning sands of Africa and learned that caution and patience saved lives. Dane had also been there, but somehow he hadn't learned—or was choosing to ignore—the lesson.

Millcutty growled at them, "Keep your eyes and ears open. You see *anything* out of the ordinary, take cover."

Dane noticed that his senior NCO stayed forward with the first line of soldiers. He thought about calling him back but decided against it. He tried not to micromanage his men. If the sergeant wanted to stay forward, so be it. Thoughts of Africa raced through his mind. He'd made mistakes there. His superiors told him his actions were warranted based on the information he had—but nevertheless, his actions had caused men's deaths, and that weighed more heavily upon him than any disciplinary action ever could have. He often wished he *had* been punished, just so he could feel like he'd paid for his decision, however insignificantly. He swore he wouldn't make another mistake here and hoped his late reaction hadn't already done so. He couldn't live with more blood on his hands.

At Stollman's urging, Tarkington and Willoth pulled everyone back from the rocks while he carefully set the timed fuse. Vick protested, but Stollman insisted and he finally relented, still keeping a close eye on his friend.

Tarkington and Willoth hunched behind a thorn bush, watching Stollman work. Willoth asked, "Why's he so spooked?"

Tarkington answered, "This climate plays havoc on the fuses—especially the time release ones. We keep 'em as dry as possible, but sometimes it just can't be done. If they're damaged, they usually just won't work, but sometimes they'll spark too early. He's just being cautious."

Willoth ducked a little lower. "Brave young man," he uttered.

Tarkington shrugged it off. "Odds are in his favor."

While they watched Stollman carefully insert the fuse, Willoth asked, "So, move south towards Wau or back to the river and try hooking up with Nance and his men?"

Tarkington frowned slightly as he adjusted the short sword strapped to his waist. "After this, we don't have many more explosives. Probably a good idea to head south and get in contact with Wau. I imagine they're wondering what the hell's going on up here."

"I agree. We still don't have an exact enemy head count, but at least we'll be able to tell them exactly where they are. Maybe they can call in a bombing run."

"Wishful thinking. Last I heard, there're more pilots than planes."

Willoth shook his head. "When's the brass going to get around to taking this part of the world seriously? The Japs are at our bleeding doorstep. They've already bombed Darwin once."

Tarkington answered, "I'm not on the general's staff, but you've heard the term *Europe first*. We're in a holding pattern here. Keep 'em bottled up until they take care of the Nazis."

Willoth spit into the mud. "Wait much longer, there won't be any place to stage from."

"They won't take Australia. We're making headway despite the supply problem."

Stollman finished inserting the fuse. He carefully covered up his work. He checked the small trench they'd dug, connecting the first bomb to the second. It was well hidden. The det cord connecting the two would increase the power of the bomb twofold. He stepped back and gave his work one last look, then trotted to join the others.

Tarkington breathed easier and stood. "We'll head south downslope a half mile. Henry, find us a suitable spot to lie up for a few hours. We'll push to Wau after the fireworks go off."

Stollman rubbed his hands together and grinned. "It's gonna be a big one, Tark. Sure hope the Nips enjoy it."

Tarkington nodded. "Even if they're not close, they'll waste more time checking it out."

They spread out and moved downslope. The thorny scrubs thinned the further they descended, and soon the lush, waist-high grasses returned. The clouds darkened and rain washed over them, making them shiver. They couldn't see the sun setting, and it seemed the world went from light to dark in an instant.

The plateau continued for a mile before it dropped off into a dark valley. Trees dotted the area, and they stopped and waited beneath a cluster of them. They draped ponchos over themselves and shoveled soggy C-rats into their mouths before they turned to mush.

Stollman watched the horizon like a child in front of a fireplace waiting for Santa Claus on Christmas Eve. Vick huddled nearby. "What if it doesn't go off? This rain might fuck the whole thing up."

Stollman shrugged and checked his watch. "It's tucked pretty deep. It won't get wet enough to make a difference." He leveled his gaze at Vick. "You wanna put some money on it?"

Vick learned a long time ago never to take a bet against Stollman, but he threw caution to the wind this time. "Why not. Five bucks says it doesn't go off."

Stollman grinned. "Deal."

Winkleman piped up, "I'll bet a fiver it goes off at," he gazed at his watch, "2130."

Raker added, "I'll take 2045."

Henry drawled, "2105, but by whose watch?"

Stollman's eyes glowed. He was in his element. "We'll sync them to mine." He went around to each man and collected the money. Some commandos stepped forward, and money exchanged hands rapidly. Stolly held up his hands. "No more bets." He looked at his watch. "I'm at 1940 right...now." He grinned at Vick. "Your bet's just with me." He looked at the officers and asked, "What about you two? You want any action?"

They both shook their heads. Willoth leaned close. "Your Corporal Stollman's quite the character."

Tarkington grinned and wiped his nose. "I never bet against him." He raised his voice. "Keep alert for Japs." He lowered his voice again and growled, "Just our luck to be ambushed 'cause of a stupid bet."

The time ticked by slowly. The miserable conditions were more tolerable as they wondered who'd win what. As the clock ticked past the early-time bets, men cursed their luck. At precisely 2100 hours, the sky lit up with a bright orange-and-yellow blast that reached fifty feet into the sky. The sound crashed into them even a half mile away. Leaves shifted and a few dropped onto to the ground.

Stollman danced in a circle around Vick. The soldiers had the sense not to hoot and holler, but everyone grinned and laughed beneath their hands. Vick cursed and dug into his pocket. He came up empty and shrugged. "I've got it back in Wau."

Stollman shook his head. "You bet with money you don't have? Shame on you. You'd get gutted back home."

Henry stepped forward. "I believe that's my pot."

Stollman closed his eyes, seeing the bets play out in his head. "That it is." He handed the mixed wad of US and Australian bills to Henry. "Congratulations."

Vick shushed everyone, and Stollman looked annoyed. Vick dug into his pack and pulled out the radio. "I thought I heard something," he mumbled as he put it to his ear.

~

The explosion caught Captain Dane and his men by complete surprise. They'd just passed through a foreboding forest. He'd slowed the men, figuring it was probably the forest where the Americans had encountered the snipers. Passing through was stressful, and they'd just left it behind them and relaxed somewhat when the explosion happened. Dane nearly pissed himself.

The rumble finally reached their ears many seconds later. He hissed, "Get on the radio, Corporal." Huggins turned up the volume and listened, but there was nothing but static.

Sergeant Huggins said, "That blast was a ways off. A couple of miles, at least. We're probably still too far away to make contact."

Dane stood and waved the men forward. "Well, now we know where they are, let's get a move on."

Huggins passed on the order, and the two platoons moved across the grassy field at a fast walk. He stepped beside Captain Dane and asked, "What's our plan, sir?"

Dane huffed, "Hasn't changed. Establish contact and help them out if they need it."

Huggins pressed, "Sir, we don't know what the hell that was. For all we know it might have nothing to do with the Japs. It might be where the Japs are, but it might not be, too."

Dane hesitated before answering. "I see your point, but if it has nothing to do with them, it'll still draw their attention, which means they won't be watching their tail as closely."

Huggins nodded and added, "Just don't want us rushing into anything, sir."

Dane said, "We won't. This rain will help too." He pointed. "Looks like another tree section coming up. Once we're through it, we'll have a much better idea where the Nips are."

13

Captain Dane moved as quietly as possible through the trees and shrubs. His men spread out to either side, and everywhere he looked, he saw their shadowy shapes. Finally, they reached the far side and faced another open plain of grass. Even in the darkness, the grass seemed to shimmer, inviting them in like a Siren's song.

He watched the swaying grasses for a few minutes. He tried to gauge where the explosion had occurred, but there was no sign of it. Indeed, the area felt completely devoid of human activity.

He whispered to Sergeant Huggins, "Try the radio again." He heard Corporal Klug keying the radio and whispering softly. Only low static answered his calls. Dane conferred with Sergeant Huggins. "We must be close. Move First Platoon ahead, we'll follow in a few minutes. I don't like this open field. See what cover you can find."

"Yes, sir." Huggins moved off, and soon First Platoon moved from the woods and entered the field.

Dane could still hear Klug trying to raise Willoth. "Put that thing away, Corporal."

Dane nervously watched First Platoon move across the plain. He expected to see winking muzzle flashes and burning tracks of tracer rounds at any moment, but nothing happened. He waved Second Platoon forward and stepped into the open with them. Stepping from the cover of the trees made him feel exposed and vulnerable, and he hunkered as he pushed through the waist-high grass. Memories of the wide open deserts of Africa crossed his mind. This field, although devoid of solid cover, was much better than crossing those empty sands.

He searched the sky. Breaks in clouds allowed stars to shine through. Unlike Africa, he didn't need to worry about German Stukas strafing and bombing his men. So far, the weather kept the Japanese out of the air, and for that, he was eternally grateful. He doubted he'd ever get over the banshee-like scream of a diving Stuka. The mere thought turned his sweat icy, and he shivered involuntarily.

First Platoon crept along fifty yards ahead, and he had to slow Second Platoon to maintain their separation. He wanted to move faster, but now wasn't the time. They couldn't be far from where the explosion happened. There'd been no sounds since, and again he wondered what had caused the massive blast. He hoped to see a residual flicker of light on the horizon, but the night gave nothing away.

The private in front of him held up a fist, and Dane noticed First Platoon had stopped and crouched into the lightly swaying grasses. He crouched and focused his senses, searching for anything out of the ordinary.

The blocky, black shape of Sergeant Huggins appeared, and Dane stood and gave a quick wave. Huggins moved to him and whispered, "The terrain changes from grass to scrub ahead. At the far end, there's what looks like a large rock. Hard to tell what it is exactly, but it's the only cover I can see." Dane lifted his chin, struggling to see through the darkness. Huggins pointed forty-five degrees left. "It's that way—guessing it's a half mile away."

"Any movement?"

Huggins shook his head. "No, sir, but it's hard to tell much of anything in the dark."

A slight breeze shifted the grasses and blew directly into Dane's face. He immediately smelled smoke. Huggins noticed too and turned to sample the air. Dane hissed, "Smoke, coming from the rock. Maybe from the explosion."

Huggins nodded. "Seems about right."

"Can we approach it without being seen?"

"Hard to tell. Like I said, the terrain changes from grass to scrub."

Dane squinted into the night, wondering how to proceed, then pointed west. "Let's stay in the grass and move until we're directly in front of it. Maybe we'll find cover to make our approach."

Huggins nodded but added, "There's been nothing since the blast, sir. No small arms fire, no more explosions. It's been quiet for hours."

Dane leveled his gaze at him. "So? What's your point, Sergeant?"

"Well, we came out here to support Lieutenant Willoth and the Yanks. But they're obviously not still in contact...if they ever were." He licked his lips and asked, "What's our end game, sir?"

Dane thought about that for half a minute before answering, "Our primary mission is to find the Japanese and report back to General Moten. Willoth may have blundered into them and been wiped out for all we know." The more he spoke, the more sure of his answer he became. "We need to find the Nips and report in."

"Yes, sir."

"Move First Platoon, we'll follow at fifty yards. Avoid contact. We'll locate them, then go around until we can contact Wau." He glanced at the glowing hands of his wristwatch. "We've got plenty of night left." He pointed in the rock's direction. "I'm guessing the Nips are close to that rock."

"We'll find out soon enough, sir."

An hour later, Sergeant Huggins and First Platoon stopped their slow trudge through the thinning grasses. The distant rock looked like a massive black hole against the dark sky. He'd seen no movement and heard nothing to indicate enemy soldiers laagered nearby. The occasional burnt smell wafted over them, reminding him of their danger.

The grasses thinned with each yard, giving way to the thorny scrubs that dominated the area. So far, he had seen nothing resembling a good approach. The ever-decreasing cover made him move slower and slower, and he noticed Second Platoon closing their gap. As Captain Dane and the rest of Second Platoon approached, the rain started again.

Huggins waved, and Dane came forward and hunkered. Dane listened and watched for any movement, then said, "Quiet out there. Not much cover, but this rain'll help." He focused on the outline of the boulder. "I'd say it's about an eighth of a mile away." Huggins nodded his agreement. A tense minute passed before Dane ordered, "Take First another five hundred yards. We'll wait fifteen minutes, then approach carefully. If there's anyone there, one of us will see them. Use the handheld."

Huggins gritted his teeth, not liking the idea of splitting up at night in hostile territory. "Yes, sir."

Dane slapped his shoulder. "Timer starts now." Huggins moved off, waving First Platoon to follow along.

The rain intensified, and soon Huggins couldn't see the other platoon members. He weaved in and out of thorny bushes, which snagged his clothes and cut exposed skin. Soldiers cursed in low tones. He checked his wristwatch. Only a few minutes before the fifteen-minute mark. He doubted he'd made five hundred yards. The rain shrouded the outline of the boulder, but he could see that it was now off to his right at forty-five degrees.

He crouched and listened. The others hunkered and listened too, but no one could hear much beyond the pounding rain. Huggins glanced at his watch again. It was time to move out. He leaned close to Sergeant Clifford's ear and whispered, "Keep your interval and move Second and Third Squads forward. I'll come behind you with the rest of the lads."

Sergeant Clifford gave him a curt nod and touched the brim of his floppy jungle hat. Rain water spilled from it and ran down his hand.

Huggins added, "If you see *anything*, stop and let us catch up."

Clifford moved off, whispering commands to the squads.

The ground quickly became saturated, and their boots sank into the sticky mud, which stuck to the soles, making each step heavier than the last. The rain muted their squelching steps.

They made slow, steady progress, and the boulder's wispy outline grew. Huggins glanced right, wondering where Captain Dane and Second Platoon might be. He looked behind and saw Corporal Monk a few steps behind. He hoped the flighty young man had the radio wrapped tightly in his poncho. Wetness wreaked havoc on the short-range units. He stopped to allow Monk to catch up.

Huggins heard a dull pop, so faint he thought he might have imagined it. He held his breath and froze. Suddenly the night exploded in light as a flare burst overhead. He dropped to the ground immediately but watched in horror as his green troops hesitated, transfixed by the sudden light show. He hissed, "Down! Get down!"

An instant later, the sound of gunfire erupted from the night. His men finally dropped to their bellies. The enemy fire quickly intensified, and Huggins heard and felt the familiar snap of bullets passing overhead. Men screamed, but he couldn't decide if they were screams of terror or agony.

He squinted through the rain and darkness, searching for muzzle flashes. He couldn't see anything but gloom. A couple rifle shots from his men made him call out, "Cease fire! Don't give them a target." But his words were in vain. Rifles cracked, firing blindly into the night. "Clifford! Cease fire, dammit!" The Japanese fire intensified, and the ripping woodpecker sound of a heavy machine gun joined in.

Huggins cupped his hand around his mouth and bellowed, "Fall back! Fall back!" Soldiers to either side pushed themselves backward, and Huggins followed suit. He bumped into his radioman, Monk. He kicked his shoulder. "Snap out of it, man. Get moving!" No response. Huggins turned and brought himself nearly on top of him. He shook him and finally pushed him onto his back. In the dimness, he saw Monk's staring, lifeless eyes unblinking against the incessant rain. He felt for a pulse. "Dammit." He called to the nearest man, "Nolan!" Private Nolan's wide eyes stared at him through the gloom. "Help me with Monk."

Huggins got to his knees, slung his rifle, and gripped Monk beneath one arm. Nolan did the same with the other, and they dragged Monk through the brambles. The thorns cut and scraped their arms and legs, but they barely noticed. Huggins yelled at the men around him, "Fall back! Fall back, now!" He had no idea if Sergeant Clifford's men were coming, but his men heeded his call and hustled back the way they'd come.

Huggins stopped after one hundred yards and between heaving breaths yelled, "Form up on me. On me, lads." He released his grip on Monk, and

Private Nolan did the same. They both unslung their rifles and faced back the way they'd come. Huggins yelled at men still fleeing, "On me! On me!" He finally got control of them, and soon panting, panicked soldiers surrounded him. The occasional bullet zipped overhead, but the fire had shifted.

Huggins yelled, "Spread out. Don't fire unless you're absolutely sure of your target. Remember, our boys are still out there." Another flare burst overhead, and Huggins saw distant darting shapes running his way. He leveled his rifle but saw familiar features and yelled, "Don't shoot—those are your mates. Easy does it, now." A screeching whistle overhead made him yell, "Mortars! Take cover!" He dropped and covered his head with his arm. The first dull thump exploded well to his front, and he lifted his head in time to see flashes among the retreating squads. Men flew sideways, their arms outstretched.

Huggins cursed and got onto one knee. He waved frantically and yelled, "Take cover, dammit!" The men of Second and Third Squads didn't listen. They kept on coming despite the scything shrapnel. Huggins saw two more men cut down before the rest finally sprinted out from beneath the barrage.

He got to his feet and waved at an oncoming soldier. "Stop! Get down." The soldier showed no signs of slowing. Huggins dropped his rifle, stepped into the oncoming soldier, and rolled him as though tackling a rugby player. He ended up on top of the panicked soldier, pinning him to the muddy ground. "Knock it off," he yelled. Their noses nearly touched. He felt the soldier relax, and he pushed off him and lunged for another sprinting soldier. He caught his arm and spun him around, causing him to trip and sprawl into a thorn bush.

The other members of his squad followed his lead. Men cursed and yelled and a few even fought their assailants, but finally, the headlong retreat stopped.

A few more mortar rounds exploded far forward, but the rifle and machine gun fire ceased. Huggins searched through his dead radioman's pack and finally found the handheld. He keyed the mic, but there was nothing. He tried again, then realized the unit had a bullet hole through the center. He dropped it, wondering if the same bullet had taken Corporal Monk's young life.

He yelled, "Sergeant Clifford!" Clifford emerged from the darkness and rain. His wide eyes suggested he'd bolt at any moment. Huggins asked, "You hit?" Clifford licked his lips nervously, and his eyes darted around like a cornered animal. Huggins gripped his shoulders and shook him. "Focus, Sergeant. Focus on me."

Clifford's eyes finally keyed on him, and he nodded quickly. "I'm—I'm not hit. They're all dead—dead." His voice broke, and Huggins saw the panic rising.

He tightened his grip until Clifford winced. "Get control of yourself, Sergeant. Now."

Clifford shut his eyes, then opened them. He looked calmer.

"Give me a bloody head count of your squads," Huggins said. "We're not leaving men out there." He slowly released his grip, and when Clifford hesitated, Huggins slapped him lightly and repeated with more venom, "Get a head count." Clifford's mouth tightened into a thin line and his eyes seethed with anger, but he nodded and turned away.

Huggins barked at the nearby soldiers, "Stay in pairs, but spread out. Don't shoot unless you absolutely must. Nolan, stay with me." Private Nolan nodded and moved beside his staff sergeant.

A minute later, Clifford appeared from the gloom. He'd regained his composure and looked more embarrassed than scared. He stated flatly, "I'm missing Randall, Jenkins, and Winkauer." He looked down and shook his head. "I—I'm sorry, Glen, I—"

Huggins didn't let him finish. "Forget it. Stay here. I'm taking First Squad forward to recover our men." He looked behind him and pointed at Nolan. "Send Meng up here. I may need a medic." Nolan darted into the darkness and soon returned with Corporal Meng. Huggins raised his voice, "All right, First Squad, we've got three men out there somewhere. Stay low and quiet."

Clifford lifted his eyes. "I should go. I was in charge."

Huggins shook his head. "Not up for debate. Just keep the men from firing on us when we return." He slapped Nolan's shoulder. "Move out." Nolan nodded and moved into the murk.

∾

An hour after contacting the American Alamo Scouts on the radio, Captain Grumskey and his commandos joined up with them. Tarkington and Willoth brought him up to speed quickly. It rained with purpose, helping to solidify their decision to vacate the area and get back to Wau, or at least Wardumi.

Speaking with Vick, Stollman cursed the decision. "We'll never know how many Nips we took out, dammit."

Vick replied, "Maybe those NGVR fellas will have some idea."

"What *about* those guys? We just gonna leave 'em out there?"

Sergeant Omar overheard them. "Don't worry about those blokes. They've been surviving out here without our help for years now."

They continued packing up their meager supplies. Lieutenant Tarkington gathered the Scouts together in the darkness. "We're moving toward Wau with Grumskey. We know the Japs' approximate position and need to let command know as soon as possible."

Winkleman asked, "What about Dane and Nance and company?"

Tarkington shrugged. "Grumskey's not worried about Nance. He'll send word for a runner to let Dane know what's happening. We don't have time to work our way back around the Nips to let 'em know ourselves. Some reinforcements have arrived, but Grumskey tells me they're still thin and will need every swinging dick they can get down there defending the airfield."

Winkleman shook his head. "This sounds more and more like the damned Alamo."

Henry grinned and drawled, "Maybe old Krueger knew something after all."

Raker looked at him sideways. "What the hell you getting on about, Henry?"

Henry spit and shook his head, not bothering to answer. Winkleman finally filled in the blanks for Raker. "Alamo Scouts, dummy. General Krueger came up with the name. He's from Texas...get it?"

Stollman smacked the side of Raker's head. "You get it, dummy?"

Raker's head still hurt from the fistfight, and he tried to smack Stollman back, but Stolly deflected his hand. Raker seethed, "Fuck off, you..." but he didn't finish his tirade. The sound of distant gunfire made them stop. They looked north and listened to the familiar sounds of a firefight. Through the gloom, a faint glow appeared.

Grumskey and Willoth stood beside Tarkington and gazed into the night. Grumskey asked, "The NGVRs?"

Willoth shook his head slowly. "They're long gone by now. More likely to be Captain Dane's men."

The firefight's intensity increased. Tarkington surmised, "Must've heard the explosion and come to investigate."

They listened a few more minutes and heard dull thumping explosions. "Mortars," Grumskey said.

Willoth added, "Dane doesn't have mortars."

Grumskey shook his head. "Dammit."

Willoth faced him and asked, "What are your orders, sir?"

Grumskey took off his jungle hat and raised his face to the falling rain. He wiped his forehead, then jammed the hat back on. "Orders stand. We head back to Wau and report the enemy position." He added, "Hell, Dane's stalling them even more. The best way to help him is to get the word out. Moten can send help from the Black Cat Mine."

Tarkington glanced at Willoth, seeing the doubt and anger stewing just beneath the surface. He said what he supposed Willoth wanted to say. "A regiment of Japs against two platoons ain't a fair fight."

Grumskey's eyes hardened. "Dane's a veteran. He'll break contact. They'll be all right." He said it as though trying to convince himself.

14

Captain Dane swallowed the bile rising in his throat. The acidic burn nearly made him gag even more. Corporal Myer reached up from the ground and pulled on his sleeve. "Get down, sir."

Dane snapped from the instant of sheer terror, as though awakening from a bad dream. He dropped beside Myer and watched the flare drifting lazily through the rain. "They must've spotted First Platoon," he hissed.

"Yes, sir."

"Dammit, I told him to be careful."

Corporal Myer saw the anguish in the captain's face. Before he'd pulled him down, he'd been frozen like a damned statue.

Long seconds passed as Dane watched the flare get lower and lower. The stillness shattered with the sudden popping of rifle fire. "Shit, they've been spotted for sure."

As the intensity increased, Corporal Myer asked, "What should we do, sir?"

Dane gave him a withering look, then rose to his haunches and surveyed the area. The rain and darkness made it impossible to see more than a few yards, even with the dying glow from the flare. He saw a flash from his left and realized Huggins's men were returning fire. He heard the distinct sound of a heavy machine gun join the fight and caught sight of the muzzle flash. He pointed. "There, to the right of the boulder." Myer kept his head down, taking his word for it. "Get on the radio," Dane ordered. "Try to raise Huggins."

Myer pulled his pack off and found the bulky handheld. He unwound the poncho he had it wrapped in and keyed the mic, calling frantically. There was no response. Muted yelling from the pinned-down squads reached them. Now the only fire came from the Japanese position.

Dane called out, "Sergeant Murtaugh." He startled when the technical sergeant spoke from right beside him.

"Here, sir."

Dane pointed. "I saw the enemy machine gun in that area, maybe five hundred yards away. Just a flicker, but it had to be them." Murtaugh, another veteran from Africa, nodded. Dane continued. "They're chewing our guys up. We need to take the pressure off." A distinct popping sound made him stop his train of thought. "Mortars." The realization made him queasy all over again, but he bit back his fear. "We'll hit their flanks. Quick hit-and-run, then retreat back here. We'll use grenades; they won't see muzzle flashes. Pass the word." Murtaugh moved off. Myer continued trying to raise Huggins. "You can stop that shit, Myer."

Soon the rest of the platoon closed ranks and formed a perimeter, with Dane at the center. He could only see outlines in the darkness. Murtaugh stepped forward. "We're ready, sir."

"Okay, move out. Keep close—I don't want to lose anyone in the dark." He waved them forward, and the platoon wove through the thorn bushes in a relatively straight line. Murtaugh kept a quick pace, trying to move while the battle still raged. Mortar shells continued to pepper the area to their left and shots rang out, but the volume of small arms fire decreased quickly. When they'd gone a few hundred yards, Murtaugh crouched and looked back at Captain Dane.

Dane studied the terrain. The outline of the boulder seemed to loom nearby, but in the darkness, he guessed it was probably still a ways off. He couldn't see muzzle flashes, but the popping of the mortars sounded closer. "Remember, just grenades," he whispered. Murtaugh nodded, and Dane waved him to the left.

Murtaugh led the men slower now. The mud beneath their boots squelched and sucked with each step. Dane prayed the Japanese would be too preoccupied to hear the threat approaching from their flank.

Murtaugh slowed until they barely moved. Dane couldn't see more than a few yards ahead. He fought the urge to stand and get a better look. A popping sound in the distance was followed by a volley of rifle fire. Dane surmised it had to be Huggins and his men again. They were still in contact.

The lead man suddenly stopped and held up a fist. Dane stopped and crouched, gripping his rifle tightly. He heard the rustling of equipment and low chatter of conversation. He gritted his teeth, wanting to wring the neck of the trooper making the noise. He held his breath when he realized it wasn't his men he was hearing. The Japanese were close and, he surmised, discussing the distant firefight. More popping explosions and more rifle fire filled the night.

Time seemed to stand still. Dane tried to figure how many enemy soldiers were out there and how close. But the pounding rain made it impossible. He heard the clicks of pins being pulled from his men's grenades. He braced himself for the coming blasts. The low chatter ended abruptly and was quickly replaced with a night-shattering yell...in Japanese. Dane threw himself onto his belly as the first grenade exploded. More followed quickly, and he saw flashes in the darkness, lighting up dashing and darting figures.

For an instant he felt frozen to the mud. Perhaps if he stayed where he was, they wouldn't notice him. An agonized scream pulled him to his senses, and he got to his feet and yelled, "Fall back! Fall back!" Dark shapes sprinted past him, and he kept waving and encouraging them to hurry.

Sergeant Murtaugh nearly ran him over in his haste to leave. He gasped, "Come on—that's everybody." He pushed Dane, and they weaved and darted through the thorns, not feeling their skin ripping. Shots rang out behind them and bullets zinged and buzzed through the air, but there was nothing close.

Dane caught up to Murtaugh as he slowed. Men continued their mad dash to get away, but the shots had stopped and soon everyone slowed and levitated toward one another like a school of fish after a shark attack. Dane had his hands on his knees, trying to catch his breath. The distant wail of a wounded Japanese soldier carried through the darkness. "Every—everyone okay?" he asked between breaths.

A smattering of affirmative replies. He glanced back the way they'd come. If the Japanese were pursuing, he wouldn't see them coming, but he'd most certainly hear them.

When he caught his breath, he waved them forward. "Let's get back and find First Platoon."

~

Sergeant Huggins, along with First Squad, followed Private Nolan through the murky darkness and rain. The mortar and rifle fire had stopped. The Japanese couldn't see any better than they could. Huggins wondered why they hadn't put up another flare. Perhaps they were low on supplies, or perhaps they were using the cover of darkness to advance. The thought chilled him.

They found Winkauer's shredded body first. Nolan kneeled beside him, and when Huggins approached, he shook his head. Winkauer was dead. Huggins pointed at the two nearest troopers, Huff and Plansky. He whispered, "Take him back." The two privates nodded, slung their rifles, and hefted Winkauer's body between them. When they disappeared into the gloom, Huggins motioned Nolan to move out.

The rest of the squad wove their way between the thorny bushes, taking care with each step. Smoking craters left by the mortars dotted the area. A low moan from the darkness made them all stop and crouch. Huggins thought it came from his left but couldn't be sure. He cupped his hand over his mouth. "That you, Randall? Jenkins?" There was no response.

The moaning resumed, and Corporal Meng shuffled forward until he was close enough to whisper into Huggins's ear, "He sounds wounded. I'll check it out."

Huggins nodded but said, "Careful. Could be a Jap trick." Huggins got Nolan's attention. "Go with him, Nolan." Nolan nodded and moved toward the moaning. When the pair was out of sight, he hissed, "Rest of you keep your eyes peeled."

Long minutes passed. The pattering rain was the only sound. Finally,

Nolan returned. "It's Jenkins. He's hurt bad. Meng's trying to patch him up, but it doesn't look good."

Huggins gritted his teeth, picturing the happy-go-lucky soldier. "Take us to him."

Nolan nodded and led the rest of the squad back to Meng and Jenkins. Corporal Meng had Jenkins's top off, and he'd just finished securing a bandage over his abdomen. Huggins could smell bowel and blood. "Can we move him?"

Meng noticed them for the first time. His hands dripped with blood and shit and shook slightly. "Only chance he's got is getting to a surgeon. I've done all I can out here." Huggins stared at him, and Meng shrugged and said, "He'll die whether or not we move him, Glen."

Huggins sighed, then said, "Then we move him."

From the darkness, another voice called out, "Help me." Everyone turned toward the sound. "I hit."

Meng sat up and strained to see into the gloom. Before Huggins could stop him, he called out, "Randall! Is that you?" Huggins clasped his arm and pulled him down sharply. Meng glared at him. "Lemme go. He needs help."

Huggins gripped his arm tighter. "Shut up. That didn't sound right."

The call came again but louder this time. "Help me. I hit. Help me."

Meng tried to pull away, but Huggins didn't let him go. "Knock it off." He took a grenade from his harness, pulled the pin, and before Meng could protest, threw it toward the voice. He ducked, pulling Meng down with him. "Fire in the hole," he yelled.

The blast sounded pathetic in the rain and gloom. It abruptly cut off another plea for help. Meng's eyes looked like saucers in the darkness. He stammered, "Wh-what the hell's the matter with you? You killed him. You—"

Shots and muzzle flashes erupted from the darkness nearby, cutting Meng's protest short. Bullets whizzed and snapped overhead, but the Japanese only had a vague idea of where they were. Huggins hissed, "Stay down and don't return fire."

The shots finally stopped. Huggins estimated they were less than twenty yards away. He heard excited chatter, which was quickly cut off by a guttural order. He couldn't hear them anymore but decided they must be moving toward them, trying to flush them out. He slapped Nolan's leg and signaled for him to use a grenade. Nolan nodded and pulled his single grenade off his belt. The man beside him, Private Polk, did the same. They rolled onto their sides and lofted the grenades over the brambles as best they could, then dove and buried their heads in the mud.

The two explosions happened almost simultaneously and lit up the area momentarily, outlining two enemy soldiers. Surprised screams and rifle shots rang out. A bullet slammed into the ground in front of Huggins's face and showered him with mud. He brushed the mud from his eyes and aimed his rifle at where he'd seen the muzzle flash. If he fired, he'd give away their position, but he had to do something or the Japanese would step on them and simply skewer them with their bayonets.

He hesitated for a moment longer. Muted explosions erupted farther back and to the right. They sounded like grenades, but his men hadn't thrown any more and they were too far away. He heard a Japanese soldier call out and caught movement only yards away. He adjusted his aim and pulled the trigger. The rest of the squad opened fire. He worked the bolt action and yelled, "Grab Jenkins, and get the hell outta here. Go!"

He crouched and fired into the blackness. He couldn't see his targets, but he fired where he'd seen muzzle flashes. Men ran past him. He saw Meng struggling with Jenkins. Huggins slung his rifle and ran to the other side of Jenkins. Together they lifted him and dragged him through the grass. Enemy rifle fire continued. Huggins expected a bullet in the back at any moment. More screaming and yells of terror ripped through the night, and Huggins realized their grenades had done more damage than he initially thought. Bullets ripped past them, but nothing concentrated or accurate. He pushed his body, ignoring his burning legs and lungs.

They nearly ran into Private Huff and Plansky, returning from delivering Winkauer's body. The soldiers looked beyond Sergeant Huggins, searching for pursuing Japanese. Huggins felt his lungs would explode with the effort of carrying Jenkins, who'd mercifully fallen into unconsciousness. "Take—take over," he uttered between breaths.

Huff and Plansky slung their rifles and took Jenkins's weight between them. "Now get going," Huggins said. "We'll cover you. Go." He unslung his rifle and aimed back into the darkness they'd come from, ready to drop anything that moved. Where the hell were Japs? Huggins wondered.

Meng followed Huff and Plansky, not willing to leave Jenkins's side. Soon Huggins found himself alone in the darkness and rain. He heard distant firing and yelling, but nothing close. He wondered if the enemy had moved back to address whatever was happening near the rock.

He stood and trotted to follow his men. He caught up to Meng and the others, and they joined the rest of the nervous platoon members. Sergeant Clifford couldn't hide the relief of seeing his staff sergeant and long-time friend emerge from the darkness. "Glen, you're okay. What the hell happened?"

"No time to explain. Let's meet back up with Captain Dane and get the hell outta here."

The rain slackened as Dane and the men of First Platoon retreated back to the grasses. The darkness seemed to grow thicker and a mist rose from the saturated ground, making each step a mystery. They stopped occasionally to make sure the Japanese weren't following them, but they could barely see a few yards. There'd only been a smattering of rifle shots since the engagement and nothing close by.

With each step, Dane felt better and better. He'd engaged the enemy, delivered a blow, and hadn't lost anyone. He hoped Second Platoon had fared as well but knew it unlikely based on the volume of fire and mortars he'd seen and heard. For all he knew, they'd been wiped out, but even that thought couldn't turn his mood sour. He'd been doubting himself for months. The debacle in the African desert had stained his soul and his reputation. Perhaps he'd turned the corner on that chapter of his life.

He halted the men when they'd pushed deep into the waist-high grasses again. He whispered to Sergeant Murtaugh, "We've gotta hook up with Second Platoon. Take Third Squad and find them." He pointed further north at the stand of trees silhouetted against the dark mountains. "We'll move back to the tree line. Meet us there."

Murtaugh nodded. "Yes, sir." He gathered the squad and moved. Dane watched them disappear into the misty darkness. When they were out of sight and sound, he waved the rest of the men forward. "Let's go," he uttered.

The rain stopped, and they moved through the grasses quickly. Without the rain, the night suddenly seemed brighter. Their boots sank into the soft mud and clung to their soles, but despite that, they felt lighter with each step they took toward the tree line.

It didn't take long before Sergeant Murtaugh and his squad reappeared, out of breath and leading what was left of First Platoon. Jenkins and Winkauer were dropped in front of Captain Dane, and he cursed under his breath. While he'd been congratulating himself for a job well done, his men had been dying. He felt the old familiar feeling of desperation creeping its way into his gut.

Staff Sergeant Huggins emerged from the gloom. Even in the darkness, he looked tired and worn out. Dane asked, "What happened, Glen?"

Sergeant Huggins gave him the brief version, and when he'd finished, Dane asked, "What about Randall? Is he still back there?"

Huggins shook his head slowly. "We never found him. The Japs were too close. We had to get the hell outta there." He looked Dane in the eye. "He's dead, though, sir. Clifford saw him take the brunt of a mortar round."

Sergeant Clifford stepped from the shadows and lifted the brim of his jungle hat. "No way he could've survived. His body..." He hesitated, remembering the grim scene. "Well, he just came apart."

Huggins pointed at Jenkins's body. "He was alive when we found him, but he was gut shot and died on the way here." He glanced at Corporal Meng, who hovered nearby, looking dejected. "Meng did all he could for him."

A sudden commotion made everyone turn and clutch their rifles. "Who goes there?" someone called out nervously.

The familiar lilt of Corporal Nance's voice put them at ease. "Easy does it there, mate. It's just us."

The four Volunteers made their way through the gaping AIF soldiers. In their woven hats and shredded shirts and shorts, they looked more like farmers than soldiers. Nance's grin turned to a smile upon seeing Captain

Dane and the NCOs. It dimmed slightly, seeing Jenkins's and Winkauer's bodies sprawled on the ground. "We found another man. He's dead, too."

Huggins looked up, startled. "You were back there with us? We didn't see you. Where's his body?"

Nance's smile faded, and his lips disappeared behind his thick beard. "We were there. Took a few of the buggers out by hand after you took off." He patted the long knife strapped to his side with affection. "We left your man back there, though. He was dead and would've slowed us down too much."

Huggins didn't like the description of taking off, but he supposed it was as accurate a phrase as any. He stated flatly, "We could've accidentally shot you."

Nance exchanged an evil grin with the other three Volunteers and sneered. "We weren't too worried about that."

"Criminy sakes, man. We threw grenades."

Nance nodded. "That you did. Gave us a bit of a scare, too. Once the Nips gave away their positions, it was easier for us, though."

Huggins pinched the bridge of his nose and said, "So that's why they didn't pursue us, then." Nance didn't answer but gave him a theatrical stage curtsy. Huggins shook his head. "Well, I'll be damned."

15

Tarkington didn't feel right leaving the area while a firefight raged in the distance. The further they moved toward Wau, the less they could hear, but the distant pops hadn't stopped, and occasionally increased in tempo. Whoever was back there was having a tough time, and it pained him to simply walk away. Captain Grumskey's decision to report in was on mission, but it didn't make it any easier.

The rain stopped, and even though they had hours before dawn, the darkness seemed to lift slightly. They made good time and soon found themselves walking along a dirt track that eventually turned into an actual road. Grumskey spread them out to either side and told them to keep a lookout for C Company occupying the farm near Wardumi.

They couldn't hear the firefight any longer, and Tarkington wondered how it had played out. He decided he'd volunteer to lead the relief effort back up the Black Cat Track. The thought of trudging back up the trail made him want to sit down and weep, but he'd gladly do it. He didn't like leaving loose ends.

He glanced at his men. Henry's shoulders slumped, a sure sign that his point man felt fatigued. Winkleman's gaze never left the ground as he slogged, putting one foot in front of the other like an automaton. Even Stolly, his indomitable BAR man, looked tired. They'd been through much worse than this, though. He decided they looked more dejected than tired. They didn't like leaving the battlefield any more than he did.

He swelled with pride. These were good men. For the hundredth time, he wondered how he'd come to lead them. When the war started, he was a mere rifleman in a combat squad. Now he wore a first lieutenant's bar and the small Indian head emblem of an Alamo Scout. All that in just over a year. It didn't seem possible.

He thought of his little brother, Robert. He realized he hadn't thought about him for a long time, and it startled him. *He's my brother. Is he even alive? Why can't I picture his face?* Mail to New Guinea wasn't what could be called reliable. When the mail did occasionally come through, he'd usually have a letter from his parents, and five to ten from Robert. Once he'd entered basic, or what the Marines called boot camp, the letters grew more infrequent.

Last he'd heard, Robert and his unit were heading for combat somewhere, but that was a month ago. He wondered if he were a part of the Solomon Islands campaign. Scuttlebutt said Guadalcanal was a hellhole. Was Robert fighting the Japanese there? *Was he in a firefight at that very moment?*

Tarkington suddenly wanted to get the hell out of New Guinea and check on his little brother in the worst way. He shook his head and suppressed the ridiculous notion. Once again, he told himself, *The more Japs I kill here, the fewer Robert will have to face.* He steeled himself and picked up the pace.

The next few days passed with little action. Grumskey had reported the suspected whereabouts of the enemy massing in the hills, and Captain Dane and his two platoons had reported that they'd safely disengaged and returned to the Black Cat Mine. They'd sustained casualties, but under the circumstances, it sounded like they'd gotten off easy.

The third morning back from their patrol, Tarkington awoke to the sound of more C-47s landing and offloading troops and supplies.

Winkleman stepped next to him and rubbed the sleep from his eyes. "How many is that now? I've lost count."

Tarkington shrugged. "They've been averaging six to eight flights a day or so, I figure. I overheard Moten say they've gotten another two hundred fifty men in since our little foray."

Winkleman shook his head. "Not nearly enough. Japs got at least a regiment up there."

Tarkington sipped the watery tea he'd procured from the makeshift mess hall. Coffee wasn't on the Aussies' food list, and he'd been forced to drink tea for the past few weeks. He curled his lip as he sipped. He took a gulp, then stated, "Who knows how many they've got up there. But I agree, we're outnumbered at the moment."

Winkleman dumped the rest of his tepid tea onto the ground. He looked up at the increasing cloud cover. "Weather gets worse and worse. It's a wonder they can still get in here at all." The surrounding hills to the east had a layer of fog inching down toward the valley. The Owen Stanleys remained relatively clear, but the deeper they got into the rainy season, the earlier the fog shut down the air lane.

Winkleman squinted up at the hills to the east. "At least Tojo's getting the brunt of the weather, too. Wonder why they haven't tried anything yet?"

Tarkington ran his hands through his hair, which was getting close to being out of regulation length. "Probably making sure all his ducks are in a row. It's a long trip over from Salamaua, and we gave him a bit of a bloody nose, too." He tilted his battered cup to his lips and drained the rest of the tea, then said, "Probably watching us right now—biding their time."

"That's not a pleasant thought."

"Moten's got men spread out all over the damned place."

Winkleman rubbed the stubble on his chin. "Think they're spread too thin?"

Tarkington thought it over for a moment. "We don't know where they'll hit us. Hell, Tojo may even split his forces and hit us from two different directions. Moten's got no choice. He's got men north at the old coffee plantation and spread all the way south to Wardumi."

"And all this rain's brought the water level up on the river. That'll act as a good natural barrier."

Tarkington nodded his agreement. "Which is why he's got men at the bridges and choke points. I think he's doing all he can with what he's got. What we really need is artillery support, but they take up too much room on the transports. He's gambling on getting more men in versus firepower."

"At least we didn't see any sign of Jap artillery up there on the Black Cat Track."

Tarkington nodded slowly. "We'd already be getting hit if they had. We know they've got mortars, though...but so do we."

Major General Okabe scanned the Wau Valley through the shifting layers of fog and rain squalls. After two weeks of misery and pain, his harried force of three thousand men from the 18th Army were finally in position. He couldn't see the airfield they had tasked him with overrunning, but he could hear the droning of aircraft circling overhead.

He doubted the American C-47s could land today. The airfield must be shrouded in fog. The Imperial Japanese Airforce, who were supposed to be bombing the airfield, faced the same problem. They couldn't bomb what they couldn't see. Perhaps a fighter sweep would destroy the circling transports.

He let the binoculars hang from his neck and noticed his First Battalion commander, Major Jima, standing nearby. "Major Jima." Jima raised his chin and stiffened his back. Okabe asked, "Did you find the enemy force harrying our rear?"

Jima bowed slightly, keeping his eyes on Okabe's boots. "No, sir. They have retreated north. We suspect they are heading toward the mine. I have a platoon in pursuit, sir."

Okabe frowned, and he shook his head. "Recall them. They are an insignificant force, trying to draw us away from the airfield. We'll waste no more time on them."

"Yes, sir."

"A message from General Adachi informed me that our forces at Buna-Gona are performing a strategic withdrawal." He let the news linger. He understood what it meant, they'd suffered a crushing defeat, but to say so out loud would be tantamount to heresy against the Emperor. He continued, "General Adachi expects the enemy air operations to increase here as a result." He punched his closed fist into his open palm. "We must attack and destroy the airfield in the next few days, before they can effectively reinforce themselves." Jima nodded curtly, and Okabe continued, "Gather the other officers for a battle order, Major. Meet at my tent in one hour." Okabe saw Major Jima brighten with the news.

Jima bowed stiffly. "It will be my pleasure, sir."

An hour later, the twenty officers of Okabe's force sat on mats on the floor of the command tent. Okabe looked them over as he paced with his hands clasped behind his back. They'd been through a lot over the past few weeks. The boat trip from Rabaul to Lae had been plagued with incessant air attacks. Despite nearly constant fighter coverage, the Allies succeeded in destroying many *Maru*-class ships carrying troops and supplies. He'd lost nearly half his force and most of his medical supplies.

After offloading at Lae under near constant enemy air attacks, they were finally transported to Salamaua via smaller barges and transport ships. From there, they marched over endless tracks and trails, often having to hack their way through the thick jungle with machetes.

January brought the rains, making the trails and roads quagmires of mud. Everything had to be carried upon their backs. Native laborers helped, but they proved unworthy and often treacherous. More than a few soldiers had their throats cut in the night. The other officers desperately wanted to torture and kill the remaining laborers in retaliation, but he needed their strong backs. Having to watch and guard the natives didn't help his men's morale or health, but it kept them alive.

They'd succeeded in slipping past the Australians without being spotted. The Australians finally found them and harassed their flanks, causing more casualties and more delays, but now they were finally in place. A few days of rest would be optimum, but he needed to attack sooner rather than later.

He stopped pacing and began the briefing, "We have suffered over the past weeks." He let that set in for a half a minute before continuing, "Our efforts and sacrifices will lead to our inevitable victory." The officers straightened their backs proudly.

Okabe used a pointer stick on a wall-sized map of the area. Unlike the Allied maps, it was detailed and relatively accurate. "Wau airfield is our objective. By taking it, we cut off the Allies' ability to reinforce the area. Their focus is shifting from Buna to Lae."

He smacked the pointer into his open palm with a loud slap. "We must deny them this vital airfield." He lifted his chin and pointed to black lines drawn onto the map in diverging arcs. "First Battalion, led by Major Jima, will move southwest toward Wardumi. Second Battalion, led by Captain Ho, will move northwest and hit Wau village from the northeast. The Bulol River is rising, limiting our crossing options. Our scouts report there are weak forces arrayed against us."

He turned from the map and looked out over the sea of battle-hardened faces. "We will crush their defenses simultaneously from two directions. Once we're through their front lines, there'll be nothing standing between us and our objective." The officers' eyes sparkled, seeing their inevitable victory playing out before them. They'd known nothing else in their young lives and only wanted the opportunity to be let loose on the enemy.

Okabe pointed at an area on the map along a low ridge overlooking the Wau Valley. "We move into our jump-off point tonight. We'll move out at first light tomorrow morning." He gave a slight grin and continued. "They have promised us air support, but the weather will make that difficult for our brothers in the air corps." He sneered. "As usual, it will be up to us." He lifted his chin. "As it always is and always will be." There was a smattering of indistinct murmurs of appreciation and derision for their pilot comrades. The only true warriors fought on the ground and were members of the Imperial Japanese Army. He let the murmurs fade, then raised his voice, "Lead your men to victory for the Emperor and family!"

The officers stood as one and raised their voices and arms together. "Banzai! Banzai! Banzai!"

～

Major Shima shaved carefully, using the small metallic mirror he had propped into a crease in his makeshift table. Even in the less than perfect reflection from the tiny bent metal, his face looked older than he remembered. More creases, deeper lines, and touches of gray hair alarmed him.

He looked forward to attacking the Allied forces defending the airfield but wished they had given his men at least one day to recuperate from their long trek over the mountains from Salamaua. He understood Major General Okabe's need to strike quickly, but he worried it might lead to mistakes. He kept his fatigue at bay by a strong force of will—knowing he was far better off than most of his men.

Okabe had ordered the men to half rations during the trek, in case their transit took longer than expected. He'd learned this lesson the hard way while battling the Chinese. The intent had always been to conserve food on the way over, then allow a few days of full rations and rest to bring the men back into fighting shape and boost morale. Now, with the timeline moved up, the troops wouldn't get the full benefit.

Just before Shima had left his commander's tent, Okabe had clasped his shoulder and said, "Our men will have all the food they can eat once they take Wau."

Shima finished shaving. He wiped the excess soap from his face and turned away from the mirror. He adjusted his uniform and thought about his commanding officer. He respected General Okabe. He treated the men relatively well, which wasn't the norm in the IJA. He'd heard grumblings about it from time to time, officers saying he was too lenient and familiar, but nothing had ever come of it, because everything Okabe touched turned to gold. That was why he'd been sent to this vital part of the world—to achieve a much needed victory.

Shima turned from the mirror and adjusted his sword, sheathed in the embroidered black scabbard. He wondered briefly if he'd get a chance to use it in the coming battle. He frowned, thinking about Okabe's plan. He thought it a mistake to split their forces.

He'd be leading First Battalion and planned to hit the Australian defenders hard and fast. He thought his mission goals would be easier to attain if he had the direct support of Second Battalion. Splitting their forces kept the Allies guessing, but it also kept both battalions weak. A powerful, quick thrust with both battalions would have negated the need to pin defenders in the north. By the time they reacted, the airfield and the town would have fallen into Japanese hands, and up against nearly three thousand troops, the Allies could never take it back without reinforcements.

He pulled his shiny pistol from the holster, checked the action, and made sure the magazine was firmly in place. He sighed and uttered, "One day, I'll be in command." He stepped from his tent and out into the incessant rain. Soldiers scurried everywhere, their uniforms and boots filthy from the deepening mud.

He looked to the sky. The rain forced his eyes closed, and he felt it pool like tears. Now that they weren't in the mountains, the air temperature was actually pleasant. If not for the rain, it would be a good day for a walk. He pictured his wife, Yasui; she wouldn't care about the rain. Little Arai and Kaya would run wild and find mischief in the puddles, drawing the ire of his wife, who'd lightheartedly scold them. He pushed the memory to the back of his mind, holding them in protection to be enjoyed when there was more time for such things. There were a hundred things he needed to get done before they marched that night.

16

Lieutenant Tarkington and the squad attached themselves to Lieutenant Willoth's platoon after General Moten sent the commandos off to join the regular AIF troops on the line just past Wardumi. As they walked along the rutted and muddy road, Willoth voiced his displeasure to Tarkington. "You'd think after all the successes we've had, Moten would understand we're not regular bloody infantry, for chrissakes. We've got a golden opportunity to hit the blighters up there, but instead we're used as bleeding cannon fodder."

Tarkington knew Willoth couldn't share such things with his peers, so he was using Tarkington as a sounding board. Tarkington nodded sagely. "We've run into the same thing. They're set in their ways, and getting them to do anything different's like pulling teeth from a hyena."

Willoth looked exasperated. "I don't mean to complain; we had a good run while it lasted. Just wish it would continue."

"Moten sounds like a good tactician, at least."

Willoth scowled. "He's got his head shoved so far up General Blamey's arse he can probably see just how far Blamey's got his head up MacArthur's arse."

Tarkington grinned at the image Willoth painted, then suddenly turned serious. "That's no way to talk about our esteemed commanders, Lieutenant."

Willoth gave him a sideways glance and saw Tarkington trying to keep from laughing. Willoth grinned and smacked Tarkington's arm. "Oh, bugger off, mate." They walked a few more yards, gazing through the rain and fog and catching glimpses of the hills and mountains beyond. "I didn't know you blighters would be coming along with us."

Tarkington looked back at his squad and said, "I made an executive decision." Willoth looked quizzically at him, and Tarkington explained, "I'd rather fight alongside men I know and trust. If we would have stuck around much longer, Moten would've been forced to put us somewhere—and God knows where. He'd probably have us cleaning latrines or counting boxes of ammo." He grinned and elevated his enunciation. "I saved him making a decision which might've adversely affected our country's ambassadorial relations."

Willoth guffawed. "You Yanks are full of shit, you know that?" Tarkington just smiled. Willoth added, "Well, we're glad to have you. Ever think you'd be regular infantry again?"

Tarkington looked bemused. "To tell you the truth, since becoming Alamo Scouts, we've done more regular infantry fighting than anything else."

Willoth shook his head. "I shouldn't complain. At least I'm taking orders from fellow countrymen. They've hijacked you blokes."

As they approached the tiny town of Wardumi, they spread out and went quiet in case the Japs had been up to no good. As they entered town, AIF troopers emerged from trenches and foxholes and greeted them, calling them all sorts of names that Tarkington could barely decipher through their heavy accents. The commandos gave as good as they got, and soon the verbal sparring ended. Tarkington thought it was all in good fun, however, he detected an edge to the tone.

A few villagers dressed only in loincloths and gaudy body piercings watched the newcomers. Tarkington noticed one wore a dirty, bloody bandage over his shoulder. Tarkington found Corporal Vick and asked, "You have any extra bandages?" Vick nodded and veered from the road to assist the man. Tarkington raised an eyebrow to Lt. Willoth. "What happened to him?" Willoth shrugged.

An AIF captain strode from an alley and answered, "He took a sniper's bullet meant for one of my men. Stepped in front at exactly the wrong time...for him, at least. He probably saved Private Miranda's life."

Tarkington and Willoth stepped from the road, and the officer extended his hand to each of them. "I'm Captain Warren of A Company, Seventeenth Brigade." He grinned, looking Tarkington's uniform up and down. "Who the bloody hell are you? American?" Tarkington nodded, and Warren added, "Didn't think any of you blighters had made it over from Buna just yet."

Tarkington answered, "We weren't part of the final act, but yeah, we were there for a bit of it."

Warren waited for more, but when it was clear Tarkington was done, he turned his attention to Lt. Willoth. "Can't say I'm happy to see you commando-types. Moten said we'd be reinforced, but I was hoping for some proper infantrymen."

Willoth's eyes hardened and his mouth thinned to a tight line, but he didn't rise to the bait.

Warren looked disappointed. He sighed and pointed. "Why don't you buggers head up to the farmhouse and reinforce Lieutenant Pringle's Third Platoon. We've got enough here already, and you'll just get in the way."

Willoth ignored the rebuke. "That's where Moten assigned us in the first place, sir."

They walked through the rest of the tiny town, ignoring the jeers and taunts from the regular infantrymen. Once they were outside the town, Tarkington leaned in and asked, "Those assholes have any idea how long you and your men have been fighting here?"

Willoth shook his head and answered, "As you Americans say, they can all fuck off."

Tarkington laughed. The rest of the squad heard the exchange, and they joined in. Tarkington felt good about his decision to join Willoth and company. He'd fight beside these men any day of the week. These untested, green-as-grass AIF soldiers of the Seventeenth Brigade weren't qualified to hold their toilet paper rolls. *Ignorance is bliss*, Tarkington recited silently.

They arrived at the farmhouse, which was little more than a shack with a waist-high stone fence stretching into a field for a hundred yards. AIF troopers dotted the fence line, some watching the field, others snoozing, cleaning weapons, or shooting the breeze.

They met Lt. Pringle soon after arriving. He strode toward them with a smile and a handshake. Tarkington thought he might be the skinniest soldier he'd ever met, barring men who'd been on starvation rations in Buna. His angular cheekbones gave him a skeletal look, but his blue eyes sparkled goodwill. "You blokes must be the reinforcements General Moten promised. I was beginning to wonder."

Lt. Willoth tipped his jungle hat off his brow and said, "Moten gave us our orders no more'n two hours ago, mate. Came here straightaway." He noticed Pringle giving Tarkington and his squad a long look. He explained, "Lieutenant Tarkington and his men are American Alamo Scouts." Pringle furrowed his brow, and Willoth continued, "They got pulled into this foray while on a different mission. They're on temporary assignment to us. They've forgotten more about jungle fighting than you or I will ever know, so consider yourself lucky."

Pringle nodded. "Welcome to the farmhouse. We'll find work for you, I'm sure of that." Pringle motioned them to stand behind the shack. "Come out of the open—we've had problems with snipers lately." He adjusted the sling of his brand-new Owen submachine gun.

The commandos and Alamo Scouts had already spread out and taken knees in the grasses. Tarkington and Willoth followed Pringle to the back wall of the shack. The rain had slackened, but the thatch roof continued dripping water into puddles with loud dollops. Another stone fence extended from the shack in the other direction. In the middle, a water-cooled Vickers machine gun sat atop a tripod. Two AIF soldiers had their backs pressed against the wall, watching the newcomers while the gunner kept vigil over the wide open field and the scrub forest beyond.

Pringle pointed toward the machine gun position. "That's the only big gun we've got. Plenty of .303 ammo for it...if we can keep it from overheating." He pointed down the length of the other stone fence. "Got a Bren and a Lewis down that way." He glanced at Tarkington's M1 carbine. "Hope you brought your own ammo—doubt we've got your caliber."

Tarkington nodded. "We brought plenty, and there's more in Moresby if we get low."

Pringle looked into the low overcast sky. "Won't be getting a resupply if this weather's any indicator. Socked in tight."

Willoth said, "Least it keeps the Japs grounded, too."

"You're right," Pringle agreed. "Noticed more and more Jap planes out and about...but not since this." He lifted his chin toward the sky. He pointed behind them at a low depression fifty yards back. "We've got two mortars in that defilade. Don't have as much ammo for them as I've got for the Vickers, though, but every little bit helps. Your platoon would fit in nicely along the wall to the left of the Vickers, Lieutenant."

Willoth and Tarkington both gave the defenses a good look. Willoth finally nodded. "We'll settle in, then. You've got a good line of sight with all this open ground. Have you scouted the left flank? Looks like those trees get up pretty close."

Pringle nodded. "Yeah. There's a little creek running through there. It's a possible Jap attack route. I'd planned to put a squad there to keep tabs, but now that you're here..."

Willoth crossed his arms across his chest. "We'll cover that flank, Lieutenant."

"You can call me Willard, if you like."

Willoth didn't acknowledge that he'd heard. He raised his voice to his men and motioned left. "That's our new home, lads. Get 'em dug in near the end of that fence line, Sergeant Mills." Sergeant Mills got the men moving. Willoth turned to Tarkington. "You're welcome to join us."

Tarkington nodded at Winkleman, who passed it along. "Don't mind if we do."

∽

A few hours later, the sun finally set. It always came as a surprise in this region. One moment, blazing daylight, the next, darkness. There never seemed to be an in-between. Tarkington wondered if he'd ever get used to it.

He sat on the side of his foxhole, facing the little ditch leading to the sparse forest. He spread jelly onto a soggy cracker, shoved it into his mouth, and silently chewed. His last hot meal had been back in the native village on their way to Wau. The thought made him wonder about Sergeant Omar. He'd lost track of him after they'd returned from the hills. Saving him from the villagers seemed like a millennia ago, but he realized it had been less than two weeks.

Henry and the rest of the squad huddled nearby, slurping down the last of their C-rats. Henry pointed toward the ditch with his utensil. "I bet they come through there. Why would they come straight through the grass? They'll get cut down."

Raker buried his garbage in the soft soil and asked, "Think they'll come tonight? What's that sixth sense telling you?"

Henry looked annoyed. "It's not like that. I can't just tap into it like opening a C-ration. It just comes to me. It's a feeling...and don't pretend you don't know what I'm talking about. We've all got it to some degree. It's why we're still alive."

Winkleman spoke up. "Well, you've got it in spades."

Stollman poked his head forward. Even in the darkness, his mop of red hair shone slightly. More than one Australian officer had given him second and even third glances. "I've got some pyrotechnics leftover, Tark. Should we set up a little surprise for 'em?"

Tarkington thought it over, then said, "Nothing like the blast from the rock, I hope."

"I wish—that was beautiful. Still wonder about the effects. But no, I have nothing like that. I've just got a few of those nasty poppers. At the least, they'll alert us to anyone coming."

Tarkington nodded. "Do it. Take Raker and Henry for cover. I'll pass it back to the others so you don't get shot on your way back."

Stollman's smile glowed through the darkness. He clapped his hands and said, "Hot damn."

A few minutes later, Stollman followed Henry and Raker from their holes. They stepped into the muddy ditch. The rains had brought the little creek to life, and it lapped at their boots as they carefully moved upstream. The rain came down steadily—just enough to keep them wet and cold. Moving helped keep them warm, and Stollman relished the added benefit to his spur-of-the-moment mission.

Henry reached the first stand of trees and hunkered. Raker moved right and watched uphill. Stollman continued until he hunched beside Henry. All three of them watched the night for anything out of the ordinary. Satisfied that they were alone, Stollman took his pack off and opened the top, careful to keep as much rainwater from entering as possible.

He gingerly pulled out a wrapped cylinder. He'd made the bomb himself out of an old partially rusted pipe. It was wrapped in oilcloth, and the weight felt good in his hands.

Raker said, "Thought you only had poppers left."

Stollman shrugged and whispered, "I lied."

"Is it a big one?"

Stollman couldn't keep the smile off his face. "Pretty big, yeah." He gazed at the bomb lovingly. It would pack a wallop and take out anyone within a fifteen-yard radius.

Raker moved back until he lay beside Henry.

Stollman slung his carbine and moved forward until he found a suitable spot. He glanced back and saw Raker's and Henry's silhouettes against the darkness beyond. They were in the blast radius. He went ahead anyway, thinking, *I'll be extra careful.*

He carefully unwrapped the oilcloth and inspected the bomb as much as he could in the dark. He'd lashed the trigger to the outside of the pipe bomb for quick and easy access. He unwound the tightly wrapped trip line and stretched it across the ditch, extending between two medium-sized trees. He anchored it to the far side, as close to the ground as possible, then went back to the first tree and scraped out a hole near the trunk. He shoved the pipe into the hole and slid the cap off. He pushed the handmade trigger device into the guts of the bomb and attached the line carefully to the metal ring he'd saved from a spent grenade. He made sure it was secure and the line wasn't stretched too tightly across the ditch. He pulled leaves over the hole, then stacked as many rocks as he could find around the buried bomb. He hoped they'd act as missiles and cause maximum damage.

He tidied up the area and turned back toward Henry and Raker. He immediately froze. Henry and Raker had disappeared. He'd been so engrossed in planting the bomb, he hadn't seen a hand signal or heard a whispered warning. He cursed himself silently.

He kept his carbine slung on his back and eased himself onto his belly, moving glacially slow. Suddenly the bomb, only a few feet away, felt ominous. He pulled and pushed himself back downstream. The cold creek water lapped against his right arm. He would've shivered if not for the warming effect of his fear. Perhaps he should turn and shoot whoever might come before they triggered the bomb and blew them all to hell.

He stopped and listened, but the only thing he could hear was the damned creek. He kept moving downstream, hoping Henry and Raker would take care of the problem.

He finally made it to his ruck. He stopped and looked at each side. He couldn't see much beyond the lip of the ditch, and the babbling creek kept him from hearing anything else. There could be an enemy soldier feet away and he wouldn't know about it down here. He figured if the bomb went off now, he'd most likely survive as long as he stayed on his belly. He'd have a raging headache, but he'd survive...probably.

He eased his carbine off his shoulder and hoped it hadn't gotten mucked up during his crawl. He remembered Raker had been on the right and Henry on the left. *Did they leave me?* He shunned the idea as soon as it formed. Of course they wouldn't leave him; they were a team.

He gripped his ruck and pushed himself backward. Henry and Raker could be anywhere, and if he poked his head over the lip, he might get in the way or expose himself to whatever was out there. He wondered if instead of an enemy soldier, they'd spotted a tiger, or perhaps a panther. For a brief moment he contemplated which he'd prefer, Japanese or wild carnivorous beasts. He'd killed Japanese...not toothy animals.

He pushed himself another fifteen yards before he stopped and listened again. The creek had flattened out and didn't burble as much, allowing him to hear better. Still nothing. Were Henry and Raker in trouble? Perhaps they'd been outmaneuvered and killed. The thought almost made him laugh out loud. Both of them were master woodsmen and deadly in hand-to-hand combat...*any* combat, for that matter.

He decided it was time to come out of the ditch. He slithered to the right and stopped at the top of the lip. The grassy field to the right shimmered in a slight breeze. He sniffed the air, but it held no surprises. From the corner of his eye, he spotted quick movement in the shadows beneath the trees he'd just vacated. He aimed his carbine but kept his finger off the trigger.

He heard a muffled, surprised cry that quickly cut off. The movement stopped, and Stollman worked to calm his charging heart. His breath came in quick gasps, but he finally got control and eased his finger from the trigger guard to the trigger. Something moved in the ditch.

He nearly pulled the trigger in surprise when something gripped his boot. He turned and saw Raker holding a finger to his lips. Stollman eased his finger from the trigger and swallowed the bile that had worked its way up his craw like a striking snake. Raker eased forward until he lay beside him. He grinned and pointed toward the ditch. "Henry bagged a Jap sniper."

Stollman moved the barrel from the ditch and hissed, "Holy mother of God, you scared the holy hell outta me, Raker. What the hell's the matter with you? I nearly fired."

Raker's teeth gleamed in the darkness. "We signaled ya, but you never looked back, not even once. You get your charge set?"

Stollman just nodded, not trusting his voice.

Raker patted his shoulder. "I told Henry your bomb's more'n a popper. The Nip came out of the field and was coming straight down the ditch at you. We didn't want him to trigger it and blow you to hell, so Henry bounded forward and jumped him before he reached it."

Henry slithered out of the blackness of the ditch and joined them. They couldn't see his face, but he wasn't smiling. He whispered, "Jap sniper." He pushed a Type 38 rifle with a scope attached to the top forward. The scope sat off to the side of the rifle and was less than a foot long. "We should probably get back before more come and cook off that damned bomb you planted."

17

Major Shima hunkered beneath a poncho and shivered alongside his men in the chilly rain. Rabaul had been pleasantly warm and humid, and so had Lae and Salamaua. But once they ventured into the mountains, the temperatures dropped. Not uncomfortably so, but combined with the monsoon season's rains, the days felt cold. His men stoically did their duty despite the conditions. The prospect of combat in the morning had varying effects on the men. Some relished it, others feared it, but most thought of it as the inevitable purpose of their lives. It was simply something they must do.

Finding the takeoff point had been easy enough. He ground his teeth, wishing Okabe's plan had them attacking that very night rather than waiting for sunrise. Captain Ho and Second Battalion had a longer march north to their staging area, and Okabe wanted the attacks to occur simultaneously, so he had to wait.

He itched to engage the enemy. After taking their abuse all the way from Rabaul to Lae, then Salamaua to here, he yearned for retribution. The Japanese fighting man is built for offense, he mused. Quick surprise attacks at night were the very backbone of their military tactics. Yet here he sat...waiting.

He'd ordered his men to get rest, but he knew that would be impossible.

Even he couldn't sleep before an upcoming operation. He faked it and called it meditation.

He closed his eyes and tried to slip into a trance, which might make the time pass faster. His mind raced, though. Had he missed anything? Was there anything he could do at that moment to assure their success? He'd sent his snipers out an hour earlier with orders not to engage until the main attack commenced. He envied those young men for their single-minded purpose.

He wished he could move closer to the enemy but didn't want to risk alerting them of their impending attack. He sighed and feigned sleep while listening to his men nervously whisper among themselves. They were veterans. None of this was new, but that didn't make the time pass any faster, nor did it dull the fear that was always there in the background.

Major Shima resisted the urge to check his wristwatch, relying instead on how the night felt. When he sensed its gloaming grip loosening, he checked the time and felt relief. Time to roust the men and get ready for the assault, finally.

The rain had slackened and eventually stopped around midnight. Fog and mist rolled past like the spirits of long-dead armies. But as dawn approached, even those lessened. He looked up and saw a few glimmering stars through the thinning cloud cover. It would be good weather to fight in, although he hoped it stayed sufficiently cloudy to keep enemy aircraft off his men's backs. Air support would be nice, but he certainly didn't need them to vanquish the enemy. By the time this day ended, he would either be dead or victorious.

He found Lieutenant Takeda and touched his shoulder. Takeda's head snapped upright from meditation or sleep. "It is time," Shima said. His words passed through the ranks silently, and his men rose and readied themselves. He heard murmurs as men spoke in hushed tones. Some moved off a few meters to shit or piss. Shima wondered how many of his men would die today. Sacrifice was a part of being a warrior of the Emperor. It had always been this way; young men died in battle.

An hour later they moved off along a broad front by company. Shima respected his company commanders. Indeed, all his officers had earned his respect over these long years of war. He'd lost so many, but now it was time to teach the Allies a hard lesson.

Tarkington and his men slept in shifts. After hearing about the sniper encounter, they stayed in their foxholes. The rain and the saturated soil seeped into the holes. But they'd become experts at drainage by now. The rain stopped halfway through the night. The smells of rain mixed with soil and decay wasn't unpleasant. Mists rose from the field, drifted into the trees, and covered the fence line.

As dawn approached, the air took on a distinct chill, and Tarkington pulled his jungle hat lower around his ears. No one slept now. Even without Henry's sixth sense, no one doubted the Japanese were on their way. The sniper's presence helped cement that feeling, but even without that, the air felt heavy with anticipation—like a dam getting ready to break.

As the sky lightened in the east, the mist and fog rose and exposed the field. The grasses looked impossibly green, and the dollops of rainwater sparkled, reflecting the colors of the sunrise. The dull thumping sound beyond broke the spell. Near the shack, someone yelled, "Incoming!"

Tarkington spotted the arcing shells overhead, cutting holes in the mist. The first salvo landed a few yards in front of the stone wall to the right of the shack. The next salvo landed a few yards deeper and straddled the wall. Tarkington marveled at the skill of the shooters. Three more salvos wreaked havoc among the Australians. Men not in holes either died or dove for cover.

A roar from across the field—a battle cry—and Tarkington saw Japanese soldiers emerge from the forest. The Vickers opened fire, sending a short volley to get the range. Rifle fire rippled down the line, and soon the sound was one constant roar.

Tarkington watched Japanese stumble and fall as .303-caliber bullets swept them, but more replaced the fallen. An enemy machine gun opened fire. The distinct staccato told him it was somewhere straight across from his position. The wall in front of the Vickers sparked, and rock chunks and dust covered the position. The Vickers gun crew stopped firing, and Tarkington wondered if they had hit the gunner. Losing the gun that early would be a bitter blow, but it soon rejoined the fight with renewed vigor, sending long bursts of devastating fire into the charging enemy.

None of his men had fired a shot yet. They kept their eyes on the left flank. Stollman and Vick crouched at the far end of the stone wall as though they were still a BAR crew. Old habits die hard, Tarkington thought.

A few bullets chipped the stone wall to their front, but most of the enemy fire concentrated on the shack and the MG positions. Stollman suddenly switched his muzzle from the left and zeroed in on the field directly in front. He yelled, "Japs in the grass! They're crawling!" He fired his carbine and burned through half his fifteen-round magazine before ducking back down. Beside him, Vick fired, taking careful shots before ducking. The rock wall exploded with bullet hits, and ricochets made bizarre, otherworldly sounds.

Tarkington's carbine rested upon a piece of wood he'd placed there for the purpose. He shifted his muzzle to the field. From his ground-level view from the foxhole, he couldn't see what they were shooting at, but that changed a moment later when Japanese soldiers rose from the grasses only fifty yards away. He and the rest of the squad immediately poured fire into them, and men dropped and spun as the .30 caliber tore into them.

Tarkington moved from one target to the next, but more soldiers appeared and they closed the gap quickly. He saw Vick hurl a grenade, then ducked back down, yelling, "Grenade out!" The muffled explosion landed close to the leading men and they dropped as shrapnel tore into their bodies.

Vick came up firing, and Stollman sent another grenade flying. Tarkington saw a soldier near the back, waving a pistol and screaming, exhorting his men forward. The grenade exploded, and from the corner of his eye, Tarkington saw more men fall. He applied pressure to the trigger, but before he fired, the officer's chest erupted in gore. The officer dropped his pistol and fell flat onto his face.

Tarkington glanced left in time to see Henry cycling another round into the Japanese sniper rifle he'd acquired the night before. Tarkington quickly found another target and sent rounds downrange, and the soldier dropped into the grass.

He swept the field, but the only Japanese he saw were distant, attacking the center defense line. The din of fire continued unabated along the rock wall. But from his foxhole, Tarkington didn't have a target.

Mortar rounds impacted in the field. Tarkington glanced toward the mortar pit Lt. Pringle had pointed out yesterday and saw smoke rising from the spent shells. *About time*, he thought.

The Vickers stopped firing, and Tarkington saw the gun crew working to unstick a jammed round. The Japanese had made it halfway across the field, but they'd taken heavy losses. More mortar shells exploded in the field. Tarkington remembered what Pringle had said about limited ammo.

He stood in his hole, his carbine at his shoulder. He figured he had five rounds left in the mag. Stollman and Vick continued firing, but not as fervently as before. Tarkington fired at movement until he emptied the magazine. He dropped down. "Reloading!" he yelled.

He swapped magazines quickly, then propped his carbine back onto the wood. An explosion from the ditch surprised him. The hot air from the concussive blast blew the brim of his hat back. He shifted his muzzle left and saw dark chunks of dirt and debris raining through the trees. Stollman whooped like a damned cowboy, and Tarkington saw him pumping his fist from the corner of his eye. *Popper, my ass*, thought Tarkington. *More like a damned howitzer shell.*

Henry fired the sniper rifle. Tarkington strained but couldn't see what he'd fired at—he waited. Panicked yells mixed with enemy mortar shells as the Japanese resumed their deadly barrage, landing among the AIF soldiers defending the right wall. The Vickers crew continued struggling to clear the jam.

He saw Lt. Pringle tucked tight beside the back wall of the hut. He kept yelling into a radio but soon flung it away in frustration. Mortar shells exploded beyond him and walked their way along the line, shredding soldiers not in foxholes. The Vickers crew finally cleared the jam, and the gunner sent a long, sustained burst into the renewed Japanese push. But it wasn't enough.

Enemy soldiers vaulted the wall and thrust and slashed long bayonets into anything that moved. Willoth shifted his section's fire. They peeled off the rock wall and filled the trenches and foxholes facing the shack and the right flank. Owen submachine guns and rifles barked a steady beat, but they couldn't fire on the main thrust for fear of hitting their own men. Pringle fired his Owen into a charging soldier, and he dropped at his feet. He yelled, "Fall back! Fall back!" The AIF infantrymen didn't hesitate. They took off with their commander.

Tarkington cursed, "Shit. Right flank just collapsed."

The Vickers crew worked to free the big gun from the mount, but Japanese soldiers were nearly on them. They left their smoking, hissing gun and ran. Willoth yelled for them to stop, but it was useless.

Willoth waved his arm, and five commandos ran forward. They hosed the Japanese coming over the wall with their Owens and rifles. Two men lifted the gun from the tripod while two more hefted the tripod. The rest took the ammunition and the containers of water used to cool the barrel. They ran everything back to Lt Willoth's position.

Beyond them, the Japanese flowed over the right wall like high tide. They chased the fleeing soldiers, stopping occasionally to take a knee and fire. Tarkington's attention turned back to the left when he heard Winkleman yell, "Here they come."

Through the settling dust from Stollman's bomb, Japanese soldiers appeared. They weren't yelling and screaming, but running fast, using the trees and ditch for cover. Tarkington estimated fifteen soldiers. He aimed at a soldier who'd just fired his rifle and was working the bolt action as he ran. Tarkington fired three times, and dust and blood erupted from the soldier's chest. He sprawled and fell into the ditch, tripping another soldier who splashed face-first into the bottom of the ditch.

Henry calmly fired the sniper rifle, moving from one target to the next. The others poured .30-caliber rounds into them, and they fell in writhing heaps. Raker stood and chucked a grenade into their midst. It exploded in the creek and sent shrapnel and bloody water cascading in every direction. The few remaining soldiers burst through the mist and then dropped as the Alamo Scouts emptied their magazines.

The Vickers machine gun barked, pulling Tarkington's attention back to the right. Hundreds of Japanese soldiers flowed past the wall, heading straight for Wardumi. The Vickers knocked a few down, but their angle wasn't quite right, and soon the enemy soldiers were protected by the slight defilade they attacked through.

Tarkington barked, "Keep an eye on the ditch. I'll check with Willoth." Winkleman finished reloading and nodded. Raker fired twice, putting a wounded Japanese soldier all the way down.

Tarkington stayed low and hustled up to the dug-in commandos. They continued taking pot shots at streaking enemy soldiers, but the main body had passed. Tarkington found Willoth and joined him in his foxhole. "We stopped the thrust from the left flank."

Willoth noticed him for the first time. He wiped the grit from his face. "Pringle couldn't hold the line long enough for us to help them out. Japs went right on by, but now we're stuck out here."

"You got radio contact?"

Willoth shook his head. "Tried the walkie but couldn't raise anyone."

Tarkington pointed. "Just before Pringle took off, I saw him toss his radio receiver. Radio's probably still next to the shack."

Willoth nodded. "They had a landline buried. If it's broken and we can fix it, we can coordinate our efforts."

"That's what I was thinking."

The mortars fired right on time from the relative safety of a low ridge overlooking the small farmhouse and the village of Wardumi beyond. Major Shima watched as the skilled gunners dropped the salvos right on target.

The scouts and snipers he'd sent out the night before had little trouble finding the first line of Allied defenses. When they'd first reported and took him forward to observe them himself, he'd barely been able to see beyond the foggy mist. He caught glimpses of the stone wall and a shack beyond the open field. A farmer's field, no doubt. It would serve as a good killing ground for the Allies, but his men would make it across given their over-whelming numbers and unmatched ferocity.

Shima waited until the third mortar salvo had slammed home before he nodded to Lt. Takeda. The fourth salvo was airborne by the time his men broke from the woods and charged into the field with cheers and battle cries. He desperately wanted to join them but held back. His days of charging across battlefields weren't behind him just yet, but he chose when and where, and until his forces were safely across, he needed to command.

The awful sound of the enemy machine gun opening fire and the bullets slamming into flesh made him cringe inwardly. The smell of burnt gunpowder and sulfur wafted over his position. Some battle cries changed to agonized screams, but his men continued pushing through the storm of lead. His heavy machine guns opened fire, and he watched in satisfaction as the bullets swept enemy positions and quieted their machine guns. He saw Australian soldiers being flung backward as heavy-caliber bullets found their exposed bodies. The mortars continued falling farther back, seeking out their commanding officers and supply dumps.

From the right, the platoon of men crawling through the grasses, hoping to surprise the Allies' left flank, were suddenly taken under fire from soldiers behind the furthest section of rock wall. His men rose and charged. Small explosions erupted among his men. They were the sideshow, meant to confuse and keep the defenders guessing, but the main event crashed toward the middle. Straight at the farmer's hut.

The enemy machine gun continued slaughtering his men, and he thought about ordering the mortars to target the crew, but his men were too close. Just a little farther and his men would close with the enemy and overrun their position. From there, it was only a short distance to Wardumi, and once it was captured, the airfield would be next.

The battle ebbed and flowed. The Allies put up a better fight than he expected. He ordered the mortar crews to bring their shells closer—to rain their fire onto the wall and the troopers cowering behind. He risked hitting his own men but decided the risk was worth the benefit.

The explosions erupted in the enemy ranks. Defenders had no choice but to duck as the air came alive with hot shell fragments. His men surged forward beneath the cover and were soon vaulting the wall and driving their bayonets into the hapless soldiers beyond. He ordered the mortar crews to cease fire and prepare to move forward.

The majority of his men still hunkered in the forest—awaiting their turn to enter the fray. A large explosion from his right pulled his attention. He wondered if they had somehow brought artillery to the battle. His attention didn't linger—his men were through and the Australians were breaking and running. Joy and pride filled him, and he pulled his pistol and screamed, "Forward!" His men rose up as one and surged into the body-littered field with screams and yells of triumph.

His adrenaline surged, and he felt like a twenty-year-old again. He leaped over wounded and dead and dying soldiers, determined to make their ultimate sacrifice meaningful in the best possible way: victory.

He jumped over the stone wall. He saw vanquished enemy soldiers everywhere. Some grievously wounded, others torn to shreds and obviously dead. Some of his men bayoneted the wounded. They screamed with fierce battle cries, then moved on to the next—one after another.

Machine gun fire suddenly erupted from the right flank, and he realized in a flash that not all the defenders had left their posts. Bullets whizzed and zipped past his head. The sickening sound of bullets meeting bodies kept him moving fast and low. Most of his men diverted their charge to a slight defilade, which made them harder targets.

He cursed the holdouts, but they wouldn't pose a threat once his forces entered and took Wardumi. He couldn't tell exactly how many soldiers held their ground, but he figured it wasn't more than a platoon. He could deal with them at his leisure. They'd probably fade into the woodwork like cowards. He waved and yelled, "Keep moving! Keep moving to the village!"

18

Captain Warren, company commander of A Company of the Seventeenth Brigade, watched the attack from a slit trench dug in front of the shacks and huts of Wardumi. He'd been sipping his first cup of tea when the first salvo of mortar rounds slammed into Third Platoon's position at the farmhouse.

He sprinted along the trench line, men hugging the dirt walls to let him pass. Corporal Onkmeyer looked relieved to see him as he handed the radio off. "It's Lieutenant Pringle, sir. They're under attack."

"Your powers of observation are truly stunning, Corporal," he chided. He swiped the radio and spoke, "This is Warren. Over." He listened to Lt. Pringle's frantic words. The sounds of the explosions forced Pringle to yell. Warren raised his voice. "You're sure about those numbers, Pringle? Over."

With the radio at his ear, he stepped from the sandbagged bunker and looked over the edge of the slit trench. He saw dark plumes of smoke and dirt in the distance. He nodded. "Okay, Pringle. I'll relay it to command. Can you hold? Over." He gripped the handheld tightly as he listened to the platoon leader and then said, "You've got an excellent position there, Lieutenant. Get the mortars working, but remember the ammo situation. Hold until I get back to you. Out." He yelled to Corporal Onkmeyer, "Get me HQ."

He relayed the situation happening at the farmhouse. General Moten himself got on the line, causing Warren to unconsciously stiffen even though miles separated them. He listened, nodding over and over until Moten finally finished and signed off without waiting for a reply. Warren scowled at the handheld, then barked at Onkmeyer, "Get me Pringle again."

It took thirty seconds before Pringle got on the horn. He sounded harried, and the sounds of machine gun and rifle fire were loud in the earpiece, forcing Warren to yell, "Moten says their hitting the boys up north too. You need to hold as long as possible, but don't wait too long to retreat if you have to. Over." An explosion drowned out the response, and the radio suddenly cut out with a loud click. Warren pulled it from his ear and looked at it as though it had transformed into a piece of dog shit. "We got cut off. Mortar round must've cut the line." He tossed it back to Onkmeyer.

He took a few steps down the trench line, cupped his hands over his mouth, and yelled, "Sergeant Ronk."

A burly staff sergeant emerged. "Sir," he growled.

"Line from Third Platoon's been cut. Get men on it. I need to know what's happening up there." Ronk nodded and used his baritone NCO voice to get the men moving to correct the issue.

Two men carrying a spool of telephone wire leaped from the trench and followed the track left by the men who'd buried the line in the first place. Depending on the damage, they'd either repair it or run a brand-new line.

The sounds of battle intensified. Warren peered through his binoculars and slowly swept them from side to side. Even from a quarter mile away, he heard Third Platoon's Vickers machine gun barking. Sergeant Ronk stood close by, watching and listening. Warren ordered, "Make sure the men have their weapons and ammo close. They may order us forward at a moment's notice."

Ronk said, "They're ready to go, sir. Champing at the bit."

Warren let the binos hang, bit a fingernail, and spit. "Hate sitting on my hands while they're in contact."

Ronk nodded sagely. "Worst part's always the waiting."

They listened to the thundering firefight ebb and flow. From this distance, they could hear just enough to guess what was happening. When the heavy thumping of the Vickers ceased and the enemy mortar shells increased, they looked at one another with worry.

Warren heard Corporal Onkmeyer trying to contact Lt. Pringle every couple of seconds. Warren cursed, "Dammit. Why's the repair taking so long?"

Ronk didn't bother replying. The answer was obvious: there was a firefight going on. Warren called out, "Any word from HQ?" Onkmeyer interrupted his pleas and shook his head.

Warren pinched the bridge of his nose. "I can't just sit here any longer."

The sound of battle changed slightly, and Staff Sergeant Ronk pointed. "Sir?"

Warren pulled his binoculars to his eyes again for a long minute. He licked his dry lips, finally seeing something other than smoke. "Our—our boys are coming, and the Japs are right on their tails." He continued watching and barked, "They're coming fast!"

He dropped the binoculars and yelled to his men, "Third Platoon's coming, and the bloody Nips are right on their arses. Make sure of your shots and make room for our lads. We'll stop 'em right here!"

He barked an order at Ronk, "Get the mortars dialed in, and be sure the Vickers crews are ready." Ronk nodded and hustled down the line, sending men scurrying in different directions.

Lieutenant Pringle was living his nightmare. His men had no chance of stopping the overwhelming enemy force. They'd doled out plenty of pain, causing massive casualties, but the Japanese just kept on coming. He'd heard about the human attack waves the Japanese were known for, but hearing about it and experiencing it were two very different matters. It disgusted and terrified him at the same time. What kind of men would hurl themselves straight into concentrated machine gun fire? How could they ever hope to stop soldiers willing to throw their lives away so wantonly?

His men were in disarray, in full retreat. At first, he'd tried keeping the retreat orderly, but his men quickly fell apart as screaming, charging soldiers pursued them. He watched his men being cut down with bayonets and being shot at point-blank range.

He ran with the rest of them, the overwhelming fear creeping into his guts and making him run, run, run. He struggled against it, knowing he should stop and fight, slow the enemy advance, but he couldn't seem to make his legs stop. He'd lost control of himself and his men.

He felt sickened. His father's voice suddenly entered his head and spoke to him as though he were standing beside him. "Mathew, stop!"

He'd only been a boy when he'd last seen him. His father had gone off to fight the war to end all wars. The only thing that returned was a wooden box and a stack of colorful, shiny medals. Young Mathew Pringle had spent endless hours imagining how he'd won each medal—saving his men by cutting down countless scores of the evil Hun in their spiked helmets and long pointy mustaches. "Stop!" his father thundered in his head.

Lieutenant Pringle felt the fear fade, replaced with shame. He stopped his headlong retreat and forced himself to turn back toward the enemy. His men streamed past, bullets chasing them like a disrupted hive of hornets. He brought his Owen to his shoulder, trying desperately to control his breathing.

He searched for a target and didn't have long to wait. An enemy soldier with a blood-tinged bayonet leading the way screamed and charged. Pringle aimed low and walked his five-round burst up the right side of the man's body. The soldier's yell abruptly cut off, and he spun before falling onto his back.

Pringle sent another volley toward a soldier following close behind. The ground erupted in clods of dirt and grass as his .45-caliber bullets chewed up the dirt in front of the soldier, but the soldier burst through, aiming his bayonet at Pringle's guts. Pringle steadied his aim and emptied the rest of his magazine. The enemy soldier's rifle splintered and bits of his own weapon eviscerated him, along with the heavy-caliber bullets.

Pringle rose from his crouch and reloaded as he ran backward. Bullets zinged overhead and thwopped into the ground all around. He waved his men onward. "Keep moving! Keep moving!" His father's voice faded, along with the debilitating fear. After twenty yards, he crouched and aimed back the way he'd come. His men were mostly past him, but a few stragglers struggled, obviously wounded. The Japanese gained on them, and he watched in horror as one of his men turned in time to take an enemy bayonet to his chest. The enemy soldier pushed and drove him to the ground, pinning him there. He viciously cut back and forth and gouts of blood sprayed his hands and face.

Pringle stood and aimed his Owen but didn't want to hit his own man. He ran forward, the Owen tucked tight against his shoulder, ignoring the surrounding chaos. He felt hot fury in his gut. He yearned to make the enemy soldier pay. The soldier saw him coming and pulled savagely to free his bayonet and rifle, but it was firmly stuck between his victim's ribs. The Japanese soldier finally placed his boot on the gasping man's chest and yanked. The sound of scraping metal against bone and the Australian soldier's scream enraged Lt. Pringle even more.

Just as the bloody Japanese soldier brought his weapon to bear, Pringle pulled the trigger. His first burst missed, but he quickly corrected and obliterated the soldier's chest, neck, and face. He kept firing, following the body to the ground, only stopping once he hovered over the man and his firing pin slammed against a dry breech.

He quickly reloaded and turned to his man dying in the mud. He recognized Corporal Leach, a rifleman, who liked to crack jokes. Pringle kneeled and hefted the soldier onto his shoulder, then stood on quaking legs. He spun and fired the Owen one-handed, his bullets spraying wildly, causing the oncoming enemy soldiers to pause. Then he took off running. He felt the soldier's blood drenching his back.

His men, seeing his actions, stopped their headlong retreat and turned to fight as they withdrew, covering their platoon leader. Mortar shells exploded among the enemy, helping to slow their advance and allowing what remained of Third Platoon to withdraw.

Pringle finally hurled himself into the nearest trench. Corporal Leach had to be pried off Lt. Pringle's back. "We've got him now, sir. It's okay, we've got him." Pringle finally relented, and Leach's body slumped to the bottom of the trench. The medic checked him over quickly, then sat back and shook his head after a moment. Leach's vacant eyes stared into the cloudy sky and his skin turned grayish white, as though all the blood in his body had drained from him.

Lieutenant Pringle growled, "Let's make these blighters pay."

～

Captain Warren watched Third Platoon's fighting withdrawal. He hadn't been impressed with Lieutenant Pringle to that point, but now he'd changed his mind. He watched through binoculars as the fighting got closer. He picked out Pringle by his Owen and watched him crouch and fire, fade back, then crouch and fire again. His men followed his example. When the enemy troops were in range, he ordered, "Mortars, open fire."

Staff Sergeant Ronk relayed the order, and soon the light 60mm mortar rounds arced overhead and slammed into the enemy ranks. Warren yelled over the din, "Get Lieutenant Covington on the horn, Corporal. Tell him to open fire." Corporal Onkmeyer gave a quick nod and called Second Platoon, dug in on the right flank along the road leading into Wardumi.

Warren watched what remained of Third Platoon stream into the slit trenches and foxholes. A few continued running to the cover of the shacks and trees of Wardumi itself. He glimpsed the impossibly skinny Lt. Pringle running with a wounded man on his back. Blood and grime marred his face. Streams of sweat streaked down, making him look as though he had tiger stripes.

Warren focused his attention on the Japanese beyond him. A few had made it through the mortar barrage, and his men engaged them with lethal fire. The main force still advanced steadily further back. The mortar barrage lifted. They had strict orders to conserve ammo, and the four crews had cycled through their allotted five salvos already. That was when Lieutenant Covington opened fire on the charging Japanese's left flank.

Warren watched with grim satisfaction as they swept the Japanese with fire from the protection of the wall. The Japanese that weren't hit outright dove for cover behind sparse trees, boulders, and slight defilades. He took his eyes from the binoculars momentarily and nudged Sergeant Ronk. "Have the lads fire at will. We've got them pinned, and I'd like to keep it that way."

The crack of rifles mixed with the Vickers, Bren guns, and Owen submachine guns, sending a hail of lead. Warren watched more Japanese fall. He dropped his binoculars and yelled, "Lieutenant Pringle."

Pringle maneuvered around soldiers firing from the top of the slit trench and reported, "You wanted to see me, sir?" Warren looked him over. His back and side glistened with blood. Pringle shook his head. "It's not mine. I'm not wounded."

Warren nodded. "Thank God for minor miracles. That was a bloody good job getting your men back without losing the entire platoon, Lieutenant."

Pringle couldn't hold his gaze. "Lost a lot of men. They're—they're still out there."

Warren's lips thinned, and he gave a slight nod. "You did all you could, Mathew. Don't know how you managed getting that wounded man back like that."

Pringle shook his head again. "He didn't make it either."

"We'll have time to mourn later. How many men made it back with you?"

Pringle braced and looked Warren in the eye. "Preliminary count's thirty-five, sir. But some of those men are wounded and out of action. Probably twenty-nine effectives."

Warren nodded, hiding his shock. Half the platoon was gone. "Where are those commandos and Yanks? I haven't seen them."

Pringle startled, realizing he hadn't seen them either. "They were on our left flank. The main thrust came right at our center. They—they must still be back there." He poked his head up as though he were about to lunge over the top and charge back to them.

Warren grabbed his arm. "Easy, Lieutenant. If they're still alive, they can take care of themselves."

Corporal Onkmeyer called out from the bunker, "Captain. Lieutenant Covington's on the horn. They're being outflanked." He held up the radio.

Warren moved past Pringle and said, "Get your men organized. We'll need every weapon and bullet for this fight." Pringle nodded and moved back toward his platoon. Warren took the handset. "This is Warren. Go ahead. Over."

Covington's normally cool demeanor had vanished. His voice cracked, rose, and fell as nearby explosions and bursts of machine gun fire crackled in the background. "At least two companies attacking on our right flank. They're getting behind us."

Warren briefly closed his eyes. He'd expected this to happen. Second Platoon's position was perfect for engaging enemy crossing the relatively thin cover stretching from the farmhouse to the eastern edge of Wardumi, but only a full regiment would be enough to block the Japanese from running an end around and rolling up their flank. He didn't think the Japanese would exploit the weakness this quickly.

He keyed the mic and said, "Wait for the smoke, then move back to the primary. Repeat: wait for smoke then move. Acknowledge. Over."

Covington didn't try to hide his relief "Acknowledged. Wait for smoke and pull back to primary. Over and out."

Sergeant Ronk had already sent the word to the mortar crews. Captain Warren clutched his staff sergeant's shoulder and had to yell to be heard over the constant din of gunfire. "Once Covington's back in Wardumi, we'll move back too."

Ronk nodded but said, "Shame to leave these nice dugouts, sir."

"I know, but there's at least a battalion of Nips out there. Holding Wardumi's a pipe dream, and Moten knows it."

Ronk's sun-drenched face resembled hard leather. "What about Willoth and the Yanks?"

"They're on their own. God help 'em."

Outgoing smoke-round canisters erupted a few hundred yards out, and the firing dropped off to a trickle.

The fighting passed the farmhouse. The battle still raged only a quarter mile away, toward Wardumi. Tarkington and his squad, along with another squad of commandos, tucked close into the stone wall, watching for more enemy that might trickle into the field. Willoth and the rest of his men searched for the broken telephone line.

Ten minutes later, the rest of the commandos gathered around Tarkington and the others. Willoth shook his head. "Line's broken in multiple spots. Doesn't matter, though, 'cause it looks like Pringle must've put rounds into the radio."

Tarkington said, "Smart thinking. Carrying it back woulda slowed him down too much."

Corporal Vick and the commando medic, Corporal Edmunds, came back from checking bodies. They looked grim and pale. Vick gave them the bad news. "They're all dead. The Japs skewered them as they passed by, I'm guessing."

"I returned the favor," Edmunds said. He patted his sheathed bayonet, and Vick gave him a quick, disgusted glance.

Tarkington noticed the look and wondered about it. They'd all killed wounded Japanese. They'd learned through hard experience that wounded Japanese soldiers sometimes played possum, waiting for the opportunity to kill roving medics and GIs. Vick and the rest of the squad had learned it in the Philippines. The face of a well-liked sergeant flashed into his mind. He'd fallen victim to a wounded enemy soldier when he'd tried to help him and been blown up for his trouble. He wondered if the Australian commandos had similar experiences or were simply doing what came naturally.

Lieutenant Willoth glanced over the wall at the field. Arms and legs poked up from the grasses, marking the spots where enemy soldiers had fallen. A few rifles poked up, their bayonets having dug into the ground and stuck in like arrows. Beyond the killing ground, the trees swayed in a light, midmorning breeze. The mortar crews, which had been so devastatingly accurate, had undoubtedly fired from there. They must have already joined their attacking comrades.

The sound of battle from Wardumi increased, and they all shifted their attention back that way. Willoth glanced at the only other officer, Lieutenant Tarkington. Willoth finally said, "Well, I suppose we should give the Nips a surprise and hit 'em from behind." The commandos nodded and murmured their agreement.

Tarkington looked at his own men. Henry chewed on a piece of grass, rolling it side to side along his lips. He held the Japanese sniper rifle in his hand, his M1 carbine slung over his back. He'd already collected as much Type 38 ammo as he could carry. Winkleman and the others simply watched Willoth and the commandos, knowing what Tarkington was going to suggest instead.

Tarkington narrowed his gaze. "We could do that. Might do some good, I suppose." The only sounds were the distant battle and the wind as it passed over and through the gaps in the rock wall as they waited for the other boot to drop. He flicked his thumb over his shoulder, back where the Japanese had come from. "Or, now that we're behind 'em," he went on laconically, "we could head east and see about lopping off the head of the serpent."

19

Reports poured into General Moten's command center. As near as General Moten and his second-in-command, Major Connaway, could tell, they were being hit by two separate forces. One from the southeast, the other from the northeast. "Sir, Captain Warren with A Company doesn't think he can hold Wardumi. He's asking permission to fall back, sir," blurted the radioman, Sergeant Kippler.

Major Connaway joined Moten at the map spread out on a rickety table. He put his finger on the penciled-in micro-town of Wardumi. His voice sounded clipped and tense. "They're getting awfully close. Just a couple miles."

Moten pushed his sizable gut against the table and grunted his agreement. "Hmm, yes." He put his finger closer to the airfield. "We'll have him fall back to B Company. They can link up and keep them from crossing the river."

Connaway tilted his head. "They'll have the river at their backs. Could get dicey if they have to retreat in a hurry. All this rain's bringing the river level up, but for now, it's still wadeable."

General Moten considered that. "Yes. Last I checked, the bridge is still operational, too. It's a rickety old thing—rather take my chances with the crocs in the river, but if it comes right down to it, it's a viable option."

Major Connaway went to the radio and put the phone to his ear. "Captain Warren. Is that you? It's Major Connaway. Over." He could hear bursts of fire and explosions in the background.

"Yes, Major. It's Captain Warren. Japs are hitting hard. We're low on ammo and won't be able to hold them much longer. Over."

Major Connaway nodded and gave Moten a concerned look. "Fall back to the river, Captain. B Company is dug in there. You will join Captain Lynch and stop the enemy advance at the river. Over."

"Roger. Copy all. Can you give us any cover? Over."

"Negative on cover. Weather's keeping planes grounded. There've been no reinforcements. Good luck, Captain. Out."

Moten watched his second-in-command hand the phone back to the sergeant. He saw the concern on his old friend's face. Moten said, "He's a competent officer, Dan. He'll be all right."

Connaway nodded curtly and returned to the map. He spoke to Corporal Bust, directing him to put the new situation on the map.

Moten pointed to the northeast and asked, "Any more word from Grumskey at the coffee plantation?"

Connaway answered, "Not since his initial contact alert. Should we raise him, sir?"

"I suppose no news is good news..." He stroked his chin. "But yes. Get a report."

Connaway went to Sergeant Kippler's side while he rang up the commando company commander. They got through right away. The buried phone lines had proved reliable so far. It took five minutes before Captain Grumskey's harsh, low voice answered, "This is Grumskey. Go ahead. Over."

"Captain. This is Major Connaway. What's your status? Over." Connaway listened, his brow furrowing as he digested the news. When Grumskey finished, he told him to wait one moment and reported to Moten. "He's having a bit of a bad time of it, I'm afraid. They stopped the initial charge, but he thinks the Japanese are changing tactics and trying to flank them, sir." He hesitated and finished, "He's not sure he can hold with the ammunition they've got on hand."

Moten slammed his fist down, rocking the table. "Dammit. If this weather doesn't lift, I'll lose the whole command," he blurted.

Soldiers looked at their boots or busied themselves, embarrassed by the sudden outburst. Connaway looked concerned. It wasn't like General Moten to show such emotion, particularly in front of the men. Moten quickly got control and leveled his stony gaze at Connaway. "Tell him there's nothing between him and Wau. We can't send him any help at the moment, there's no one close enough." He lowered his voice. "He has to hold—no matter the cost."

Connaway gulped hard and relayed the message. "Look, old boy. The Nips from the southeast are nearly at our doorstep. We need every rifle keeping them from the airfield. You have to hold your section at all costs. Over."

There was a longer pause, but Grumskey finally answered, "Roger. Copy all. Out."

~

Captain Grumskey handed the radio back to his radioman, Corporal Gaines. Lieutenant Blakely noticed his grim look. "What'd command have to say, sir?"

Grumskey stared at the platoon leader with cutting, icy blue eyes. "We're on our own out here. They've got their hands full with the southern thrust. Japs are almost at the airfield. We have to hold at all costs."

Blakely gulped. "Bloody hell."

Grumskey tapped his radioman. "Better get your kit. We're gonna need every rifle out there."

Gaines hung his headset on the radio and stood and stretched his back. "Been getting a bit stuffy in here, anyway, sir. Could use some fresh air." He grabbed his Lee-Enfield rifle, ducked out of the bunker, and trotted to join the other commandos dug in all around the coffee plantation.

Grumskey turned his attention back to Blakely. "How's your ammo situation?"

Blakely answered immediately, "Got enough for one more hard fight. But after that, we'll be down to throwing stones."

Grumskey nodded. He ducked from the bunker and looked out over the top of the unfinished trench. Dead Japanese soldiers littered the open ground in grotesque, unnatural contortions. The initial attack had been a straight-in human wave. His men, and particularly his Vickers crew, had cut them down almost to the man. The Japanese attack had finally faltered and failed.

The few survivors had retreated back to the thin forest beyond the open fields. Harassing mortar fire dropped among the commandos' foxholes, keeping their heads down and their adrenaline flowing. A few men had been lightly wounded in the frontal assault. Grumskey knew he hadn't broken the attackers. There were hundreds, if not thousands, of troops forming up out there for another attack.

He glanced skyward. Low clouds spit rain, and the wind had whipped up a bit. No one was flying today. Grumskey stated, "Look, I don't think they'll do that bit again." Blakely nodded and tilted his hat off his forehead. Grumskey continued, "I think they'll come from the river and hit our left flank. Maybe from the right, too, but it's more exposed. They can use the riverbank to get close on the left side. It's what I would do."

"I agree. That frontal attack cost them dearly but didn't break them."

Grumskey made up his mind. "Shift your men left. Stay in the trees but get as close to the riverbank as possible. I'll keep the others here in case I'm wrong. Either way, be ready to move at a moment's notice. General Moten needs us to hold this plantation. If they get through, they've got a straight shot at Wau. The airfield won't last long after that, and we'll lose any hope of resupply and reinforcements."

Blakely looked grim. "We'll hold, sir. We have to." He left Grumskey, who continued shifting defenses and checking the rest of the commandos' positions.

Blakely found Sergeant Omar. He and one of Captain Dane's platoons had journeyed back down from the Black Cat Track and joined the defense of the coffee plantation. Captain Dane remained at the mine to block any more Japanese that might attempt to use the track. "Sergeant, we're moving to the left flank. We'll set up right along the river bank. Get the men dug in." Omar nodded and got the men moving along the trail leading to the river.

They kept inside the tree line. The river was rising inch by inch. The water, always murky, looked like flowing chocolate milk now. Bushes and uprooted trees rolled along the bottom, branches rising and falling like ancient serpents. Although rain swollen, the river had a long way to go before it would flood the banks. A long stretch of gravel and mud extended from the forest to the river. The many tendrils of water cut through the gravel, making deep channels and inlets. The surrounding air smelled like tilled soil.

Digging foxholes in the soft ground didn't take long. They couldn't dig more than three feet because of the high water table. The rainwater trickled in from all sides, and soon the commandos kneeled in six inches of water, shivering.

Lieutenant Blakely hunkered near a large tree trunk, watching upstream. He'd placed his Bren gunners nearby. If the enemy came from that way, they'd be exposed for a deadly fifty-yard stretch. He had checked the other positions, visiting each man. They were wet, cold, and miserable but ready to repel the enemy once again.

The harassing mortar fire ceased. He thought he heard the droning of an airplane like a distant afterthought. He glanced up through the thin tree branches. The clouds hung low and didn't appear as though they'd ever leave. If there was an airplane nearby, it had to be way above the clouds. *If the weather doesn't break soon, there'll be no resupply, and soon we'll be out of ammunition*, he lamented to himself. Then they'd be forced into the bush and unforgiving jungles of New Guinea.

Blakely remembered the days when he'd first arrived in this dark valley. They'd had very little supplies to work with then, but they'd still managed to nibble away at the enemy, even succeeding in assaulting and killing nearly two hundred Japanese stationed at Salamaua airfield in a daring raid. Since then, the Japanese presence had grown, curtailing their ability to raid and ambush. What had started as a featherweight boxing match between two cautious fighters was devolving into a heavy-weight slug fest.

Blakely heard the distant sounds of fighting to the south. It had tapered off significantly but never completely stopped. Rain squalls moved from the hills and swept through the valley, sometimes bringing unbelievable deluges. He felt his body stiffening, and he concentrated on working the muscles of his calves and legs to keep the blood moving.

Noon came and went with no sign of enemy movement. At 1430 hours, the popping of mortar tubes, followed by the whistling shells, made them all cringe and hunker lower. The explosions erupted behind them, along the main line of defense.

He checked his Owen submachine gun. He'd only had the weapon since it arrived from Port Moresby a few weeks prior, but he'd fallen in love with the simple design. He had yet to have a single issue with jamming, even in New Guinea's relentlessly harsh environment. He tapped his ammo pouch, feeling the six stick magazines each holding thirty-three rounds. He'd overloaded his pouch, knowing he wouldn't be able to resupply easily.

He moved from the base of the tree and into his foxhole. Cold rainwater seeped into his already soaked feet. He and every other commando in the unit had long since given up on wearing socks. Indeed, some men resorted to sandals or even bare feet. Some of the more staunch officers didn't like it, but footwear often rotted off their feet in a matter of days. The rainy season simply accelerated the process. Simple sandals made with old tire treads lasted considerably longer.

Blakely heard Sergeant Omar hiss a warning, "Something's coming down the riverbed."

Blakely poked his head up. Soft drips of water hit his hat as he peered from beneath the soaked brim. The rain fell light and steady, slightly obscuring the riverbed, but movement caught his eye. A Japanese soldier moved along the edge of the cut riverbank. Jungle plants stuck from his pith helmet, breaking up his outline. More soldiers funneled in behind him, moving slowly. Beyond the riverbank, he saw more soldiers pushing through the thick brambles along the edge of the forest.

He pulled the well-wrapped walkie from the top of his ruck and keyed the button. "Lead. This is Three. We've got enemy moving down the riverbed. Over," he whispered.

It took a moment, but finally Captain Grumskey's distinctive low voice answered, "Copy. Strength? Over."

"At least a company. Can't see far. Over."

"Copy. Shifting two squads your way. Out."

Blakely slowly wrapped the radio into the tarpaulin, keeping his eyes on the advancing enemy. His men had their weapons up and aimed, waiting for the order to open fire. Blakely kept the muzzle of his submachine gun leveled. He moved the bar selector switch from safe to semi-automatic fire—another feature he liked about the weapon.

More enemy soldiers appeared around the corner. He wanted to allow as many soldiers into the open killing ground as possible, but he had to worry about the soldiers advancing along the edge of the woods, too. If they got too close, he'd have a hard time clearing them out. It was a balancing act.

He centered his sights on the closest man's chest. The soldier continued to hug the bank only fifteen yards away. Blakely could see his anxious, pinched features as he expertly moved. Blakely put his finger on the trigger and felt his heartbeat through the digit. He blew out and slowly applied pressure until a single shot broke the silence. The soldier's concentration turned to horror and shock and he fell backward into the wall, as though taking a seat. Blakely fired twice more, and gouts of blood mixed with the misting rain.

The rest of the platoon opened fire nearly simultaneously, and Japanese soldiers jolted and dropped in the devastating storm of lead. Blakely pushed the selector all the way forward and fired controlled bursts.

The doomed men in the riverbed dove for any cover they could find. Bullets kicked up gravel and rock shards, making it seem as though a dark curtain had descended upon them.

Return fire finally came from the trees as the Japanese there found cover. Blakely yelled, "Shift fire right. Shift fire to the trees." His men shifted aim and fired into the trees. Blakely didn't have a good angle, so he continued firing at survivors in the riverbed. His two Bren guns swept the trees, gouging chunks from men and trees alike.

Blakely fired his last shot and pulled the top mounted magazine and tried to insert another. He wasn't as smooth with the new weapon yet and fumbled. He cursed under his breath and concentrated on what he needed to do. When it snapped into place, he looked up in time to see a mortar round explode only yards away from his hole. He instinctively ducked, but instead of an explosion, he heard hissing and sputtering.

White and gray smoke billowed from multiple smoke rounds, covering the area in a dense fog. Dark apparitions appeared, running fast and hard.

"Smoke," he yelled.

He fired at a silhouette, and his target stumbled and fell hard. Smoke wafted into the trees, and he could see darting shapes moving like ghosts. His men killed many, but soon the enemy closed and the fighting was point-blank range.

Blakely immediately understood that they would cut his men off from the rest of the company if he didn't do something fast. He yelled, "Grenades! Use grenades and fall back!" He heard Sergeant Omar repeating the order.

Blakely stood and unleashed the rest of his magazine into shapes emerging from the smoke, sending a lethal hail of lead into the riverbed. He dropped into cover, pulled a grenade, and hurled it. Before it exploded, he'd already swapped his spent mag for a fresh one.

He jumped from the muddy hole and fell onto his face. He rolled and got to his feet. Grenades exploded in dull flashes, and he ran a few yards and tucked behind a tree. His men streamed past him, turning occasionally to fire. He saw Private First Class Jocklin firing his Bren gun from the hip like something out of a comic book.

Blakely screamed, "Fall back! Fall back!" He unleashed a short burst and followed Jocklin, who'd expended his magazine and struggled to reload as he ran. "Move it, Jock!"

They bobbed and weaved, and bullets smacked trees and snapped twigs over their heads. Blakely felt his shirt tug and rip from a near miss. He kept running. Behind him, he heard roaring Japanese soldiers in pursuit.

The platoon hustled into the main line and took cover. Blakely found Captain Grumskey and said between heaving breaths, "Couldn't hold 'em. They nearly cut us off."

Grumskey just nodded, his eyes on the commandos still streaming into his lines. Grumskey yelled, "Here they come!" The last of the commandos emerged from the trees. They turned to cover one another, but the enemy was right on their heels, and two dropped as bullets tore into their bodies. The Japanese stepped over them, screaming and firing their rifles and submachine guns from their hips, bayonets gleaming in the wetness. Grumskey ordered, "Open fire!"

The initial onslaught cut the leading line of Japanese down like a massive scythe through wheat. But more surged over their fallen comrades and were soon among the foxholes and trenches. Slashing bayonets and clashing rifles mixed with screams and grunts of men in desperate hand-to-hand clashes.

Blakely ran forward, enraged at seeing his men being cut down. He clutched the front grip of the SMG and fired a short burst into the back of a Japanese soldier who'd just been thrown back by one of his men. Blood and bone mixed as the 9mm rounds sliced through vital organs. The commando glanced his way, but there was no time for thanks. More enemy soldiers poured into the line. Blakely swept his SMG across charging soldiers, and they dropped and spun away.

He went to a knee and brought the stock to his shoulder. He aimed and fired at an officer, waving a sword in one hand and a pistol in the other. One shot, then an empty chamber. He'd missed, and the officer continued charging. Blakely cursed himself and tried to reload. But there wasn't enough time.

He felt a sudden and dire presence closing in. He gripped the front of the Owen SMG and swung it blindly, like a cricket bat. The charging infantryman ducked beneath it and thrust his bayonet forward. Blakely tripped and fell, his clumsiness saving him from being skewered like a wild boar. He rolled away and fell into the bottom of a trench with a splash of mud. He lost his wind and gasped for breath like a fish out of water.

Distantly, he heard Grumskey's booming baritone voice, "Fall back! Retreat!" He forced himself onto his belly, expecting to be run through at any moment. He still gripped the muddy SMG. He willed himself to put one foot in front of the other until he was sprinting through the bottom of the trench. Shadows darted overhead as they leaped the trench. He had no idea if they were friend or foe. He kept running and hoped he was going in the right direction.

20

Captain Grumskey and his commandos hunkered two hundred yards from the southern edge of the coffee plantation. They'd retreated alongside the road, paralleling the river. They pulled into a stand of trees and boulders and assessed their situation.

The scowl never left Grumskey's face as he spoke. "Our orders were to hold that damned plantation at any cost." Lieutenant Blakely knew his commander well enough not to interject. Grumskey asked, "How much ammo we got left?"

Lieutenants Blakely, Cavanaugh, and Mueller had already gotten ammo and casualty counts from their NCOs.

Cavanaugh and Mueller both looked to the more experienced Blakely to pass the news. "After we redistributed what we have, each man has two more mags or clips. The Brens have one each." He tapped his own SMG. He'd split his magazines with the other officers. "We've each got two thirty-three-round magazines, sir."

Grumskey shook his head. "It's not enough." His scowl deepened. "Losses?"

Blakely sighed and answered, "We have eight dead, four others missing and presumed dead. Ten wounded, four seriously and are out of the fight, sir."

Grumskey rubbed his forehead and murmured, "Can't let this stand."

Blakely didn't quite hear him and asked, "Sir?"

Grumskey looked from one officer to the next and raised his voice. "We've gotta take the plantation back." Silence greeted his announcement. "If we stay here, they'll roll over us like we're not even here. We'll make 'em pay, but they'll push through us and hit our boys from the rear and take the airfield." His voice hardened, and his eyes took on a cold glare. "I'm not gonna let that bloody well happen."

He straightened his back and looked the men over. Instead of proud, confident warriors, he saw defeated and scared young men. He raised his voice. "Listen up, men." The commandos stopped what they were doing and moved closer, drawn by their commander's strong voice and withering gaze. He pointed back toward the coffee plantation. "We're gonna take that plantation back from the bloody Japs." The men stared at him without a word. "We're gonna do what they don't expect us to do. We're not going to sit back and play by their rules. We're going to attack." A devilish grin crossed his face. "And here's how we're gonna do it."

Lieutenant Blakely and the other officers, including Captain Grumskey, traded their Owen submachine guns for Lee-Enfield rifles. The two Bren gunners had the SMGs slung over their shoulders awkwardly.

What was left of the company snuck through the tall grass and thin woods along the bank of the river.

Blakely whispered to Sergeant Omar, "This is crazy on a grand scale. A bloody bayonet charge? Feel like were reliving the Great War all over again."

Omar whispered back, "Hope it works out better for us."

The company halted on a signal from Grumskey. He pointed and waved the two Bren gunners to move. They kept low and hustled to the right until they reached the road. When the lead scouts gave them the all clear, they scurried across the road and disappeared into the grasses and trees beyond. The rest of the company waited in the wet grasses for five minutes before Grumskey waved them forward again.

Blakely's legs and back ached from being hunched over, but he ignored it as best he could. Success hinged on taking the enemy by surprise, and that meant approaching low and slow. None of the other commandos looked to be bothered, so he kept his discomfort to himself.

The lead scouts went onto their bellies and crawled the final thirty yards. The rest of the company followed their example. Crawling actually helped relieve Blakely's screaming back but brought new aches and pains for his hips and knees. He wondered if at the ripe old age of twenty-three, he was already too old for this crap.

The commandos bunched up as they ran into the men in front. The scouts had already reconnoitered the area soon after Grumskey told them the plan. They'd snuck to within twenty-five yards of the first enemy position. That was where the grass turned to wide open ground. Ground they'd need to cover quickly or die trying.

Blakely felt fear edge into his gut. He gritted his teeth and tried to fight it off. He needed to be brave—lead by example—but he could feel it building. He hoped Grumskey wouldn't wait too long or he wasn't sure he'd be able to force himself to get to his feet and charge. He bit his lower lip and tasted blood. The sharp pain helped him focus. Five long minutes passed before Grumskey finally stood up calmly, as though his mother had called dinner in the middle of a hide-and-go-seek game. For a moment—he stood alone—it was surreal.

Blakely pushed himself up, along with the rest of the company. Being suddenly exposed after such a long sneak felt wrong. The nearest Japanese soldiers, only twenty-five yards away, stared at them as though looking at ghosts.

Without a word, the lead scouts jogged forward, gaining speed with each step. The others followed, and soon Blakely had enough room to run. The long bayonet on the end of his rifle looked deadly and archaic, like something from the Bronze Age.

The enemy soldiers finally reacted when the lead commando was only five yards away. An enemy soldier yelled a warning and fired his rifle. His shot shattered the lead commando's leg, but as he went down, he hurled his rifle and bayonet like a spear. It buried itself to the hilt in the enemy soldier's chest. He gaped at it until blood filled his mouth and he toppled forward.

A great yell went up from the commandos, despite Grumskey's orders to keep quiet as they attacked. Blakely felt his own yell building in his gut, replacing the fear rising like a fiery mass. He bellowed like a dying ox, his voice foreign to his own ears. Over the blood pounding in his ears, he heard the Bren gunners open fire.

He leaped over the first foxhole filled with panicked soldiers. The Japanese reacted slowly, unsure of what was happening. Bullets stitched exposed men. Blakely ran straight toward an officer emerging from one of the plantation's buildings. He spun toward Blakely with surprise and fear in his eyes. Blakely thrust his bayonet into his guts. The officer's air escaped in a whoosh, and his mouth opened in a silent scream. Blakely, filled with adrenaline, lifted him off the ground, then slammed him back to Mother Earth, pinning him there. Blakely tripped over the officer and had to let go of his rifle as he somersaulted and rolled to his feet like a trained gymnast doing a floor exercise.

He spun back to the dying officer and extracted his rifle from his belly. A thick fountain of blood and intestines came with his blade. His adrenaline surged, and he felt superhuman. He saw movement inside the building. He took the short stairs in one stride and stepped into the room. NCOs and officers gaped at this bloody, crazed apparition. Blakely kept his rifle at his hip, fired, worked the bolt, and fired again until they were all down.

He backed away from the blood pooling and flowing around his boots. He tore his eyes from the gaping wounds and dying men and stepped out the doorway. One of his men nearly shot him but recognized him in time and grinned, then ran after his charging, blood-crazed comrades.

Everywhere Blakely looked, commandos and Japanese were locked in deadly hand-to-hand combat. The Japanese fought valiantly, but the commandos' blood was up, and soon the Japanese gave ground.

Blakely saw Private Jocklin, the Bren gunner, wielding one of the Owen submachine guns. He must've moved forward as the battle did, Blakely surmised. Jocklin had the gun on full automatic and swept it from side to side, cutting the enemy down. When he ran out of ammo, instead of reloading, he simply dropped the weapon, unslung the remaining SMG, and continued his bloody rampage with short, controlled bursts.

Blakely turned from the scene and reloaded his rifle. He jogged forward, searching for targets, but most of the enemy was fully engaged or dying. He watched in amazement as Japanese soldiers broke and ran. He'd never seen that happen and never thought he would. He'd seen retreats, but never a flat-out fleeing Japanese soldier. The commandos had put the fear of God into them. He knew it wouldn't last long.

He aimed at a fleeing soldier a few yards ahead and fired. The soldier's back bloomed red, and he tripped and fell hard. Blakely searched for more, but the rout was complete. The Japanese fled. All that remained was the stench and the agonized screams of dying men.

He suddenly felt light-headed, and he couldn't control his breathing. He went to a knee and clenched his fist until his skin turned white. He finally got control when Sergeant Omar gripped his shoulder. "You hit, sir?"

Blakely jolted, then stood next to his blood-covered NCO. "No. You?"

Omar shook his head, seeing his bloody arms and feeling the stickiness dripping off his chin, "It's not mine."

Blakely shook his head, almost unable to comprehend the scene. "Jesus, Joseph, and Mary. I can't believe that worked."

Omar handed him one of the discarded Owen submachine guns. It was covered in mud, and the barrel still smoked. "Think this is yours."

Captain Grumskey looked the bloody battlefield over in astonishment. His insane plan had actually worked. The Japanese had been taken by complete surprise. Now he had to hold what he'd taken back. He directed his men, "Clear out the bodies and get back into the foxholes and trenches. Gather their weapons and ammo, too. We'll use it until we're resupplied." He pointed at an NCO. "Take three men back to Wau and tell General Moten what happened here. Tell him we need more ammo...and men." The NCO nodded and took off with three bloody soldiers trailing in his wake.

Grumskey oversaw the grisly work, helping collect and stack rifles and ammunition. He saw Corporal Winningham, the Bren gunner he'd given his Owen submachine gun to for the attack. It was still slung over his shoulder. Grumskey walked up to him and pointed. "I'd like that back now, Corporal."

Winningham looked embarrassed. He grinned and handed it back. "Of course, sir. There's only half a magazine worth of ammo, I'm afraid." Grumskey took off the magazine and checked for himself. Winningham said, "Shoots like a dream, sir."

Grumskey nodded. "Yes. Hope to get more of 'em soon." He pulled a rag from his back pocket and wiped the weapon down. He saw Lt. Blakely enter a building with his SMG leveled.

Grumskey held his SMG at port arms and followed his platoon leader into the room. Bodies littered the floor. Blakely noticed his boss and stiffened his back and said, "Making sure they're all dead, sir."

Grumskey nodded, trying to ignore the smell of death, which covered the room like a wet blanket. "Officers," he stated bluntly.

Blakely nodded. "I killed one at the bottom of the stairs, then came in here and..." His voice trailed off as he remembered their startled faces turning to fear and pain as he shot them down one at a time.

The edges of Grumskey's mouth turned down. He put a hand on Blakely's shoulder and murmured, "It's a nasty business we're in, Lieutenant."

Blakely nodded again, then leaned down and picked up a leather case. He righted the overturned table the officers had tried to use for cover and placed the case on top. The case had a locked bronze latch. He pulled his bayonet and pried the lock until it snapped. Grumskey stepped close as Blakely pulled out documents and spread them over the table. Everything was in Japanese, but they recognized the map of the area, which had marks and arrows drawn in.

Grumskey slapped Blakely's shoulder. "Good work. We'll get this sent to Moten."

Blakely asked, "Anyone read Japanese?"

"Believe it or not, Corporal Nance does."

Blakely looked at him sideways, clearly stunned. "You mean Nance of the NGVRs?" Grumskey nodded and Blakely asked, "Where is he? Haven't seen him for a couple of weeks now."

"He was at the mine last I heard. Hooked up with those Yanks and your pal, Willoth."

Blakely pushed his hat off his head. "I saw Willoth before coming over here, but Nance wasn't with him."

"Blighter might be hard to find. Probably having the time of his life with all the Japanese around."

Blakely pushed the documents back into the bag and handed it to Grumskey. Grumskey took it and gave the room one last look. "Get these bodies out of here and look for anything else the higher-ups might want, then get your men dug in tight. It's going to be a long night."

Blakely watched Grumskey leave, then turned back to the carnage. He'd smelled death countless times but never got completely used to it. The thought of spending one more second inside made him nauseous. He had to get out now. He descended the steps, taking in deep lungfuls of semi-fresh air. He barked at two passing commandos, "There's a pile of Jap officers inside. Go through their stuff and stack their bodies with the others."

The commandos scowled but did his bidding with a grumbled, "Yes, sir."

21

Tarkington and his squad led Lieutenant Willoth and his commandos up into the hills to the east of the farmhouse. With each yard, the sounds of fighting faded behind them.

Lieutenant Willoth gazed back occasionally, as though wondering if he were doing the right thing. While his countrymen fought for their lives, he moved away from the danger and closer to the unknown.

Tarkington noticed Willoth's furtive looks. He'd grown to respect the veteran Australian commando. He asked, "Having second thoughts?"

Willoth equivocated and seemed to have trouble finding the right words. "It feels odd moving away from battle. My mates are fighting for their lives down there, and we're heading the other direction." Silence for a half a minute while they wound their way through vine-covered trees. Willoth finally shook his head. "But no. We can do more good cutting off the head of the serpent."

Tarkington pointed at the chewed-up ground. "Nice of them to leave us such a nice, easy path to follow." Willoth just nodded, and Tarkington thought he was either suffering from exhaustion or indecision. Either way, he didn't seem himself.

The further uphill they ascended, the denser the layer of ground fog became. Spits of rain pelted them occasionally, but the combination of climbing and moving stealthily kept them warm. Willoth's pace slowed, and Tarkington pushed ahead with his men.

Minutes later, Henry and Raker stopped the procession with raised fists. They didn't crouch, so Tarkington strode forward. Willoth finally joined them. Henry pointed at the muddy ground. Two distinct paths diverged. The main boot prints continued up the hill. Henry drawled, "This must be where the northern group split off from our friends back there."

"Sure looks that way," Tarkington agreed.

Henry continued, "Can't see much in this pea soup, but I'll wager we're gettin' close to the bigwigs."

Tarkington nodded. "We'll move off the path and slow things down. Don't wanna run into any pickets and give ourselves away."

They spread out into a loose combat spread, with the Alamo Scouts leading and Henry at the tip. They kept the track on their right as they moved directly uphill, slowly. By the time they crested the hill, evening was setting in. The fog lifted, and a passing swath of heavy rain thundered down upon them. Tarkington called a halt, and they ate and drank water. The rain came down in sheets for nearly an hour before it finally let up and the squall passed into the valley like a physical gray wall.

Tarkington shivered. Night would be upon them soon, and their misery would increase as the temperature dropped. With the rain gone, they could finally see more than a few feet in front of them. They were on the edge of a thin forest of hanging vines and dripping leaves. Further along, they could see a field of kunai grass stretching up a slope, but the most distinct feature was a black cliff wall just beyond the grass.

Tarkington had patrolled this area once before but didn't recognize that particular feature. He wasn't surprised. There were countless hidden valleys cutting through these hills, which he wouldn't have time to explore in two lifetimes. He pointed. "Looks like that might be a good vantage point."

Henry nodded slowly. "The trail leads that way, too. Probably can't make it up there before dark, though. Be tough climbing."

Tarkington waved Willoth forward. His sallow cheeks made him look half-starved. Tarkington pointed to the cliff face. "We were thinking we might be able to see better from up there."

Willoth's face darkened, and he looked miserable. "Won't be able to see anything in an hour," he uttered.

Tarkington noticed the dark bags beneath Willoth's eyes for the first time. He looked tired, more tired than he'd ever seen him. "You okay?"

Willoth's face looked gray, and his eyes were bloodshot against a yellowish background. He suddenly shivered violently and his teeth chattered. He gritted them but couldn't keep them from banging into each other.

"Christ, you're having a bout of malaria, aren't you?" Tarkington said.

Willoth stared vacantly and could only nod as another wracking, bone-shaking shiver coursed through his body. Tarkington signaled Sergeant Mills, and he trotted forward with fatherly concern. Tarkington said, "You need to bivouac for the night. He can't operate out here like that."

Everyone knew the signs of malaria. Indeed, most had contracted the debilitating condition themselves. Even with the constant intake of quinine, no one was immune to the mosquito-borne disease. The only way to avoid it was to not get bitten by the infected mosquitos...and that was like trying to dodge raindrops in an open field during a summer thunderstorm.

Mills rifled through Willoth's ruck and found his poncho. He wrapped it around Willoth, who protested weakly, mumbling, "I can make it...I'm fine."

No one believed him, and he couldn't resist their efforts. He got passed back through the ranks, and men wrapped him with whatever clothes and ponchos they could spare.

Tarkington took Sergeant Mills aside. "Stay here with him. Stay out of sight." He pointed toward the cliff in the distance. The colors of the setting sun danced across the rock, bathing it in soft reds and yellows. "We're going up there. Keep your walkie close-by. If we find their HQ, we'll contact you tomorrow."

Mills didn't look too happy. "Just you six? I'll grab a few and join you."

Tarkington shook his head and answered, "We're used to working alone, Sergeant."

∿

They pushed through the kunai grass, which rose above their heads. They veered away from the path the Japanese had left. It continued winding south, disappearing into a sloping valley beneath the cliffs.

Tarkington hesitated, wondering if they should push their luck and simply follow the track all the way to the suspected camp. He discarded the idea. The Japanese would have pickets out defending the base, particularly since they'd been harassed the entire way there. He waved at Henry to keep moving toward the cliff face.

They made it to the cliff face with fifteen minutes of light left. The cliff looked vertical from a distance, but now that they were close, they could see the columnar formations formed little ramps here and there. They scrambled up a scree slope as quietly as possible until they could go no further. They each pulled a length of rope from their rucks and tied the ends together to form one long rope.

The rope had been a constant joke for them since the Alamo Scout instructors had insisted they carry them. They'd griped about the extra weight and valuable space the ropes took up in their rucks, but the instructors insisted that one day they'd wish they had it...that day had finally arrived.

They'd all passed the climbing portion of training fairly easily, but only one of them had shown exceptional skill. Vick didn't hesitate to step forward and hook the end of the rope to his belt. He slung his carbine across his back and cinched it up tight. As the last bit of light disappeared, he lunged upward and clutched the first handhold. He cursed the wetness but managed to pull himself up once he'd gotten a good foothold.

The columnar rock had good shelfs and ridges to hold on to and to jam his feet into. Even with the wetness, the climb was relatively easy for him. Higher and higher he climbed. The rope got heavier with every inch of the vertical climb as more and more of it lifted off the ground and hung from his belt. By the time he was close to the top, it felt like it might pull his pants from his slender hips.

He finally reached the top and sat for a moment to take in the view. The rope dangled beneath him, disappearing into the abyss one hundred feet below. He found a sturdy boulder and wrapped the rope around it once, then tied it off to a stout, vine-covered tree. He went to the edge of the cliff and heaved the rope up and down five times, signaling that it was time for the others to come up. He sat back, sipped water, and looked out over the distant flashes coming from the valley. The rope tightened as another climber started up.

Henry appeared over the lip. He'd also excelled during the climbing course, and he had made it up quickly. He hauled on the rope, signaling again, and he joined Vick in the darkness. Henry whistled low and said, "Looks like Wau's still getting hit. Must be mortars."

Vick agreed, seeing the distant flashes. "Means they're probably pretty close to the airfield, I guess. They didn't have anything bigger than 60s, unless they were holding out on us."

Henry looked up at the dark sky. He could see stars shining through breaks in the clouds, something he hadn't seen in days. "If this keeps up, they'll be able to resupply us tomorrow."

Vick added, "Might be quite a show tomorrow. The flyboys from both sides'll be out in full force."

Henry grinned, plucked a length of grass, and shoved it into the side of his mouth. "And we'll have the best seats in the house." He got to his feet. "You check the area out yet?"

Vick answered, "Just the immediate area. Nothing beyond that little rock wall there."

Henry left the Japanese sniper rifle and moved off with his carbine ready. "Be right back."

One by one, the rest of the squad scrambled up and joined Vick. Before long, they all stood staring at the view.

Tarkington was the last man up. He looked around and asked, "Where's Henry?"

Vick pointed over his shoulder. "He went to check out the rest of the ridge."

At that instant Henry stepped from behind them, opposite the direction he'd gone, and said, "Hiya."

Tarkington jolted. "Dammit, Henry." He gave his lead scout and oldest friend a withering stare. "Well, did ya find anything interesting?"

Henry grinned and nodded. "Uh-huh. Sure did, Tark. You're gonna love this."

Winkleman shook his head. "Crazy, mysterious damned Cajun—always speaking in riddles. Just come out and tell us already." His voice still wavered from having to deal with the height of the cliff.

Henry motioned them to follow. Vick and Stollman pulled up the rope and coiled it neatly on the edge of the cliff, then followed them past the rock wall and onto a flat piece of ground flanked by another low cliff. They followed the band of flat ground for forty yards. Henry finally stopped and extended his arm. A figure sat on a rock facing the valley. The figure stood, and even in the darkness, his thick beard and woven straw hat left little doubt.

Tarkington stepped forward to get a closer look. "Nance? Is that you?"

Henry chortled. "Found him up here asleep. I coulda slit his throat... nearly did, in fact."

Corporal Nance's teeth shone through the darkness. "Wasn't expecting company, that's for bloody sure." He pointed at Henry. "He moves like a damned ghost, he does."

Henry laughed. "I smelled you before I saw you." Nance ignored the jibe.

Tarkington asked, "What the hell you doing up here?"

Nance shrugged and answered, "Probably same as you. Good observation post."

"How long you been up here?"

"Got here about four hours ago, I guess."

"Did you see anything interesting before it got dark?"

Nance gave an exaggerated nod. "Indeed I did. I decided to sleep on the situation, sometimes I wake up with a plan, but you blighters arriving changes everything." He pointed into the dark abyss. "Can't do anything until morning, so you may as well pull up a rock and rest awhile."

Tarkington moved to the edge of the precipice and asked, "What did you see, Corporal?"

Nance stepped forward and stood beside Tarkington. He pointed. "Right about where I'm pointing, there's a camp. An enemy camp. It's too far off for any kind of shooting, though."

Tarkington strained to see anything in the darkness. "Can't see a damned thing," he uttered. "Did you get a sense of their defenses? Can we sneak close enough for sharpshooting? Henry borrowed a scoped Jap rifle."

Nance looked over his shoulder at the grinning Cajun. "That'll certainly help," he said, "but they've got men spread out all over the place. I saw at least two machine guns, and a few snipers strung up in the trees. I suspect there's even more on the ground that I didn't see." He sniffed the air. "Rain stopped. That'll be to their advantage. That's what I was sleeping on—how to get close without being seen."

Tarkington took it all in. The others had joined them near the edge. Winkleman stayed back a safe distance but could still follow the conversation. He said, "That type of thing's kind of our specialty, Corporal."

The squad shared C-rats, drank water, and discussed the upcoming operation. Nance assured them no one would bother them on the top of the cliff, so the conversation grew more and more animated as they worked out each detail. Nance wracked his brain, remembering all he could about the enemy positions. He drew a map in the muddy ground under a red-lensed flashlight.

With a semblance of a plan in place, Tarkington used the walkie and for once was able to contact Lt. Willoth's unit. Willoth didn't answer, still too sick, but Tarkington filled Sergeant Mills in on the approximate position of the enemy camp and let him know their intentions. Mills had nothing new to report and wished him luck.

At midnight, they went back to the coiled rope and descended one at a time. Nance and Henry stuck together, and the rest of the squad moved off silently, following Raker. Henry watched the men he'd been through so much with disappear into the gloom. He hated splitting up, but the plan called for Nance and Henry to provide support as a sharpshooter team.

Without a scope, Nance would have to get close to use his weapon, and after the first shot, his position would be compromised. So he'd hidden his rifle beneath a marked pile of rocks and now had an old pistol in a holster and a pair of powerful binoculars tucked safely in a hard case and wrapped securely around his shoulder. Henry had offered his carbine, but Nance refused, referring to it as little more than a popgun.

The sniper team had been Winkleman's idea. Growing up, he'd often hunted as a pair with his uncle. They would take turns holding the scoped rifle or the binoculars. Straining through the scope's limited sight picture sapped energy, but scanning through binoculars was easy and much more ground could be covered. Invariably, whoever held the binoculars spotted the elk, then they'd talk the shooter onto it. They'd bagged over twenty elk and even more deer using the method. Now, Henry and Nance would use it to hunt men.

Clouds drifted overhead, sometimes exposing starlight, other times blotting it out completely. Henry followed Nance through fields of kunai grass, then sparse forests. Nance moved extremely well for a bigger-than-average man, and he quickly earned Henry's respect. They snaked their way silently around suspected enemy sniper and machine gun positions. They never saw or heard the enemy, but Henry sensed their presence.

It took hours, but Nance finally tucked them into a thick stand of trees on the front side of a hillock overlooking a field of swaying grass. Beyond the field was where Nance suspected to find the enemy camp. Before darkness descended, he'd seen smoke and distant activity from the cliff vantage point.

They silently pulled grass and huge jungle leaves over their position. The extra layer served two purposes: concealment and warmth. The rain had stopped, but their clothes never completely dried out.

Henry whispered, "Be light in another two hours. Why don't you get some sleep." Nance nodded, laid his head onto his hands, and was asleep a few minutes later. Henry shook his head in amazement. He fell asleep faster than Stollman, and that was saying something.

The rest of the squad moved silently, carefully skirting the suspected enemy positions. Their circuitous route took them around the right side of the plateau and through a thicker section of jungle. Nance hadn't mentioned seeing snipers in this area, but it hadn't been his focus.

Raker moved cautiously, keeping his eyes scanning both the ground and the trees. Their camouflage and silent passage would keep them from being seen unless they stumbled directly into an enemy position. Raker wasn't about to let that happen. His sixth sense wasn't as highly tuned as Henry's, but he could sniff out trouble with the best of them. So far, things had gone perfectly. He'd seen no sign of the enemy, and despite their slow movement, they'd made good time.

Moving through the jungles of this massive island sometimes made Raker feel as though they'd dropped off the face of the earth and ended up in an alternate universe. The massive fields of grass, the sprawling forests and jungles spread over low hills and high mountains, made a man feel small and insignificant. It wouldn't be difficult to simply disappear into the jungle and live out the rest of your life.

The thought had crossed his mind once or twice. He always pictured himself surrounded by a harem of beautiful women feeding him grapes as he lounged...

A sound brought him back to reality and stopped him in his tracks. He strained, filtering out the constant hum and click of insects and the screeches of night birds and other animals. He'd heard something subtly out of place, and it was close. The others stopped and slowly crouched. They were spread out in a loose wedge formation, with Raker at the front.

The sound of water splashing onto a broad leaf focused Raker's attention. He heard the soft, unmistakable tinkle of a belt buckle. Raker struggled to keep his heart rate under control as he reached out and dragged a leafy barrier down. Beyond, he saw the outline of a soldier taking a leak. He looked small, and the outline of his pith helmet made him distinctly Japanese.

Raker silently cursed himself. He'd been self-absorbed and if the soldier hadn't chosen that exact moment to relieve himself, Raker would've led the patrol straight into him, and he probably had buddies nearby.

Raker released the bushes, allowing them to rise back to their natural position. He touched his knife handle, wishing for a moment that he had Tarkington's short sword. He hoped it wouldn't come to that. He'd killed men with his knife and didn't relish the act. He'd much rather shoot them, but using the carbine was out of the question.

Raker heard the flow of urine slow to a trickle, then finally stop. Through the leaves he saw dark movements and heard the belt buckle again. The soldier turned around and moved to Raker's right. He lost him in the darkness but continued to hear his light footfalls disturbing the flora and fauna.

Raker turned around and found the dim outline of Sergeant Winkleman. He could only see the whites of his eyes, but he got the feeling he glared at him. Raker motioned left and turned that way. Winkleman gave an exaggerated nod, and Raker thought he must be saying, "No shit," in his head.

The rest of the way, Raker stayed hyper-vigilant. They didn't encounter any more enemy outposts.

Tarkington stopped him an hour after the near miss, and the squad conferred on their whereabouts in relation to the suspected enemy camp. Tarkington pulled out his compass and the scrap of a map. The only landmark was the distant outline of the cliff against the sky.

Tarkington pointed and whispered, "Time to move southeast. It'll be light soon, and we need to be in position before that happens."

As Raker led them into the grass, Winkleman pulled Tarkington aside and whispered, "I don't like this much, Tark. What're we gonna do once we get there?"

Tarkington could barely make out Winkleman's blackened face. He answered, "You know I don't have an answer for you, Wink. Maybe nothing. We'll just have to see how things look when we get there."

Winkleman watched Tarkington's back disappear into the darkness. He sighed, glanced at the outlines of skittering clouds overhead, and mumbled to himself, "Don't like this one little bit."

22

Major Shima watched through binoculars as his men rose from their fighting positions in the early morning predawn and assaulted the nearest side of the riverbank. They'd exchanged fire with the stalwart Australians all night long. He'd called a meeting of his surviving platoon leaders and ordered them to attack just before dawn and push the Allies into the river. He explained that once they took the riverbank, they could shell the airfield and keep reinforcements from flooding in.

He watched as the bulk of his battalion ran forward. He'd ordered a silent assault, and so far he'd heard no shooting. Had he caught the Australians by surprise, or had they simply retreated? Either would be a success.

A burst of yellow tracer fire reached out from the opposite bank of the river. Soon more streams joined the first and swept his men as they continued their advance. No fire from the near side of the bank, however, and he realized they must have retreated sometime during the night. How had he not noticed? Their incessant rifle fire throughout most of the night must've come from a rear guard.

More and more of his men streamed across the plateau, darting in and out of half-destroyed and smoldering huts and shacks. Most of the thatch roofs had burned the day before under his mortar attacks. Rifle shots rippled and little sparks of muzzle flashes dotted the area, but nothing heavy, and it was short-lived. Probably his men firing at shadows.

Soon, his troops made it all the way to the riverbank. The unexpected absence of resistance left Shima momentarily stunned. He didn't have a plan for advancing across the river. General Okabe's revised orders were for him to secure this side of the river and harass and pin down the enemy until Captain Ho and the Second Battalion swept down from the north.

Major Shima's battle instincts kicked in, urging him to continue the attack. He had momentum. He could push across the river and take Wau over the next few minutes. Corporal Nori's voice broke his concentration. He poked his head from a captured native's house and held up the radio receiver. "Sir, General Okabe."

Major Shima cursed under his breath but quickly strode the few meters and ducked into the hut. "Vulture here, sir. Over."

"Vulture, stand by for Alpha One." Scuffling on the other end, then he heard the distinct voice of General Okabe. "Report. Over."

"The attack is a success, sir. We've met little to no resistance. The cowards must have left during the night. We hold the eastern edge of the river. Request permission for plan Y, sir. Over."

"Excellent news. Plan Zeta in effect. Repeat: Plan Zeta. Acknowledge. Over."

Major Shima gripped the receiver until he thought it would crush. Plan Zeta was the original attack plan—hold, harass, and wait. Against his better judgment and everything he'd ever learned about dealing with superior officers—particularly this superior officer—he tried one last time. "Plan Y has a high probability of success. Over."

Momentary silence, and Shima thought he might get his wish, but his hopes were dashed when Okabe's voice lowered and the words came through the radio with bitter finality. "Plan Zeta. Acknowledge. Over."

Shima closed his eyes and answered curtly, "Plan Zeta. Acknowledged. Out." He handed the receiver back to his radioman and uttered, "Fool." The young corporal pretended not to hear and busied himself with the radio knobs.

Shima clenched his fists until they turned white. He turned and looked out over the river. The Australians fired on his men as they scattered into the Australians' old positions and returned fire. The river separated them— only fifty meters in spots.

The river had risen considerably overnight, but it still had a long way to go before it flooded the banks. His men could probably still ford the river in most places. If they crossed the bridges, the bottleneck would lead to massive casualties. They'd be cut to pieces by machine gun and rifle fire.

He shook his head. One heavy smoke barrage and one good push would put his men into the Australian lines. He had enough men to get the job done now. General Okabe probably couldn't see the developing situation from his faraway, safe HQ in the hills. If he could, he might change his mind. Perhaps Okabe would move west with the good news, wanting to see the final push into the airfield. Perhaps he'd want to lead the attack himself.

Shima barked at the radio operator, "Get me Lieutenant Takeda." Moments later his First Platoon commander's excited voice greeted him, "Takeda here, sir."

"Excellent work, Lieutenant. Over."

Takeda's pride beamed through the tinny radio. "Thank you, sir. What are your orders? Over."

For a moment, Major Shima struggled. He desperately wanted to send First Battalion across the river—his gut screamed that it was the right thing to do. He nearly blurted out the attack order but caught himself in time. "Plan Zeta. Plan Zeta. Over."

He thought he could discern Lt. Takeda's own disappointment. "Plan Zeta. Understood. Out."

Minutes later every mortar in the battalion began lobbing mortar rounds over the defending Australians and onto the airfield.

Major Shilansky of the USAAF and nine other P-38s crossed over the top of a string of C-47s crossing the Owen Stanley Mountains. Each transport plane carried twenty-five to thirty Australian troopers from the Seventeenth Brigade. The AIF soldiers had been champing at the bit in Port Moresby, waiting to get into the action as they'd listened to the desperate radio chatter from Wau relaying the hard, desperate fight.

The last few days, the weather had shut down all flights into the Wau Valley, keeping half the brigade out of the fight. The unusual break in the weather the night before came as a welcome surprise, and Shilansky and his mates from the Thirty-ninth Fighter Squadron of the Fifth Air Force had been up well before dawn, preparing.

Shilansky led the two flights of four flying out of Port Moresby, and flying top cover for the C-47 transports, all the way. They'd been in the air for two hours, searching for enemy fighters who would also use the good weather to their advantage. So far, the only other planes in the sky were a flight of Australian-owned P-40 Warhawks out of Dobodura airfield near Buna.

Shilansky's radio buzzed in his headset. He could tell by the distant, tin-can sound that the message was from command back at Moresby. "Red One, this is Falcon Two. Over."

"Falcon Two. Red One. Go ahead. Over."

"Red One. Multiple reports of enemy bombers and fighters entering your airspace from the northeast. Estimated elevation from two thousand to fifteen thousand. Suggested vector of three zero degrees. Over."

Shilansky cringed at first, hearing the word *zero* in the transmission. Before getting the P-38s, they'd flown P-39 Airacobras, and tangling with the Japanese Zero in a 39 had caused the deaths of many pilots. Those harrowing missions still lived in his head, but with each mission in the P-38s, the memories and fear faded as the squadron's confidence in the new twin-engine fighter grew. "Copy. Turning to three zero degrees. Out." Shilansky relayed the message to his flight. "Keep your eyes peeled. New heading three zero degrees. Combat spread. Remember, our priority's defending the transports. Out."

He turned slightly to thirty degrees and pushed the throttles forward, feeling the powerful Allison engines propel his aircraft. He scanned the sky in twenty-degree increments, searching for the telltale glint of metal or reflected glass. Large columns of cumulus clouds towered up from the higher mountain peaks, but mostly, the day was clear.

The lead C-47 broke into a turn and dropped toward the dirt airfield near the small town of Wau. Even from eight thousand feet, Shilansky saw red tracer fire reaching up from the plateau and riverbank. The airwaves immediately lit up with a call from the C-47 pilot: "Taking fire from the river." The pilot's calm voice belied the situation in stark contrast.

Before Shilansky could see whether or not the transport arrived safely, a call from one of his veteran pilots: "Bandits twelve o'clock high."

Shilansky looked up through his bubble canopy and immediately saw glinting metal and tiny black dots. If he'd been in the P-39, he would've ordered his pilots to scatter and hope for the best, but in the P-38, he confidently raised the nose a few degrees and pushed the throttle, gaining altitude and easily maintaining speed. He keyed his throat mic and said, "They'll have to come through us to get to the transports. Maintain formation and keep your heads on a swivel. Over."

Another pilot's calm voice: "I see Bettys mixed in up there. Over."

Shilansky saw the bombers, too. "Leave them for the Aussies. If the Zeros make a move, we'll engage. Over."

As the dots became more like flying crosses, it became obvious that the Zeros were there to protect the bombers. They stayed high. Shilansky scanned the deep greens of the jungle below and keyed his mic. "Keep your eyes open for low Zeros trying to squirt through."

Seconds later, the excited voice of one of his newer pilots, Second Lieutenant Myles, broke the silence. "Zeros at eleven o'clock low. They're heading for the transports."

Shilansky didn't see them immediately but ordered, "Break into them." He turned left and pulled the nose down, cutting the throttle back. He didn't have to look for his wingman. He knew he'd be watching his tail like a hawk. Shilansky immediately saw the green-painted Zeros slashing low across the jungle. He counted two sets of four, one group slightly higher and tailing the other. "Blue Flight, take the tail-end element."

First Lieutenant Connor gave a curt, "Copy."

The physics and math played out in Shilansky's head. The Zeros were flying hard and fast, but his sharp-eyed young pilot had seen them in time. Like a hawk, Shilansky's P-38 stayed above and slightly behind the lead group of four. He pushed the throttle forward and watched his airspeed indicator reach four hundred mph. The P-38 had a tremendous speed advantage over the Zeros. The Zeros could still outturn them, but Shilansky didn't intend to fight them that way.

He lined his nose up on the lead plane, most likely the flight leader and probably the most experienced pilot. The Zero grew steadily in the orange-glowing gunsight picture. He pulled the throttle back, not wanting to over-shoot the slower enemy plane. He moved his thumb to the gun button on his flight yoke. He'd use the four .50-caliber machine guns mounted on the nose. He'd reserve the 20mm cannon for the bombers if he got a chance.

The Japanese pilot must have seen his impending doom. He suddenly pulled up hard, spoiling Shilansky's shot for an instant. Shilansky quickly corrected and pulled his nose up, watching his pipper rise through the target, which grew impossibly large in his windscreen. He mashed the trigger, and yellow tracer fire erupted from the nose and swept through the lightly armored fighter. A fireball filled his view, and he instinctively pulled up hard. The burning wreck passed only a few yards beneath his fuselage. "Hot damn!" he whooped.

He continued climbing and turned on edge, searching below for more targets. The enemy planes darted away from his attacking pilots, scattering in every direction. He heard his pilot's chattering as they engaged and gave chase. Streams of yellow fire filled the sky, some ricocheting off the ground wildly. He noted the burning wreck of his victim had created a mini-conflagration in a grassy field.

The enemy pilots' attempts to hit the transports had been thwarted for the moment. He called his pilots, cutting through their chatter, "Don't get pulled away from the transports. There might be more." Another Zero suddenly glowed orange as the engine caught fire and consumed the cockpit. Shilansky heard his rookie pilot's exuberant voice, "I—I got one. Hot damn!"

Shilansky wondered why Second Lieutenant Myles wasn't watching his wingman's tail but decided they could work that out later over a beer in Port Moresby.

He climbed to four thousand feet and looked for more enemy fighters. Spurts of yellow and red tracer far overhead caught his attention, and he could see dots and smoke trails as the Australian P-40 pilots tangled with the Zeros and Betty bombers. The P-38s were better platforms for that mission, but that wasn't his mission today. The veteran Australian pilots could hold their own against the superior Japanese Zero because of their vast experience, but it would be a hard fight, and there'd probably be losses.

He tore his eyes from the deadly dance overhead and searched for more Zeros. His green-painted P-38 flashed over the top of Wau airfield, well above the pattern altitude. Puffs of smoke erupted near the edges, and he realized the airfield was under attack while the transports were landing and quickly offloading men and supplies. Tracer fire crisscrossed over a muddy river to the east of the airfield. He shook his head, marveling at the size of the transport pilot's balls.

He keyed his mic. "Blue Flight. Stay on task. Over." He got a quick affirmative from Connor, then addressed his flight. "Red Flight. Follow me for a strafing run on the east side of the river. Let's try to clear a path for the transports." He heard clicks and affirmatives as he pulled his plane into a climbing turn to the north. He checked his knee board for the C-47's call sign and pressed the mic. "Gallant. This is Red Leader. Over."

There was a brief moment of static, then a laconic Southern voice said, "Red Leader, this is Gallant. Go ahead. Over."

"Gallant. Stay off the approach while we clear it out for you. Over."

"Copy, Red Leader. We'd be obliged. Out."

Shilansky leveled off at two thousand feet and paralleled the river. He craned his neck, seeing his target, then pulled sharply right until his nose lined up on the east side of the river. Outgoing red tracer fire marked the enemy position, and he pushed the nose down slightly. He opened fire with all four of his .50-caliber machine guns. He worked the rudder pedals, yawing his nose back and forth—spreading the .50-caliber rounds gratu-itously. His rounds ripped a long swath of dirt and mud. He pulled up slightly and pushed the throttle to clear the area. The other three ships in Red Flight strafed at fifteen-second intervals, stitching long lines of destruction. Shilansky grinned. "Gallant. Red Leader. That should help. Out."

The Southern lilt dripped through, "Red Leader. Rounds are on me. Out."

~

Major Connaway couldn't believe their luck. The weather had finally broken, allowing troops and supplies to be flown in from Moresby. Command had informed them they'd be coming in for as long as the weather held.

He heard their droning before he actually saw them. He hunkered near a heavily sandbagged bunker, scanning the sky with his powerful binoculars. The Japanese on the far side of the river had been dropping mortar shells all night long. The small shells did minor damage to the airfield, but soldiers and engineers stood by with shovels and risked their lives when they deemed a crater needed to be filled in. They'd dashed out three times during the night, and thankfully no one had been injured.

Connaway finally spotted the first transport. "I see them. Here they come. Looks like they've brought a fighter escort too."

General Moten emerged from the depths of the bunker and raised his own pair of binoculars. He found the aircraft, then peered across the river to the east. "The pilots will have to fly right over the damned Japs on the river. They're parked right on their final approach. They'll be taking fire coming and going."

Connaway shifted his gaze to the battle raging along the riverbank. The Japanese seemed to have endless ammunition. Their own troops didn't, so most of the fire came from the enemy. The AIF soldiers had been ordered to only fire if they could be assured of a hit. Now that they could see, more shots rang out.

General Moten stated, "The commandos held off the Japs overnight at the coffee plantation but expect an attack at any moment. Once the first load of soldiers land, I want them sent north to bolster Captain Grumskey's men." He looked up at the relatively clear day. He slapped Connaway's shoulder and exclaimed, "By God, this came just in time. We may just keep this airfield after all."

In the early morning light, they both watched the first C-47 come in steeply and level off. Red tracer fire arced up from the river. Connaway held his breath, watching the pilot yaw and bank side to side. The transport landed hard and rolled up the ten-degree slope quickly. At the end of the runway, the plane turned abruptly and faced back the way it had come. The engines continued to roar and the plane shuddered against the brakes, eager to fly off again.

Soldiers spilled out the side door, carrying packs and rifles. One last piece of gear flew out and landed in a heap. Once the door closed, the pilot released the brakes and the transport shot down the runway and lifted off.

Normally, departing aircraft stayed level as they built up speed, but this pilot didn't relish flying through more enemy fire and so pulled into a shallow right turn. Connaway thought it would dip into the ground, but it kept flying and soon outdistanced the enemy tracer rounds nipping at its tail.

Another plane was already on short final. This one seemed to drop nearly straight onto the airfield. Connaway, having some experience flying before the war, explained, "He's cut his speed and he's using full flaps to lessen his glide slope. He's gotta be careful—there's no time to recover from a stall." They watched the plane drop onto the muddy strip and charge up the slope. Connaway blew out a breath he didn't realize he'd been holding. "Damn good bloody pilots, those Yanks."

Moten hustled from the bunker and strode toward the airfield with purpose. Connaway followed close behind. "Is it wise to risk yourself out here, sir?" he asked.

Moten ignored him and kept walking. Mortars continued to rain down and bullets snapped overhead. Newly arrived soldiers hunkered, wondering what they should do. A young lieutenant gaped at General Moten standing over him. The lieutenant cringed as a mortar shell exploded only twenty yards away.

Moten put his fists against his hips and addressed him, "You there. Get your men up and out of the way." He pointed north and barked, "Take them north and report to Captain Grumskey at the coffee plantation." The officer's eyes looked like saucers, and he made no effort to move. Moten leaned down and yelled, "Now, Lieutenant!"

The officer gulped and jumped to his feet, fearing the crazed general more than the mortar fire. He waved at his cowering men and yelled, "Let's go. Grab your gear and follow me."

Moten lifted his chin and looked down his nose. "Now that's better." He slapped the officer as he hustled past. "Off you go!"

Connaway cringed beside him. Moten pointed to the next batch of soldiers gathering their gear from the offloaded transport. He ordered, "Take those men to the river. We need to bolster B Company and keep the Japs from shooting at our transports."

Connaway unholstered his pistol and said, "Yes, sir." He ran, hunched over, toward a second lieutenant organizing his newly arrived men. When he got there, the lieutenant saluted, and Connaway slapped his hand down. "Not out here, you bloody fool."

"S-sorry, sir—I—"

Connaway interrupted, "Never mind that! What's your name?"

He stuttered, "Foley. Samuel Foley, sir."

"Follow me to the riverbank, Lieutenant Foley. We need to keep the Nips from firing on the transports." The young lieutenant's wide eyes swept the battlefield. His eyes settled on General Moten, still standing like a statue amid the chaos, directing traffic.

Connaway looked at Lieutenant Foley's troopers. Some looked terrified, others calm—veterans. "Come on, lads," he ordered. "Let's get into the fight."

He led them to the right edge of the airfield. Another transport landed hard and raced uphill, the wheels spewing muddy water. Connaway saw jagged bullet holes near the fuselage, and the side window had been spider-webbed. He ran as fast as he could, dodging mortar craters and trying his best not to slip and fall in the mud.

When he reached the leading edge of the airfield, Connaway noticed more cracks and whips as bullets passed nearby. He hunkered lower but continued his headlong sprint. He finally slid into a filthy trench. The bottom had six inches of water and another six inches of mud. More soldiers piled into the trench, some slamming into soldiers already tucked against the wall. They cursed their clumsiness.

A sergeant facing away from Connaway fired his rifle and worked the bolt action. Connaway slapped his back. "Hey, Sergeant. Where's Captain Ligget?"

The NCO spun around with fire and hatred burning in his eyes. "What's the..." He noticed the rank, and his face changed immediately. "Oh, sorry, sir—I..."

Connaway waved it away. "Answer the question."

"The captain got hit. Captain Warren's in charge now." He pointed to the left. "He's down that way somewhere."

Connaway nodded his thanks. "Brought some reinforcements for you. Tell Lieutenant Foley where you want 'em." The sergeant smiled through his mud-encrusted face and found the petrified lieutenant.

Connaway didn't wait around. He needed to find Captain Warren and find out what had happened to his friend, Captain Ligget. Whatever happened must've happened recently, or they would've been informed back at HQ. He sloshed past men with their boots jammed into wall slots, aiming and occasionally firing their weapons. A Vickers machine gun crew was setting up after relocating, and he heard an officer directing them. "Come on, lads, hurry up."

Connaway touched the captain, and the officer stiffened and turned. "Major Connaway. Where'd you come from, sir?"

Connaway ignored the question. "Reinforcements are arriving. The Japs are hitting the transports as they fly overhead. We need to stop that from happening." The officer nodded, and Connaway shouted, "Pour it on, Captain. If those transports get shot down, we'll be in trouble."

Warren understood immediately. He cupped his hands and barked, "Okay, lads, let's give 'em what-for. Cover the transports."

The Vickers crew quickly finished setting up. The gunner pointed at the box beside him. "This is the last of it, sir."

Connaway barked, "There's more coming in right now."

The gunner gave him a crooked grin. "Well, in that case..." He gripped the handle, aimed, and sent a long volley of fire across the river. The spent hot brass casings hissed as they hit the muddy water.

Warren pointed left and asked, "Those ours?"

Connaway looked and saw four twin-engine planes wheeling toward them. Connaway couldn't keep the smile off his face. "P-38s! Yes, they're ours." He cupped his hands and yelled, "Friendly strafing run. Heads down!"

Despite the order, he kept his eyes peeking over the lip. The ripping sound reached him a split second after the ground beyond the river erupted in massive black geysers of dirt. Each plane made a devastating pass, and when they'd gracefully arced away, men cheered and pumped their fists up and down the line.

23

Lieutenant Blakely hadn't slept a wink since they retook the plantation the evening before. Thinking about the successful bayonet charge made him physically ill, so he tried to block it out of his mind.

The Japanese had faded into the forests and grasses along the river's edge. Everyone expected a counterattack during the night, but it never came. He didn't have as much experience fighting the Japanese as some, but he knew they loved their counterattacks...particularly at night.

Grumskey had kept the men vigilant all night long, and now, despite the very real probability that they wouldn't survive another day, Blakely could barely keep his eyes open.

He bit his lower lip, feeling a scab break away. He tasted blood and felt the twinge of pain reawaken his mind, but that trick wasn't as effective as it had been, and the wakefulness was fleeting. He needed to sleep.

The droning of aircraft made all the commandos look up with a mixture of dread and hope. Sergeant Omar looked as tired as Blakely felt. Black circles hung beneath his eyes like he'd never slept in his entire life. He pointed, and his voice cracked, "Transports. Ours."

Blakely's eyes itched and burned, but he looked skyward and saw many glinting shapes wheeling overhead. "Bloody weather broke just in time."

The cracking of distant fire increased from the direction of the airfield. "Sounds like they're pushing on the airfield again?"

Omar shrugged and tore his gaze back to the lightening jungle and grasses beyond. "If they are, they'll bloody well try the same thing here, I expect."

Captain Grumskey moved along the line, checking and encouraging the men. He got to Blakely and Omar. Grumskey's eyes looked bright and fresh, as though he'd gotten a full eight hours. Blakely knew he hadn't gotten a bit of sleep. In fact, he never remembered seeing Grumskey even take a rest. He'd seen him all night long, either checking on the men or relaying their situation to General Moten. He hadn't slowed down for a moment and still looked fresh somehow. His example shamed Blakely, and he shook his own fatigue off like a heavy wool coat in summer.

Grumskey asked, "Any movement out there?"

Blakely shook his head. "Nothing. Thought sure they woulda come last night."

Grumskey nodded. "Me too. We musta hurt them more than we thought." He poked his head up and scanned the mist-shrouded grasses and forest. He ducked back down and uttered, "Got word from Moten. He's sending us fresh troops from those bloody transports."

Blakely tried to wet his dry and cracked lips. "Hope they hurry the hell up about it. We're down to the last of our ammunition. Got enough for one short engagement."

"I sent a squad from First back to guide them here...so we'll be short for a few minutes." He tapped Blakely's arm. "Keep your men sharp, and we'll make it out of this mess. Moten knows about our ammo problem. We're certainly not alone in that." Grumskey got to his feet. "Come with me, Omar. Let's check on the rest of the men." Omar glanced at Blakely and followed Grumskey to the next group of men.

Blakely checked his SMG and wiped a smudge of dirt off the bolt. He only had two more magazines remaining. He pushed up and peered over the top of the muddy trench. Besides the stench, the bodies, and parts of bodies, the morning reminded him of home.

The droning airplane noises increased, and he saw more and more planes darting and dashing overhead. The partial clouds and distance kept him wondering about aircraft type until he saw the distinctive twin tails of American P-38 fighters. A group of four flew straight toward him, and he wondered if they'd been directed to attack the tree line. Instead, the planes pulled into steep turns and shot back toward Wau. The throaty roar of their twin engines increased as they flashed overhead, and Blakely forgot about his fatigue momentarily.

His attention was ripped from the skies as a flurry of mortar shells erupted inside his perimeter. Dirt and mud cascaded down upon him, and he clasped his floppy hat against his head and cowered into the bottom of the trench. Screaming and yelling erupted from the tree line. Rifle and machine gun fire mixed with the exploding mortar shells. Bullets zipped and snapped overhead. He heard Grumskey yell, "Here they come! Hold your fire!"

He ignored the hollow pit in his stomach and scurried back to the lip of the trench. He peeked, seeing dark shapes sprinting and weaving through the mist, despite their own mortar barrage. He pulled back and cupped his hand and yelled, "Fix bayonets!" Most still had their bayonets attached. Those that didn't quickly remedied the situation.

No one had opened fire yet. Blakely rolled to a better firing position. His men looked at him with their rifles ready. Their exhausted, hard faces and eyes made Blakely wonder how he'd gotten lucky enough to lead such men. Finally, the word came down the line. "Open fire! Fire at will!"

Blakely lunged forward and propped his submachine gun on the dirt. It didn't take long to find a target. Japanese soldiers ran and weaved, closing the distance quickly. He fired a short burst into a shape emerging from the mist. The soldier's pith helmet flew off his head, and he dropped into the grass. Blakely adjusted slightly and squeezed off another short burst.

The two Vickers machine guns cut large swaths through the rushing Japanese. Interspersed Bren guns added to the carnage. Rifles cracked, and his own men cursed and yelled as they met the onrushing wave of humanity with lethal fire.

An explosion to Blakely's left silenced the Vickers gun suddenly and violently. Blakely spent the last of his magazine into a group of three Japanese soldiers who'd gotten bunched together. He half-rolled and inserted his last magazine. "Reloading," he yelled. He took one last look at the sky and spotted a dark smear of smoke tracing a sinister line to the ground. He rolled back to his stomach, found another target, and carefully aimed and fired.

∾

The attack didn't come as a surprise for Captain Grumskey; indeed, he expected to be hit during the night, but the timing was particularly bad. They were dangerously low on ammunition, manpower, and morale. The droning aircraft overhead promised resupply, and he'd enthusiastically relayed that reality to his men, but they'd received no help overnight as expected and knew they wouldn't be able to hold off a big push with their limited ammo. The men had gone above and beyond, and he couldn't blame them for feeling abandoned. Enemy strength estimates told them they were facing the same number of enemy troops but had less than half the men holding the airfield. But somehow, Moten hadn't felt the need to send them reinforcements. Grumskey tried to play it off, but the men knew the situation only too well. They were getting the shitty end of a short stick.

After ordering his men to open fire, Grumskey sprinted along the trench. He needed to get in contact with Moten. He needed support now, or they'd lose the position. Exploding mortar shells sent mud and shrapnel in every direction. He stayed low and finally arrived at the bunker. He pulled up short, taking in the grisly scene.

Smoke billowed from inside, and a good portion of the roof had collapsed and was on fire. A blackened soldier staggered from the white smoke and orange flames. He tripped into Grumskey's arms. His charred skin felt hot and flaked off in pinkish strips against Grumskey's hands. He carefully set the soldier down, trying to recognize him. He uttered, "Gaines?"

The soldier's eyes focused for an instant on Captain Grumskey, and he gave a slight nod. The slight move caused him to grimace. He tried to speak but could only manage a sickening gurgle.

Three commandos slammed into the trench beside Grumskey. Private First Class Joffee asked breathlessly, "Are you okay, Captain?"

Grumskey nodded. "I just got here."

Joffee said, "We were over there. Saw the bunker take two direct hits. White phosphorous rounds." He gazed at Corporal Gaines. "Bloody hell."

The other two commandos took positions along the bunker and fired their rifles repeatedly. Grumskey stared at Gaines and saw him take his last pain-filled breath. Joffee gave him a strained look, then joined his comrades on the firing line and quickly opened fire. He looked back at Grumskey, who seemed to be mesmerized. "Sir. Captain. We're almost out of ammo."

Grumskey tore his eyes away from his radioman's body. The world of chaos and war flooded back into focus. Sergeant Omar sprinted to him, his torn and muddy boots sloshing through the deep muddy bottom. His eyes blazed, reflecting the fire from the bunker. He looked questioningly at Captain Grumskey.

Grumskey stood and saw Japanese soldiers only yards away. He raised his Owen and quickly fired a burst into the closest soldier. The commandos struggled to get to their feet and meet the charging soldiers. Private Burrill got to his knees but slipped onto his face when he tried to stand. The nearest Japanese soldier thrust his bayonet. Grumskey aimed from the hip and pulled the trigger, but nothing happened. He watched the bayonet bury into Burrill's back. The private screamed and arched his back unnaturally.

Omar launched from the mud and drove his own bayonet into the side of the Japanese soldier. He pulled the blade out and thrust again, driving the soldier off Private Burrill.

Grumskey inserted his last magazine and pulled the bolt. The other commandos parried and thrust, locked in desperate combat. Private Joffee pushed his opponent backward and slipped into the bottom of the trench. Grumskey suddenly had a clear shot. He stepped forward and fired point-blank into the enemy soldier's chest. The stricken enemy reeled back and fell to his knees.

Grumskey yelled, "Fall back! Fall back!" He stepped out the back of the trench and crouched, bringing his SMG to his shoulder. He fired methodically into a seemingly endless line of charging Japanese.

The call to retreat went up and down the line. Grumskey saw his men sprinting from foxholes, trenches, and burning thatch huts, but many men were locked in hand-to-hand combat and could not break away. Grumskey pulled his last grenade and threw it directly at a surging line of soldiers as though throwing a fastball from a pitcher's mound. The grenade bounced off an enemy soldier's chest and exploded an instant later, shredding two others. He emptied his magazine and yelled until he thought his throat would bleed. "Fall back!" He slung his Owen and pulled his service revolver.

Sergeant Omar pushed him. "Move it." The commandos that were able had disengaged. Some sprinted while others crouched and fired. Grumskey ignored Omar and aimed his pistol at a bloody soldier charging through the trench. He pulled the trigger, but his bullets seemed to have no effect.

Omar sensed the danger at his back and spun just in time to bury his bayonet into the soldier's belly. Omar held on, but the soldier's momentum spun him back toward Grumskey. The soldier landed on his back. He clutched at the bayonet and gasped for air like a Koi fish out of water. Grumskey stepped forward and shot him in the forehead.

Omar pulled but couldn't extract his stuck rifle. Grumskey pushed him. "Leave it. Get outta here." Omar reluctantly released the rifle and ran. Grumskey emptied the revolver toward more charging soldiers, then followed his sergeant.

He sensed the pursuing Japanese only yards behind but kept running. They entered the grass and veered toward the more protected riverbank. What was left of his men sprinted in disarray all around him. Some splashed through the river, others weaved through brambles and thin trees. Bullets smacked and zinged all around, and a few found their marks with sickening results.

Lieutenant Blakely finally stopped running when he ran over an embankment and nearly had his head blown off by three other commandos. He recognized them immediately, despite most of their features being covered with blood, mud, and soot. "Don't shoot. Don't shoot," he stammered between heaving breaths.

Corporal Scott kept his rifle aimed but shifted the barrel back the way they'd come. "Glad to see you're alive, sir."

Blakely crouched. He still held his Owen SMG, but he'd burned through the rest of his ammo. "Glad to be alive, Scott. How much ammo you got left?"

"May as well be a spear. I'm empty. We're all empty."

Blakely slung his SMG and pulled his revolver. "I've got some pistol ammo but might as well be shooting spit wads through a straw. Why'd you stop?"

Scott shrugged. "Seemed like a good place to catch our breath."

Rifle fire cracked, and Blakely saw darting shapes in the distance. "Seen anyone else?"

Scott pointed with his thumb. "A minute ago."

The others kept scanning the trees and grass while Blakely finished checking his revolver. "Come on, then. Let's find Grumskey and the others. Don't wanna get caught behind the Nips." He took one last look, then rose to a crouch with his pistol ready and backed away from the embankment. The others got to their feet and trotted across the shallow water near the bank. Blakely turned and followed them, adding, "The river leads straight to Wau. If we don't run across the others, at least we'll be near friendly lines."

Scott said, "If our guys still hold Wau, that is."

Blakely was thinking the same thing. "Now, now, Corporal. Chin up. That's no way to talk about the Regulars. I'm sure they're doing all they can."

Scott turned, and Blakely gave him a grin.

"Right...," Scott said.

The sporadic rifle shots suddenly grew in intensity and volume. The commandos exchanged glances and moved back to the embankment. Through the grass and thin trees they could see darting shapes, explosions, and chaos. Almost as though the Australians were attacking.

Private Hussey looked at Blakely and asked, "What you think that's all about?"

It struck Blakely how blue the young commando's eyes looked against his blackened face. "Gotta be our reinforcements. Our boys don't have enough ammo."

Scott nodded his agreement. "I think you're right. It's the only thing that makes sense."

Private Logan couldn't keep the excitement out of his voice. "Reinforcements means we still hold the airfield." He went to stand up. "Let's join 'em."

Blakely grabbed his arm and pulled him back down. "Get down," he hissed, and the urgency made them all duck. Blakely went silent and hugged the embankment. He whispered, "Japs moving this way. Might try a flanking move."

Corporal Scott eased his head up, then came quickly back down and whispered, "At least ten of 'em. They're upstream of us. Probably use the river the whole way and walk right into us. We gotta go now."

He started to move, but Blakely held up his hand and hissed, "Stop. It's too exposed. They'll see you and shoot you in the back."

Scott hissed back, "Well, we've got no ammo...we're out of options. We have to try."

Blakely held up his pistol. "I do."

"There's no way. You might get one or two, but—"

Blakely interrupted, "I'll get 'em to follow me. When you hear my shots, you run like hell and don't look back."

Scott looked as though he'd eaten rancid bully beef. "That's suicide, sir." He shook his head. "I won't let you do it."

He made a quick thrust, trying for the revolver, but Blakely deflected him. "When you hear the shots," he repeated. He got his feet beneath him and moved upstream a few yards.

Scott exchanged worried glances with the others. He hissed, "Blakely, dammit. No." Blakely looked back at him and grinned, then put his finger to his lips for silence. The firefight from the east continued, joined now with mortar and machine gun fire.

Blakely broke eye contact and lifted his head over the embankment. The Japanese weren't trying to be quiet, and he spotted them easily. They'd nearly made it to the edge of the river. He had to strike before that to keep them from seeing the others.

Blakely closed his eyes and tried to calm his thumping heart. He felt sick to his stomach. He thought of his home and his family, eagerly awaiting his return. He hesitated for a moment but didn't allow his fear to get the better of him.

He stood, leaped onto the riverbank, and ran straight at the nearest Japanese soldier. He sprinted with the pistol held straight out. As the soldier turned in surprise, Blakely pulled the trigger twice. He knew he had little chance of hitting anything, but that wasn't the point. His shots sent the soldiers onto their faces.

Blakely immediately turned and sprinted toward the sounds of battle, screaming at the top of his lungs to keep the enemy's attention. Bullets chased him, and he heard his pursuers yelling. He dove behind a thin tree and waited. The firefight raged behind him. He chanced a glance toward the battle and saw muzzle flashes and mortar explosions.

He refocused his attention forward and heard soldiers moving steadily but cautiously toward him. He got his knees beneath him and peeked around the edge of the thin tree. A bullet smacked the tree, and he saw the puff of smoke from the muzzle. He reflex shot twice, then rolled away from the tree. A red hot poker suddenly jabbed into his stomach, and he wondered if he'd rolled over lava.

His mind reeled in waves of agony, and he closed his eyes. Images of red-hot pain tormented him. He sensed a presence and opened his eyes. A huge looming figure stood over him, blocking out the rays of sunlight streaking through the thin layer of leaves. The figure said something he couldn't understand, but he desperately wanted to. "Wh-what?" he pleaded. A sudden flash, then nothing.

24

Tarkington tried to shut his mind to the countless insects crawling over his body. He'd hoped the rain-soaked ground would keep them to a minimum, but that wasn't the case. As darkness gave way to morning light, the need to stay motionless became more pronounced.

In the wee hours of the morning, Raker had led them through a maze of enemy outposts, and with only an hour before daylight, they finally found a good thicket to lie up in. With each passing minute, the GIs realized they'd placed themselves much closer to the enemy camp's perimeter than expected.

The muddy wetness seeped into their hand-scraped depressions. Tarkington willed himself not to shiver for fear of rustling the leaves and branches he'd pulled over himself. Daylight revealed more and more enemy soldiers.

Tarkington studied the camp. A line of hammocks strung between the sparse trees held enemy troops. The nearest, only thirty yards away, suddenly came to life. A soldier pushed his way out and stretched his arms over his head, arched his back, then performed a few deep knee bends. It reminded him of watching a monarch butterfly emerge from a chrysalis. The thought chilled him and reminded him of the creepers moving on his arms and inside his pant legs.

He looked right and finally saw Raker's hiding spot, but only because he gave him a slight wave. Camouflage had kept them alive up to this point, and today would be no exception. He had little doubt they could remain in position and never be discovered, even if an enemy soldier stepped on them.

He slowly moved his eyes back to the camp, which was quickly becoming a hive of activity. He thought about Winkleman's question a few hours before. What was the plan? He didn't have an answer then, and he didn't now. He only knew they'd found what had to be the enemy's HQ.

The lone tent he could see had a constant flow of soldiers in and out. He suspected the head honchos were inside, planning and directing the assault on Wau. But what could he do? He couldn't charge in guns blazing. Sure, they might kill a few officers, maybe even the man in charge, but they'd be gunned down in a hail of bullets. Tarkington shook his head to himself. *We're not a suicide squad.*

He soon noticed a new sound. It started as a low buzz and grew steadily. He slowly lifted his head but couldn't see the aircraft he knew must be there. Soon, the sound was a constant drone, adding to the ever-present buzz and squawks of insects and birds. *Ours or theirs?* Probably both, he decided. He wished there was some way he could contact them and have them strafe or bomb the HQ. He discarded the thought, knowing their radios barely worked even with line of sight, and he did not know if it was even possible to talk directly to pilots.

He thought about fading back the way they'd come. If they got close enough to Willoth and his commandos, they could get in contact and confirm the HQ's location. Willoth could radio the information to General Moten, who could contact Moresby, who could talk to the attack pilots. But even that was futile. Without accurate maps, he couldn't give them coordinates. Even if they got the information in time, it would most likely be a waste of munitions and just chew up empty jungle.

He bit his lower lip. The enemy was close—too close. Even sending one man back would be risky. Japanese infested the area. Moving in daylight—even with their highly tuned training—might get them killed.

He closed his eyes, took a deep breath, and let it out slowly. *Patience.*

They were well-hidden and would remain so, as long as they stayed in place. Like he'd told Winkleman, *We'll just wait and see what happens.*

~

As dawn broke in the east, Henry nudged Nance. Nance stiffened but didn't make a sound. Henry heard the difference in his breathing. He whispered, "Welcome back, sunshine."

Nance lay only a few feet to Henry's right. Nance whispered back, "Thanks, mate. Did I snore?"

Henry grinned. "Nah, but you're a twitchy son of a bitch. Like you were running a race or something. Got any dog in you?"

Nance gave him a confused look. "Dog?"

"You know. When a dog sleeps they twitch, like they're dreaming of chasing a damned squirrel or something."

Nance grinned and stroked his beard. Bits of dirt and scruff came off in his hand. He itched around his cheeks, and the noise grated on Henry's nerves. Nance said, "I don't think my mother ever laid with any dogs, mate. Although she probably thought of my dad that way once or twice." He took the binoculars out of the case, adjusted the strap, and scanned. "Have you seen any..." He stopped his scan and worked the focus knob. "You see this?" he asked.

"You mean the Jap HQ?" Henry spit out the piece of grass he'd chewed down to a nub and put a fresh one in. "Yep."

Nance adjusted himself and continued to scan the area. "Not an easy shot through those trees, but there's plenty of targets. You want me to call 'em out for you?"

Henry ran his finger across his tongue, then wiped a smudge off the lens of the scope. "I've been watching them, but your binocs have better reach and a wider lens. Hard for me to figure ranks from here." He sensed Nance growing more and more excited as he scanned Japanese officers. Henry said, "I've been searching for the rest of the squad. I know they're down there, but I can't see 'em." He tapped the walkie by his side. "Nothing on the radio, but that's nothing new."

Nance grunted and continued scanning. "I'll keep watching. So far all the officers look young. I'll know the high-brow when I see 'em. Once I find him, I'll keep track of him until you're ready to take the shot."

Henry shook his head. "Whoa, there. Our mission's covering the rest of the squad. I'm not shooting unless it's covering them."

Nance took the binoculars from his eyes and stared. Henry returned his withering gaze. Nance itched his beard, then said, "We have a chance to kill their commander. We can wreak havoc on their entire attack plan, perhaps even stop it altogether."

Henry pursed his lips, considering his response. "Killing their commander won't stop the attack. I'm no expert on Jap military doctrine, but I'll bet they've got layers just like we do." He shook his head. "We shoot now, we'll stir up trouble, which may get my friends killed." He put his eye back to the scope and lowered his voice. "I'm not gonna do that."

Nance's face reddened, and he clenched his fists. Henry thought he felt the heat coming off him. Henry drawled slowly, "You try taking this weapon from me...you'll pay the price."

Henry took his eye from the scope, and they stared at one another for nearly a full minute before Nance finally nodded and looked away. "All right, Yank. We'll do it your way."

Henry's eye went back to the scope. "See if you can find the squad. My guess is they'll be to the right of the camp, but they could be anywhere."

Nance raised the binocs but instead of searching the forest, he scanned the sky. He pointed skyward and said, "Bunch of planes up there. Maybe they'll see the camp and do the dirty work for us."

"Can you tell if they're friendly?"

Nance adjusted and readjusted the focus and finally answered, "See a few with twin tails. Never seen those before. The rest are just dots...can't get a good read on 'em."

Henry remembered seeing the P-38s parked at Port Moresby's airfield. "The twin tails have gotta be P-38s...American. I don't think the Nips have anything that looks the same."

Nance pointed and waved his arm.

Henry reached out and pulled Nance's arm down. "Knock it off, dammit. You'll give away our position. What the holy hell's wrong with you?"

Nance never took the binoculars from his eyes, and he couldn't keep the smile off his face. "Sorry. But they're fighting up there. Can you see the tracers? Beautiful. Like a light show or a dance routine."

Henry strained to see better. He could see dots, twisting contrails, and dim spurts of tracer fire. "Dance or not, those are real bullets."

Nance raised his voice. "Whoa, look at that."

Henry had had enough. He yanked the binoculars from Nance's hands and seethed, "Keep your voice down before you get us both killed."

Nance looked like a scolded child. He pointed to the sky, beseeching Henry to look. Henry sighed and finally looked up. He saw a black streak spiraling down. It disappeared behind the crest of a hill, but the rumble a few seconds later left little doubt about the outcome. Henry handed the binoculars back. "Okay, you've had your little show—now keep your damned head in the game and find me the rest of the squad."

Major Shilansky led the three P-38s of Red Flight to eight thousand feet. Far overhead, the remnants of white contrails mixed with darker, more foreboding black smoke trails. He strained to see the P-40 Warhawks, or as the Aussies called them, Kittyhawks, but soon gave up. He called Blue Flight, "Blue Flight leader, this is Red flight leader. Over."

The response came immediately: "Red Flight lead, read you loud and clear. Over."

"We softened up the approach for Gallant. Any more bogeys try to sneak through? Over."

"Negative. Nothing. Over."

Shilansky could hear Captain Connor's disappointment. He keyed the mic again. "Red Flight is at eight thousand. Heading is zero nine zero. Over."

"Copy, Red Flight. Tallyho. I have you in sight. We're at your eleven o'clock high. Over."

Shilansky searched and finally saw the glinting of sun off a cockpit canopy. "Tallyho, Blue Flight. Maintain racecourse pattern and call them if you see 'em. Out." Shilansky called his flight, "Keep your eyes peeled. I've gone through most of my ammo. Red Two, how you fixed for ammo? Over."

"I've still got plenty, Skipper. Over."

"Copy. Johnson has the lead on any bogeys. Out."

From eight thousand feet, the battle raging along the river didn't look like much. Tracer fire crisscrossed the river. He saw puffs of explosions and a few streams of smoke swirling upward. He thanked his lucky stars that he wasn't down there slugging it out alongside the infantry.

A steady flow of C-47s landed, unloaded, and quickly took off again. The planes stacked up as they waited for the runway to clear, making perfect targets for enemy Zeros. A large line of explosions west of the airfield caught his attention. He squinted, searching for the Japanese Betty bombers he guessed had dropped their loads, but gave up after a few seconds.

His radio came alive. "Zeros coming out of the sun!" He recognized Second Lieutenant Myles's shaky voice. Before he could spot the threat, red tracer rounds sliced past his canopy. He heard and felt a sickening thump, and his right wing dipped as though he'd hit turbulence.

He instinctively spun the yoke left. His normally agile plane felt sluggish and heavy, but it turned as more tracers ripped past his wing. He pushed the nose down and pushed to full throttle, but something was amiss. He quickly studied the gauges, seeing his oil pressure dropping and the heat rising in the number two engine. A quick glance out the windscreen confirmed his fears. Heavy black smoke spewed from the cowling. Through jagged chunks of metal, he could see the guts of the engine.

He shut the engine down with quick efficiency and feathered the big three-bladed propeller. It spun freely, creating as little drag as possible. The smoke continued, but he'd cut the prospect of fire down considerably. He ignored the radio chatter as much as he could until he'd taken care of his ship.

He'd named her Maiden's Bounty—a reference to his wife's voluptuousness. If his wife ever saw the suggestive paint job on the nose, she'd blush deeply, then smack the crap outta him.

He tore his mind from her sexy image, amazed how the male mind could think of such things at a time like this.

With the engine under control, he swiveled, searching for Zeros as he continued his dive toward the valley. Nothing. He pulled the yoke back, feeling the mushiness all over again and hating the feeling. He maintained a shallow dive and keyed his mic. "This is Red Leader. Any one see the bogey that got me?"

"He's off you. You okay, Ski?"

Shilansky recognized his wingman's voice, First Lieutenant Lance Johnson. Shilansky answered. "I lost my number two and have some aileron issues, but I'm still flying. Where are the bogeys?"

"Two of 'em came out of the clouds. They hit you and took a bite outta Myles, too. They pulled into the clouds, and the others are still looking for the sneaky bastards."

Shilansky pulled into a turn back west toward the airfield. He saw Johnson's sleek P-38 off his port wing, giving his plane a once-over. Shilansky keyed his mic and motioned emphatically. "Get back to the transports. Japs might try to pull us away from 'em. They'll be sitting ducks."

Johnson replied, "With one engine, you are, too. I'm staying with you, Skipper."

Shilansky saw red. "Negative, Red Two. Cover the transports. That's an order, Lance." He added, almost as an afterthought, "I'll be fine. I'll make my way to Dobodura. Good luck. Out."

Johnson gave him a tip-o'-the-hat salute and turned west. The radio chatter had slackened but suddenly intensified again. He heard C-47 pilots calling out incoming bogeys from the north. He recognized Captain Connor's calm voice, answering the call for help. Now that Shilansky was out of the game, Connor was in charge. Shilansky listened to him quickly and efficiently vector his flight onto the Japanese Zeros.

Shilansky punched the flight yoke. "Dammit." He desperately wanted to join the fight, but with one engine, he'd just be in the way. He consoled himself with the one confirmed kill and the devastating strafing run. He'd done all he could, and now it was time to nurse his stricken Maiden's Bounty to a suitable airfield.

He trimmed the aircraft to lessen the strain on the rudders and shredded ailerons. Flying on one engine wasn't optimal, and the folks at

Lockheed didn't recommend it for long periods of time. But he was confident he could nurse her to Dobodura.

He leveled off at two thousand five hundred feet and listened to the radio chatter as he adjusted the map on his knee board. Dobodura airfield was listed, but he knew it was an approximation at best. The only thing he knew for sure was the course from Wau airfield to Dobodura, but distances tended to be a guestimate. Fuel wasn't an issue as long as he nursed the engine. If he missed Dobodura, he could ditch in the ocean and swim to shore. Natives were generally friendly, unless he was unlucky enough to run into one of the headhunter tribes he'd heard whispered rumors about.

He turned south and swept the skies, realizing in a brief panic that he hadn't done so in at least two minutes. *That's a good way to get your tail shot off, Ski.*

He'd just completed his search when a flash out of the corner of his eye caught his attention. He knew he was in trouble immediately. The two Zeros dropped from the cloud cover at just the wrong time. His green paint scheme would make it difficult to see against the backdrop of the jungle, but the wisp of black smoke streaming from his dead engine pinpointed him like a beacon.

The Zeros hesitated for an instant, and Shilansky thought he might make the distant cloud bank before they saw him. He felt a lead weight in his gut as both agile fighters banked toward him like lions finding the weakest wildebeest in the herd.

Shilansky considered using the radio, but he didn't want to pull anyone away from the primary mission: protecting the transports. Besides, they sounded busy.

He took a deep breath. He wouldn't die running away. He pushed the single engine to full power and turned into the oncoming Zeros. The turn felt agonizingly slow, but Maiden's Bounty made it with a few seconds to spare.

Their closing speed increased to nearly seven hundred miles per hour. Shilansky centered his aiming reticle on the lead plane, growing steadily larger. His thumb rested upon the 20mm cannon. The Zeros' wings twinkled and tracer swept out. He distantly felt impacts. Shilansky pressed the trigger. The cannon's slower cadence and heavy clang always reminded him of his father's workplace at the steel factory.

The next instant both Zeros passed by him in blurry-green flashes. He let out the breath he'd been holding, and the blood pounding in his ears gave way to awful sounds of wrenching, grinding metal. Every instrument gauge told him that Maiden's Bounty had taken critical damage. He didn't need the instruments to tell him that, though. He could feel her dying through the yoke.

The cockpit smelled of burning electrical wires, and he worried about a fire. Keeping one hand on the yoke, he struggled to open the canopy. Glorious wind filled the space, and he worked to unfasten his harness. The forces of gravity seemed to work hard against him, but he finally managed to unsnap himself. He glimpsed blue sky overhead. He pulled on the yoke, then turned it all the way to starboard. His number one engine burned brightly, and he hoped the self-sealing gas tanks would keep the fuel from igniting.

He didn't remember bailing out. Gravity took over, and he simply fell out of the cockpit. His head yanked viciously, sending lightning bolts through his brain. He distantly realized he'd forgotten to unhook the radio cord. Pain flashed like lightning. But then he was falling, falling, falling.

Through a hazy fog, he remembered he should do something—something important. He clutched at the parachute rip cord. He finally found it and yanked hard. He felt a massively uncomfortable slap and pull around his groin before the world went mercifully black.

25

The activity within the perimeter of the enemy HQ increased as the morning crept on. Tarkington and the other GIs stayed still and silent and took it all in. Tarkington could just make out the outline of an open-sided tent through the trees. He figured it had to be where most of the officers were. Soldiers entered and left as though delivering constant messages. At least a company of soldiers milled about the area. Too many for the five of them to take on, even with the element of surprise.

Tarkington searched the northern highlands. He saw the outline of the cliff they'd climbed the night before in the hazy distance. Somewhere between him and it, Henry and Nance lingered. He wondered how close they were and whether they'd spotted their position. He doubted it; even Henry's eagle eyes wouldn't be able to spot them. But he'd have a good idea of their whereabouts. Even with their help, though, there were too many enemy soldiers protecting the HQ.

Time passed slowly. Being beneath multiple layers of leaves and dirt, and with the relatively warm day devoid of rain, he felt warm for the first time in a long time. Sure, it was dank and wet and crawled with insects, but he felt relatively comfortable. If not for the nearby enemy, he might've even tried for a nap.

He shook the thought off and went through the motions—moving first his toes, then each foot, then his fingers and hands. He moved as many parts of his body as possible to maintain blood flow and avoid cramping. It was excruciating, but helped to pass the time.

The droning of aircraft engines increased, and he raised his eyes to the sky. The thin treetop cover allowed him to see streaking contrails. The flyboys were at it again, mixing it up with the Japanese Zeros and bombers, he suspected. He saw a streak of tracer fire. He could only see dots. Dark smoke mixed with the white contrails, reminding him that those pilots faced death the same way they did down here, they just didn't have to deal with bugs, rain, and mud. He wondered if he knew any of the pilots fighting overhead. He'd met a few Australian P-40 pilots when they'd been stationed in Milne Bay months before.

He kept his eyes on the dot spewing black smoke. The pilot had brought the plane low, and Tarkington saw the distinct outline of a twin-tailed P-38. It passed nearly directly overhead, and he could see that one engine was shut down. The propeller spun freely in the wind but still smoked slightly. He watched the lone plane turn south and streak away. It was nearly out of sight when Tarkington heard the roar of more aircraft. Two green-painted Zeros had dropped from the clouds and turned to give chase.

Tarkington remembered where he was. He tore his eyes from the sky and saw enemy soldiers pointing skyward, obviously just as enthralled by the dance of death transpiring overhead. Soldiers abandoned their positions and moved to the clearing for a better view. Tarkington licked his dry lips. Perhaps this would be a good time to get themselves out of the area. Were the Japanese distracted enough?

He glanced toward Raker, who looked like a mound of dirt with eyes. He stared back at Tarkington. The sound of distant machine guns pulled his attention skyward again for an instant. He glimpsed the fight overhead. The stricken P-38 pilot had turned into the Zeros. It looked as though they were playing a lethal game of high-speed chicken. The soldiers in the clearing raised their voices and pointed. Soon the entire camp was watching.

The guns rose to a cacophony of sound. The buzz saw staccato combined with screeching engines and rending metal. Some of the Japanese raised rifles, but the range was too far.

Tarkington decided. He signaled Raker. Raker nodded and signaled the next man in line. Tarkington pushed himself from the wet mud and immediately felt cold again. He shimmied his way from beneath the leaves and dirt, careful not to make too much noise but wanting to move fast enough and optimize his time while the enemy soldiers were occupied.

Staying on his belly, he turned away from the HQ and crawled west as fast as feasibly possible. The other four GIs moved with him. They still had piles of dirt and leaves on their backs, reminding Tarkington of some ancient lumbering troop of tortoises.

They'd made it twenty yards when the yelling from the camp made Tarkington glance back. The soldiers were even more excited, continuing to point and call out to one another. A deep rumbling crash rolled over the area. Tarkington saw a fireball through the trees. Thick gouts of black smoke curled into the sky. *Poor son of a gun.* Then he saw an olive drab-colored parachute beyond the fireball. He lost sight of it an instant later.

One loud yell cut off the enemy soldiers' excited voices. Tarkington figured it had to be an NCO barking orders and getting control. There was no other sound like it. An angry NCO's bark was universal and recognized across all branches and nationalities.

The distraction allowed the GIs to move one hundred yards from the camp without being spotted. Tarkington pulled himself into a thicket and waved the others to join him. They faced one another on their bellies. Winkleman was the first to speak. "I saw that P-38 pilot bail out. The Nips saw it too. They're going after him."

Tarkington had only seen the chute and didn't know who it belonged to. "You sure it wasn't one of the Zero pilots?"

Winkleman nodded emphatically. "I'm sure. One Zero flew off, spewing smoke but kept flying. The American bailed out."

Tarkington nodded. "I saw the chute, but didn't see who it was."

Winkleman's eyes blazed. "We have to go get him before the Japs do. They'll torture him for sure."

Tarkington looked around the group. They all looked just as determined. "Okay. Raker, lead us around the camp. The Japs'll focus on the pilot, but we don't know how many are out there. We'll have to hurry. Once the Nips have him..." He didn't need to finish the thought.

"There they are," Corporal Nance exclaimed, unable to keep the excitement from his voice. "Found your Yanks, mate."

Henry adjusted his captured rifle and peered through the scope. Nance described where they were, but Henry interrupted, "I've got 'em. They're damned near inside the perimeter. No wonder they weren't moving. Looks like they're taking advantage while the Japs are distracted watching the flyboys."

Nance shifted his binoculars. "That P-38 pilot's bailed out. He's gonna land in the valley to the southeast of the camp." The smashing rumble of the P-38 blowing up on impact rolled over their position moments later. Nance added, "Got out just in time. Lucky bugger."

Henry drawled, "Lucky? Son of a bitch is about to be captured. That ain't lucky at all." He kept watching his squad through the scope. They looked like moving lumps of earth. He could only see their hands and feet occasionally. He had to concentrate to keep from losing them in the small reticle of the scope. They finally moved into a thicket of bushes, and Henry lost sight of them.

Nance continued watching the Japanese camp. Two separate squads formed and moved southeast in two lines. "The Nips are going after the pilot. Two separate squads."

Henry moved his scope off the GI's position and rubbed his stubbled chin. Nance took his eyes from the binocs and watched Henry contemplate. A full minute passed before Henry made up his mind. "We're moving."

"Moving? Where?"

Henry was already slinging the rifle over his shoulder and collecting himself. "We're gonna support the others while they try to snatch that pilot before the Japs do."

Nance looked exasperated. He glanced through the binoculars, trying to find Tarkington and the others. "I can't even see them. How do you know that's what they're doing?"

Henry didn't look at him, just kept packing. "I just do. That's all. Now hurry the hell up."

Major Shilansky hit the ground hard. The jolt and pain pulled him from the blackness. He opened his eyes. Everything looked blurry and distorted. For a moment, he didn't know where he was. But as his eyes cleared, he saw green grass swaying over his head, and beyond that a blue sky dotted with clouds and streaks of oily black smoke. He suddenly remembered his P-38 being shot out from beneath him. *Maiden's Bounty.*

He tried to roll onto his side, but something kept him tethered to the ground. Spasms of pain shot through his body as though electric current were being forced through him.

He shifted onto his back. He reached up and felt the parachute lines. He felt for the release, but his hands didn't seem to want to work. He finally managed to unhook the right side. He felt the tension release from his body. He rolled right and this time succeeded in sitting up. The grass towered above his head and swayed in a light breeze. He unclasped the left side, and the silk caught the wind and blew away a few feet. He stared at the flowing silk and distantly thought he should collect it and send it back to his wife. She'd make a beautiful dress from it.

He shook his head, trying to rid his brain of the cobwebs. He closed his eyes and took deep breaths in and out, evaluating his body. Everything ached. He felt sharp pains from his left arm and saw splotches of blood seeping through his torn sleeve. He pulled back the fabric, wincing as the pain magnified. His forearm dripped blood, but he couldn't determine the severity of the cuts and slashes. He pushed his sleeve back into place and fumbled for the medical kit on his belt. It wasn't there. He must've lost it when he bailed out. What else had he lost? He felt for his pistol strapped to his lower leg. The pistol felt good. He pulled up his pant leg and unsheathed the Colt .45. It looked to be unscathed. He chambered a round.

He tried to remember his approximate location. He'd been flying southeast toward the sea when the Zeros jumped him. He'd turned into them, west. He thought he must still be east of Wau. Were there Japanese this far in the hills?

He pulled himself gingerly to his feet. He staggered as pain shot through his body. He swayed on shaky legs. Nausea suddenly overtook him, and he fell to his knees and threw up violently.

He wiped his mouth and tried to stand again. He took his time and kept the nausea at bay. He took in his surroundings. He'd landed in the middle of a vast field of kunai grass. He spotted the inky black smoke of his burning aircraft.

He felt remorse for losing her. She'd gotten him through so many missions. He felt as though he'd let her down. He searched the sky. He saw distant contrails but couldn't see any of his comrades. The airfield must be hidden behind the peaks. He listened for the sound of aircraft but only heard the light wind rustling the grass.

The wind gusted his chute, and it billowed. Seeing no immediate threat, he holstered his pistol and pulled the shroud lines toward him. No reason to make it easier for the Japs to find him. The edges of the grass cut, sliced, and held the silk as though trying to claim it for itself. He finally pulled the rest in and wrapped the lines around the silk, making as small a package as possible. Doctrine said he should bury it, but he wasn't about to waste the time and energy. He left it at his feet. Which way to go?

He oriented himself. He contemplated moving to the wreckage but decided against it. There'd be nothing to salvage. His head cleared with each passing second. He thought perhaps he should stay where he was. Someone might've seen him crash and were on their way. He spit, trying to rid his mouth of the acidic taste of vomit. No one saw him. He'd been alone. His flight assumed him to be halfway to Dobodura airfield by now.

He drew his pistol again and took his first steps west. He'd made it forty yards when he heard a sound carried on the wind. He stopped and listened, cocking his ears to the east. Voices. He spun, searching for the source. Someone *had* seen him, and they were on their way to rescue him. Three hundred yards east, he saw movement in a lightly forested area. He nearly waved but stopped himself. *You don't know who they are, fool.*

He crouched, keeping just his head above the grass. He could see rifles and funny-shaped helmets. The sweat on his forehead turned icy cold. *Japs.*

He ducked down and felt the nausea again. He tasted the acidic bile rising and kept it down. He fought to control his spiking heart rate. He could hear it pounding in his ears.

There had been many discussions in the various O clubs talking about the possibility of being captured by the Japanese. Stories from infantry troops, both Australian and American, told of horrific treatment, disfigurement, and beheadings. The few Allied airmen that had bailed out over enemy territory had rarely been seen again. Had they been tortured and beheaded, or consumed by the jungle? No one knew for sure. He figured if even half of what he'd heard was true, he wanted no part of it.

Would they go to the wreckage? Would they find the parachute? He cursed himself for not burying it or bringing it with him. The thought of backtracking all the way to the chute made his bowels loosen. Would they be able to track him? The soft, muddy ground left perfect boot prints. Of course they'd be able to track him, and of course they'd find the chute. He had to get the hell out of there fast. Once they found the chute, the hunt would be on in earnest.

Staying low, he trotted through the kunai grass, ignoring the countless micro-cuts across his hands. He angled toward the nearest clump of trees. He hoped the ground would be more solid and he could lose them. He forced himself to keep moving. *Don't look back. Keep moving. Don't look back.*

∾

Raker moved quickly, weaving through the thin forest, using whatever cover presented itself. After conferring with the others, he took the squad southeast, far around the enemy camp, before turning them back east. He used the oily black smoke from the burning plane's wreckage as a sort of landmark. From what he'd seen and what Winkleman confirmed, it looked like the pilot had landed within a mile and west of the wreckage.

The Japanese would beeline it for the parachute. If the pilot was dead or unconscious, they'd get there first. But if he was alive and uninjured, they assumed he'd head east toward the airfield and friendly lines. They planned to get in front and hopefully intercept him. The immense area and nearly innumerable possibilities could make all the assumptions and efforts null and void, but they had to try.

After being cooped up watching the enemy camp, it felt good to be moving. They'd trained for long laagers behind enemy lines, but it didn't make the inactivity and mind-numbing hours any easier to get through.

Finally, Raker came to the edge of the forest. An immense field of kunai grass extended for at least a mile before it disappeared into another valley. The smoke from the plane had dimmed but was still visible, snaking into the partially clouded sky. It came from beyond the grasses to the northeast. He guessed it wasn't more than a mile away. He scanned the grasses as the rest of the squad took positions to either side. There was no sign of movement.

Tarkington stood beside him. Raker mused, "Wonder if he went to the wreckage."

Tarkington shook his head. "He must know he's in enemy territory. The Japs have probably already searched the area."

Stollman pointed. "There. Japs." Everyone turned and strained to see what he'd seen. "The last of 'em just went into the trees. I was lucky to see 'em at all."

"Shit," Tarkington cursed. "We got here too late. They're already in front of us."

Raker looked sheepish, but he couldn't have gotten them there any faster. He looked out over the swaying grasses. "We could hustle across this field and get there quicker than going around and through the trees."

Tarkington squinted as he looked over the field. "Still won't put us in front of the Nips." He looked northeast toward the enemy camp. "They must've seen the chute and gone straight to it. It didn't take us long to get here. They got across this field fast—probably didn't even search through it. They must've picked up his trail and are in pursuit." He looked around the group and got nods. "You get any idea how many?"

Stollman shook his head. "Saw at least three..."

Tarkington continued through his logic. "Doubt they'd send less than two squads, maybe three. Either way, we're outnumbered. I don't relish gallivanting across this field and running into the Jap rear." He stroked his chin. "Let's just assume the Nips are gonna capture the poor S.O.B." He looked each man in the eye. "That doesn't sit well with me." He looked out over the grass. "I'll bet they'll be so excited about their prisoner, they'll come straight back through here with him."

Winkleman grinned, reading his mind. "Ambush." Tarkington nodded. Winkleman's grin disappeared. "In the grass? Not much cover."

Vick pointed toward the tree line back northwest. "We could hit 'em from there."

Tarkington shook his head. "Too close to their camp. The bulk of their forces would hear the firefight and be on us too quick." He pointed to the middle of the field. "We find their track and set up on it."

Vick looked skeptical. "Even if there's just one squad, we'll still be outnumbered—and what keeps 'em from killing the pilot as soon as we spring the ambush? Or us killing him accidentally, for that matter."

Tarkington explained, "My guess is they'll be in single file. They'll use their old track to avoid having to cut a new trail. We'll set up alongside the track and wait till we see the pilot. We'll snatch him right from under their noses." He got more doubtful looks. "I know it's not optimum. There's a lot of variables." He held up his palms. "I'm not trying to get any of us killed. If it's not perfect, we won't attack. We'll let 'em pass and come up with some-thing else, or call the whole thing off and let the pilot fend for himself." The GIs searched each other's faces and finally nodded.

Stollman said, "Wish I had more demolitions. We could really put 'em through the ringer."

"Too risky for the pilot," Tarkington replied. "We've got plenty of ammo and grenades. We'll snatch the pilot, lob grenades, and shoot through the grass. They won't know what hit 'em...then we'll fade away."

Vick smiled. "I'm liking it more and more, Tark. Let's find their trail."

26

Major Shilansky stopped running where the grass turned to forest and looked behind him. He saw distant bobbing heads snaking their way through the grass. They moved slowly, obviously searching for him. He watched, hoping against hope that they wouldn't find his parachute. He'd wadded it well, and it was an immense field. Perhaps they wouldn't find it or his tracks.

He knew he should keep moving, but he couldn't help watching their progress. He'd seen enemy soldiers from the sky, but they looked like dots that he could simply file away as targets, devoid of humanity. But down here, he could hear them talking, could hear them coughing and occasionally sneezing. He could hear their humanity, and it terrified him.

He knew ground troops especially reviled pilots. Even Allied soldiers held them in contempt for their grand accommodations out of the blood and mud. Enemy troops would hold a special hatred for him. Especially these soldiers. As the squadron commander, he'd been briefed on the enemy ground forces—air attacks along their entire journey from Rabaul to Lae had harassed them daily. Reports estimated they'd lost half their force. They'd love to take their revenge on a captured airman.

He heard yelling. He watched one soldier jumping up and down, waving and yelling. His stomach dropped. They'd found his chute. It was only a matter of time before they picked up his boot prints. Panic rising, he looked at his surroundings. The sparse forest provided little cover. The ground wasn't as spongy soft here, but it wasn't hard-pack either.

He searched for roots and rocks to step on, but the ground consisted mostly of fallen leaves and dirt. He glanced back and saw the bobbing heads of Japanese in single file now jogging directly at him. He clutched the pistol in his sweaty palm. Perhaps he should find a good place for a last stand. He had three magazines of .45-caliber ACP. He could do serious damage and save the last bullet for himself.

The thought staggered him. *Am I about to die? Are these my last moments?* He pictured his wife, Maryann, sipping an old-fashioned on the deck overlooking the garden. Her sultry dark eyes perfectly matched her thick, dark hair. She never failed to arouse his interest, even after fifteen years of marriage. He craved her like he craved air. He knew there was no way he could end his own life. He'd survive to see her and hold her again. He had to.

He holstered his pistol and snapped it securely in place. He took off running, not trying to hide his tracks now. He had to get as far away as possible, then try to figure out how to lose them.

He ran until his breath came in great heaves. His legs burned as much as his lungs. He stopped and clutched a tree trunk. He couldn't see the Japanese soldiers. He took that as a good sign, but he didn't have time to catch his breath. He pushed forward, not running but settling into a comfortable, mile-eating pace. He didn't have a destination in mind, just distance. So far, Lady Luck was on his side. Perhaps she'd present him with a solution. He just had to keep moving.

What seemed like a long time later, he stopped again and leaned against a tree. His feet ached. He had no sense how far he'd run. It felt like a long way, but his fear of being captured and tortured tended to twist and distort his mind.

He heard branches breaking and heavy footfalls coming from behind. His adrenaline spiked, and he took off running again. A rifle cracked, and a tree beside his head shook with the impact. He weaved to the right, and another rifle cracked. He felt it pass by his ear, and he covered his head instinctively, then dove into a thicket of bushes. He landed hard and stifled a desperate groan as pain shot up his arm. He felt dripping blood—he'd reopened the scabs. He tried to stifle his own breathing. He clasped his bloody hand over his mouth, trying to keep the noise to a dull roar.

A slow footfall only yards away made him hold his breath. He lowered his head and stuffed his nose into the soil and breathed. He smelled the mossy soil, tinged with rot. More footfalls were all around him. *They must see me. They're playing with me like a cat with a cornered mouse.* The thought enraged him, and he considered reaching for his pistol. He imagined himself rising up like a phoenix and striking them down with perfectly placed shots—one after another.

The fantasy ended when he felt the tip of a bayonet in the small of his back, followed with the guttural sound of a very foreign language. He lifted his head and saw a stocky soldier wearing a dirty, torn uniform. His features looked nothing like the propaganda posters of buck-toothed, bespectacled monkey men. He looked young and, despite his unfamiliar foreign features, handsome.

He said something low and menacing. Shilansky showed him his hands. The soldier barked something and stepped away. Shilansky pulled himself to his knees and looked the young soldier in the eye and smiled. Fast as a striking adder snake, the soldier whipped his rifle's buttstock into Shilansky's jaw.

He saw stars, and the world wouldn't stop spinning. He felt himself being lifted—rough hands beneath his armpits. *Maryann*, he thought. *I'll make it home to you...somehow.*

∼

It didn't take the GIs long to find the Japanese tracks in the kunai grass. Once they found it, they backtracked until they found where the ground looked trampled excessively.

The squad stayed low, keeping their heads below the level of the grass. A half an hour had passed since Stollman had spotted the Japanese moving into the tree line.

Tarkington said, "I'd say this is about halfway across the field. We'll set up further along. The farther from their base camp, the better." A distant rifle crack made them all crouch low. "They've found him," he hissed. "Let's move." Another rifle crack. "If they're bringing back a corpse, we'll let 'em pass."

Winkleman furrowed his brow, obviously not liking that plan, but Tarkington would not risk the men's lives for a corpse.

Raker led them parallel to the path until he came to a slight bend. He stopped and waited for Tarkington. When he arrived, Raker whispered, "We'll be able to see the column from here—hopefully see where the pilot is, too."

Tarkington checked the area and nodded. "Good a place as any."

Stollman whispered, "Haven't heard any more shots."

"They could be using him for bayonet practice right about now," Vick spit out.

"Nah, we'd hear screaming."

"Could be the stoic type."

Tarkington hunched in front of them. "Look, this is how we'll play it. I'll stay on this corner. You guys spread out where it straightens out again, but not too far. I'll be able to see the situation and give the thumbs-up or down on the whole thing. Thumbs-up means he's alive and we'll make the snatch. Down means we fade away and do nothing."

Everyone nodded. Tarkington tipped his hat back and wiped the sweat from his scarred forehead. "I'll give you guys a count. If I hold up five fingers, it means the pilot is the fifth man from that point on." He pointed at Vick and Raker. "Raker, I want you across the path. You'll snatch the pilot. Tackle him so he falls onto this side. Vick, you'll kill the man holding him or whoever's right behind him. Use your knife, if possible." He looked at the others. "When that happens, throw grenades. The more chaos, the better. Then we get the hell outta here." He pointed to the way they'd come from the forest. "That's our rally point." None of them looked too happy with the plan. Tarkington asked, "Questions or suggestions?"

Stollman asked, "Why don't we just mow 'em all down?"

Tarkington thought about it for a moment, then said, "If it's only a squad and the prisoner is well spaced, I'll give you a trigger-pull signal instead of a thumbs-up." He added, "I'll still give the pilot's number in line, though." Everyone agreed. Tarkington knew it was complicated, and there were far too many variables for his liking, but with short notice it was the best he could do.

When no one ventured any more questions, they moved into their positions. Raker stepped over the path, and Tarkington noted where he'd gone to ground.

Tarkington lay down and moved until he could see Raker's face. He could see Vick across from Raker and Winkleman beyond him. Stollman was last in line and out of sight. Tarkington pulled a grenade from his belt and placed it within easy reach. He made himself comfortable and settled in to wait.

Henry and Nance had worked their way around the enemy camp. They'd moved through grass and forest like ghosts. Each man had layers of branches and bits of foliage stuck into his clothing and through his hat. When they stopped, they seemed to disappear into their surroundings.

They'd seen a few enemy soldiers guarding the camp's rear flank, but they spent most of their time watching the skies. Contrails and smoke lines crisscrossed crazily as more aerial fur balls occurred overhead.

Once past the camp, Henry increased his pace. When he thought he could safely do so, he flat-out sprinted. Nance had little trouble keeping up with his fleet friend.

Henry finally topped out on a bluff overlooking the valleys to the west. Wau village was out of sight, tucked deep into the valley. The only evidence a battle raged there was a thin layer of smoke and the occasional rumbling of explosions. From this distance, they could've mistaken it for a distant thunderstorm. Henry continued sprinting until he reached a good overlook.

He took a knee and looked out over a vast field of grass. From their elevated position, they could see a distinct path starting from the middle of the field and leading due west. Henry put the scope to his eye and swept the area. He hissed, "See it?"

Nance struggled to free his binoculars from the case slung across his chest. He put the glasses to his eyes and scanned. He whistled low. "I see something at the start of a path. The color's a bit off. Parachute?"

Henry got onto his belly and rested his rifle on a wrist-sized branch. "Yep. Look about fifty yards down the path. See anything else?"

It took a few seconds before Nance whistled low again, then said, "Shifty Yanks. They're gonna try to snatch the pilot, you think?"

Henry pulled out his walkie. He nodded at Nance and tried once again to raise the others. After four attempts, he stuffed it back into his ruck in frustration. "Piece of crap."

Nance suggested, "They might not have it on. We could go down there and even the odds."

Henry shook his head. "I'm in the perfect position to cover them."

Nance whined, "But I don't have my bleeding rifle, mate. I can't do a bloody thing from here." He tapped the pistol at his side. "Least down there, I could lend a hand."

Henry didn't want to argue. Nance's eyeballs would be helpful in identifying targets, but from this range, he could probably manage without him. Nance could let the squad know he would cover them. Before he gave him the okay, he saw movement coming from the far trees. "Too late. Here they come."

Nance cursed beneath his breath and brought the binoculars to his eyes. He scanned the Japanese, emerging from the shadows and entering the bright sun. Henry had them in his sights, too. A slight quartering breeze from his right made him adjust his aim. He cursed the Japanese for not integrating their scopes with outside adjustments. The tiny sight picture might mean he missed his targets altogether.

Henry hissed, "I see the prisoner. He's staggering but walking. Looks like they worked him over a bit." He added, "Only a squad. I expected more."

Nance adjusted his sights back to where he'd seen the other GIs. He finally reacquired them; they looked like lumps of dirt and grass from here. "What're your cowboys gonna do? They'll end up killing the poor chap."

Henry kept his crosshairs on the prisoner. "They're not going to kill him...can't say the same thing for the Japs, though."

Nance shifted views and took in a sharp breath. He reached out and clutched Henry, ruining his aim. "Dammit!" Henry exclaimed. "What the hell are—"

Nance interrupted, "Another squad. They're not using the same path."

Henry put his eyes back to the scope and found the other enemy squad. "Shit, they'll end up behind the squad. There's no way they'll notice them in time." A thousand thoughts raced through his mind. He adjusted his position. "When whatever Tark's got planned happens, I'll fire on the second group. I'll keep 'em pinned down, give Tark time to get the job done and get outta there."

Nance nodded but looked back the way they'd come. "We're gonna make a lot of racket. Might attract the wrong sort from the camp." He took off the binoculars and placed them beside Henry. He got to his knees and drew his pistol. The wooden grip was worn down and smooth as polished rocks. "I'll cover the rear."

Henry looked him in the eye. He didn't like the idea of Nance facing off against an unknown force all alone. He got to his knees and unslung his carbine. "Take this. It's better than your damned pistol. Stay close enough so we can leave together when the time comes."

Nance took the carbine, hefting the light weapon. He shook his head and mumbled, "Peashooter." He slung it and raised his voice just above a whisper. "Don't wait for me. I'm used to being on my own out here." He gave him a crazed smile. "Besides, I haven't killed a Jap in days—starting to get jittery."

Henry handed him extra magazines. "Take these too—fifteen rounds each. You might need it."

Nance took the magazines and stuffed them into various pockets. "Hope not."

Henry drawled, "Don't get too attached. I want it back." He went back to the scope and readied himself for the coming violence.

Nance guffawed. "I'd sooner get attached to a thorn bush...about as useful." He pointed to the binoculars. "Don't *you* get too attached to those. They're precious."

∽

Major Shilansky's jaw throbbed, and his mouth continually filled with blood. His jaw wouldn't work, so the blood dripped from the sides of his hanging mouth. His tongue lolled, pushing out globs of blood. His head pounded well beyond the worst headache he'd ever experienced.

They bound his hands in front, and the soldier who'd butt-stroked him led him along like a dog on a leash. When he swayed and fell behind, the soldier would yank and yell angrily. Shilansky felt dizzy, and walking wasn't easy. He'd fallen once, and soldiers behind him kicked him viciously before yanking him painfully back to his feet. He began wishing he'd taken that last stand. He'd be dead, but at least the pain would stop.

He barely had his eyes open, and his swollen cheeks impinged on his vision. The day suddenly brightened, and he realized they'd left the forest and entered the field of kunai grass. The brightness made his eyes stream, but the tears pooled and made his vision even more fuzzy. He concentrated on putting one foot in front of the other. The path had grown muddy with so many passing soldiers. He struggled to keep his boots from sticking and pulling off. Losing them would make his plight that much worse.

He tried to let his mind drift away to happier times, but with each step his jaw and entire body protested and kept him in the here and now. He wished he'd pass out again. He yearned for it. Then he'd either wake up or he wouldn't, but at least he'd shorten his misery. It would anger the young enemy soldier, and that thought made Shilansky happy for an instant. He loathed the smug son of a bitch. *Perhaps I'll pretend to pass out.* The thought made him fearful for the inevitable kicks he'd have to endure. Perhaps the kicking would make him actually pass out.

A heavy force suddenly slammed into him from the side. He had no time to wonder what the hell happened before he landed hard on his left side. The rope yanked painfully, and he heard the young Japanese soldier call out in surprise.

Shilansky felt a person on top of him. He opened his eyes as wide as his swollen face would allow. Through the grass he saw the young Japanese soldier's face, streaked with fear. A black-faced apparition seemed to rise from the grass. It drove a blade deep into the soft skin beneath the soldier's chin. The apparition rode the soldier to the ground, twisting the blade. In the next instant the apparition faced him, and quick as a viper, he cut the rope linking Shilansky to the now dead enemy soldier. He felt the tension release but nearly lost his bowels when the killer stalked toward him with the dripping blade firmly clenched in his bloody hand.

But instead of slicing his throat, he sprang past him and attacked the next soldier in line. Another similar apparition appeared beside the next soldier. It gripped the soldier's hair, yanked his head back, and slashed a blade across his neck. The soldier's head nearly came completely off in his hand. A shower of blood sprayed the swaying grasses, and Shilansky heard a violent expulsion of air.

Just as quickly as they'd appeared, they disappeared. He felt someone yanking the length of rope still attached to his hands. He struggled to his knees and saw another black-faced ghoul only feet away, saying something he couldn't understand. He was pulling the rope hard, and Shilansky tried to stand up so he could run the other way, but the ghoul yanked hard and dropped him back to his knees.

It got right in his face, and Shilansky finally realized these were not ghouls but soldiers—friendly soldiers. The soldier's blazing blue eyes were centimeters from his own. He hissed, "Stay the fuck down and do exactly as I say."

Shilansky tried to answer, but his broken jaw and blood-filled mouth only produced a low gurgle. So he nodded instead. Explosions rocked the area, and shock waves swept over him. He looked around in a panic.

The soldier ignored the blasts, reached forward, and cut the rope binding his hands. He went behind Shilansky and pushed him in the back. "Go. Move out. Now." Shilansky saw another soldier a few yards ahead. He blended into the grass perfectly, his movement the only thing giving him away.

Shilansky got to his feet painfully and stood, but the soldier behind hooked his thumbs into the waist of his pants and kept him in a crouch. Every fiber in Shilansky's back and legs screamed, but he shambled along the best he could, following the man in front.

More explosions coupled with agonized screams from the trail. A nearby rifle fired, then a few more. Shilansky heard a bullet thwack into the ground nearby. Japanese screamed and yelled. Shilansky chanced a look back, and the soldier pushed him, urging him forward. He wondered why they weren't firing back.

A Japanese voice in front of them stopped the ghost soldiers in their tracks. Shilansky felt the soldier's hand on his back. He turned to him, wide-eyed. The calm soldier put his index finger to his mouth—quiet.

He felt a snap over his head, then the sound of a bullet hitting meat, then the distant crack of a rifle. Shilansky wanted to scream. What the hell was happening?

27

Through the binoculars, Henry saw one of his comrades. He recognized Raker's familiar movements, tackling the prisoner like a linebacker blind-siding an unsuspecting quarterback. At the same instant, a quick violent attack against the soldier leading the prisoner. Black-faced soldiers emerged and collided with stunned Japanese soldiers, leaving carnage in their wake. Henry saw the whole thing play out like he was watching a newsreel. He'd heard a term he thought fitting: *poetry in motion*—violent poetry in motion. He was proud of his squad mates. *Deadly sons of bitches.*

He watched the others lob grenades before most of the enemy soldiers had even reacted. From his vantage point, the explosions looked ridiculously small, but they were far from ineffectual. The blasts and shrapnel knocked several soldiers off their feet. The rest dove for cover.

Henry tore his eyes from the scene. He dropped the binoculars and put his eye back to the scope. The second squad of Japanese had dropped into crouches. He could just see the tops of their heads. Some wore soft caps, others the familiar pith helmets. Their uniforms blended well, but he knew what to look for. He took his eye from the scope, seeing his friends moving due south, straight toward the unseen squad. Their paths would cross in another fifty yards.

Henry put the crosshairs on the lead man's chest and slightly right. The sounds of panicked and injured enemy soldiers reached his ears. The first squad was in complete chaos, but the second squad was still evaluating the situation. So far, he had heard no shots from his squad mates. That was good. Grenades, yes, but the enemy wouldn't be able to distinguish the sound of one grenade from another. Perhaps the second squad wouldn't suspect an enemy presence. Perhaps Tarkington would lead the squad right past them.

Nope, they were veering straight into them—completely oblivious—putting as much distance between themselves and the first squad before they got their shit together.

The soldier in his sights stood slowly. He cupped his hand around his mouth and called out. Without taking his eye from the scope, Henry opened his opposite eye. He could see his squad had stopped. The lead enemy soldier was only twenty-five yards from them now. Henry would be forced to shoot over the top of his friends' heads. He had to act before the first squad figured out what had happened and tore off after them.

He put his finger on the trigger and controlled his breathing. The soldier turned to look at his comrades. Henry pressured the trigger, and the Type 38 rifle pushed solidly into his shoulder. He worked the bolt action smoothly. His bullet entered the soldier's chest beneath his right collarbone. He'd been aiming at his left. He adjusted his aim minutely, finding the next man crouched and staring in disbelief. His entire right side was exposed. Henry touched the trigger and watched his bullet enter low, shattering his hip and collapsing him like a domino. His victim rolled side to side, and Henry could hear his screams even from here.

He quickly chambered another round and found the next man. He was flat on his stomach, frantically pushing his way backward. Henry blew his air out and pressured the trigger. His bullet slammed into the soldier's right leg. A new agonized scream joined the first man. A nearby soldier slung his rifle and ran forward to help the closest wounded man. He looked side to side, expecting to be shot at any moment. Henry obliged, but this time his bullet only grazed his cheek. The enemy sat down hard and gripped his face. The rest of the squad stood and ran, weaving their way through the grasses.

Henry traversed his scope until he found his squad. They'd used the time to move in a more westerly direction, away from the wounded, screaming soldiers. Henry put his crosshairs on the back of a soldier from the first squad. They'd collected themselves and were pushing toward their screaming comrades. He fired, and his bullet slammed into the soldier's lower back, dropping him instantly.

The others turned away from the screaming, and Henry saw puffs of gun smoke. Bullets thunked into nearby trees and whizzed and snapped over his head. Despite his concealment, the Japanese had somehow spotted him. Time to go. He made sure his ammo pouch was secure, then backed away quickly.

He noticed the binoculars and cursed himself. Nance would never forgive him if he lost those. He reached, and a bullet smashed into them, sending them hurtling backward. Henry cursed as bits of glass cut across his cheek and lower lip. He clutched the ruined binoculars and slung the strap over his head, then pushed himself from the line of fire.

Corporal Nance finally found suitable cover one hundred yards back from Henry's sniper position. He'd only been in place for ten minutes when he heard the distant thumps of grenades and the occasional rifle shot. Minutes later, he heard the crack of Henry's captured Type 38. He desperately wanted to watch, but he couldn't see more than a few yards that way, and besides, his job was to watch for enemy coming from the rear. He held his pistol. He'd placed the carbine on the ground at his feet. He longed for his Lee-Enfield.

The terrain in front of him was widely spaced trees. If the Japanese from the camp reacted to the firefight, they'd have to come this way. He'd see them whether they came straight at him or veered into the kunai grass. Henry fired again. If the Japanese came, they might not investigate this way, since Henry was firing one of their own weapons. It sounded different from a Lee-Enfield and much different from the carbine. But all the explosions and screams would pique their interest. He could clearly hear it all, and the action took place at least a quarter mile away. Unless the Japanese were asleep, they'd have to investigate.

The tone of the fighting changed. He heard bullets smacking trees behind him. The Japanese must've spotted Henry. Nance listened for return fire but only heard incoming rounds. Perhaps Henry was hit. He glanced behind, wondering if he should check on the surly American. If he was wounded, he'd need help.

Movement in the trees. He saw Henry weaving toward him. He marveled at how well he moved through the woodlands. A true hunter. The relief Nance felt surprised him. Henry had grown on him. He gave him a quick wave, and Henry veered toward him.

Henry kneeled beside him and said, "They snatched the prisoner and are on their way out of the field. They're heading west."

Nance grinned and jabbed him with an elbow. "Good to see you, mate."

Henry asked, "Any sign of Japs?"

Nance refocused his attention forward. "Not yet, but I think they'll come. That was an awful lot of noise. How 'bout the soldiers in the field? Will they come here?"

"I knocked a few of 'em onto their backsides, but they saw my position." He plucked a piece of grass and shoved it between his lips. "I think they'll come."

"We should get outta here, then. We'll be caught in a crossfire."

"Agreed. Which way?"

Nance pointed. "They won't expect us to go north."

Henry suddenly stiffened. "Freeze," he hissed. Through the trees, from the direction of the camp, enemy soldiers emerged. They moved slowly, heading directly for the little promontory overlooking the field. Directly toward them. "Must've radioed in. Afraid of that," he whispered.

There was only sparse cover to either side. If they moved from where they were, they'd be spotted immediately. Henry put the rifle to his shoulder. "Not a lot of options here."

Nance sounded offended. "What the bloody hell happened to my binoculars? You bloody wanker. That how Yanks treat someone else's property?"

Henry looked mystified. "We're about to be overrun and you're worried about...?"

"I've been babying those for years. *Years.* And you hold 'em for a few minutes and ruin 'em? Bloody hell, mate."

Henry settled his eye into the scope. He put the crosshairs on the nearest soldier's chest. "Might want to get ready, Corporal."

Nance shook his head but finally let it go. He aimed his pistol and whispered, "Let 'em get closer. Pistols are not my specialty."

"Use the carbine."

More soldiers emerged from the trees. They had laced their helmets with branches and leaves and moved with purpose and care.

Henry switched his sights to an NCO farther back. "You fire when you think you can hit. I'll follow your lead." He pulled a grenade off his belt and held it out. "How's your arm?"

Nance took the grenade and placed it nearby. "Better'n yours, mate." Nance lowered himself and steadied his hand on a fallen log. When the lead Japanese soldier was twenty yards away, he stopped and crouched. The soldier scanned back and forth, clearly unsure about the thick cover directly to his front.

He signaled for the others to hold. They hunkered, and the point man walked cautiously forward, his rifle at the ready. When he was ten yards away, he stopped again and leaned forward, his eyes seeming to drill into them. Henry wondered what the hell Nance was waiting for.

Finally, Nance pulled the trigger on his pistol. The sudden noise, although relatively muted, sounded like the gates of hell opening. The point man's head snapped back, and he fell over backward. Henry squeezed the trigger, and the bullet entered the NCO's head at the bridge of his nose. Henry quickly chambered another round and dropped the soldier to the right, who was still staring at his dead comrade's brains.

Nance got to his knees and hurled the grenade. Henry glimpsed it flying far and true. He ducked his head. Soldiers yelled, and the grenade exploded beside two crouched Japanese, sending them both flying sideways.

The rest of the enemy soldiers flung themselves to the ground. Henry fired once more, drilling a soldier through the top of his shoulder. He smacked Nance. "Back. Move straight back." Nance plucked the unused carbine off the ground and took off, keeping the cover between him and the enemy. Henry tossed his last grenade and followed Nance, running low, his rifle nearly touching the ground.

The Japanese finally responded, firing their rifles into the thicket. They weaved through the sparse trees for fifty yards before Nance slid in behind a boulder. Bullets followed them, and Henry felt one pass through the fabric along his side. Nance had his pistol out. Henry barked, "Use the damned carbine."

Nance gave a low growl and stuffed his pistol into his waistline and took up the carbine, murmuring, "Useless peashooter."

Henry put his eye to the scope. He could see forms through the thicket, but he didn't have a shot yet. "Watch our backs. Those Nips from the field can't be far." He checked his ammo supply and cursed. "I've only got one clip left."

Nance turned and watched behind them. If the Japanese came from that direction, they'd be sitting ducks. "Not much cover on our backsides." He looked to his right and left. Right led to the kunai grass. They'd be easy targets for anyone on the ridge. Left was better, but the sparse trees wouldn't give much cover either. "I don't like this. We need to move into the trees before they come over the top behind us."

Henry fired through the thicket. He pulled the bolt and chambered a fresh round. The soldier dropped, but Henry didn't know whether he'd hit him or just made him dive for cover. "Let's do it," he hissed.

Nance cursed, seeing a soldier coming from behind them. "Bloody hell." He put the carbine to his shoulder and pulled the trigger, but nothing happened. "What the...?"

Henry spun and saw the Japanese soldier peeking his head over the ridge from his original position. He barked, "The safety. Push the safety off." Henry fired but knew he had little chance of hitting anything. He didn't have time to find the target in the scope's tiny sight picture.

Nance pushed the only button he could find, and the magazine dropped out of the bottom. "Bloody hell!"

Henry quickly reloaded the Type 38 and shoved it at Nance. "Take this." When he didn't take it right away, Henry threw it at him and viciously snatched the carbine from his hands. He reinserted the dropped magazine, chambered a round, flicked the safety, and fired three quick shots. He reversed and fired into the thicket. He yelled, "We've gotta charge 'em."

Nance fired into the thicket. "What? No!" Nance chambered another round and sighted through the scope. "There's too many. We've gotta break contact through the forest."

Henry shook his head. He fired at movement on the hillock. "There's not many this way. Probably less than a squad, and they won't expect it." He spun back toward the thicket and emptied the rest of his fifteen-round magazine. He reached for another magazine, forgetting that he'd given them to Nance. "Gimme the carbine ammo."

Nance dug into his pockets and handed him two more magazines. "You're crazy."

Henry reloaded and drawled, "I'm Cajun. We're all crazy." He got his feet beneath him. "Leave the rifle. Use your pistol. Quick, before they get around that thicket."

Nance fired the Type 38 into the thicket without really aiming and then dropped the rifle. He drew his pistol and turned toward the ridge. "Okay, crazy Cajun. Let's go!" Fire replaced trepidation. "Let's go!" he yelled.

"Fast and hard!" Henry shouted. He stood and took off at a sprint. Nance veered right and kept pace. They charged over the rise, and Henry's battle cry bounced off the trees and sky above.

The first Japanese he saw was on his belly, crawling toward a tree. Henry fired into his back three times. The next soldier, behind the first, brought his rifle up, but Henry fired point-blank into his face as he sprinted past. He continued his battle cry. He fired into stunned soldiers, but there were more than he expected.

Nance ran straight at an enemy soldier. The soldier's rifle aimed directly at Nance's face. Nance bellowed and fired his pistol as he ran. One of his bullets knocked the pith helmet from his head and staggered him backward. The enemy soldier's rifle fired, and the bullet nicked Nance's ear. Nance bellowed louder and kept charging.

His bullets seemed to have no effect. He held fire until the last instant. The soldier desperately tried to reload. Nance pulled the trigger only inches from the enemy soldier's chest. Sticky blood splattered his face as he ran past.

He aimed at the next man, cowering behind a tree. He pulled the trigger, but nothing happened. He chucked the empty pistol, and it bounced off the soldier's nose, causing him to scream and reel back.

Henry fired the last round in his magazine and reached for another. He tried to eject the spent magazine, but it wouldn't come loose. He stopped running as twenty Japanese soldiers got to their feet and aimed their rifles.

Nance faded toward him until their backs touched. He'd drawn his big knife and held it out like a sword. They breathed hard, watching the soldiers advance until they encircled them.

The nearest Japanese, an officer, barked orders. He advanced slowly with his Nambu pistol aimed at Henry's face. Henry let out a long, slow sigh. "Well...how you wanna play this, Nance?"

Nance turned his head until they could see each other's bloodshot eyes.

Henry nodded. "Me too. Been an honor."

At the same instant, they charged.

EPILOGUE
ONE WEEK LATER

Lieutenant Tarkington and the rest of the squad walked past the stinking mass grave the natives had dug for the dead Japanese. Tarkington barely gave them a second glance, keeping his eyes on the airfield and the line of Allied soldiers lined up side by side beneath bloody tarps and ponchos a hundred yards beyond. To the side of the dirt strip, a charred C-47 still smoldered.

They ignored the distant sounds of artillery and a one-sided firefight in the eastern hills. The Japanese were no longer a threat to the airfield. They were on the run, desperately trying to make their way back to Salamaua after being stopped at the river's edge by overwhelming reinforcements, including artillery. Allied planes buzzed overhead, peeling off occasionally to strafe or bomb the retreating enemy.

The squad stopped in front of the dead. Tarkington stood beside Lieutenant Willoth and a few of his surviving officers. Captain Grumskey, along with Major Connaway and General Moten, stood a few yards away. Behind them, Australian commandos smoked cigarettes and sat around silently watching. Willoth gave Tarkington a grim nod.

A C-47 banked and lined up on the runway, dropping and losing speed quickly. After offloading supplies, the ship would serve as an air hearse and shuttle the bodies back over the Owen Stanley Range.

Most of the bodies beneath the blood-soaked tarps were Australian commandos from Lieutenant Blakely's unit...Lieutenant Blakely included. One was an American.

Despite his bout of malaria, Willoth and his commandos had assaulted the enemy HQ a few hours after Tarkington had snatched the pilot. The assault forced the enemy commanders to fall back to a more secure area. Willoth himself found Corporal Nance's and Sergeant Henry's bodies in the abandoned camp. Nance's compatriots insisted on burying him near the Black Cat Mine, where he'd want to be buried.

Tarkington extended his hand to Willoth, and Willoth took it. They shook, and Tarkington said, "I can't think of a more honorable way for our man to travel back to Port Moresby—surrounded by men cut from the same fabric. Thank you."

Willoth released his hand and looked at the darkening sky. "Will we ever know men like these again?"

Tarkington felt the despair threatening to overcome him. He bit it back and took a deep breath. "They're all around us."

AFTERWORD

I portray the men of Tark's Ticks as being Alamo Scouts from late 1942 to early 1943. Historically, the first Alamo Scout units went into training on December 27, 1943. I moved up the timeline and put Tarkington and company into the program because I thought they would've been perfect candidates for such intensive training.

The battle for Wau village and the Bulol Valley was fought almost exclusively by Australian Imperial Forces (AIF), Australian commando units, and NGVR units. I inserted Tarkington and his men (US Army) into the mix because the underserved heroics of this battle fascinate me, and I wanted to write about it. I mean no disrespect to the forces involved and hope I've brought their incredible sacrifices and fighting spirit to light.

I hope you enjoyed the book and would love to hear from you. You can reach me via email: chrisglatte@severnriverbooks.com. I read and respond to all emails.

War Point: Tark's Ticks #6

One courageous squad tackles three deadly missions in the Pacific Theater at the height of World War II...

Lieutenant Tarkington is the leader of Tark's Ticks, a squad of soldiers who take on the most dangerous tasks in the Pacific Theater. After losing a close friend in combat, Tarkington struggles to keep his team on the right track —and when they're assigned three lethal missions, each team member will be pushed to his limits.

Mission One sends the squad to perform reconnaissance on a Japanese airfield, where a last-minute order from headquarters will throw them into direct contact with the enemy.

Mission Two introduces a new Japanese-American team member determined to prove he belongs, with tensions rising in a squad divided by his arrival. But when the team is tasked with taking out a Japanese general on a remote island, they must set aside their differences to complete the operation, where a lack of trust can have fatal consequences.

Mission Three raises the stakes even higher when the team learns the location of a group of prisoners, including people close to Tarkington's second-in-command. Controversial orders from headquarters collide with the squad's sense of justice when they arrive at the scene—and with so many lives on the line, making the right decision comes at a steep price...

**Get your copy today at
severnriverbooks.com/series/tarks-ticks-wwii-novels**

ABOUT THE AUTHOR

Chris Glatte graduated from the University of Oregon with a BA in English Literature and worked as a river guide/kayak instructor for a decade before training as an Echocardiographer. He worked in the medical field for over 20 years, and now writes full time. Chris is the author of multiple historical fiction thriller series, including A Time to Serve and Tark's Ticks, a set of popular WWII novels. He lives in Southern Oregon with his wife, two boys, and ever-present Labrador, Hoover. When he's not writing or reading, Chris can be found playing in the outdoors—usually on a river or mountain.

From Chris:

I respond to all email correspondence.
Drop me a line, I'd love to hear from you!
chrisglatte@severnriverbooks.com

Sign up for Chris Glatte's reader list at
severnriverbooks.com/authors/chris-glatte

Printed in the United States
by Baker & Taylor Publisher Services